THE DAY OF THE SARDINE

FLAMBARD MODERN CLASSICS

THE DAY OF
THE SARDINE

Sid Chaplin

Foreword by Alan Plater

FLAMBARD

First published in London in 1961 by Eyre & Spottiswoode
This edition first published in the UK in 2004 by Flambard Press
Stable Cottage, East Fourstones, Hexham NE47 5DX

Typeset and cover design by Gainford Design Associates
Printed in England by Cromwell Press, Trowbridge, Wiltshire

A CIP catalogue record for this book
is available from the British Library

ISBN 1 873226 72 1

Flambard Press wishes to thank Arts Council England
for its financial support.

website: www.flambardpress.co.uk

FOREWORD

Let's start by reclaiming one of our home-grown Tyneside expressions from the world of celebrity antique dealers: *The Day of the Sardine* is a bobby-dazzler of a book, a generous and humane account of a world long vanished. The 1960s were awash with novels and plays about young working-class lads from the North on the make, on the run or on the skids, but Sid Chaplin's book, first published in 1961, set down a marker for those that followed, and was never surpassed.

The central character, Arthur Haggerston, caught in 'the shadows between boyhood and manhood', is much more than the standard issue Northern anti-hero of the times, if only because he isn't at all sure who or what the enemy is. An education system that betrayed so many 11-plus failures? A labour market that could only survive with an intake of cynical, untrained muscle? A local Labour Party there to protect the dispossessed but tainted with corruption exemplified by his Uncle George? It's no surprise that Arthur finds a focus for his frustration and unfocused rage in gang warfare, street violence, and the lethal security of tribal loyalties.

Arching over the tale is a recurring theme in Sid's work: the alienation of the individual marooned in big cities, the inevitable long-term consequence of the Industrial Revolution. We know in our bones that we were designed to live in village communities. Geordies don't live in Newcastle; they live in Heaton, Byker or Gosforth, just as Londoners live in Hammersmith, Brixton or Kensington.

It is a profoundly serious book, but never pompous or solemn.

There are gorgeous comic sequences, like the saga of Harry the Lodger's pet snails and Arthur's ultimate revenge on Uncle George, though it's a revenge that leaves a sour after-taste.

That, too, is key to the Chaplin universe: a genuine hit-you-in-the-guts irony – as opposed to the glib, postmodern brand, purpose-made to give legitimacy to twenty-four carat trash. Sid's is the real thing. At the most intimate level it colours Arthur's relationships with women: his innocent love of a pretty, God-fearing girl carries the seeds of betrayal while his profane love of a lonely, older woman becomes, at the heart of its resolution, sacred.

Sid's unerring eye and ear for the small change of urban life give a unique personal texture to the tale. When he describes the minutiae of life on a building site or in a sardine factory, he knows what he's talking about, whether it's the fine and painful detail of handling a shovel or the merciless banter punctuating the tedium of a working day. Above all, when he depicts Arthur's search for some sort of moral framework within the anarchy of modern society, he speaks for all of us, poetically and passionately, as truly now as he did almost half-a-century ago. As he himself wrote of Thomas Bewick, another illustrious son of the Tyne: 'Here is art that is apt, and still needed.'

ALAN PLATER
2 April 2004

ONE

1

When I was a lot younger than I am now I thought the lodger was cuckoo, crazy, just plain loopy. But he was only in love, all the way. Otherwise he wouldn't have given me so much rope. Harry Parker is his name, and he's quite a character. Now I'm getting a bit sense, I hope, it seems hard to believe that a man could be so patient, cheerful and wooden-faced with anybody as rampageous, bigoted, and what have you as me. Especially since he was in love with the Old Lady – and he's a man – and all that stood in his way was one snotty-nosed, half-daft kid. How d'ye do? This is me, Arthur Haggerston, speaking, using a hanky now that I've five or six jobs' experience behind me, school diminishing at the wrong end of the telescope, and a taste of my own medicine running through my system.

The medicine is to see something you want and not be able to reach it. Or see somebody else pick it up. You might be drinking a jar of ale at the end of a long tiring day. You raise it to your lips. You have your eyes on the head snapping and popping. Now it's nice to have a dry mouth. Then somebody walks over and knocks the jar out of your hand. You ignore the interruption and order up again and at the precise moment the character knocks it flying again. And again. That's me and the Lodger. I was the character that knocked the glass flying at the precise moment, and several times. It was just on this one point: the Old Lady. Otherwise, we got along like a house on fire. He came rolling in from the sea, tired of donkey engines and galley cooked meals, maybe two years before I finished school. He told a good tale, didn't mind giving me the odd snout, or fag, listened to my half-baked opinions and slid in his lessons like a well-greased piston, so quietly that sometimes it would take your wits half an hour to work it out.

Just the man to have around a house with a fatherless boy running wild. And was, until maybe a fortnight before I finished school. I remember myself then, still sore but trying to hide it. The day I left school he was the first to greet me. It was late because I'd been paying off an old score or two and it had turned out to be one of those capers that isn't content to go off once, but keeps going off like a big invisible jumping jack that skips ahead in time and right in your track and waits, like the character on the jar caper, for the precise moment when you will step over it. I'd done a lot of running for no reason at all but fear and was in a lather.

Harry lit one snout from the stub of another and asked me if I'd been chasing a job, or the job me. This was a laugh. The year I left school was the tightest for jobs on record; shipyards paying off, foundries putting out their furnaces, factories locking up and nailing the doors to make sure. And I was secondary modern with an off-centre imagination and nothing in the way of concentration; brilliant, but not brilliant enough to find the shop where they sell memory photography in six easy lessons. And in the B-stream to boot. The lowest of the low.

But you have to make a joke of it until it's too thin to wear.

'Not a chance,' I said. 'Roadsweepers are two a penny and even the Army's gone choosy.'

'Never mind, kiddar,' he said. 'Forget your worries. You're strong and healthy. There's a lad wanted at Robinson's; driver's mate. With your brains you should be sitting behind the wheel in less than no time.' Robinson's was the local coal merchant, and I reacted swiftly.

'Some brains Ah'd have,' I said. 'Humping roundy coal a hundredweight at a time up the new council flats. Ah'd be punch drunk the first week.'

'It's that or Uncle George.'

'No fancy for the open air and Uncle George standing over me,' I said.

'Fancy's out of date.'

'Ah'd rather take the coal-heavin'.'

'Suit yourself,' he said. 'It's your life … What about the Youth Employment?'

'Offered me a butcher's boy, typewriter mechanic, and a vacancy in a paint factory.'

'Pick of the roasts, eh?'

'Not on your life.'

He offered me a snout. I accepted gratefully and blew rings. 'Think Ah'll slip along and see old Robinson before he locks up.'

'You'd be better off with Uncle George,' he said, looking away. 'Humping sacks is real rough work.'

He wasn't pushing me, only giving me the experience of a quarter of a century in the fish docks, the trawlers, deep sea boats and a hard hoist to a master's ticket, followed by a still harder bump back to the deck and a host of other rough menial jobs in stinking yards and factories. He knew what it was to hump. But I wasn't taking anything from him.

'Ah can take it,' I said, and ran all the way to Robinson's. The old man was checking delivery notes and barely looked up.

'It's heavy work,' he said. 'You're young.'

'Ah'll manage.'

'Get a hard cap,' he said. 'Report at seven next Monday.'

I said goodnight but he was back in his books. And, boy, if you know anything about coalmen you'll know why. Having it all in front of me I felt humiliated. Me humiliated! To him I was just another sack carrier, another beast of burden, another one to watch. He'd seen them come and go, he'd seen dozens, perhaps hundreds like me. Yet in my innocence I was offended. But it was a job, and I went home like a dog with two tails. Harry was reading and the Old Lady was rushing around making a meal, always in a hurry, always worried, nothing in her mind but frying steak and chopped onions. All she had time for was to say: 'Well, Ah hope ye know your own mind – and stick it.'

Of course I'd stick it! I was amazed at their lack of faith. Then I started reckoning times. The part-time cleaning was finished at six; ten minutes walk home, walking fast and she always walked fast, and the one thing on her mind to get a meal ready. Yet here it was, seven o'clock and nothing ready. I looked at the Lodger, not old Harry now, but the Lodger. He was stretched out in the easy chair like a big cat, turning a page once in every three or four minutes, fast reader that he was, delighted with the book, purring internally. The Old Lady had forgotten all about my job and was slipping in and out of the scullery like a fish, humming softly … So they'd been at it again. Or, to put it bluntly, he'd been at her. They'd fight and argue but he always won. He'd lost a ship but was her master, a masterful mariner by dead reckoning or the book, as soothing as a calm sea himself. A man who took some beating, otherwise he'd never have pulled through the kitten caper. This was a couple of years before I finished school …

2

Now cats can be okay. I like those blue ones with the big eyes and I like the monkey kind you see in the gardens of the big nobs that shoot off like a puff of smoke if you lift a hand to stroke them. But this was a sick kitten. Thin as a rake, mattery eyes, scabby eyes; in every way a stinker.

'Get that thing put out,' said the Old Lady.

'He's sick and needs attention,' said the Lodger.

'Then take it to the Shelter.'

'Ah'll keep it in my bedroom. Ye'll never see it.'

'And who'll clean up after it?'

'Me, of course – didn't Ah tell ye Ah was a sick-berth attendant in the Navy?'

'Ye're not nursing that thing in my house!'

'Aw, come off it; be a sport. Live and let live. It'll gladden your heart when it's fat and shiny again and purring all over the house.'

'More muck then meow – an' kittens before ye know it. No, Ah'm not havin' it, so that's flat.'

'It's a He-cat – no complications for us,' said the Lodger.

'Just your gannin' to put on the neighbours.'

'Come on,' he said. 'Ah'll pay for the extra milk.'

'That's a laugh. You're a fortnight behind with your rent.'

'Ah always pay up in the end, now don't Ah? And Ah'll pay for the animal and its milk.'

'All right: but none of that stinkin' cat food. And the first time it makes dirt, out it goes.'

The Lodger got an old clothes basket and mat from the Rag Market down on the quayside. He beat the chap down to nine-pence. Food was a problem – after a couple of days on milk the kitten tried to batter the pantry door down; retired with a sore head; strolled into the backyard, shinned up and through the pantry window, and shifted half a jar of jam and a quarter of a big pork pie intended for the Lodger's tea. Then was sick all over the pantry floor. The Lodger cleaned up after it then nipped out and bought a new jar of jam and a couple of pound of horsemeat at Donnelly's, the knacker.

The cat was almost human. He sat with his eyes fixed on the pan in which the Lodger boiled the horsemeat. Every so often he serenaded the Lodger, or the pan, or both.

He was almost human. Knowing the Lodger loved him he respected the Lodger's room. Elsewhere didn't matter. The Lodger kept a sharp eye and cleaned up after him. But the kitten was too fast and frequent.

In the end the Old Lady said she was sick of being acting scavenger, unpaid: and the Lodger walked out with the kitten, a sack, and rusty old iron.

'What have ye done with it?' asked the Old Lady when he returned a couple of hours later. He was well-oiled.

'Fat lot you care.'

'Did ye find a home for it?'

'Over the bridge,' he said.

'You're a dam' liar.'

'Never seen so many bubbles …'

'In that filthy water – who're ye tryin' to kid?'

'You could hear them comin' up … big bubbles. Dam' nigh cried.'

'Ah don't know how ye had the nerve – feeding the poor little thing up then pitchin' it into the burn. Callous, that's what it is.'

'Ah was driven to it.'

'There was no need to do that – there's plenty would've been glad an' willin' to give it a home.'

'A dam' fine sample of hospitality you gave it!'

'An' a fat lot of mercy you showed it.'

'It wasn't wanted. It never knew the death it died.'

'Well all that Ah can say is that Ah hope you never get happed up in a sack and tossed into the river,' she shouted, and started putting on her coat.

'Now where ye're off to?'

'Out to walk it off,' she said.

'Then bring some fish and chips back – Ah'm peckish.'

'Ah'll see ye in hell first,' she snapped, and the house shook as she slammed the door.

After she'd gone I boned the Lodger.

'Settle yourself,' he said. 'Gave it to the timekeeper at the factory – for a consideration. They lost theirs to a brewery lorry. So,' he concluded, pulling off his shoes, 'in a manner of speaking, killing that cat paid the brewers a double dividend.' He brooded a bit. 'Funny if their cat was the mother of our kitten …'

'How much did you get?'

'Ten bob,' he said. 'Ah'll miss her, mind.'

'Ah thought ye told me mother it was a Tom?'

He winked at me. 'Ah was leavin' the first litter to break that bit of news!'

The Old Lady didn't speak to the Lodger for a day or two; it was only after I'd let out that he'd sold the kitten that she resumed normal relations by giving him the telling off of his life. 'And Ah'm glad Ah didn't get the fish and chips,' she concluded. 'At least Ah've that to console me.'

'And Ah've got my bit of consolation,' he said. 'The way it struck home when Ah mentioned the bubbles.'

But he missed the kitten.

One morning the Old Lady was making the Lodger's bed while I was having my breakfast. She came out and poured herself a cup of tea, switched off the wireless, and said: 'We've got slugs in this house!'

'Slugs?' I said.

'Have a look for yourself,' she said. 'In the Lodger's room.'

So I went in and had a look. There were silvery trails all over the carpet, but I couldn't find any slugs. 'They went home,' I told her, and switched on the wireless.

'It took me three months to get rid of the blackclocks,' she said. 'Now it's slugs … switch that wireless off: it's time ye were away to school.'

'What's the matter?' I said. 'Listening for the slugs?'

This went on for two or three days – slug trails every morning; the Old Lady pulling the bed out, rolling up the carpet, tapping on the walls and poking about with a straightened hairpin in every mousehole. Then one day Harry left his bottom drawer open and she found this cardboard box full of chippings upon which slept a pair of dirty great snails with blood-red bands on their shells.

'The filthy lout!' she shouted. 'Arthur, come and have a look at this lot.'

So I went and had a look. She was all for throwing them on the fire, but I persuaded her to keep them as evidence – it was the only way to save their lives.

Harry didn't turn a hair when I told him. He grunted and remarked: 'Ah'm startin' to roll me own fags, so she'd better be careful.'

Not getting the point I looked at him. 'Because Ah'm smokin' a lot less an' what with the famine and the fumbling me nerves are on edge,' he explained.

The Old Lady came in stamping mad: 'Ah'm not havin' great greasy trails all over my good carpet,' she said.

'That'll be cured in a matter of time,' he said categorically.

'They'll be cured as from tonight.'

'Over the bridge again?'

'Over the bridge or anywhere you like, so long as you get rid of them.'

'Now listen, Madam,' said the Lodger. 'You never listen, an' that's your trouble. Ah said it'd be cured in a matter of time.'

'How's that?'

'Ah'm teachin' them to travel single file.'

'My God, Ah should have me head examined for listenin' to ye,' she cried. 'Now what are ye lookin' for?'

'A sack,' he said.

'Don't be ridiculous. Ye could use that fancy baccy bag.'

'Listen, Peg,' he said. 'Ah'm attached to these two snails. Let me keep them in the yard.' Seeing she was shaking her head he continued: 'Ah'm a lonely man. For three quid a week Ah get two square meals a day and a clean bed. But no company. Now these snails – they're good company. They're something to look forward to durin' the long day. Let them out o' the box every mornin', watch 'em run for the lettuce; or wander round, explorin' the great wide world. Open the box at night – wonderful to see those little horns come out and snap back like twin periscopes. Then come back again when they've registered a friend. A friend. They've made a friend of me, and me a friend of them. Is there anythin' wrong with that?'

'The house should have fell down on top of me the day Ah let you in!' said my mother. 'First it's a mangy kitten – now it's snails. Next it'll be snakes.'

'Let me keep the snails and Ah'll spare ye the snakes: God's honour truth or Ah'll slit me throat. Let me keep me two friends.'

'Ye can show ye friends to the door,' said the Old Lady. Her

16

lips were as thin as skimmed milk.

'All right, then,' he said. 'You're not a woman, Peg. You're not half a woman. You're a hard-hearted flint.'

'Ah know what you're after!'

He went into his bedroom which, I should explain, once used to be the sitting-room, and returned with the box in his hand.

'Now what are ye after?'

'Never you mind.'

'Boss,' she said. 'That's what you're after. Boss of the house. Boss in everything.'

'Shush, the lad,' he said.

'Shush you! Ye're wearin' me down wi' ye ceaseless tricks and talk. Once Ah give in, ye've got me. That's what ye're after.'

'Have Ah ever put a wrong step forward?' he asked. 'Have Ah, now?'

'That's what's got me worried,' she answered.

'Have ye ever seen me put a foot or a hand where Ah shouldn't?'

'Oh, no. Not a hand or a foot – but those little blue eyes …'

'Enemies of Satan,' said the Lodger, and went to the back-door. 'It's hard enough to keep the rest under control. Ah'd need blinkers for the eyes – and in time Ah'd be permanent blind; and that's a fact. A man's mouth may deny the good, but never his eyes.'

'Harraway wi' ye!' She was blushing.

'Then Ah keep my snails?'

'Ah've told ye what to do wi' the snails,' she said, her lips tightening again.

Then he packed his big sailor's box. He looked sort of top-heavy when he went out. The big box was on his shoulder, the snail box was hanging from his little finger. He wouldn't let me help. 'This is between me and your Ma,' he explained.

'Let him go,' ordered the Old Lady. 'Can't ye see he's only playin' on our feelin's? He'll be back in double-quick time, when they stop his beer; you'll see.'

But he wasn't. Not that night, nor the next.

'What's he up to?' she kept muttering to herself. I could see she was upset. That was the time I was on the car-door racket and getting in late. She raised hell every time; she'd have slaughtered me if she'd known. She kept saying: 'Home's a bed and nothin' more for you; and Ah'm the bloody servant.'

I kept my temper. 'Expect me to stay in every night?' I asked her. 'In a few years Ah'll be in the Army fightin' Chinks or Russians, or married. We're only young once.'

'Ah'd like to know what ye're up to,' she snapped. 'Roamin' the roads of a dark night – an' me sittin' here on me own through the long draggin' nights.'

'Should've kept the kitten,' I said.

'You shut your mouth!'

'It's the truth. Kept the kitten and kept the man.'

That's when she threw the teapot. Had to go to the out-patients and get six stitches in my cheek. Left a scar. That's why the Manor lot nicknamed me 'Pretty Boy' – behind my back. Well, she was all tears and repentance. Got Mousey Hole's old Dad to take me in his old taxi and waited till I was out. There was tripe for supper. She hates tripe in batter but this time had to grin and bear it. Then, before we went to bed, she remarked: 'It mightn't be a bad idea if you waited outside the factory tomorrow night. Don't let him see ye, mind, for God's sake. Shadder him to wherever he's holed up. Then let me know. He's a useless feller, but Ah'd hate to see him in the hands of that Shalley Street lot.'

Shalley Street is where the common lodging houses are. At the respectable ones there's always a chap waiting for you to get out of bed; at the others there's maybe one or two women; the working kind. It wasn't the dirty beds and the tough types that worried the Old Lady but the drabs. I knew as soon as she asked me to trail him down. She'd always had a fancy for him. Now it was serious. If I'd laughed about it before I wasn't laughing now. I looked at her. She flushed up and said: 'Now don't forget – better go straight from school. Here's sixpence for a bar of chocolate.'

I hadn't to remind her about the tanner when morning came. She handed it over without a word and I was even more sure she was soft about him. Could have knocked her down. What is it that makes you jealous? It had been a long time since she stopped kissing me. It wasn't sloppiness. In all my life there'd only been the Old Lady; as for the Old Lady, if she had any memories she never talked them aloud. I was all she had. That's where the jealousy came in, I think. Two against the world is a perfect set-up; three's a laugh or hard-going. Except when it comes naturally, which is what I had to find out for myself.

'What's the look for?' she asked.

'What look?'

'If looks could kill … you know what look Ah mean.'

'The way you go on gets me down,' I said. 'Always pullin' me to bits – always askin' what Ah'm thinkin' – always givin' me your dirty work to do …'

'What d'ye mean – dirty work?'

'Aw, Ma; you know what Ah mean,' I said. 'Come off it and don't play the innocent. You turned the poor old Lodger out and now ye want him back … you're gone on him, that's what it is.'

I thought I was for the teapot again. She got hold of it with both hands and yours truly got ready to jump. Then I noticed she was holding it down in case it got away. 'What if Ah am?' she said. 'You like him, don't you? You stick up for him plenty. He's a decent feller even if he does talk until you don't know whether you're on your head or your feet.'

'Oh, Ah like him,' I said.

'There,' she said. 'You've got to admit it; with all his faults he's a canny chap.'

'Canny enough.'

'Well, what are ye arguing about, then?'

'It's your argument,' I said. 'All I said was that you were gone on him – and it's true.'

'Would it matter if Ah was?'

'Not my business.'

'Never mind that. We know it's not your business. Ah'm just wantin' to know what you think.'

'Ah think ye should have learned your lesson by now,' I told her, and got ready to jump. But she didn't move for a second or two, and I relaxed, until her forehead came down on the teapot. I saw she was crying. I daresay she felt bad, but I felt bad too. I felt rotten.

Daresay I wouldn't have bothered about tracking the Lodger down because when school was finished my belly was shouting blue murder, and I'd blued the tanner on a one hundred to seven cert that should have stayed in the stable for its nap. Bullock the school bookie made the killing of his life; but he didn't enjoy it long. Couple of days later the kid that started the tip blew his top and we cornered Bullock in the lavatories and bashed him about with the day's takings – ten bob in silver and copper wrapped up in his hanky. Never mind, that's not the story. What I'm trying to say is that, despite hunger, the memory of her tears drove me on the errand.

There isn't a trolley service or a direct bus from the school to the quayside, where the Lodger works, so I had to walk. Luck was in my way: one of the old-fashioned old ladies had left a row of teacakes on the window-sill to cool. When it was down I felt a lot better; for two pins I'd have gone back and thanked her. You can't appreciate good cooking and baking until you've lived out of a frying pan the way we did when the electric oven went up in smoke. She's a dab hand really. You can eat her teacakes without butter; with it they'd bring tears to the eyes of a chef.

Well, my stomach stopped rolling and I made good time. It's about a mile from the school to the factory and it's two to one anybody with eyes would say it's far from lush scenery. Old Rattler, the school boss, says it's the wreck of an historic village. Some wreck. You never saw such a network of streets, most of them in squares or triangles, some two deep, with a bull-ring inside. Every now and then some tired types come along, strip a roof or two, then smoke a tab and drink tea while a bull-dozer has fun. Result: plenty of open spaces, some as big as a football pitch, and ideal for stacking old beds, decrepit settees, ancient prams, buckets, tin cans, dust-bins, and sometimes the odd body. The last's for true. Some of those squares you can walk across the scrap without putting your foot on the ground. But I like it – wouldn't feel at home without scrap and wrecks around me. Then there are abandoned streets and jagged ends where they've stopped demolishing. You'd laugh when they evacuate such a street. Soon as it's dark the place is alive with characters that fancy the odd door or a dozen or two window panes – ideal for greenhouses. Enough to give you the Willies: saws, hammers and axes going, torches flashing, and chaps carrying the stuff, some like coffin bearers, all like bodysnatchers hugging the shadows. That's for our parish. You pass through it to the park: a bloody flat wilderness of ashes with the odd swing or two. You skid down the south end of this under the viaduct and the road bridge and that's where the burn flows out into daylight again – out from under sixteen million tons of filth. You're in No Man's Land here. There's a house or two occupied by tinkers, hawkers and scrap men and what-not, and two gas lamps. Nobody can see what's happening at night on those big slopes which are all pocked where they used to work clay.

Five hundred yards further down the burn is tidal. The ships used to come up and you can see what's left of the old quays. Granaries have been turned into warehouses and houses into offices and small factories. For some reason they call it Venice Steps.

It's very interesting down there. From six o'clock onwards the place is deserted and you can easy break into one of these barns – trouble is there's very little portable stuff. But they're smashing for a fight, or a prayer-meeting, which is what we call a meeting of the gang. I'm still on my way to the quay, so don't worry. You pass the Motor Boat Club outfit, cross the main riverside road, then dip down to the quayside, where you're back among the wreckage again. Some good big solid houses; some corrugated-iron creations; some houses where people live (but you never see them); some lousy lively pubs; and stuck up here and there some concrete and glass monsters with hellish great pipes curling round or shooting straight up into the bright sky. On Sunday.

Harry's factory was pretty near the quayside so I dodged shunting engines and mobile cranes and gave myself a little relaxation spitting in the river. The trick is to spit in a clear bit of water.

Ten minutes later the buzzers started going and I cut over the quay and up one of the chares and watched the men come out. Even the old men were moving fast but not fast enough to kill the beautiful smell of sardines and pilchards with tomato sauce. They'd all been baptized: I didn't have a glimmering that one day I'd also be baptized and stink to high heaven myself. As usual, Harry was last out – Old One-Speed, lagging along behind the others, same at the end of the shift as in the beginning. Anybody seeing Harry running full-tilt will witness a miracle. A man walking slow and easy is hard to shadow. You never know when he's going to turn to pat a dog or stroke a dandelion – more likely the latter with Harry. In all it took us about twenty minutes to cover ground that I'd done in ten minutes coming down; and that's not including the five minutes he stopped to buy a paper, a tin of spam, and a head of lettuce.

This was on the riverside road. I watched him cross over and turn along the lane that leads to the Motor Boat Club; gave him a minute to get ahead, then nipped after him. He wasn't visible. I nosed up two or three turnings, drew a blank in each, and got into a cold sweat. I ran along the lane but I knew it was hopeless: in that short time he couldn't have made it so far.

Then I remembered the Motor Boat Club at Venice Steps. He wasn't in the clubroom. He wasn't behind the pile of timber, or viewing dandelions and rosebay willowherb on the waste ground, nor was he taking a dip in the burn, because it was low tide and there wasn't enough water to drown a dog. The little old boats were leaning all ways on the beautiful cherry-black mud, canted, coining and kelted, taking it easy. Some day I'd like a boat of my own; I'll have one with a wheel and wear a nonchalant cap, pullover, silk scarf, and knife-creased trousers. Also a bloody big pipe and maybe a beard. Thinking this, I walked along the quay making up a better yarn than the truth for the Old Lady which I knew she wouldn't believe, on principle.

Ever heard a mud-bank talk?

'Lookin' for a berth, shipmate?'

I jumped like a shot cock. I stood rigid.

Caught! Caught cold! That low-down snail-trainer had known about me shadowing him from the start. He'd been sitting laughing his guts out while I hammered hell out of the cobblestones, chasing hither and thither like a raw postman without a sense of direction whose reading is restricted to 'GENTS' or maybe 'BAR'. I could have kicked myself. Instead I hung on the dizzy heights and descended twelve feet of rungs.

Trust old Harry to drop in the jam. She was a fairly big boat and had a cabin which was roomy enough if you sat on the floor. The stove was going merry hell, the spam was frying, and the tea was black pleading for white. Condensed, of course. I knew I'd a belly. While we were eating he cross-examined me: a full mouth never stopped the Lodger.

'How's things?'

'Fine.'

'How's Peg?'

'Fine.'

Now it was my turn. 'How's the snails?'

'Don't take to a life on the ocean wave. Went off the lettuce, stopped talkin', wouldn't come out of their shells. So I stampeded them last night.'

'What's the lettuce for, then?'

'Thought they might drop in on me; you never know.'

'She's a nice boat.'

'This is the best boat they've got. Seems they've had one or two stolen. Take 'em to a strange harbour; re-paint 'em; change the engines; sell 'em to suckers. So they offered me this berth.

Ten bob a week and free board.'

'It'll be lonely.'

'Not so bad as you might think. Get the odd courting couple. Sea-gulls come down for a hunk of bread – got a promising bird with one eye. Got a tame mouse.'

He leaned back and pulled a string. A door opened in a box on the shelf. A black and tan mouse put his nose out, twitched his whiskers, came down head-first like a streak of lightning, played on the Lodger's head, skidded to a standstill on his shoulder and wolfed a quarter of a pound of cheese standing on his hind-legs.

'Ain't she sweet?'

'Sure she's a she?'

'Who're you kiddin' – my old man was a Chinese chicken-sexer.'

'You were wrong about the kitten.'

'That was diplomacy.'

'She'll not let you keep the mouse.'

'Arthur, me boyo, me and the mouse already have a roof over our heads!'

'She's wantin' you back.'

'Is she now! And what about you?'

'Things are pretty dead,' I said, because you've got to be honest. 'Furthermore, *she's* like a cat on hot bricks.'

'It was her that set you after me?'

Now it's a funny thing, but this question got me on the raw. I get along with the Old Lady but I like her and the Lodger apart; I like them best when around and not on speaking terms. Don't like either of them to be personal about each other. Don't like – as you'll see – to be second fiddle.

So I didn't answer this one. Looked at the floor, fastened a shoelace, did a bit yogi exercise. But nevertheless went into a sweat and couldn't look at him.

'All right, then,' he said. 'Give her my love. Tell her I'm comfortable. Tell her – freedom is wonderful.'

'You tell her yourself,' I said. 'She'll scalp the hide off me if I tell her you found me out. All I know is that you're here, so be a pal and don't tell her you foxed me'.

'That's a deal,' he said. 'Think she'll be down tonight.'

'Nobody knows the way she'll jump,' I said.

'I was assistant to a tiger tamer, once,' he stated. 'Worked in the cage, carried a gun in one hand and a whip in the other. He's and she's – there's no difference – they all jump through the hoop.'

He was as happy as Larry.

But I was young then. 'Was it loaded?' I asked.

'Hell's bells, no. Them dumb beasts don't know the difference.'

I thought a while. 'You'll never put the Old Lady through the hoop,' I stated.

'If you mean the golden one, yes, maybe,' he said. He stretched himself out on the bunk. 'There's a complicated woman for you! All she had to do was shake the tree – but she wouldn't. Not her. Stubborn, rotten stubborn. Wants to plough her lonely furrow with you at her side.'

'The Old Lady's all right,' I said.

'She'll really be an Old Lady when you light out,' he said. 'She knows that and she won't budge.'

'Who's goin' to light out?' For answer he just looked at me. 'But Ah'll not.'

'You'll sail the seas,' he said. 'And when I say seas, I mean deep seas, 'cos you're not the type to bide in the bottleneck. In fact,' he added, 'come to think of it, you're like me. You'll see strange sights, and ports and people. Might even end up on the moon … you're no sardine.'

My mind bit on that. 'Sardine?'

'In Norway the sardines come in from the ocean in billions and billions,' he said. 'Swimming up the fjords. The sea changes colour. First she's green as old copper, then she turns sliver, solid silver, and you can't hear yourself talk for the gulls goin' mad and divin' down to gorge themselves. On they come. They don't know why and they don't want to know why. Maybe they've got to go there to spawn. And they go bang into the nets like a hundred locomotives – the old ropes twank an' the ship heels over.'

'You've fished for sardines?'

'Fished? That's not fishin' – it's massacre; haulin' 'em in on piecework, acres of them, cataracts pourin' from the nets into the hold, flippin' and fightin', until you batten down. Then they put 'em in barrels and send 'em over here to be laid out in the tin coffins, head to tail and tail to head.

'All they know is the shoal,' he said. 'All they care about is to eat at eating time and spawn at spawning time. So into the net they run and end up in a little tin box.'

'What a come-down for you!' I said. 'Ah'd rather fish for 'em than work in a packin' factory.'

'You miss the point.'

'What's that?'

'Don't be a sardine. Navigate yourself.'

'Ah'm goin' to be Somebody.'

'And what's that?'

'Get filthy rich, hob with the nobs, drive a Jaguar, have a private swimmin' pool.'

'Another kind of sardine – plush-lined tin, that's all.'

'Better than bein' a sardine slave, anyway.'

'Thought you'd say that. But you're wrong. Ah use the sardine factory the way Ah used the sardine boats: to eat to live and not living to eat. You think Ah'm with the shoal – eh? But that's not the case. Ah'm swimmin' on me own.'

'Honest, you're a comedian!'

'Ah'm lettin' ye into the biggest joke in the world,' he said.

'What's that?'

'Explainin' the point spoils the joke,' he stated. And shut up.

That was the beginning of it all. Being only thirteen or so I didn't catch on. All I could see was new suits and maybe a Jaguar gleaming on the horizon. I didn't see any birds, because birds were then only a kind of mobile furniture. Well, practically. I'd been with one or two in the clay-holes or in those dark empty houses, but they didn't know much and I knew less and I reckoned the whole thing was a dud buy. As I say, I didn't catch on. But if my writing's bad my double entry memory is good. It all goes down and sooner or later comes shooting out. You'd have laughed. I nicked up the ladder – not so many rungs because the tide was running – and looked back.

'Tell her Ah'm here,' he said. 'Ah'll not split.'

'Oke,' I said. 'You're on a slow boat – that's the story.'

'That's my boy,' he told me.

I was a sardine boat sailing the fjords; I was a sardine swimming alone; I was a handsome man at the wheel of a Jaguar. I didn't know what I was, but I was half-cracked and part-happy. I put the wireless on full pelt and watched the walls do a shimmy. I'd be a big nob yet. I switched the American forces on and listened to Pee Wee Hunt. He played so good I had to examine the walls for cracks. They gave another for good measure. Marching to the tune of the Saints I set the table and fried the kippers. I'd wolfed mine and ten rounds of bread by the time the Old Lady arrived, yelling blue murder because her kipper was frizzled and the tea like tar. But she soon simmered down.

After supper the Old Lady washed the dishes, then herself. Both times in the sink, because the only bath we had was a zinc coffin without a lid and weighing half a ton that we kept in the yard. She hummed her favourite song as she stepped out of her working skirt and pulled off her blouse; the song that goes like this:

> There they go, full of joy,
> Lucky girl, happy boy –
> And here am I – broken-hearted …

While she sang and built up a mountain of lather I admired her nice blue-veined arms and white shoulders and thought what a pity it was about her hands. Blue soap and scrubbing had taken hell out of them and they were as red and wrinkled as a babby's face; the new-born kind.

'You goin' out?' I asked.

'Mind your own business,' she said.

'Dyin' to see that crazy old Lodger, Ah'll bet.'

'Might stroll down that way.'

'Soon be dark,' I said. 'Queer characters get down that way; types that'll tackle a girl at the drop of a hat.'

'Ain't no girl and Ah've got no hat,' she laughed.

She pulled on a flowery dress. 'You oughta wear a ballerina-type dress and show those knees,' I told her.

'What is it ye're after?'

'Nothin',' I said. 'Nothin'; but you be careful down Venice Steps.'

She got her handbag. 'Isn't it the longest day? It'll not be dark till practically midnight ... anyway, all the scrubbin' Ah've done's brought me up to fightin' pitch.'

'Those types are strong,' I said. 'Crazy strong ... ye can't hold them.'

'You know too much, Arthur,' she said. 'Where d'ye get all that stuff?'

'It's in the papers every day.'

'Don't be so jealous,' she told me. 'Wash yourself and get to bed in good time – and leave the place tidy.'

'Give us a tanner for a cup of coffee at Marino's?'

'You're not goin' out; it's far too late for a boy your age.'

'*You're* goin' out!'

'Oh, for God's sake,' she said. 'Stop actin' on. Ye'd think you had a ball and chain on me. Bad as a mean husband.'

'Let me go down there with you, then.'

'You'll stay here an' that's flat!'

'Give us a tanner, then.'

She stood with her handbag slung over her arm: 'You're determined to come, Ah see,' she said. 'Jealous eyes! All right, get your jacket on.'

'Two's better in a fight, Mam,' I told her; but she didn't laugh. Raced all the way, so hard I had to trot and I'm not kidding.

Never said a word, excepting when we passed a watchman sitting over his coke fire with a stubby pipe, waiting for adventure. 'Fine night for a bit courtin', Peg,' he said with a wink and a spit.

'Fat chance for me,' she said.

'Should be in bed, his age,' he remarked.

'If it wasn't for randy old characters like you,' I told him, 'Ah wouldn't be here.' He almost swallowed his pipe.

And the Old Lady gave me a mile of yakity-yak-yak on respecting elders.

'Just you walk into that tent some night. Ye'll sharp find out about respect.'

'One of these days somebody'll up and give ye a bashin',' she told me. All told, she was a true prophet.

Nothing happened on the way down but a dozen bats that use the Glasshouse Road, which lies between those old-fashioned six-floored warehouses, as a flight-testing ground. First one she jumped. Second one nearly got into her hair and she screamed. Third one, she got hold of my hand.

As it happened, the Lodger had company. She was a golden bird, golden hair, golden arms, golden legs; so much bullion I was surprised not to see a black van and armed guards standing by. 'What's that?' asked the Old Lady.

'That's the ballerina-type dress Ah was telling you about.'

'Not that, dafty. Who is she?'

'Just a girlfriend.'

'Girlfriend!' she said. We marched over. 'Well, well,' said Harry, who was sitting on top of the cabin where he could talk to the bird more comfortably.

'Hope you're comfortable,' said the Old Lady. 'Ah'll not mention your manners – keeping your lady-friend standin' while you sit.'

'She was only passing,' said Harry mildly.

'Seems to me to be settled for the night.'

'Hey, there,' said the bird. 'Ah'm only waitin' for me boy-friend ...'

'Funny place to wait for a friend,' said the Old Lady.

'Not if he plays around with motor boats,' said the bird, tossing her head. 'An' if he doesn't come soon he'll have his head in his hands to play with.'

But the Old Lady's blood was up. 'Fine story,' she said.

'Beg your pardon, Ah'm sure,' said the bird and walked away.

'Peg, ye've got no manners,' said the Lodger.

'An' you're too easy.'

'What's the matter – come down for an argy-bargy?'

'Come down to look you over … and high time, too.'

'Well, come down and look over the boat.' He held out his arms.

'No thanks; Ah'll take the gangway.'

'Haven't got one.'

'Ah'll stay here, then.' She glanced at the girl. 'Ballerina!'

'And very fetchin', too,' said the Lodger. 'Come on down, Peg.' Well, I left them to it. The chap belonging to the golden girl came in and got his dressing-down. They went off, so I moved further.

I waited until he'd cleared off, then walked along the quay to the boat Harry was occupying. She was rocking ever so slightly and I could hear the lap of the water between her and the quay-side, but there was no light inside. She was still riding high and I could just see the deck. Something scuttled behind a box of fishing tackle: the mouse. I felt desolate, lonely. So they'd made up and gone home. There'd be laughter and junketings and I didn't feel like being the third party. I dropped on to the deck with the idea of spending a few minutes in front of the hot little stove. It was a little bit chilly and very quiet and my hand was on reaching for the door when I heard a murmur.

'It'll be more comfortable at home.'

'No chance of bein' disturbed here.'

'There isn't enough room.'

'We're not doin' so badly.'

I could hear the boards creak as they moved around. Standing paralysed I could hear my heart thumping. I wanted to rush in and pull them apart but couldn't move. Can't tell you what I was thinking. Something about stopping kidding myself, everybody was like this and why not the Old Lady, the proof being me. This was how I'd been ushered in.

'Get up off your knees, silly,' she said.

'But Ah worship ye, honest, this is the place to be.'

'It isn't,' she said, so softly it made my blood creep.

'Oh, God,' he said.

The boat rocked and I thought of the sardines rushing into the nets like a hundred locomotives. I could almost hear them come together as the night exploded and I ran up the rungs like a crazy cat. I wanted to run for ever from the sound of the kiss as they came together, but as I ran it caught me up and was no longer a sound. The kiss closed around me like a wet cellophane sack, and run and beat as I would I'd never be free of it.

TWO

1

I wouldn't like to live those two years through again. Generally speaking I'm not one of those characters who'd jump at the chance of another take, but the funny thing is that it's those two years between fifteen and seventeen I dislike most. After these followed a year of practically useless capers, near-murder, self and other varieties of torture, sudden death, all of which I could at a pinch take again. But I shudder at the thought of fifteen to seventeen and the slow torture of six dead-end jobs. Dead-end is right. Everybody down there, heaving coal, running errands, carrying meat, watching a machine, walking about or sitting on his backside, matterless what, is either dead or dying. Don't be killed by the odd one or two exceptions that kick the slats out of a foreman or grin and bear it, because they're just the same underneath: rejects, found wanting, defeated before they ever made a start. Education is a sieve as well as a lift.

Looking up at the little hole you've come through isn't any consolation. All right, so there's still room for character? Who's kidding who? When you're down there learning the knack of lifting a sack onto your shoulder and dropping the odd empty one with it while the mistress of the house is looking at the chit, character's no asset. You've no excuse. Reject; able to count, suck and use a pencil, work a twist. The list begins with reject. There are no rough diamonds now, only pebbles with a polish.

My driver was a character named Charlie whose particular

drug was the cheapest beer in town or anywhere. He was the only genuine telepath I ever knew. Name a club where one door-keeper, senile, deaf and dumb and practically blind, was the only hurdle to cheap rich ale, and he was there. Let a pub ten miles away put out the flag for draught ale at a tanner a pint and he was knocking at the door before the locals were even at the starting point. He swore by pubs, navigated by pubs, lived for pubs and went in fear of missing opening time as good Catholics go in fear of mortal sin. He had a wife and five kids and no home sex life, unless you can include a dive into bed and you-know-where and asleep in five minutes flat.

Liking his beer meant a daily twist. I didn't like it because of old Robinson – the old man was as sharp as a needle and knew the game inside out, but knew what he could afford and let the slack run. What I was afraid of was Charlie's appetite. We'd race round corners on two wheels and tip coal like a rushed-up film just so that he could get an hour's straight boozing. Being big for my age and covered with coaldust anyway, the perfect make-up, I used to go along for company. I got a taste for the stuff; not in my neck but in my belly. After a morning lugging sacks up and down stairs, along winding corridors and through narrow doors the roots of your mouth cried out for it; two pints and there you were, merry and bright for the rest of the day. When winter came every pub sign was a passport to ease, a blessed chit for the only medicine that could dullen the gritty feeling down your back, the broken nails aching with cold, and the cold eating away at your knees and toenails. In time both of us were up to the neck in the swindle, along with the milkman, the grocer, the club and insurance collectors. The road to beer was to batten on the ladies. And what a variety!

Long, short, fat and thin, most of these discontented, so that the rare cheerful one facing up to life and what dropped from the pay-packet, cheerfully sharing her husband with the club, the darts team, and local football team, shone like a star in the darkness, a darkness with few stars. Most of them were watching every penny, council flats and semi-detached houses alike, but there are tricks to every trade. A merry line of crack with a sprinkling of compliments while you signed the chit was generally sufficient. Meantime Charlie was working the oracle with the extra, empty sack.

And, if Charlie could be believed, there were other tricks of the trade. There were women stretching out the last copper who were not above lifting their skirts for quick payment. 'Black?' I'd shout above the knock of the engine; and he'd turn quickly, white teeth flashing and tongue licking red lips. Sometimes when we'd finished our stint for the day he'd run the lorry under a leafy tree and tell tall yarns about bored and thirsty housewives. There was Polly, wife of a hard-boozing golfer-business man, fond of a drink herself, and with an ever-open door for the window cleaner, milkman and coalman. The man with the ladder got it first; a black-haired cockney with long sideboards, on a cold, cold day with a gale blowing snowflakes the size of half a crown. 'Do the bedroom windows from the inside,' says she. 'It'll be more comfortable.' Still wearing her dressing gown at two in the afternoon, but not for long; in the second room he went, where he dropped his pail, scrim and chamois in stark astonishment and sheer delight at the sight of a tall, generous red-haired woman standing on a chair and tugging at a drawer in the top of the wardrobe. 'The chair's rickety,' says she, looking over her shoulder the minute he walks in, 'steady me.' The frilly white material rippled with her movements and one high-heeled shoe keeled over and naturally brought her toppling into his arms, a warm delightful bundle but too much for one man to hold when there's a bed behind to help with the weight; the curtains drawn and not a thing to worry about but a big frisky woman with nothing to take off and nothing to learn, and enough energy to work a regiment of hard-boozing golfers to death. Many a time, said Charlie, she'd keep him at it so long he'd rush off and forget to pick up the window-cleaning money, but it was always there the next time.

'Whoo!' I'd say, eyes shining over a dry mouth. 'It's a fable.

He was having you on …'

'Not a chance,' says Charlie. 'Talky Tommy soon spread the news and before Bob's your Uncle every caller was accepting the offer of a cup of tea and enjoying the changes she'd swing on the trick of getting you where she wanted to be.' He sighed. 'She was worse than a hard day's work – reckon that's why her old man took up golf … dying for it day in and day out.'

'But black!'

'Not a chance. "Don't you feel uncomfortable!" was the word, "The water's lovely and warm." So you'd strip off and in next to no time she'd be scrubbing your back and generally playin' around, dyin' to be in with ye, but that was one caper Ah'd never stand for. Always wanting to make it last, playin' all the way, but what could ye do? Got tirin' in the end, but it was a pity they had to leave in the end. Talk of the town, and no wonder. A gift!'

He'd nudge me, 'Never mind, kiddar. You'll get your chance.'

And he'd be off again, more often than not about his favourite experience, the willing widow early in his career who'd wrestle with him on the mat before the fire, never saying a word from start to finish and never consenting to take him upstairs or take her clothes off – 'All Ah wanted was to see her stripped,' he'd murmur regretfully, 'but it was no dice.' And I'd stare at him in astonishment at a man with riches in his hand quibbling about the one treasure she wanted to keep.

But it wasn't all tales, as I soon found out. You could see the possibilities in the way they eyed you, the way some of them cracked jokes about not touching you because coalmen brought luck to childless women, and nine times out of ten these same ones would have taken a fit if there'd been anything in the superstition. The hunger used to leap out of their eyes, bored women looking for an outlet in 'True Romances' and dying to meet the big boys of television.

'Never mind, kiddar, you'll get your chance,' and he was right. But don't think life on the coal-lorry was all gossip and spicy adventures. It was grind until your shoulders ached, but the worry was worse. You can be as tough as you like, and I'm no jelly baby, but when you're working a dodge worth a couple of quid a week there's also the worry, not that you're doing wrong, but that you'll be found out. Trust Robinson for that, the old fox paying out the rope every week until at last he had Charlie where he wanted him. We were out on our necks.

I hated Robinson. Standing there that Friday night when the rocket went off I could have knocked him on the head and put him away in one of his own sacks. Because he was right. But what can you do when keeping the peace with the man on the job means diddling the boss? Even if you're not short of the lolly it's a temptation to have extra money in your pocket so that you can buy the beer and records you want, keep yourself going in snouts, and not be on your knees Wednesday and Thursday for the odd shilling or two to keep you going. That was the worst interview in my life. The old man dry and small with only his eyes alive like tadpoles behind the glasses, me burning under the dust on my face and spouting sweat under the leather backpad.

'Ah could slap you both into court,' he said.

I was shaking like a leaf, inside. All my insides were a field of corn in the wind but I managed to say: 'Ye've every right to, Mr Robinson.'

'You admit it, then?' I nodded. 'You came through a damn sight quicker than him.'

I thought of poor old Charlie's face, all streaked and working so that you didn't know whether it was sweat or tears. 'He's got more to throw away than me.'

'That's right – he's got a wife and five kids. You're as free as the air. Or are you?'

The old bastard was wringing every last drop out of the situation, but I hung my head and said, 'No – there's my mother.'

'Right,' he said sharply. 'He's got five kids and you've got a mother … how much d'ye reckon ye've swindled me out of?'

'Not you – the customer.'

'Not the customer,' he said wearily. 'They only lost money –

I've lost goodwill. That's something you can't pick up from a counter ... my God, that's something you slave for all your life. And ye stand there asking favours!'

'Ah'm askin' no favours.'

'You aren't, eh? Ye should see yourself in a mirror.' He was right. If I'd thought creeping on the floor would have done any good, I'd have done it. I'd have licked his boots, the laces, the leather, the sole. But I knew that it was no use. Whatever he was going to do he'd decided before I walked into the room. 'All right,' he said. 'You'll not pay anything back – it would take a man's wages a year to track it down anyway. And Ah'm telling ye now that if ye'd been in the clear I'd have taken it to court. But you're not, and Ah'm not going to be responsible for sending you down to a court, juvenile or otherwise. Now clear out.'

I shot away but he stopped me before I reached the door. 'Any man's lucky to have one chance, and you've had it. Remember that. And be thankful for that old woman, the one that tipped me off. If ye've got any savvy she did ye the best turn of your life.'

Lucky for me that down at my end the men that fire and hire don't ask for references. The Old Lady went up in a blue light, and old Harry sat looking into the fire the whole time. That's what hit me hardest. I wanted him out, but in a funny sort of way I respected him and needed his respect.

2

I went wandering around to the Youth Employment. It was winter and we were having a hard spell of ice on the floor every morning, and when it wasn't ice or sleet it was an east wind that would have cut a forest down. I was lucky. Got a job as a baker's apprentice. Not a two by four bakery, but a big model one employing maybe fifty or sixty girls as well as the usual muster of male bakers, most of them on the loaf turn in nightshift. I was the jack of all hoists, rushing from the lift, still rope-operated, to the scullery, and a mountain of cake tins, jammy knives, filthy trays, shapes, rolling pins and what have you, and from there to a spell with the spades in front of a blast of hot air and leaking steam. Or beguiling the time away removing clinkers from the furnace, which was away in a chamber of horrors behind the ovens and occupied by millions of crickets and dance-mad mice. I hated it. I hated the women and girls, but most especially the girls. The forewomen were most ancient, mutton-dressed-up-as-lamb, earning good money by being as hard as nails. But having to deal with girls and all the worry that this can mean they didn't mind me so much. To them I was a mobile piece of furniture. They shouted 'Arthur' as some might shout 'Fido', but without affection. But the girls were teasers one and all. It was like being in the middle of a conspiracy. Whispers and titters all around you. Times I wished I could have had one or the other in the furnace room or over a flour sack in a dark corner of the storeroom above, but they were too sly for that. I opened my big mouth too much. Kidding me about being too young to know anything one day at tea-break – a dozen girls making together like a pack of wolves, passing secrets with little giggles or, what is worse, with their eyes, all ganged up on me. In the end I let out. I blew up like a volcano. Didn't give them the lickings of a dog – and told them I'd had my share of better meat than them. Which was true, but that didn't justify it.

I saw one of the forewomen standing outside the ring and knew she'd heard everything. She was old enough to be my mother and I went red at the thought. We broke up but that particular little episode was never forgotten – from then on I was the sex maniac and they'd pretend to jump whenever I passed by, or would make little screams and back into corners, picking up a dough knife as if prepared to defend their honour to the end. Honour! There wasn't more than one or two intact among the whole bunch; every weekend you'd hear them whispering in a corner about how to make 'him' do this or that, the frights they'd had, what Mam suspected or had found them doing, and so on. Marriage was their end and aim, an easy living to look forward to, but also a kind of slavery that made them hate their men. I was too young to kidnap, so they took it out of me. But the particular forewoman watched me and was always tender, giving her orders in a low, kind voice. Not a widow, a married woman, with some kind of trouble on her hands, probably the husband.

It's funny, but I've forgotten her name. Clean forgotten it. But not her line of approach. I've mentioned the way she watched me. Whenever I left the room, she knew. Whenever I entered, without turning round or looking up, she still knew. Don't ask me how I know – there were times I'd slip in after half an hour's absence and she'd call out my name without checking I was there. Despite her age, getting on for the middle-thirties, something grew up between us, like two people in a roomful who see the point of a joke and smile at each other, or share a secret. But nothing was ever said. I never tried to get into conversation with her, or her with me, and if at the end of the day we accidentally met at the door she'd shy away, slow up so that I could get ahead or wait for me to make the pace and leave her behind. But once or twice I'd catch her looking at me, weighing me up, and I used to wonder if women were like men, wondering what lies beneath the clothes.

It was so secret that I didn't even admit it to myself. More than twice my age and I'm not going to pretend that she was a lush piece, she was trim, tidy, but not one to go breathless over.

Then one day when I was sweeping out the storeroom she came walking in like a ghost. Just my luck when there was a dozen I'd have preferred more. Not that I knew what it was all about. It was a dark lofty sort of place and all the light bulbs were covered with flour or meal. My broom had lifted all the dry dirty flour into the air and she came through it like a moth through smoke. She followed me into the far corner. I kept looking over my shoulder and she kept coming on, walking very quietly. When she was near enough I caught a whiff of some perfume or other. It went into my nose like a needle, through the heavy smell of meal mingled with ground almonds, walnuts, and the rest. In the end

I had to stop against a barricade of sacks. 'Well?' she said.

'Is there anything you want?' I asked like a softy.

'Just a little bit talk.' I sat down, holding on to the broomshank for support or an anchor. Boy, she wasn't excited or breathing hard; cool as a glass of spring water, sure of herself. She stood over me, looking down with a queer little smile, then put her hands into my hair. I must have jumped at her touch … 'You're old for your age,' she said, 'and big … where did you get that scar?' She was tracing it with her finger tips. They tingled as if they'd been dipped into shaving lotion. 'Does it hurt – you're shivering?' Without waiting for an answer she continued, 'I heard you on with the girls the other day – the bitches!' with such an explosion of pure hate that I stared at her. 'Put that broom away.' Like a private under orders I shifted it to the side, brushing her knee as I did so. Then it was her turn to shiver. That's how near she was. 'I heard you saying – saying that you knew all about girls. Was that just a boast?' Then I knew what was coming. I could hardly believe it, I wanted to be out and away and stay all at the same time. I shook my head at the question. 'Sure?' she crooned, very softly. 'Who was it?' And all the time her hands were running through my hair. 'A girl your own age – or somebody older – like me.'

'Like you,' I said.

'Ah,' she breathed, as if a bet she'd made with herself had come off. 'Ah thought it was like that.' The nice accent was wearing off. 'Y'know, Ah've wondered how that sort of thing starts. Like this?' She dropped onto my knees and came down on my mouth all in one swoop. From then on it was a free-for-all, too quick to be good. I never had time to tell her that it hadn't been like that at all, and certainly not afterwards. The other time had been slow, gentle and confident. This was a wrestling match, an ambush and a kind of attempted murder. Revenge, if I'm any judge. There'd been no hate in the other woman, only a kind of weary sadness that helped and didn't use me. But she was older.

Everything always comes out different to the way you want it.

Instead of a piece like Polly, or the kind that Charlie meant when he gave me a dig in the ribs, I lit on a woman who was old enough to have had everything but had missed most of it, a woman who wanted to give and not take. And that afternoon in the flour-loft it wasn't one of the pert birds I wanted to humiliate, but a woman who'd been humiliated herself. But dangerous. It happened again, but not regularly. She'd just jump without rhyme or reason, and I always had the feeling that it wasn't her decision, but somebody else's. Like Charlie's other woman, the one who wouldn't undress, she wouldn't talk. I never saw her outside the bakery. She was as much a stranger at the end as at the beginning. In the end she wore me down. I had to get out. It wasn't only because of her being a married woman, or appearing not to care about being safe, but her entire outlook that sent me running. I don't remember her name, but I often wonder who and what she really was, and why she picked me, and why she did it. She was the only woman I ever met without a scrap of tenderness in her. I keep wondering what burned it out. Of course, there was the scrap man's daughter, Mildred, but I only saw her from a distance, so she doesn't count. And this woman never tried to insult me in any way. She didn't need to say or do anything in the way of an insult. She folded insult and her body around you at the same instant.

So I was on the hop again, getting the reputation of a jumper as I passed rapidly from one job to another. I felt like a trawler caught in a storm with the harbour in sight. I used to look at some character on the trolley wearing a nice collar and tie, reading a newspaper or a nice cellophane-covered book and envy myself into his shoes – up and coming young feller, got what it takes, tackles a job the right way, uses his brains – and he's got plenty. Snug as a bug in a rug and not worrying about the paper qualifications because he had all the others. It's a wonder some of them didn't drop dead or go up in flames – whoosh! All things I did were simple and set to a pattern, like coopering with tricks five hundred and maybe more years old. Or lugging boxes of apples, sacks of potatoes, and nets of cabbage into the Fruit and

Vegetable Market. A variety of jobs! This simply means jobs they can't mechanise up to the hilt, and in my short time I've already lost one job to the machine – when the welded barrel replaced the wooden one. One way or another, their fault or mine – what does it matter – I went through all these jobs like a dose of physic. Moses had to die when he saw the Promised Land, but the discard has to live on. At least I managed to live on with a kick. All that worried me was the Old Lady and Harry situation. Didn't realise I was still tied to her, didn't realise that it kept coming back like a stab because I was still holding on to her skirts.

These days I can laugh at their courtship; at the kitten, the snails and the tame mouse he set free by pulling a string the night she sat in the cabin, still as porcelain until the sight of the pink nose and beady eyes made her jump into his arms and relax. But I wasn't laughing then. And it's funny when you think of it, the thought cut deepest when I was in the same boat. Take the woman I mentioned. It was building up for a week or two but came to a head about a fortnight before my career as a coalman came to an end. When Charlie told me what was brewing I thought he was crazy – a woman her age. He shook his head, 'Some like 'em young,' he said. 'Never mind, you watch her.' And this was the first thing that supported his theory. She lived at the posh end where they believe in bulk, but ordered by the hundred-weight. The first load or two had been big ones, ten or twelve hundredweights, but she gradually scaled down to four or five, and always a cup of tea waiting. Brown hair and eyes, not fat but enough to fill her dress, and always that wistful watching. Too nice to run into it like the Polly woman; in fact it wouldn't have come to anything in the ordinary run of affairs. Then one night, at a loose end and roaming around the Central Station, I bumped into her leaving the ticket barrier with one case too many, travel-worn and weary. I saw her but she didn't see me.

I walked over and said, 'Give you a hand with those cases,' and she turned. She was one of those creamy women, the type that blush really hard.

'Why, yes – you're the nice boy … how different you look!'

'Sorta civilised,' I said. 'And I feel better for it. Couldn't see you struggling, not after all those cups of tea.'

At the taxi she said, 'Can I drop you off on the way? Is it in the right direction?' And because I was bored and dreading seven o'clock coming and the feel of nobbly coal on my shoulder I lied. I think she knew I was lying too. My sort didn't live that way. The taxi driver must have thought we were crazy, that is if he'd time to notice with a road like glass and a rush of traffic and wandering drunks. Maybe he thought we were mother and son, and that's a laugh because all I was conscious of during the ten minutes zooming through the night to a big question mark beyond all the others rushing through my mind was her perfume, and weight moving beside – the ripple of woman. What I could see of her face was gentle, a few lines and a little too much fat but nothing ugly. Nothing beautiful either, but very comfortable and very secure. I didn't know what to say, then she helped me. 'I hope the house is all right,' she said. 'It's been locked up a week – but there's a fire laid ready to light.'

'And a kettle ready to boil?' I said.

She pressed my hand, took hold of it, drew it on to her lap, and I knew it was fixed. Especially when she said, 'Call me Stella.' Lit the fire and drank a cup of tea – eventually – and rolled home at two in the morning too excited even to think up an excuse for the Old Lady. But – and this is the important but – I'd thought of her and Harry, once in that house, with that kind and loving woman. And believe me or not it had hurt even then. Can you believe it?

So in the end I'd exhausted so many jobs that I'd travelled on every trolley in town, but never long enough to get to know a conductor. My cards never had time to gather dust. Once or twice the job exhausted itself but more often than not I had the honour of exhausting the job. I was big and bigoted, discontented and ripe for trouble. Also, I had a great respect for myself. They called me Pretty Boy because the scar brought out my beauty, nice skin, bright blue eyes and nice bronze hair that brushed like a shield. I knew all about my wicked smile and the devil in my eyes – hadn't the Old Lady told me about them often enough? – and used them, or used my tongue with the backing of an eye for any weakness. Always the loser, but had a lot of fun because I never let on I cared. Yet, to be honest I did care. I was sore because I lacked savvy, because I was incompetent, because I was where I was, my mother's white hope become a black cloud over her life.

3

Incompetent I might be, but not at home. They couldn't get married because nobody knew where my old man was hiding out, the Old Lady was troubled with a conscience, and I made sure it kept on working. Always needling. Used to pretend to myself that it was all for the old man's sake – but that's a laugh. His face was just a blank and any feeling I had was a kind of sentiment, and pretty high at that. It was Me, the big Me behind it all.

Yet she still continued patient with me, and even went so far as to make peace with Uncle George – dear old talky George, stuffed with self-importance and a master of the art of rubbing it in. Considering her temperament that was some sacrifice. She came in pulling her gloves off and ready for a battle, knowing – and sharing as she did – my mortal hatred of the man: 'Now Ah know what ye're going to say – Ah know what he'd like and none better. But Ah'm sick of this chopping and changing jobs; ye've touched the bottom, so ye can do the same as me and pocket your pride.'

'Ah'll get him a job at the factory,' said Harry.

'He's not going to that dead-end place!'

'Make as much money – and he'll not be beholden to anybody.'

'Sardines! D'ye know what he can be if he sticks in with his Uncle George – a Civil Engineer.'

'Well, have it your own way. But Ah wouldn't like to think a lad of mine …'

'Well, he isn't, so pipe down,' she said.

The Pasha was gobbling up his supper, and television dancing girls.

'Sit down,' he ordered.

'Aye, sit down,' said Aunt Mary.

The place was calculated to smother you, kitchen and sitting room combined: television set, radiogram, washing machine, electric boiler, kitchen cabinet, cooker and fridge. Also table, four chairs, three-piece suite, brass coal scuttle, poker and tongs stand. On the walls, two bloody big mirrors with stags painted on them, drinking from a lake; a picture of Uncle George's Mum and Dad, tinted, and two pictures of Uncle George; one of him wearing his chain of office when he was Mayor, the other of him where he belonged, come to think of it, standing inside one of those big concrete sewerage pipes I was to get to know so well during my career with him.

'It's been a nice day ...' said the Old Lady.

'Shee-ist!' hissed Aunt Mary, 'he's watching television.'

She didn't need to add that he was also tackling about a stone of French-fried chips, half a pound of bacon, and a couple of fried eggs. Butter on one side, plate of sliced bread on the other, in the centre a big jar of pickled onions. Hardly took his eyes away from the screen: a real fan; spiking the onions with his fork *ad lib*; that is to go with every mouthful.

Once he said: 'Mary, ye haven't got these chips right.'

'Well, Ah'm sure Ah did them no different.'

He grunted. That was all the conversation until the girls went off. In case you're wondering, whenever he wanted another cup of tea he rattled the edge of the saucer until the old girl came running. No wonder she's thin and miserable. In the end he batted his chest, belched once or twice, and gave me an unpleasant look.

'So ye've come,' he said.

I didn't bat an eyelid, but could see the Old Lady was having a fine old time suppressing her gorge. 'Aye, Ah've come, Uncle George,' I said humbly.

'Well, as long as ye've no fancy ideas, ye'll do well with me,' he said. 'Stick in, do as ye're told, take an example from me and there's no knowing where ye'll end.'

'Aye, mind, ye'll not go far wrong,' said Aunt Mary. 'He's worked his way up to the top of the tree ... charge o' the gang, big man in the Labour Party, magistrate and once-Mayor ...'

'Takes some beatin',' said Uncle George. 'And all on merit. Merit, me lad, ye'll never find your Uncle George gannin' round the back door, lickin' backsides or pullin' strings. Merit, pure merit. And commonsense. Like Ah tell 'em at the Housin' Committee – it's as simple as layin' a sewer – get your sights fixed properly; keep an eye on the plumb; get on wi' the job.'

'Every credit due to ye,' said the Old Lady, although it choked her.

'Ah, well, there's plenty of that, plenty of that,' he said. 'Ah've mixed with the highest, but Ah've always stood by simple merit. Ah've always been honest George. Did Ah tell ye what Ernie Bevin told me once – he said: "Ah picked ye from the platform, lad," he said. "There's a honest face – a pound to a penny that's honest George from the Tyne." Now how d'ye account for that, eh? That's true judgement if you like. By gum, that shows the man he was.'

'Who was this Ernie Bevin?' I asked.

'Ye've never heard of Ernie Bevin? The Dockers' KC? The greatest Labour leader of all time – the man that did more to win the war than Churchill! It only goes to show what the modern generation is ... *we've* toiled an' moiled – *they* ask us who Ernie Bevin was ...'

'Why, it's common knowledge,' said Aunt Mary.

'It's elementary, elementary. Ye've a lot to learn, by gum ye have. Ah know ye only went to a secondary modern but that's no excuse ...'

I saw a trap and laid it for him: 'Was this Bevin a pal of yours, Uncle George?'

'Was he a pal of mine! Old Ernie knew merit when he saw it

– as Ah've just told ye, many's the time he's nodded or picked me out in the conference room; many's the time he'd put his hand out and congratulated me on a speech. Aye, Ernie knew merit when he saw it.'

'That'll be a few years since.'

'Gettin' on, gettin' on now.'

'Never was good at ancient history,' I murmured. The Old Lady slayed me with a look, but Uncle George let the insult spatter from that thick old hide.

'History! We are where we are through that man.'

'Give me Cousins every day,' I chipped in, knowing his prejudices. 'There's a man that sticks to his principles on that stinkin' H-bomb and everything.'

God help me, he just about blew up.

'He's nowt but a trouble-maker! Far over-big for his boots – an' to think he was trained be Ernie! He's one of our own but he wants watchin'. But he'll never amount to anything.'

'What about this job, George?' asked the Old Lady.

'Ah'm interested in what Uncle George's sayin', Mother,' I said. 'What if they make Frank Cousins the Prime Minister some day, Uncle George?'

'Niver in the creation of man – they've more sense.'

'Dafter things have happened,' I said. 'Can ye see him on the steps of Ten Downing Street ... what would ye do then, Uncle George?'

'Man, he couldn't be – look, if ye knew the party the way Ah knew it ye'd know they could never make Frank Cousins Prime Minister. Never!'

'But if they did – say they did?' I pressed, pretending not to see the Old Lady flagging me down.

'Ah'd rally to the ould green banner!' he said. 'Ah'd give the man me unstinted loyalty, for that's the essence of democracy – an' that's my merit; to go with the party. Ah made the party an' the party made me and so Ah'll stick to the party because it gives way to merit, fosters merit and gives way to merit.'

His eyes were popping and the sweat was starting on his brow. I remembered a word I'd once had to write over a hundred times at school, and swiftly applied it: 'The Meretricious Party, eh?' Very respectful, very humble, very obliging; and they all fell for it. 'Varry true,' said the Old Lady; 'Aye, now, that's the livin' truth,' said Aunt Mary; and Uncle George hooked his waistcoat and grunted: 'Well, Ah'm glad to see ye've got some good from your eddication.' The atmosphere was mellow, I nearly fell off my chair killing the convulsions. I always knew he was a faker and talked off a record, but this was just too good to be true.

He pulled out a flashy cigarette case and offered it. 'No thanks, Uncle George,' I murmured, nearly breaking my heart.

'Presented by the Branch for twenty years faithful service,' he said. 'Ah'm glad ye don't smoke, young feller. Ah never smoke during the day.' It was a perfect opening to tell him that since I didn't touch the weed day or night I was twice as good as him. Resisting the impulse I told him that I didn't want to start because it was so hard to stop. The Old Lady nearly threw a fit.

'Ah've got it under control,' he said. 'Ah can stop any time Ah want. That's democracy – self-discipline. That's the strength of the older generation. They were brought up in a hard school. But the younger ones – the intellectuals: you watch 'em chain-smokin' an' drinkin' like fishes, an' God knows they can't hold it.'

'George tells 'em,' said Aunt Mary. 'Don't you, George?'

'Straight from the shoulder. Truth, not popularity; that's my aim and that's my merit.'

The Old Lady was flagging me down again – I couldn't resist mouthing his signature tune in time with him – 'That's my merit.'

'Ah'm sure he'll be in good hands with you, George,' said the Old Lady.

'Ah yes,' said Uncle George. 'But he'll have to make the grade … Ah'm no believer in pullin' strings for relatives, but Ah'll make this concession. Ah'll give him a start, then he's out on his own. Ah've got to keep discipline, so there'll be no favour shown him – he'll rough it with the rest as soon as he gets his hand in.'

'What do they pay?' I asked.

'There you are! Next thing you know he'll be wanting to know times and tea-breaks, statutory and annual holidays. Five poun' twelve and six, an' if you ask me that helped to fight for it, far too much. If ye've any sense ye'll turn the packet over to your mother, the way Ah turn mine over to your Aunt Mary. Dinnat throw it away – put it away.'

'He'll put two poun' a week away,' said the Old Lady, and her eyes were shining. 'Mark my words,' she told me. 'First pay ye'll away down the Post Office and get a book out.' In my mind I chalked up a resolution to tell her that we were due to a spending spree before we started saving the first thousand pounds. She knew as well as me that the old faker could put by with all the extras he got from union business, committees, sitting on this and that; and I won't go any further because everybody knows that in this country nobody ever makes anything on the side out of public service. Ah, Ah, Ah!

'When do I start?'

It was obvious from the way he hedged that it wasn't his decision. Before he got me the job *he'd* have to crawl the way the Old Lady and me were crawling. For two pins I'd have thumbed my nose and called it a day, but I had to think of the Old Lady. Women are queer. They don't mind crawling as long as they hit the jackpot somehow or somewhere, in the end. But they don't like to put on the act, unpaid. Also, to be honest, I'd shoved five pound twelve and sixpence on the balance along with the Old Lady's tender feelings. And I'd had a good laugh out of the old faker, and would have a better on the way home. But I still felt sick.

As soon as we got out of earshot of the house the Old Lady started on me, but there was no real conviction in the old yakity-yak; underneath, I could see she was simmering at having to roast his taties for him. 'You,' she said. 'One of these days ye'll get caught out with that silent lipping – it's not only him you do it with – Ah've seen ye do it with me.'

'Not him, Ma. He's too thick.'

'It wasn't very kind, in fact it was cruel, when ye think the poor man was goin' out of his way to get ye a job – an' a good one at that!'

'Don't kid yourself, Ma. It gives him a chance to play the Pasha. Wave his magic bloody wand an' show off in front of the poor relations.'

'Ah think he's really kind at the bottom of him,' she said.

'Until it touches his pocket – or his dignity,' I told her, 'then it turns off like a tap.'

'His merit …' she started and we looked at each other and off we went on a roller-coaster of a laugh that lasted all the way home.

We had a cuppa tea and listened to the radio gospel, which the Old Lady likes for the jazzed-up hymns. Then all the fun withered away, because they were waiting for me to get the hell out of it. Which I didn't until I was told. I lay and listened for a time but they'd found another station and it was going at strength five, which would drown out even Uncle George, and for all I knew they might be holding hands or going to town. There was nothing I could do about it so I lay and looked at the stars, and thought what a zipping hell of a day it had been, and wondered what it would be like being a working man. I'd an idea the wages of work, over and above five pounds twelve and six, and all that this would buy, would be something a little worse than death.

4

It was a fortnight or so, add or lose a day, before we heard from Uncle George again: waiting to get the right man in the right mood, I suppose. The Old Lady was up to all sorts of dodges to keep me out of mischief. First job was sloshing whitewash on the kitchen top; if the plan had worked out there was a spell of painting to follow. So I took my time over that ceiling; I worked on it like an artist making a masterpiece. Harry remarked it was the most fascinating spectacle he'd ever seen. 'I could watch him for hours,' he remarked.

'Reckon you'll be drawin' your pension by the time he's finished then,' said the Old Lady sourly. She was sick and tired of putting sheets over the table and sideboard, etc. and of washing same sheets out, since part of my technique consisted of a bold sweep that zipped any surplus paint from the brush.

When the ceiling was finished she'd forgotten all about the painting, so I settled down to enjoy my last hour of freedom. It was high summer and I spent long hours down by the ravine, the one leading down to the Motor Boat Club. I found a tidy clay-hole, borrowed a sickle from old Charlie Nettlefold, a hawker chap, and cut sufficient long grass to make a bed upon which I could lie in the sun, and relax. Then I stripped off to my bathing costume and cooked myself medium rare. When I wasn't lying on my belly I viewed the sky through my fingers and watched those clouds rolling by. If ever I got tired of the clouds I'd turn on my side and watch the road bridge with all the cars, lorries and what not whooping over it and the people crawling like ants, sometimes an odd bird in a bright dress; or turn on the other side and watch the trains rattling over the other bridge. Sometimes I'd stir myself and have a gander down the Motor Boat Club, but never got a taker, because during the day the blokes were mostly crazy fishermen who didn't like company, and couldn't see it anyway. That was the best holiday I ever had and the only regret was that I never bumped into the quiet bloke that once gave me a river trip. He took me to Shields and back and never said a word. A character that doesn't want to talk, up or down, preach or insinuate, but is content to let things float, is a treasure worth meeting more than once in a lifetime.

One day I was discovered by a character named Crab Carron. I was lying face and belly in the hay, feeling the sunshine needling into my back and having a series of golden dreams about the times I'd have when I was a millionaire: private plane, personal yacht, my own island and a regiment of personal slaves, including girls. The only free woman on the place would be the Old Lady, and Harryboy, the Lodger; if she insisted. All this was drifting and I was working up a pleasurable plot whereby the Prime Minister flew down in his personal helicopter to consult me about something or other when I began to feel uncomfortable. I turned over and found Crab Carron, standing over me, only it took me a long time to make him out, firstly because he looked twice his normal size and secondly because the sun was right behind his head.

'Hey, man, you put the wind up me for sure,' I told him.

'Wonderin' what ye'd be doin' up here.'

'Gettin' to be a handsome man for when I take my annual holiday in the West Indies,' I told him.

'Boy oh boy, you've got a right lush tan already. You come here every day?'

'Accordin' to the weather. Naturally, come wet or wind I stay at home an' pick my nose.'

'Still the old joker,' said he. 'You ever notice anythin'? Around here, Ah mean.'

'When the sun goes in, that's all I notice, Crab,' I said. 'That's when I go home. What's the caper? Anythin' to do with you?' With characters like this Crab Carron, and his brother Nosey, who's about my age, you've got to come back sharp and nasty; that's their language.

'Just interested, that's all.' He squatted beside me and started chewing a straw. Both these Carrons look good, but if you looked between their ears with an x-ray you'd find only solid ivory and not very good quality ivory at that. Crab, I reckon, would then be just short of six feet and nicely-nicely made.

He was dark, with black hair and long sideboards; black as tar. He'd a long Red Indian face. Maybe his eyes were brown, maybe black, but they certainly went with his hair. He was wearing a pair of red jeans without a crease that he must have put on with a shoehorn, and a woolly sports shirt. They reckon his Old Man's Dad was a Spanish sailor. Could be. Plenty of the toreador about him and his brother, anyway.

'You workin', Crab?'

'Oh, workin' on and off – when there's a pitch. Ah run a barrow; otherwise odd jobs is my line.' He looked away from me. 'You seen old Charlie Nettlefold today?'

'Not today – to talk to. Mebbe saw him pull out with that old mangy hoss of his. Borrowed a sickle from him mebbe four or five days ago. What's he got you want?'

'Never you mind,' he said. 'Now listen. Got a little bit of business in his house. All on the level but Ah wouldn't want the old man to know – or anybody else for that matter. Easy business. Mebbe some day Ah'll let you in the game. Keep your mouth shut?'

'Ah'm dumb,' I told him.

'See,' he said, pointing with his straw, 'you've got the view from here. See anybody comin' or goin'. Glad Ah spotted ye.'

'Wouldn't have made any difference if Ah had,' I told him. 'None of my business.' Howsoever, I still wondered what the caper was.

'Shift over,' he said. 'Ease off and Ah'll have a rest.'

Well, we both lay down and dozed. I think he did, anyway. But I was never away again with wondering what his caper was. In the end I sat up. It was getting on to tea-time, late tea-time, and the sun wasn't so hot. I saw old Charlie coming down the rough road to his house, ambling along beside the nag and holding down a mountain of rags. He pulled up in the yard. A big fat man wearing a frock coat with a smooth fur collar about a century old and a greasy bowler pulled down over his ears. I heard him shouting. The door opened and a woman came out. She was old, thirty or forty maybe, and a little bit on the stout side. Plump, anyway. She'd hair as black as Crab's.

I'd often seen her around – old Charlie's daughter. Never knew her name until it was in the papers, but for the sake of the record here it is: Mildred. I could see her hair shining like a crow's wing. A bit of wind came up and blew her skirt up. She didn't hold it down the way most women do. It blew right up but she just went on talking to the old man, handling the rags on the cart. It occurred to me then that she might be the business that Crab had mentioned.

For a ragman's daughter she was clean. Never made up. Never talked, never smiled, but walked along the street with her bag on her arm and her nose in the air.

'It isn't what you think,' said Crab.

'Okay, let go my hand – Ah'll not run.'

Along his brow where it met his hair was all little beads of sweat which contradicted his smile. 'That's the craziest woman you ever saw,' he muttered, biting his fingers. That Crab certainly had the shortest fingernails I ever saw – and the longest fingers.

'Crazy old women are dynamite,' I told him. I was uncomfortable and wanted to say something. He laughed and remarked: 'That's my piggy bank, boy: money for jam.' I looked at him.

'Tell you some day,' he said, then pushed me back into the hay. I shouted something, his hand went over my mouth, and he whispered: 'The ould man's lookin' up this way; keep quiet.'

He took his hand away and never knew how near I'd been to biting off a finger or two in my panic. 'There's nothin' wrong,' he said. 'Wouldn't want old Charlie to know anythin'. Might think we're casin' the joint and before we know the slops'll be on …' I nodded, and he continued: 'You ever get thirsty down here?' I told him I did.

'Slip down some time and ask her for a drink.'

'No fears. Ye won't catch me gettin' mixed up with a crazy woman.'

'Second thoughts, might be best to leave her alone,' he told me. 'You're too young to understand.'

'Know all about it.' Which was practically true.

'You'd never guess this one in a month of Sundays, man,' he said. 'This isn't straight. This is a comedy. Enough to send ye scatty …'

'Come on, tell us.'

'Some day Ah'll let ye in,' he told me. 'Not yet. But some day

Ah'll let you in, for the simple reason you're doin' me a favour.'

We lay about ten minutes or so then scrabbled round and had a gander at the old man leading the nag into its stable. The woman was standing with legs apart and hands on her hips, looking our way.

'What's the joke?' I asked Crab.

'What d'ye mean?'

'She's laughin'. See?'

He didn't say anything for a few seconds: 'Some day Ah'll make her laugh the other side of her face,' he said at last. 'She'll not make a fool of me. You watch.' At that moment I was watching and man, I'll tell you, I didn't like the look on his face.

After he'd gone something struck me. As I've told you, this Mildred is often seen about. Now, everybody has some trick. Hers was a dead-pan face. Yet she'd stood there and looked up and laughed.

Lying there in the sun gave me a quiet contentment, and, when I thought about it, a big kick because I was free of school. Sometimes, going around, I see these modern schools built of beautiful wood, nice bricks, and acres of glass reflecting acres of green, green grass. Now, I don't want to give you any sob-stories. As far as I'm concerned all I want to give is the true strength of my educational career, which was a pretty funny one; and that involves saying that I went to a couple of schools that reached an all-time low. The first one, which you might call the sorting centre, was built about the same time as the county gaol, with the object of keeping out light and cutting down on ventilation. The steam pipes leaked and the whole place smelled like a gents' toilet. There I made my first big discovery – in their estimation I didn't have what it takes to make a boy-genius, modern type. My first major mistake was accepting the findings of their crumby court.

That's not to say I was one of the herd. While building up black marks among the teachers, who were a pretty decent lot and mostly women, I also won a reputation for being tough and witty among the clients. I didn't look for fights, but when I had to, fought hard, which was essential since my area produced some hard cards. Didn't like fighting and soon discovered that I could play off some of the characters otherwise, but also the teachers, by making a funny remark which was true but not recognised as such. You might say I discovered my talents by their abuse.

Reckon the Lodger helped in this development because it was about this time that he came to live with us. Apart from his interest in the Old Lady, which I always resented, he'd a pretty slick tongue which I admired and emulated.

But when it came to most subjects I was a dud. Let's say it didn't come easy. I was no camera eye. Anything useless, you could guarantee it would stick to my mind. But the stuff those old ladies taught me didn't have a chance. Came the 11-plus. I was under starter's orders but never ran. That morning was the most miserable of my life because for a couple of months the Old Lady had been giving me the works, and I believed it and wanted to please her, but ended up chewing my pen. Never saw such a collection of questions in my life and all the answers were elsewhere and anywhere but in my mind. About all I produced was a fine collection of doodles on my scrap paper.

So, in the end, I landed up in the Dump, so called because it was the finishing school, and boy I mean finishing, for about five hundred wild characters – and that's about two hundred above maximum capacity – who hadn't made the grade and if they didn't know were soon informed. Rejects, you might say. Headmaster was a character called Rattler and you can guess what we called him behind his back. Latter was essential because he was and had to be a hard type. Voice like a rasp. Only half the size of some of the lads but that made no difference. Would have made a good gangster or lion tamer and could certainly crack the whip – with his eyes. Had an assistant called Carruthers-Smith, big and grey and shambling like a teddy bear, temper like a lady's, a sneak in suede shoes.

Old Carruthers-Smith used to dance and shout like a maniac, and when he really let go the blood and snots used to fly. But he was most dangerous when he was quiet. It was old C.S. who did me most dirt, in more ways than one, and also gave me what you might call a last epic day at school.

Most of the teachers didn't count; in fact, few of them ever stayed long enough to make their mark – the Jungle Boys took care of that. They'd come bouncing in full of psychology, science and rich ideas and leave leaning on two sticks. I've seen big tough-looking characters break down and cry. Being rejects, we acted like rejects, and it was only the hand of tough cynical old Rattler that kept us down below the point of riot.

At the bottom of the tension was the snout situation. Between us we consumed about 5,000 cigarettes daily. A hard-smoking boy without cash for snouts is a pitiful sight. He's nervy, mean and lacks concentration for anything but getting hold of his particular drug; if he can't knock off a packet in the routine way he'll pay a midnight visit to some shop or ware-house with a pal, and a pinch bar. We also played the horses and had a school bookie with six or seven runners operating for him. He never made a motor bike let alone a Jaguar, but it kept him cosy, thank you.

It was a bad week when the detectives didn't call, in fact old Rattler used to worry if they hadn't turned up by Thursday; they said he used to ring the gorillas to make absolutely certain there was no business for him. Cash and snouts were short, and the only outlet for most was to break and enter or pilfer cars. For this reason the workshop was popular; whenever old Jones turned his back there was a rush for the inch flat steel, and you couldn't get near the shears and forge. That workshop was the greatest production centre in the country for pinch bars, mainly because a character only used his bar once. There were other tricks. Free rides on trains and trolleys were routine stuff; and the thickest character in the school could find a buckshee road into a cinema. We'd sell a scrap merchant his own stolen scrap, could size up the price of cable, copper and brass at sight, and while we never robbed the blind we could go one better by diddling the barrow boys when ripe pears were in season – and that's an operation that takes sweet organisation.

Nosey, Crab Carron's younger brother, once pinched a gorilla's bike just for the hell of it, made a quick trip to town and on arrival simply abandoned the transportation on the kerb and walked innocently away.

Mainly because I wasn't a really hard smoker and could always cadge enough for a packet of tabs from the Old Lady or Harry I didn't run into any of these capers until the close of my educational career. In fact, had it not been for the pigeon feast, I'd probably have left school with all possible honours; I was already a prefect, and might have finished as head boy, going forth with a laurel leaf around my head and my certificate of merit under my arm.

Old Rattler always had a soft spot for me and, since all my black marks were for inattention and general cheekiness, decided to pull me in on the side of law and order. I used to be pretty sore about old Rattler but all that's passed now. He's the victim of his own delusions – I mean, he was brought up in an era when miners became cabinet ministers, ploughboys poets, and middenmen millionaires, and still thinks it's possible. I used to dream of going back to the Dump and thrusting that old certificate, which I never won, under his nose and telling him just how much use it was. I knew two or three lads that used to take it around with them, but pretty soon it began to dawn upon them that this piece of paper had a bad smell or something. So they stopped using it. When you want a lad to carry a hod or a bale, you're more interested in his shoulders than his educational standards. And, boy, if a would-be tea-maker offers you a certificate of merit you'd cross him off the list – pronto as the Lone Ranger says to Tonto. For that lad wouldn't have intelligence enough to make tea, if he thought that certificate meant anything. See what I mean?

But, as I say, I wouldn't bother old man Rattler that way now. He's a tryer even if he's a thousand miles out. He liked me, and

I liked him, and if I met him tomorrow I'd offer him a pint to ease that rasp – and, come to think of it, he'd be a taker.

I'll admit that I was the sole founder of the pigeon feast. It wasn't my fault that Nosey tried for the trimmings. How it happened was that we nipped into the News Theatre one night and saw one of these Barbecue affairs, in colour; steaks, chops, sausages and what have you. So I said let's have a barbecue, just like that, and the three lads that were with me thought it was a good idea, and before we could turn we'd a bag of onions somebody had scrimped from the Fruit and Vegetable Exchange, a couple of dozen members of the Barbecue Club, and no steaks, chops, or sausages.

What put the crazy idea into my head I don't know: it just lighted like a big fat pigeon in my mind. 'Pigeons, we'll have barbecued pigeon!'

There are roughly a quarter of a million people in our city and to each person there are roughly maybe ten pigeons. Since there are many churchyards which have been turned into little parks, frequented by sentimental old persons who pass the hours away feeding them, most of these birds are plump. They are also agile. We picked the larder – the bedroom of one of those empty houses; got a store of wire upon which to hang the birds; and picked a pad, son of the third chef at the local restaurant, to pluck and clean the birds on the night. Lastly, we fixed the night of the barbecue.

All that was left was catching the birds. We reckoned we'd need at least two each; that made about sixty with reserves in case of unexpected company. We hadn't the birds, but we had ideas. Some suggested nets, others air-guns, bird-lime, electrocution, hawks and what have you. In the end we picked sites, two to each to get their quota by hook or crook.

Nosey Carron and me got a building site back of one of these churchyards. We had a council of war. First, we decided to do the job at five a.m. That way, we'd have only the occasional busman or railwayman passing by, when they wouldn't have time to stop even if their eyes were open, which they wouldn't be. There'd be the odd gorilla on the beat, but as the site was well down below ground level there wasn't much of a risk.

Second, we decided to use two methods and cut the odds. Old Nosey got some bird-lime – trust him. That was method one. Method two would be a trap made of materials on the job.

What we didn't discuss was my personal problem of getting out of the house at four-thirty or thereabouts. Nosey would have laughed at that one. From what I'd gathered there was a regiment quartered in their house, all getting their living after locking-up times. But you might guess that this kind of caper wouldn't suit the Old Lady who has a photo-electric detector cell built into her alarm system, and who sleeps with one eye open anyway. In the end I decided on a good yarn. The Old Lady's always a sucker for prestige and it went down well.

Four-thirty on the morning I was moving like a ghost. I'll swear there wasn't a creak all the way down and that's a miracle when you consider all the loose boards which have outlived their nails. I even sat on the floor to pull on my socks, remembering how a chair can yell. I should have used gloves: she came down upon me like a wolf on the fold.

She looked a sight with her hair in curlers and her big suspicious eyes. 'What's all this about?'

'Aw, Ma, told ye Ah was in trainin' for the inter-school sports.'

'It's half-past four and the baths don't open until seven, you told me.'

'Thought Ah'd give me breakfast time to settle.'

'There's something fishy on. Now what is it?'

'Listen, Ma – Ah want to be in good trim for the swimmin'. That's all.'

She heard old Nosey whistle outside.

'What's that?'

'What's what?'

'Somebody whistled – you're not goin' for burglary. All right, we'll see.' And away she scampered to the front door, nightgown, curlers and all. There was nothing to do but follow.

'Hey, you!' she shouted to Nosey, who was kicking a stone on the other side of the road. 'Come here.' He walked over looking as if butter wouldn't melt in his mouth, which was a mistake because the Old Lady always goes on contraries. That you can blame on me.

'What's on the go?' she asked.

'Aw, Ma, he's in the back and breast stroke events like me ...' Nosey picked up quick. 'And the high dive.'

'Well, it's far too early.' Her look stripped us both to the bare bone. I'm sure she suspected a shop-break or something worse. Arson, maybe. 'Just you come in and have a cup of tea. Have you had anything this mornin'?'

'Slice of bread and butter.'

'Ye've no sense – come on in and Ah'll give the pair of ye a good breakfast.'

I reckon it was the best breakfast Nosey Carron had packed in for centuries. Being used to worse upsets and liking his grub he was in no way put out. It was half-past six when she allowed us to leave and I was halfway up the street when I heard her shouting.

I'd forgotten my trunks and towel.

'Fine swimmer!' she said. 'And what's he goin' to do without his gear?'

'What d'ye mean, Ma?'

'You know what Ah mean – he's got none either.'

I pulled a quick one about Nosey wearing his trunks under his trousers and drying himself on my towel. I was past caring whether she believed it or not. She'd spoilt our chances of any pigeons that morning.

When I caught up to Nosey I was stinking mad: 'Well, that's a crazy woman, all right,' I told him. 'Wasted our morning. What do we do?'

'Get a move on,' he said. After a while he added: 'She's okay.'

'Who's okay?'

'Your Old Lady,' he said, patting his stomach.

Letting that one slide I said: 'What's the use of goin' now – the men are on the site by seven.'

'Let's go anyway.'

Well, it was one way of passing the time and so I went along. To cut a long story short, we cut down into the site and found six pigeons waiting. He'd been down last thing to spread the bird-lime and the corn. I felt a fool because I'd no idea of what to do; it was Nosey that despatched the birds. All I did was carry my share under my shirt. It was a funny feeling, all that weight with the claws and the beaks raking your skin and the feeling that they'd been alive and on the wing maybe at sunrise. I felt a butcher and also a fool because when all was said and done I was just a pigeon carrier. No thanks to me we'd won more than our quota. Yes, I was sore.

All that week there was havoc among the pigeons. Fat and friendly, full of confidence in the kindness of humanity they stepped into traps, were tangled in nets, and fell to point-blank blast. Any that survived obtained a new outlook. Friends of pigeons found themselves cut dead; even the statues were ignored. But the pigeon barbecue was a great success. We took over the main shed of the old foundry at the knuckle-end of the ravine. We built a fire under steel netting pinched from a site. We didn't have charcoal but got some good dried-out driftwood and burnt the guts out of it before we started roasting. You should have seen those lads when the first couple of dozen began to sizzle. Some of them were sitting round on old moulds and others were plucking birds ready for the fire. Some of the hard characters were having a game of brag. That old fire was glowing like a furnace ready to tap. That dark old place had never looked so cheerful. Then those birds began to sing. The fat dropped through the grid and made little bursts of flame and the smell was out of this world. In fact, it was lush.

I reckon that was the best time of all, when I was turning those birds and the fragrance was filling the place, drawing the braggers from their brag and the pluckers from their plucking. We all stood round and sniffed. Those birds never tasted so good as they smelled.

Then Nosey came in lugging a big cardboard carton. It was full of tinned beer. Ask no questions and you get no lies. Nobody asked for details. Maybe it fell off a dray; maybe it walked out of the brewery; maybe it was sold over the counter to a benevolent old gent who wanted to make life happier for a gang of working boys. We didn't mind. It was a great barbecue, even if somebody did forget the salt.

Had it not been for the pop it would have been my happiest memory. That pop certainly caused some trouble. As a matter of fact, it had been bought over the counter, all in one go, and that was the mistake. Nosey handed over a lifted bag to his brother, the one I told you about, on condition that he bought the case of tinned beer. The notes were marked, and the detectives came down on Crab Carron like a ton of bricks.

Well, naturally Crab tried to shy them off his brother, and just as naturally those sneakers tripped him up. The detectives knew what he didn't know, having caught him off-guard when Nosey couldn't give him the strength. So they got Nosey pinned down in the end and the whole story came out about the pigeon barbecue. It appears that Nosey had just found a car door open on the way up; same car belonging to the careless lady of a wealthy ship-owner – don't ask me what she was doing visiting the Shalley Street area; maybe she was dishing out soup for fun – and lifted her bag.

It carried twelve nicker and a lot of valuable fur-bound compacts. He went to the Juvenile and just missed Borstal. Bound over for twelve months and came back to the Dump looking as if he'd just conquered Everest single-handed.

Old Carruthers-Smith singled him out at Assembly; right from the rostrum he said: 'You're lucky to be back among us, Carron. Keep your nose clean.'

Also, he walked into our class, which was the B section of the A stream, and said to the current chunk who was straight from college sharpening his wits on us: 'Watch your desk when you go out, Thompson. With pigeon fanciers and cracksmen about the place there's nothing safe.'

Well, nobody minded the bit about the pigeon fanciers, but all of us with the exception of old Nosey himself resented keenly the reference to cracksmen. Of course Old Carruthers-Smith had been playing the goat considerably over the whole affair. Rattler was off with a bad cold and he was reigning in glory and couldn't resist the temptation to play private eye. Ham-handed as always. Had us all in one at a time, gave us a spiel about Nosey being a bad lot and he wanted the whole truth and nothing but the truth; and whatever was said nobody would ever know who said it.

Success came his way and he collected as many tall stories as would fill a book. But nothing about Nosey, because fundamentally Nosey was a lone wolf as you may have guessed from the pigeon-trapping yarn, and nobody had anything on him even if they'd been that way inclined.

I told him straight: 'Nosey's all right. Normally he wouldn't dream of doing anything like that. If he's got a fault, it's generosity.'

'It was his contribution, eh?'

All round-eyed and innocent I said: 'Yes, sir. Like I told you, he's big-hearted.'

'Did you know he was going to do this – just tell me the truth and you have my word it's between the two of us. Nobody'll ever know.'

'Why,' I said, 'Ah thought everybody knew. Everybody knew before the night.'

'That he was going to steal from a car?'

'Goodness, no, sir. About his Dad's pedigree pigeons. He brought three of the best along because he couldn't catch any wild ones; one of them won the Cross-Channel last year. But please, sir, don't tell his Dad because he'll murder him for sure.'

'Oh, get out!' I never saw a man so slumped.

But he got his own back. I lost my prefect's badge and with it all my ambition. From that moment I was a waster and even old Rattler lost faith in me. He'd pass me in the corridor, shaking his head. Once or twice he told me that I was his biggest disappointment. 'In my own mind,' he used to remark, 'I always believed you would make the grade.'

Always forgot to ask him what and where was the grade.

THREE

Day-dreaming in the sun you try to focus on the good things, but failure has a bitter taste. When you've been on the pop it only hits your mouth and your belly, but failure hits the whole system. Worse, if you're vain and like the look of yourself. Every time I got fixed on something easy this damn rotten failure would keep seeping through. It wasn't just looking down a line of jobs, or knowing that in all of them, or in any that were due to be filled, you were less important than a dough machine, an endless conveyor, or a piece of fencing. It wasn't only the sure fact that any older digger, concrete mixer, or dumper truck was not only bigger and better than you could ever be, but also a bigger and better investment that was worth more as scrap than you would be dead or alive. It was the entire set-up that marked you down for a failure before you had time to turn.

There were times in the Dump when you felt a ray of hope through listening to one of those college characters talking about builders of Empire, industry, science and what not. Get out into the great factory of life, brother, and the hope soon dies.

And don't give me that gum about further education. Further education for what and with what? Anything resembling a brain or aspirations meets a slow death in the overcrowded, over-strained and hopeless Dump.

Sometimes I thought about these things lying on the banks. One thing I didn't think about, because it was too near, and this was what we did to poor old Carruthers-Smith on the last day, the day of judgement.

But then, lounging in a corner of the yard with Nosey and a few more characters with a grudge, it didn't seem a bad idea at all. Wednesday was glory for anybody that had won glory, and none of my gang got within a mile of it. We didn't mind; our glory was coming. Thursday, everything was set; the ammunition was ready; the safety catch was off. Of course, some character talked and pretty soon the whole school knew there was something in store for C.S. Last day's an easy day and everybody does pretty much as they like. In the classroom there were plenty of admiring looks and a lot more whispering: as soon as the teacher left the room lads were asking the score and saying we hadn't the nerve, or pinning the medals on before the battle.

It was certainly our day. But with all the talk I was as nervous as a kitten. By a miracle it didn't leak. The teachers knew there was something up, but put it down to holiday exhilaration. At least they didn't try to sort it out. Sometimes I wish they had.

As it was, the leak nearly spoilt the plot. We rushed out and made along to one of those derelict streets where we'd hid the stuff. On the way along old Nosey looked over his shoulder and said: 'Look at them spectators!'

The whole school was milling in the yard or outside the gates. It was a circus. 'That's done it,' I said. 'He'll smell a rat – we might as well call it off.'

'Ya, give him a run for his money,' said Nosey. 'You got the wind up, Pretty Boy?'

I nearly slammed him then and there. Nosey was the only one to call me Pretty Boy and get away with it. But only once. I marked that one up, and nearly broke the chalk doing it. I'd a feeling that it wasn't such a good idea; and maybe it was because the feeling was so strong I pulled off that punch, also walking out on the caper, and said: 'Let's get cracking then.'

Which we did.

Standing in my doorway I was all out in a sweat. All I could think of, his face when we let blaze. I knew then that he wouldn't stand. I knew he'd run. And that was the part I wasn't looking forward to. Seeing his face when he decided to run.

One of the lads was stationed in an upstairs window and that's how I know the beginning of this caper. What this character saw was old Carruthers-Smith walk out smartly with his brief-case in his hand, full of the anticipation of the long holiday stretch, never noticing the unnatural quiet that fell when he passed. This character says he came through the gates and was twenty yards along the road before it hit him. Then he turned and looked. All the kids started milling again but a little too slowly. Some had already started tracking him. One or two of these made the mistake of turning back. From that moment old C.S. knew there was something in the wind.

He didn't like it. Once he slowed up as if to turn again, but pride wouldn't let him. You could see by the stiff way he was walking, said this character, that he'd the heebie-jeebies. When he was maybe halfway down the street he broke. This character says he turned and lifted his brief-case, maybe to tell the crowd to knock off and go home. Only they didn't. Something was working. I've seen it two or three times since and, boy, I don't want to see it again. Blood was up and they weren't missing anything. This character says that when C.S. set off walking again his face had slipped completely. He was walking hard as if he meant it. He kept looking at the empty doorways and windows but we were too wise and kept out of sight. He didn't see anything but knew we were there. Only the wire-net fence of the sports track kept him from making a break away from those simmering houses. But he had to keep going on because that was the only way out.

It's a bad thing to see a grown man break. It doesn't make any difference what he is, or how much you hate him. It's still a bad thing. It was my idea but I didn't throw the first rotten orange. And when I did throw, it wasn't at Carruthers-Smith but at my idea. But I threw all the same.

All hell broke loose. Nobody tried to keep under cover. They were throwing rotten fruit, etc. like maniacs and enjoying it. What it was they were getting rid of I don't exactly know even now, excepting that I'm sure that old C.S. was no more to blame for it than my Old Lady.

The aiming was good. In a minute he was marked all over with yellow runny stuff from oranges and the red of tomatoes. He ran a bit and ran into a storm, stopped and spun round, tried to say something, then dropped his brief-case and put his hands to his face. From then on he didn't know what he was doing. The stuff was pelting down like hail. He went down on his knees.

Then he got up and ran. The pack went after him and I went along. I was hoping that nobody would get near him and that was the way it was. He went off like a rocket. Everybody was shouting. He went over the edge of the clay-holes with his coat tails lifted, caught his foot in a hole and went flying. He rolled over and over. Everybody was quiet now, watching him. He rolled to the bottom and lay still. After a while he shifted a bit. He rested his forehead on his hand. He was shaking or breathing hard or maybe crying. I don't know because I never saw his face.

All that happened after this was that a dog came along and nosed him. A half-bred terrier dog. He nosed along until he reached about the neck. Then he started licking. He must have been a hungry dog.

Old C.S. just lay and let the dog lick.

This was when practically everybody felt ashamed or frightened. 'Well, that settled *his* hash,' said Nosey.

'That's for sure,' said Mousey Hole.

Nobody laughed. 'All right, you kids scram,' said Nosey.

They broke up without a second telling. Me and Nosey and some of the others sat on our hunkers and watched for maybe five minutes but in all that time C.S. didn't make a move. All the time the dog was licking and finally got round to his face. Then Carruthers-Smith got up and sort of limped away down to those old cottages they have down there. The dog followed him. Neither of them looked back. If they had, I think I'd have cut and run. Even if that half-bred dog had looked back I'd have run.

I got this from Nosey. When old C.S. started moving it seemed to be the end. We all wanted to get moving, but Nosey wanted to stay. In the end we left him. Don't know what he expected to see. All that happened was that old C.S. knocked at the first door and asked for a drink of water. Nosey says that he was taken inside by one of those ancient women we seem to breed around here. About eighteen stone with ankles overlapping the shoe tops, never been washed for a month, dressed in greasy black. Maybe she cleaned him up and gave him a cup of tea; maybe he was too far gone to care much, because Nosey never saw him come out. And I can guess that old house smelled pretty rank.

Well, as I said, we left Nosey to it. I set off walking home myself. Then somehow I got the wind up. It was pure imagination because I'd no reason to think there was any danger but I turned about. Perhaps I didn't want to walk up that street of empty houses again. Perhaps I was running away from something I couldn't beat. But, boy, I was in a panic. I ran fast and I did the complete circuit. I turned my back on the old homestead and ran along the edge of the ravine and then over the road bridge, without stopping. Looking over the bridge I could see old Nosey, still squatting. Without stopping to observe him I pelted on. I turned off by the Central Library and ran hard uphill to the furniture repository. That's where I wanted hard to stop and get my wind, but something wouldn't let me. I knew I was all right. I also knew there wasn't a chance of old C.S. telling the slops and putting them on to me alone, out of a couple of dozen, but boy, there was nothing I could do about it. I crossed the road and nearly got knocked by a scooter. His vocabulary didn't impress me, or his space-helmet, because when you've a tiger on your tail everything assumes correct proportions; particularly when you don't know the shape of your tiger. I reckon I ran three miles without stopping. Didn't go straight home; turned into the back street and got my wind back. Sat with my hand on my sweat-greasy chest and felt it surging. Argued with myself:

'What's bitin' you?'

'Don't know. Haven't a clue, boy.'

'You just ran three miles an' you tell me you haven't a clue.'

'No, it was just instinct.'

'Sure of that?'

'Ah'm not sure of anything, anymore.'

'Isn't he a two-faced twister? Didn't he ask for it? What you're worrying for?'

'Ah'm not worrying. Didn't expect it would turn out that way. That's all. Took the run for the good of my health.'

'Boy, you want to grow up and face the facts of life. You can't take it. How'd ye be if ye had to face up to a broken bottle, or a bicycle chain, or maybe a flick knife?'

'All right ... that would be *me*. So it wouldn't matter.'

'You're yeller; ye'd crumple first second. Anybody can take it. It's givin' it that's hard. Ye've got to lash out. Ye've got to learn to give it.'

'Okay, all right. Ah'll give it with the next.'

'Ye'd better, boy, or ye'll go under. They'll wipe their feet on you – it'll be Pretty Boy all the time, like Nosey tonight.'

'Okay, pipe down. Ah know about Nosey and he won't do it again. Not him or anybody else. Ah'll skuttle the next one that does it.'

'That's ma boy.' But I'm not kidding myself that a pat on the back from myself can wipe it out. And it was still with me when I lay on the claybanks waiting for my big chance in the sewer-line.

Sunshine days came to an end when Uncle George called.

'Strong boots, he'll need strong boots,' he told the Old Lady. Meanwhile I'm sitting like a dummy. 'And a cap: hate to see a workman without a cap.'

'He'll have one. What about overalls?' asked the Old Lady.

'Not on my job.' For a second I thought he was going to add that down there in the trench all you needed was naked merit. 'Get him some stout trousers – cords or moleskins. He's in for a lot of bendin' and stretchin', an' if there's anything Ah hate to see it's bare skin.'

'Ah'll get him some.'

'Better make it moleskins. They're heavy but safe and they'll keep him respectable … he'll have to do his share of the humpin'; there'll be no favourites. Got to keep up the family name, eh, Arthur?'

I muttered or growled something.

'We're bonny and grateful, George. Say thanks to your Uncle George, Arthur.'

'Thanks, Uncle George.'

'Best thing's not to let me down. Don't trade on me bein' your Uncle. Live on your merit.'

There it came!

'He'll not do that – will ye not, Arthur?'

'Wouldn't dream of it.'

'Well that's that. Ah'll be seeing ye then. Up wi' the lark, seven sharp at the site – oh, and better come on your bike.'

'What's wrong with the trolley?' I asked

'Saves the fare peddling. Also it'll come in handy if Ah want ye to run a few errands for me – see?'

See? Boy, I was sitting there seeing the whole saga through high-powered field glasses with crystal-clear clarity. Personal slave, runabout, undercover man, stooge, straight man, cabin boy, whipping boy, yes-man, etc. All that was missing was a sex-angle.

'He'll bring his bike, George.'

It suddenly struck me that the Old Lady was certainly giving a good impersonation of the woman that couldn't say no; dishing out promises like a fast-talking barker at a sucker's auction. I particularly resented the business about the bike. That bike was as good as new and represented movable capital; a smooth, shiny, low-slung colourful extra-lightweight job that I kept mainly for prestige on account of the fact that cycling's too hot in summer, too cold in winter. But I didn't want it lying around a site or bashed to hell getting help, aid and comfort for Uncle George. That's not counting the wear and tear on myself.

'Ah'm not usin' me racer, Ma.'

'So it's a racer, eh? Well, lad, ye'll learn to sacrifice everything you have on the altar of honest labour.'

'Not my bike,' I told him. The Old Lady was working her mouth like mad and getting no takers. 'She'll have to get me a second-hand boneshaker ... there's plenty goin'.'

'If ye've the money to throw away ...' began Uncle George.

'Can have my old boneshaker,' said Harry who'd just arrived and was standing, like death, in the doorway. The Pasha gave him a long sloping look.

'So this is the young feller ye've got livin' with ye, Peg?'

'Lodgin', not livin',' corrected Harry.

'Naturally,' said Uncle George. 'Now if the lad sticks in, there'll be no need ... but Ah'll mind me own business. Well, must be on my way. Lot to do. No rest for the righteous. Full meeting, couple of committees, stack of letters after ... slaves of democracy.'

'Aye, ye'll be up to the eyes no doubt,' said the Old Lady. 'By the way, Mary was wantin' the lend of me sewin' machine. Perhaps ye'd like to take it up wi' ye? It'll not take me a minute to put it in the box ...'

'Haven't a minute to spare,' said the Great Man. 'Must be on my way – tell you what – how about Arthur bringin' it up?'

For once the Old Lady didn't give him the straight yesser. In fact, she was having the most sensational personal all-in wrestling bout with herself I've ever seen. Boy, she was breathless. 'Well, now,' she said at last. 'Mebbe Ah'd better bring it up mysel' and run the curtains off for Mary while Ah'm on.'

But the shot only bounced off his armour plating; 'By gum if ye could Ah'm sure Mary'd appreciate it! Well, good nights all.'

As they say in the plays – exit Uncle George, leaving me and the Lodger to take the rap. 'A fine pair. One with a job put in his lap sits and shouts the odds about his bloody fancy bicycle, the other shovin' his nose into anybody's business but his own ... Who the hell d'ye think ye are?'

'Men wi' a little bit mense about 'em,' said the Lodger. 'But there's no need to bring the house down – Ah only offered the lad me old bike.'

'Panderin' to his whims!'

'Well, Ah wouldn't pander to that old drummer – that's for sure.'

'Meanin …?'

'Meanin' you were as near kissing his backside as makes no difference.'

'Better take that grin off your face or Ah'll wipe it off,' she told me. 'And as for you, you tuppence ha'penny sea captain with nowt to your name but a cargo of empty bottles and a ship on the rocks, Ah'll sink me pride any day to give the lad a decent start in life …'

'There's a limit.'

'He'll have me runnin' around like a shot cock,' I said.

'And it'll do you no harm. A bit worry and work never did anybody any harm.' The steam was just about blown off. Chief indication was that the Lodger had taken off his soggy boots and laid them on the hearth without a word from her. 'What's the alternative?' she asked, shaking the teacloth over the table. 'Ah'll tell ye … you'll pull the wires with the foreman down at your place … better be beholden to your own than a stranger …'

'Why, thanks,' said the Lodger quietly.

'Now ye know Ah wasn't meanin' you. Ah'm only sayin' think twice before beholding yourself to anybody.'

'In that case, your slip's showin',' he said. 'Ye've just presented a fine picture of a woman bein' as beholden as it's possible to be.'

'Somebody has to do the necessary.'

'You went just about twice as far as necessary, and by God he lapped it up.'

'All right then,' she said. 'That's the finish. In future – are ye listenin' to me, Arthur – somebody else can do the hettlin' in this house … Ah'm finished.'

Fine dramatics, but they didn't make any difference. All I had was a scrap of information about the Lodger's past and, knowing his talent for talk, not very reliable. And the lend of his bone-shaker. Also, the stiffest pair of moleskins that ever cased legs. I'm not kidding, they were like armour, had the colour of old mushrooms and a smell that was all their own.

I'd have given those trousers the discard, only the Old Lady was in one of her frosty moods and I wasn't risking another flare-up. But when I pulled them on the following morning a slow feeling crept over me that my ears were going to burn long before the first wrinkle marred their stiff, virgin surface. Wearing them was like walking in water.

Even the Old Lady had her doubts. There she was in her dressing gown, frying the bacon and eggs: whistling like a lark. 'Come on, Harry,' she shouted, 'here's the working man all set and ready … My God, they look like bleached drainpipes. Will ye manage?'

I nodded, not knowing the virtue of starting a new job in unremarkable clothes; but if I'd known then what I know now, then man, I'd have gone in my short pants. When the Lodger came in, he whistled; and when I departed he followed me into the yard: 'Thought maybe you'd need some help hammerin' your bicycle clips on,' he said. Trying to cheer me up. 'You'll be all right. Keep your mouth shut; think twice before ye ask a question; and when they pull a joke on ye laugh twice as hard as the rest.'

'Won't catch me with any of those old tricks,' I said.

'Take my tip and fall for the odd one,' said the Lodger. 'Well, good luck, lad.'

The Old Lady was standing at the yard door.

'Well, aren't ye goin' to wish him luck?' asked the Lodger.

'Take care,' she said, 'Do as you're told.' Then went in.

'Why man alive; she's full up,' said the Lodger in wonderment. 'Well Ah suppose it's a milestone.'

'As long it isn't round me neck,' I said.

'Any time you want you're as free as the air,' he told me. And that was one thing that stuck in my mind.

Having been up early before there's nothing you could tell me about the pre-seven o'clock. It's a world composed mainly of bicycles, with few motor cars or buses. Everything's slow and quiet, with panic below. Like a television picture with the sound turned low. The pedals go round like lead. Smoke's lazy. Nobody smiles. On every face is a lingering memory of sleep and a conviction that work should be abolished pronto. Pre-seven is the time to start a revolution.

There's nothing nicer than this silence when you're off on a trip. But boy it's certainly moody when you're going to work for the first time. Give me the full blast of the orchestra any day. That pre-seven solitary oboe still gives me the creeps. It was like peddling in cotton wool. The old boneshaker gave me trouble from the start. Reckon it was churning out rust like a coffee mill turning out the straight blend – only not so easy to turn. I'd three miles to go to this site, which was on the west side, and halfway there with a mile of hill to face, got a flat. Checked the valve and the rubber cracked in my fingers. Hadn't a repair kit, naturally.

I limped in at ten past seven. A fine start.

The site was a fifty-yard strip of waste land gently descending to the river a mile or so away. There was a little burn running through it. The trench ran parallel. There was a concrete mixer with a couple of feeder bunkers, the big digger, stacks of concrete piping maybe six feet in diameter, a compressor, and a shed. Apart from the hum of voices in the shed it was the picture of a quiet Sabbath morning, lacking only the bells.

I put my bike against the shed and stuck my nose through the door – and that's all there was room for. The place was jammed tight. Some characters sitting around the sides were getting their beauty steep out. Those conscious were sitting or standing around a table at the head of which was a character with a face like a frog writing bets on a sheet of paper and checking up on a pile of change.

Nobody noticed me.

'Where's the foreman?' I asked.

Character near the door stitching a patch on to a pair of overalls shouted back. 'What you want?'

'Ah'm lookin' for the foreman.'

'Pipe down everybody,' said the bookie. The funny thing was that they did pipe down. 'Now what's it all about?'

'Ah'm lookin' for the foreman.'

'Now that's a change!' he remarked. 'Soon knock that out of ye. You the gaffer's nevvy?' I nodded.

'You don't sound it. Didn't he tell ye to report to the assistant bumper-up?'

'All he said was to be here at seven.'

'Kiddar, you certainly started well – it's ten past seven.'

'I got a puncture.'

'Here – wait a minute,' he said. 'Stand on that step – that's right, up a bit.' He put his thumbs in his waistcoat and stood up to get a better view. Everybody was looking. 'Why, man, it must be all of twenty years since Ah saw a pair of pure-bred moleskins,' he said. 'Just look at them.'

'Brightness as well as whiteness,' said the character with the needle.

'Where's his gun belt?'

'Well, well,' said the bookie. 'First thing you can do is drag them trousers through the burn an' make yourself a man.'

'You go an' stuff yourself,' I said. Feller with a long nose gave a low whistle. Didn't take any notice – I was starting as I intended to finish. No bookie's runner was going to rub my nose in the dirt.

'Hey,' he said. 'It's a comedian.'

'Listen,' I told him. 'These trousers'll take off but you've got to wear that face.'

He didn't like it but put on a good laugh. 'Listen to that,' he told the others. 'Like his uncle he's a good talker ... now just wait a minute, son, till Ah get the job organised and then we'll have a bit talk.'

He told the gang off and cleared the place in next to no time. In a couple of minutes I could hear the compressor going and the lorries rolling. Could see what he meant by bumper-up.

After they'd gone he counted up the suckers' money, and made out some timesheets. Getting bored I sat down. He finished his work and sat tapping his pencil, buff-end, on the table. At the same time he was grinning.

At last he said: 'Think a bit about yourself, son, don't ye?'

'Don't like havin' the soft picked outa me.'

'What's your first name?'

'Arthur.'

'Well, Arthur; you better get to know the strength of the job. Don't lean on Uncle George too much. In fact, don't lean on anybody. Not that ye'll get much chance to lean on Uncle George because most of the time he isn't around. He's a very busy man, is Uncle George, an' depends upon me. My name's Sprogget – Mr Sprogget to you.'

'Okay, Mr Sprogget.'

'That's a good lad. Now hop over to the mixer an' tell George Flack to show you a shovel.'

'What's that?'

'George Flack. And, son …?'

'Yes?'

'Better not mention my face again.'

I didn't say anything. Just gave him a dead-pan look and walked out. Strike like a snake and never give, that's the technique. But underneath I was as nervous as a kitten. I didn't like the look of the assistant bumper-up. He was the original snake.

Flack was the character with the big nose. The lorries were dumping loads of pebbles and he was shovelling the stuff through a sheet screen. My job was to load the stuff on to an endless conveyor that fed the bunkers feeding the mixer. Old Flack gave me a shovel and showed me where to put it, then stood watching my paces with a genial sneer which set his face askew. In the end he took the shovel and showed me how to hold it, and I thanked him.

He walked back to the other side of the screen and scratched his nose. 'You got a nerve,' he said. Then his face crumpled into a grin. 'Yes – he's got a face all right – can't do anything else but wear it.' He kept shovelling hard and every ten minutes or so let off a burst of machine-gun laughter. But he didn't say anything else until about nine o'clock maybe. 'Better go and mash some tea, kiddar,' he told me. 'Kettle's in the shed.'

I laid the shovel down gently but it was no good. My right hand had been operated on. There were aches all over the territory. 'You'll learn to let the shovel do the work,' he said. 'And you go canny with Sprogget; he's a naughty character.'

I was an inch short of six feet and getting on for twelve stone. 'Reckon Ah can look after myself,' I told him.

'Well, it gets monotonous,' he said. That's all. And picked up his shovel again. I made the tea and the gang gathered round. That's when Uncle George arrived. He wandered over. He looked at everybody but me, then said to Sprogget: 'How's she goin'?'

'Fine, George,' said the bookie. 'New man came late, that's all.'

He just grunted. 'Let's have a look at the pegs,' he said; and they wandered off together. I reckon that's when I knew what he was. He didn't look at me, or say a word, and it all added up to the fact that I was dirt or something of that order. You can imagine me standing there with the big teapot in my hand, jaw on my chin, eyes mad. Some character said: 'Let's have some tea, Cowboy.' That teapot was big and heavy and what was inside was hot. Flack knew what was in my mind. 'Fill her up, son,' he said, holding out his can. I gave him a look. He shook his head. So the teapot stayed where it was and nobody had to send for an ambulance. And that was nine o'clock and two hours on, but boy, it felt like two long years to me.

FOUR

1

These days the shifts aren't so long and less happens. Once mentioned this to the Lodger and he said: 'Every day you die a bit and there's less of you to feel.' Seems a bit far-fetched to me but maybe he's got something there. Little valves winking, then fading out. Sitting there, useless, until at last there's rows and rows of them dead. So you're receiving little and sending out less.

Work also wears more than your hands, and it's just as well. Drive you crazy if you had to stay sensitive all the time. Boy, you've got to toughen up. But it's sad that you have to lose the full sense of a day. Now week follows week like somebody flipping a pack of cards. Times you want to scream – 'Stand still, you bastards.' But it's no use.

Maybe you'll laugh at me but that first day was like shifting a mountain. It seemed it was never going to end. Didn't need a ball and chain: the shovel served. Yet it wasn't the shovel. It was that sun blazing down, that beautiful sun, and knowing that it was going to blaze all a long day of lost chances. Yet it had nothing to do with the sun. It was being tied and knowing that you were tied for life.

That's when I understood a bloke like the assistant bumper-up, or Uncle George, selling his soul for a chance to hang around. They're still tied to the job but can pretend they're not. And the other characters rushing the job so that they can take time to light up. But not old Flack. That man was a miracle with the shovel. He was just going along with that shovel for a ride. Never grunted or sweated. Just went along with the shovel and that old shovel just kept going as if it had a little engine beating away in the middle of the shaft.

But every now and again he'd call a halt and pick up one of the pebbles. Turn it around in his hand and shake his head. Then drop it and start again. God knows what he'd been thinking. He was a leathery old man with a big nose and you'd think all he lived for was Scotch Ale. At least that's what I thought. When I got to know him better I discovered that he'd been around a bit in his seventy years and had helped to kill a lot of men. And had lost a wife. And had sacrificed a lot for one of his sister's boys. A great believer in education. 'Read books,' he used to say. 'Get learnin'. Be a somebody.' And he'd notice you looking at him with a question in your face and say: 'Wasn't time for me to get it, but Ah helped me sister's lad. And he's been a credit to me.'

When I went home that night it was like leaving a chapter in a history book behind me. Contractor with a lorry lived down our way and put me off at the bridge and I walked along past that old sports arena as if I'd all the time in the world, one sore hand on the handlebars, the other in my pocket. One half of my mind was relief that it was over for that day, the other half was full of tomorrow and all the tomorrows that would follow.

'How did it go?' asked the Old Lady.

'Fine,' I said. 'Fine.' I stripped to the buff and gave myself a good old soaking. She was watching me all the time as she set the table.

'Rough was it?'

'Oh, it wasn't so bad.'

'Get there all right?'

'Got a puncture – had to walk.'

Seeing the mood I was in she didn't say anything about me taking the old boneshaker instead of the brand-new modern roadstormer. Was so hungry that I dived into and demolished a two-decker dinner; beef, veg and Yorkshire pudding followed by tea and homemade gingerbread. All the time the Lodger was sitting in the armchair, smoking and reading a book. When I reached the tea it suddenly dawned upon me that there was something wrong.

'Hey,' I said. 'What about your cleanin'?'

'Oh, Ah'm goin' in late – thought you'd like a nice hot dinner.'

'You guessed right.'

'Oh, go on,' she said and pulled on her coat. 'Ah told them Ah'd be late today. Will ye be all right?'

'He'll be fine,' said Harry, handing me the green packet. I took one out and eyed the Old Lady and wondered what she'd throw. I'd still half an eye on her when I stuck the snout in my mouth and leaned over to the Lodger's light. But it was all right. In fact, she was laughing to herself as she turned to go.

2

You know how it is when you've had a rough time – you want to give yourself a reward. Not having any fancy ideas or much money, I decided to go to the pictures. Told Harry. 'Good idea,' he said. 'Rest up your bruised body in the one and ninepennies. Okay for cash?'

'Fair,' I said. 'There's only one thing – I've got the puncture to fettle.'

'Leave it to me.' I decided old Harry wasn't such a bad sort after all. Got spruced up, dried the dishes for him, then left feeling not so bad. The heat of the day was off and I was feeling good: maybe something better would turn up. Walking along in the cool of the evening I thought of what pal Flack had said and decided to take up some reading, preferably on electricity, and maybe invent a super spaceship. I'd save up my pocket money, build a shed, get hold of some spare parts and become an experimenter. Be a lone-wolf scientist, working into the small hours, and eventually that shed would grow into the biggest building in the city. Maybe they'd even stick a plaque on the old homestead: ARTHUR HAGGERSTON: INVENTOR OF THE ANTI-GRAVITY ENGINE; EXPLORER OF THE MOON: BORN 1942 – DIED –. As you can guess, I couldn't decide about the last bit – didn't want my glory to end.

Came out of the dream. This was essential since I was now walking across the 'battlefield'. The kids were having a high old time. Some were having a battle, darting about from one bit of cover to another, shooting each other with silver-plated pistols and making a pretty good imitation of the bullets with their mouths. One kid was doing a fine job of ricochets. Every bullet he fired was a ricochet. Girls were putting on a mannequin parade – very stately, with arms out and fingers pinched – in faded old dresses a mile too big for them. Hungry cowboys were roasting potatoes without salt over scattered campfires and enjoying it.

There was a house standing at the end of what had been a street. In fact, I think it had been a pub, and a pretty old one at that. There was an archway into the backyard stuck on one end. Nothing was left of the front but a bit of the wall below the ground-floor windows. You could see down into the cellars and you could see into all the rooms at the front because that particular wall had gone for a Burton.

Standing in one of these rooms on the third floor and looking like a monkey all alone in a big cage was Nosey Carron. Didn't see him. In fact I was just about to step through the arch when I heard his voice saying 'What chay' from nowhere or pretty near the edge of it. Stepped back and there he was in all his glory, tight jeans and bright blue jacket, seaside straw hat, cigarette dangling from the corner of his mouth.

'Step up, Arthur,' he said.

'Goin' to the pictures.'

'Nothin' good on. Come on up an' have a bit crack.'

'Only for a minute, then.'

I stepped over the wall and went up what had been the stairs. Somebody had left in a hurry – there was an entire iron bedstead in that room. It had a spring foundation, but the brass knobs had gone.

Nosey bounced on the bed. 'What d'ye think of it?'

'It's a bed.'

'It's five bob of scrap.'

'Then you've got five bob.'

'Help me break it up – we'll sell it to old Nettlefold.'

'Take spanners.'

'All we need is one of them shiftin' spanners.'

'Listen, Nosey, Ah'm off to the pictures. Haven't the time.'

'All right, then. You nip over tomorrow night, same time, with a spanner an' we'll take it to bits and carry it down to Charlie's.'

I said I'd do that and asked him how about the pictures with me. 'No dice,' he said. 'It's all soft stuff anyway. Ah want to keep an eye on this bed. Sure as pop somebody'll be after it.'

'Fair enough, if you're daft enough to do it,' I told him.

'Got any fags?'

'Got a couple.'

'Leave 'em with me an' Ah'll pay ye back when we get the money off Charlie Nettlefold.'

It seemed a fair risk, so I gave him two snouts. He drew his knees up, set his straw hat back to act as a pillow, and lit up from his old stub. He was chuffed to death. 'Me an' you can have some fun, boy,' he told me. 'Ah like you – how about comin' in with me? There's one or two lads interested. Knock about together. How about it?'

'No soap,' I said.

'What for? No harm in it.'

'Thinkin' about goin' to night classes and betterin' myself.'

He whistled. 'Didn't ye get a bellyful before, boy? Now's the time for a bit fun. Protect ourselves, see. Them Quaysiders been interferin' with our area. Couple o' lads got knocked up in the milk bar last Friday.'

'Let the slops look after them.'

He spat. 'Slops! Too busy pullin' money outa Shalleys or

watchin' cars. We got to protect ourselves.'

'No soap,' I said. 'Ah've got plenty to think about.'

He waved his cigarette about, like a big shot. All smooth and smiling but underneath he was dead narked. 'Okay, okay … But you'll help with the scrap?'

I took a look at the nuts to make sure I had a shifting spanner the right size, then mickeyed off. Went down the stairs and along a short passage, stepped over a kiddy chair, skirted a divan carrying a load of filth and a large rat which sat and looked at me, and stepped out the back way. I was in the battlefield again. Maybe a hundred yards on I felt somebody looking at me. Could have kicked myself for turning because I'd guessed right first time. It was Nosey, smoking hard, watching me through the rear window. Maybe the idea was to smoke all he had, then settle down and concentrate, or, maybe, go into training. Some of the salvage characters around there are pretty fierce characters. He might have a fight to keep that bed.

Looking back now I can see there was a good soldier wasted in Nosey. It wasn't only that he didn't get nasty when I refused to join up with this fancy gang of his: it was as if he'd foreseen that I'd be back asking to join. Almost as if he'd arranged it.

This was the way it happened.

Paid my money at the box, picked up a new packet of snouts, then set off climbing Everest, which is what you've got to do if you're in the cheap seats at the Albion. You go upstairs where the restaurant is, and parking space, with a couple of pair seats and a couple of tanks in which the light is either dead or the fish missing. You carry on up some more stairs and then you need your ice pick for an anchor, because that old gallery goes back to the days when the Albion was a music hall and for a low price you get a pretty steep seat, and that's the way they've kept it. That Everest part is always a bit rough. Back's a snake pit where the young lovers play boa constrictor; front's a shooting gallery where they drop orange peel, snout packets and anything handy on anybody below, depending on the quality of the picture.

Well, anyway, I reached the assault base and found it practically deserted, since the last show had started. What stopped it from being empty was a girl who lives up our street. Name's Joan Clavering and I've known her from the old hitchy-bay ring-a-roses days. Reckon she always had a yen for me, which I've never encouraged, for one or two simple reasons, one being that I never know what to talk about, the other being that with her kind you double your expenses and end up with empty pockets and the feeling that you're a kind of sad clown.

Also, it's the convention among the lads that you get your money's worth, and up till then and maybe a bit after I'd no fancy for getting my money back that way. At the end of a street, I mean. I like my love in luxury.

Joan was standing looking into one of the tanks. She whipped round when I walked up. Don't get the idea that she's not much to look at. She's not bad. But I knew she was wearing a coat she'd worn the winter before last, and this was summer. Maybe this made me feel a bit sympathetic. This and the fact that she looked a bit humped. So I said, 'Hiya Joan,' and she answered likewise, and passed on. I shouldn't have looked over my shoulder. That was the start of it all. She gave me a funny sort of look that pulled me up in my tracks.

'What's the matter – been stood up?' I asked.

She went all gay girl and said: 'He must be workin' overtime.' My reaction was that he was certainly putting all the overtime in his savings when he arranged to meet the girl well past the moneydown area, but I didn't say anything. All I said was that she was missing the show; and she came back quick with: 'Can Ah sit beside you, Arthur? On account of it's sometimes rough up there, specially when you're on your own.'

Well, what could I do?

In next to no time we were sitting watching the corniest B-feature you ever saw – all about a character who runs a lorry service up in Alaska and keeps getting punctures and running behind schedule, which is what you'd expect in Alaska; only his partner doesn't believe it and comes up from New York with his blonde wife to get the lorries on schedule, only instead the wife also goes off schedule for the single character. Played a game which is to shut your eyes and count up to any number you like and guess what's going to happen by the time you've finished counting. I won so often it became monotonous. Once or twice Joan kept inching over and I reckon she wouldn't have been disappointed if I'd gone into a clinch. Instead I offered her a cigarette. Usual caper blowing out a couple of matches before she got a light, giggling, and eventually getting hold of my hands to steady the match, as if that was the trouble. I was glad when the lights went up even though it meant having to buy her an ice.

Then this gang came in. I knew they were Quaysiders from the red jackets and long sideboards – sideboards went out maybe eighteen months ago – and I hoped there wouldn't be any trouble. They settled in the seat behind us and made a few cracks; then one, a tall thin character with a pimply face, leaned over and poked Joan in the shoulder. 'Hey, you – didn't wait for me long, did you?'

She gave me a look then drew her shoulder away and flung back her head. 'Brought plenty of company with you – what's the matter? Want somebody to look after you when you're out?'

'You come back here an' Ah'll show you!'

'Had your dice now,' she told him. 'Ah'm with somebody else.'

'Listen, Joanie,' I said. 'You go with him if you want.'

'Who's that – the village idiot?' said this character.

'You want shot of me?' she asked; and told the character: 'You keep your big mouth shut or my friend'll shut it for you.'

I was thankful when the lights went down. You don't have to be a chicken to like peace, especially when war is five or six to one. I was praying that the picture would be a five-star success because, while never chickening up on a fight, I dislike an audience. It's all right if you've plenty of support and have a chance of winning but nobody likes to be hammered in company. But that quiet little Joanie didn't understand the position. Then again, maybe she did. Haven't worked it out yet. She kept snuggling into me but I wasn't taking. Then, in the end, she tucked her arm through mine and got hold of my hand. One of those hot hands. Come to think of it, mine wasn't so cool either and I don't have to tell you that sex appeal had nothing to do with it.

Next thing I knew the thin one was hammering my back with his fist. I turned round. Slit my throat if it's a lie, but it was the first word I'd spoken to him: 'Listen, marrer,' I told him. 'Pipe down. Keep knockin' and Ah'm liable to open the door and clock you one.'

'You couldn't clock a one-armed dwarf,' he said.

'Listen: Ah don't want trouble. So pipe down.' Folk around us where shushing and saying what a shame and they should be shut up or put out, and these Quayside characters went into hysterics. All the time Joanie was snuggling up and I was edging off; and that damn picture was going so slow you could smoke two fags between pistol shots. I could hear these characters gagging under their breaths and I was ready for them. I knew it was a build up for some caper but not the kind they eventually pulled.

Two of them got hold of Joanie. The thin character was sitting smoking in the aisle seat. He was also giving orders. 'Put the baby in my lap,' he ordered. 'Lift her gently: like a barrel of beer.'

Getting sore, I got hold of the nearside character by the arm. Joanie was halfway over and I never saw so much leg in all my life. She was kicking and screaming. I wasn't getting anywhere with the nearside character, because when I took hold of his arm his pal, sitting behind me, had his hand on my face with a couple of fingers creeping towards my eyes. So I let go of the character giving Joanie the lift and punched the other character: I can raise a good punch in less than ten inches. He let go double-quick. By this time Joanie was over the seats so I jumped into the aisle and got hold of the thin man.

Well, from then on it's a short story.

I got his thin black tie with my left hand and swung my right. But it never landed, because the character unexpectedly followed his tie. Then something came between my ankles, and over I went.

The character that tripped me was stationed in the opposite aisle. Good planning. One of the house guards was flashing his lamp on me where I lay, down among dead ice-cream cartons and monkey-nut shells. 'Come on, you,' he said. 'Out for you.'

'Ah didn't start it.'

'That's what they all say,' he told me on our frogmarch up the long flight of steps. 'Ask the girl Ah was with – they set on her,' I protested.

'Which girl?' he asked me.

'That one; they pulled her over the seats.'

He flashed his torch and that was the end of the evidence. Joanie wasn't exactly on the thin lad's knee but was on her way with her eyes shut and her cheek up against the sideboard territory. So out I went into the cold, cold world.

Walked slowly back home hatching various plots. I'd forgotten all about Nosey. It certainly did me good to see him standing there in that old picture-frame, watching me walking through the smoky blue dusk, calm and easy like a cool Western gunman. I told him all about it and he never even raised a told-you-so. Just sat and listened, smoking one of my cigarettes. I wanted to go back and wait outside the Albion.

'Take it easy – he'll come to us; you watch,' he told me.

'He'll steer clear of this district.'

He shook his head. 'Pin to a penny he'll bring her home.'

But I was so worked up that I still wanted to go back to the Albion.

'Be patient,' he told me. 'Use your noddle. Go there and they'll gang up on us. Wait here, and we'll gang up on him.'

'All Ah want is a fair chance to clock him.'

'You'll get that,' he promised.

It was uncanny sitting there on the old bedstead, listening to the rats down below taking turns to chew up the old settee, and the salvage operators sliding past. Or hearing the smack of a hammer; kids crying in bed: the most miserable sound in the world; singers in pubs, and the odd couple having a row. Wondering what you'd do when it came to the pinch; wondering if you had it in you to do more than dent the odd pimple. About ten-thirty we took turns to watch out of the back window, but after five minutes we chucked the turns and stood together. Nosey saw them first.

'Can't see them,' I said.

'Coming along the footpath.'

'What do we do?'

'Nothin' – the others are liable to be sneakin' along behind.'

After a while it became obvious that they were without an escort; they were going coach-and-horses style, only he was practically carrying the girl. 'It's Mick Kelly,' said Nosey.

'Let's go down,' I said.

'Calm yourself. It's too quiet … Ah don't like the set-up.'

'He'll get away.'

'Better that than make a mistake.'

So we waited until they walked out of sight. 'Let's take him,' said Nosey. 'But quiet.' We nipped downstairs. They were walking along exchanging a kiss in going every now and again. 'Hang on a minute,' whispered Nosey. 'Ah don't like it, Arthur.'

'Seems a pity to spoil their fun,' I said.

'Let's see if we can,' said he.

We came out quick and quiet, me on my toes and Nosey on his high-deck American shoes, but he heard us coming. Letting go of Joanie he put his fingers in his mouth and gave a whistle. Never saw anything so neat in my life.

'That's for his bodyguard,' said Nosey. 'Smack him sharp and Ah'll keep a lookout.' Without waiting for any more parley I smacked him hard in the kisser and was dancing back like a comic boxer the way we worked in the schoolyard – blow for blow style – when Nosey shouted out. Thought I knew what it was all about and came in to give him a clout on the lughole: knew I had to finish it quick because I could hear feet hammering round the backstreet. What Nosey had seen was a length of chain coming up like a whip. That's what I'm told. I didn't see it. Caught me under the chin where it's soft; he was getting ready to swing on me the next time when Nosey came in for his wrist; this was necessary because I was staggering like a decapitated chicken. The next thing I knew was Nosey getting hold of me and yanking me along.

Joanie was standing with her hands twisting, giving out like a wounded soprano. The thin lad was saying his prayers. So we had twenty yards lead. Well, we made it, primarily because the characters stopped off to ask Kelly a question which he was unable to answer. Also, we were running hard. We finished up in the old iron foundry. I remember distinctly what Nosey said. It was simply, 'See what Ah mean?' Because I was still busy with the heavy-breathing session I didn't answer; additionally, I didn't have one.

Has anybody here seen Kelly? This was the question from henceforth.

In fact, time was when my eyes were bloodshot looking for him, keeping him in focus when I found him, thinking about him when they were shut.

3

There was a welt under my chin which the Old Lady was not late in spotting. 'What's that under your chin?'

'Resting it on the balcony all night.'

'Less o' your cheek – now what is it? What have you been up to?'

That's what you might call a shorthand summary. Boy, with this technique it takes a dozen questions to raise one answer and then maybe not.

'Caught it at work.'

'It wasn't there when ye went to the pictures!'

'It's what ye call a slow bruise.'

'Now will ye give me a bit sense for once in a while – ye're always hidin' something. Never a straight answer to anything. Just puttin' me off.'

'Well, you will go on and on; ye've got to know; ye're never satisfied.'

'Ah've a right to know – Ah'm your mother. Ye've been mixed up in a fight. Next thing we know ye'll be carrying a flick knife.'

'Aw, leave me alone, Ma.'

Thought I was weakening and came in quick: 'Ah'll leave ye alone as soon as Ah get some truth outa ye.'

'If ye don't know, ye won't grieve.'

'Ah've done me best for ye – and this is what Ah get. A thug for a son ... Well, Ah'll keep at ye until Ah get the story.'

'Stubborn as a mule.'

'What did ye say? just repeat that!'

'Ah said mule – m, u, 1, e – and Ah mean it. Why don't ye leave me alone.' Shouldn't have been so arrogant with it. Should have kept my mouth shut. But she was tired and I was sore in more ways than one and I didn't give her a chance. So she landed me one and, more by instinct than intent, my hand came round and caught her on the cheek. Next thing I knew I was lying in the corner with the radio set on top of me. Fortunately, it's a dinky set.

I never saw anybody move as fast as Harry: in fact, I never saw him move at all. And there he was looking down on me, still smoking and the fag still carrying half an inch of ash.

I reckon I came up crying. The Old Lady came and helped me up. 'Here, sit down,' she told me. 'And as for you,' she informed Harry. 'Never interfere with my lad again.' He threw away his fag.

'He'd better keep his hands off you, then.'

'Ah can deal with him myself ... ye're takin' too much on yourself. He's my lad.'

'And by God ye can have him,' he said, walking out. At the door he looked back: 'A fine whip you're makin' for your back, me lass.'

You'll not believe it, but when he was out I told her practically the whole story. What you might call the telescoped version. She took it all right and I was patting myself on the back; accidentally, you might say, I'd pulled off one victory. That's what I thought. Never heard her say goodnight to him. Lay awake but never heard any creaking on the stairs, then slept like a top. You'll remember this was the man that loaned me his boneshaker, and mended the puncture. Never thanked him then, or in the morning or ever afterwards. Not that it matters now. But it did then – to him.

4

The next day was pretty much the same as far as work goes. Took a note from Uncle George to a character running a builder's yard three miles from the site. Carried my repair outfit but pulled through without a puncture. Which was natural since there was a new front tyre and tube, bought after the shop had closed and after a lot of banging at the door by Harry. Didn't discover the substance of this and other messages until much later, but might as well tell you now that there was a racket going on in double runs, and surplus concrete which wasn't surplus: tell you how I set that rabbit off in the course of due time.

In the afternoon it rained, and rain stopped work and made play. Cards came out in the old shed, but me and old Flack sat in one of the big pipes, with an old sack between us and its curve for comfort, and talked. I'm telling you now that this was the first sensible man I ever met. Deep and quiet. Very, very observant, like Nosey but from different angles, and very shrewd. NO I'M TELLING YOU. He treated you like an equal. He gave you credit for understanding a thing without nailing it in and home a thousand times. And no bragging and boasting: when that man told you a thing it was a fact and he told it like a fact and not a fairy story with himself as the clever Jack that knew the answers before the questions were put.

One thing led to another.

Happened to ask him if he'd been doing this sort of work all his life. He told me no; he'd been on some big road jobs, built some big reservoirs, put through some under-river roads. 'In fact,' he said, 'Ah've done a lot of tunnelling in my time. Started as a pitman.'

'How far down did ye work?'

'Not very far. Mebbe six or seven hundred feet. Coal's pretty shallow around here. Bends in a basin. Scratch the soil up west here and ye'll find stacks of coal; shouldn't be surprised if we cut into a seam with this drain afore we're finished.'

'How old were ye?'

'Pretty young when Ah went down – thirteen or so. Trapper boy, opening and shutting a door for ten hours a day. Sat playing myself at noughts and crosses on the door stanchion. Monotonous. Then went pony driven' – pullin' the tubs of coal out. Then went into me own place – coal hewer. Made a bit o' money when Ah wasn't in Dry Bread Flat.'

'What's that?'

'A place where the coal's hard and the roof's bad; or mebbe's faulted or full o' water.'

'Rough?'

'You get used to it. It's not money for jam, that's certain. But Ah liked it all right until the first War came … then Ah got pitched in.'

'You joined up?'

'Pitched up more than joined up. Called outa the pit one day to go and see the manager, old Charlie Lawson: hard-bitten ould cuss, he was. Told me the Army wanted volunteer miners, one from each pit. "Well," he told me, "they've asked for volunteers – and Ah've picked you for ours!"'

He told it in little bursts. Had to encourage him with a lot of questions and even then he wasn't very forthcoming. It came out like a bad dream, and the dream became my own:

There was a street that leaned on a hill. I'd a big nose that everybody made game of. Every day was the same. At two o'clock in the morning: 'Get up, get up for God's sake,' shouted the knocker-up, beating the door like a big drum till you rolled out of the cocoon of sleep and shouted back that you were awake. Downstairs you lit the lamp and boiled the kettle on a big glowing fire: pulled on your pit-gear; made a pot of tea and filled your bait-bottle; fitted yourself for seven hours underground with two or three slices of bread and dripping or, maybe, wowie-and-bread, which was black treacle spread on butterless bread. Walked down the hill with the cold nipping your bare knees. Picked up your lamp at the drift-mouth and walked out of darkness into double-darkness, the tunnel getting lower and lower, shot-fumes in your nostrils and water dripping on your back to tell you that the coalface was near. Two of you drilling by hand, firing down, shovelling until you didn't know which was water and which was sweat. There you were master. No kidding about the big nose when you had the tools of your trade in your hand.

Then, in the middle of the war, the call to come out of the pit. The bugle call. The open door. Chance to be a hero.

Never forget old Charlie Lawson as long as I live. Called for me at ten o'clock that night with his horse and trap to drive a common pitman to Newcastle station. There was a big sergeant with a slack mouth and a dirty tongue who feared neither man nor devil. Charlie handed over a parcel containing a hundred Woodbines and a bottle of his favourite cough medicine and left me with this sergeant and about twenty other chaps. All the way to London we shivered, not with cold, but fear of what the sergeant told us on the subject of death and No Man's Land. At King's Cross we picked up some more and then there was another station, milling with more bewildered pitmen and shouting sergeants.

We steamed across the sea to France: it was thirty-six hours from coalface to frontline. It was flat land full of broken teeth and pockmarks; a wilderness that was all the worse for being in daylight. It was clay, clay all the way. Bloody great ponds and sometimes the road went straight through them; the clay clagged to your boots and built up until you lifted the whole earth with every step. Over on the skyline puffs of smoke kept coming and going. Down the road came a stream of soldiers, some bandaged and being helped along. They shouted they were sorry about not having had time to tidy up. They sang their own song:

> We're here because we're here,
> Because we're here, because we're here;
> We're here because we're here,
> Because we're here, because we're here.

It was not what I'd expected. Twice a passing soldier shouted: 'Better watch that conk, mate.' That wasn't what I'd expected either. It was raining and everything was slow-motion misery. We didn't know where we were going, or to what. We didn't carry guns and that made us uneasy because of the flashes and the thuds away in front. Then the road became a shallow trench turning and twisting until we lost all sense of direction. Then we got into the front line but didn't know it: just the odd rifleman every so many paces keeping watch. Glow of candles coming through the sacking stretched over the dugouts; from the other direction came a sweet sour smell.

There was a place along a communication trench. Looked like a dugout, only it had a notice which said: DEEP WELL. We went inside, travelled maybe sixty or seventy feet down and found our quarters. It was just like a coalmine excepting that there was no stone: it was clay, solid clay. When it was dry it was like iron; when it was wet it sucked like summer jam. Got settled in, then went down to the main level; and that went level out under the Jerry: under a place called Hill 60.

Alive with men under there; twenty tunnels, dimensions three by six; bloody great pumps and pipes, listening posts; thousands of men living, breathing and sleeping with clay in every pore, clay in their taste, clay on their testicles, clay on the brain. They had a kind of wireless and they were listening to Jerry working up above.

Maybe he'd an idea what we were up to; maybe he didn't want to believe it possible. Went off course once. Told the officer. He was a cocky little chap and said we were below their level and had to go to the rise. Knew that rise would take us into trouble. He wouldn't listen. One day the clay broke like a window into a place where two Jerries sat, quietly smoking.

We jumped on them and smashed them dead with our spades, the way we'd learned to smash the rats. It was easy because they'd taken their helmets off. Then we went back and blew her up at the bottom of the rise, without waiting for permission. Never saw the cocky officer again. That was one we got the better of; the Jerry had found one of ours and blew it up: they should have taken warning. Didn't know we could be so rotten cruel. I helped to lay a million pounds of explosives, but somebody else set it off. The place was thick with men and you couldn't hear yourself talking for the noise of a thousand guns – our guns. Shook down to the front line. The men were all ready, behind a starting tape. Nervous as kittens, especially when the guns stopped. Chatting with a sergeant, pale as chalk, and he showed me over the top, a hummock. Smell of bacon frying. Lovely. A bird started singing and the sergeant said it was a nightingale in Battle Wood over in the enemy lines: below the bird were thousands and thousands of Jerry, four or five divisions, some watching, some sleeping; some frying bacon, or writing letters, or telling dirty jokes.

They should have been praying.

The sergeant told me that Hill 60 and all in front of us was a mountain of men, sandbags, machine gun emplacements, snipers' nests, pill-boxes; and that nothing in the world could take it; you could take Gibraltar easier, he said, and he knew because he'd been there six months. He didn't believe that what we'd done would help; knowing what one pound of black powder would do I knew, or thought I knew, what a million pounds of that powerful stuff would shift. But I didn't tell him, didn't argue. Wish I had now, because of all the men there that day he was the deadest when it happened.

It was ten past three in the morning and our guns started up again. Not all of them – just a few to put the Jerry off.

The guns were going. Then they stopped. Something bigger was happening out there and it stopped the guns; nineteen shoots of flame went up and up and up: and the earth danced. The sound hammered your head until you thought you would go mad. I was flat on my face. Then the whistles began to blow. It was the biggest football match on earth. Men poured over the top in a khaki river. All but the sergeant. He was standing with a rifle in his hand; and the first thing I noticed was that it hadn't a bayonet. Then I looked at his hand and saw a hole in it. Lastly, I looked at his face, which had two holes instead of eyes. His jaw had dropped as if he'd died. I think he had. Lifting his rifle I went over the top. It was very quiet over there in spite of all those men running. Then you heard a humming noise: the wounded and the half-dead over on the ridge. Feet never touched ground all the way over. The earth was still dancing. I looked for Jerries to fight: but all I found were weeping, or wandering like sleep-walkers without weapons, or sitting on the ground with their heads between their knees. Nobody wanted to fight.

After this they said I could go home, but I said I wanted to be a soldier. So they let me stay. I thought they should have a chance to kill me. I'd killed my share and one or two more wouldn't make any difference: at the same time there was a fair chance of being killed myself. So I stayed. And then I found out that I was dead anyway.

How does one man's life become your dream?

I don't know. Old George Flack and me talked a lot after this; not always about the Hill 60 business; just now and again the odd throwback. Sitting in the pipe with the rain pelting down, looking into his face, made the story mine. So that ever after, a word or even a look in his eyes was enough to send me back to Flanders, 1917. Maybe the Carruthers-Smith episode being on my mind helped to bring this dream upon me; somehow there was a similarity between that and the other. Don't ask me to explain it.

It was the dying part that intrigued me. 'After that I found I was dead anyway.' In my own dream I always heard Flack's voice say this and generally I'd waken in a cold sweat at the thought that both of us, not just George, but me as well, were dead. But he knew and I didn't; that was the difference.

How could a man die in this way, yet live on? I couldn't grasp it, and what made it all the more difficult to grasp was that old George Flack was the most alive man on the site. All the others were trying to live, but he lived as naturally and easy as a bird. Maybe it's a great thing to believe you're dead.

FIVE

1

You will remember that I'd arranged to meet old Nosey that night. Having been out of work a while I was eager to earn half a dollar on scrap iron. All was normal at home, which is to say that the Old Lady had gone off to work as usual. If she'd left a message for me the Lodger wasn't relaying it.

'Ah'm off,' I told him.

'Enjoy yourself.'

Didn't look up from his evening paper. Set off whistling, then felt his hand on my shoulder. 'Where are ye off to?'

'Out.'

'Don't tell me if you don't want,' he said. 'You can go where you like and do what you like. But Ah wouldn't be too late in – you know how she gets worked up if you're out late.'

'No good in that for you, eh?' I said.

'Listen, young 'un – what have you got against me?'

'Nothin'; so long as ye don't interfere between me an' the Old Lady.'

'Ye needn't worry about that,' he told me. 'If you're afraid of gettin' a new Daddy, forget it. She could've had a divorce from the other ages ago but held off because of you. Thinks he'll come back.'

'He'll come back.'

'You're kiddin' yourself,' he said. 'After three months' married life he went missing. He's not comin' back now.'

'Well, let's wait an' see,' I told him. 'It won't harm anybody.'

'It might harm her.'

'The Old Lady …? She's all right. Ah'm all right. You're the only one that's worryin' about anything.'

'It's like talking to a stone wall,' he said. I could see from his face that he was holding back a mouthful. Also that he would dearly liked to have clipped me over the lughole. But he didn't and naturally I jumped to the conclusion that it was the two inches advantage I possessed.

I walked out high and cheerful at cutting him down to size. If I had to have a father, I preferred the one I'd never seen and was never likely to see. Let things stay as they are, was my philosophy. Me and the Old Lady were snug enough as we were; the only reform I wanted would come when I was making enough to buy her out of the charlady caper and expel all boarders.

Nosey was waiting for me – he's the kind that's always there first. Tongue hanging out for a fag. I gave him one. He sat watching me with careless interest, the fag hanging unlit. Of course, the studs were rusted in and I hadn't a hammer. 'Got you beat?' he asked.

'Need a hammer; maybe if you can spare the time you'll look around and find a piece of iron or something to hammer the spanner.'

'Gimme a light first.'

'Why couldn't you ask before?' I said, irritated.

'Could see you were boilin' to get on with the job and didn't want to hold you up. Always a mistake. Have a fag with me, and take it easy.'

After throwing him the matches I started looking around for a substitute for a hammer and failed. 'Told you to take it easy,' he said. 'Now sit down and have a draw. Inhale, man, and Ah'll fix you up by the time you're finished.'

Could have smacked him down. Instead I smoked. It occurred to me that maybe he was trying to prove something to himself and that getting me mad was part of it. So I sat and smoked and thought, and my eyes lit upon a length of piping. If it would fit over the end of the spanner it would give me the necessary leverage to shift the rust.

Stubbed my fag, picked up the pipe, and set to. The studs came like magic. 'See?' said Nosey. 'Told you a draw would do it.' So he got his victory after all. But not the one he wanted. I always had the feeling that Nosey didn't mesh with me. We were never natural marrers. I respected him and maybe he respected me, but he always kicked against his respect. Apart from this the only link was that he'd a big nose and I'd a scar on my face; in fact it was only after I got the scar that he began to take an interest in me. He'd stroke and look down that big nose of his at me with a peculiar expression. As if wondering how much we were alike, and how far apart.

Maybe he was trying to prove that we were both in the same boat. Well, anyway, he had one point: he thought the world of my Old Lady. 'Remember that breakfast she gave us?' he would say, and I'd look at him wondering what there was about a breakfast.

'What's a breakfast?' I'd say.

'Well, she *made* it, didn't she?'

I'd nod as if I understood, because I didn't want to hurt him or look like a dimwit. 'Sat us down like Lords!' he'd continue. 'Poured our tea and cut our bread, and hung around and all.' Used to think that maybe it was the novelty of being waited on that pleased him. I had to have a look at his place before I understood. New and ancient smells floating around, dirty clothes and a crummy table from which you helped yourself at any time in the day. And nobody watching to see that you ate, let alone prepare a meal to make sure you ate well.

The sprung mattress was intended to be a permanent feature so we left it – in any case, it was too heavy to carry. No slops turned up to catch us dragging along the ends and the angle-iron connections and once we reached the bankside it was easy to skid the stuff down. Not wanting to create a stir we went around by the back of the old cottages where old Carruthers-Smith had sheltered. Being rough ground it was pretty hard going; in the end we left the angles and rode the bed-ends like sledges. Even at this we were winded when we arrived. Old Charlie's place is a twisted old house with whitewashed walls and a pantiled roof, a tall, slanting chimney, and a great number of windows. Being a scrap depository it is surrounded by a high fence with barbed wire nailed along the top.

The big door swung open at a bash of my shoulder and we went in one at a time of necessity to be received by a dirty great Alsatian, all white fangs, foam and fight. We dropped the bed-ends and did a bunk. The beast was on a long lead.

We stood and watched it snarl, then Nosey said: 'Ah'll away back for them angles – that'll settle him.'

'It's not a him, it's a her,' I told him. 'Furthermore, if we brain this hound dog there'll be no sale. You wait, Nosey.'

I'd been waiting to score on him ever since we stripped the bed; funny how you like to score, and how the liking grows stronger. That little score on the sex of the dog put two inches on my height. Anyway, we stayed put while that old dog lifted her head and snarled sideways, or wrenched so hard at the rope that the house shivered and shook, and in the end the door came open. It was this Mildred, dressed in a towel-robe, with her long black hair hanging down over her shoulders. Stood all blurred, like a big moth, in the doorway, telling the dog to shut up. Instead of running to her it walked back maybe a dozen yards and sat down. Then she came over the yard.

'What's up?'

'Got some old iron we thought ye might like,' I told her.

'Well it's no use; he's out. Better come back tomorrow.'

'We'll wait,' said Nosey.

'Do what you like, but you might wait a long time,' she said. Nosey sat down on an old anvil. 'Never sit on cold iron,' she said. 'Anyway, it's no use waiting. He's on a nine-days wonder and God knows when he'll be back.'

'Closing time's ten,' said Nosey.

'He wanders,' she said. 'He might be down the road – he might be twenty miles away. And he'll be paralytic. You'll get no sense out of him.'

'You make us an offer,' said Nosey.

'For that stuff! We've got a stack of beds.'

I could see she wanted rid of us. 'Can we leave it?'

'Okay, put it down and come back tomorrow,' she said. 'But before six: he's got seven days to do yet and he never stops.'

'Aw come on, give us half a dollar,' said Nosey. 'Bring the angles, Arthur.'

So I went for the two angles and when I returned old Nosey was rubbing the Alsatian under the jowls. Mildred was gone. Old Nosey was whispering to the bitch. 'Come on an' stroke her,' he said. 'She's all right – wouldn't hurt a fly.'

'Let's scram,' I said.

'For God's sake don't look so frightened,' he told me.

'Ah'm not frightened, only cautious,' I told him; but he was absolutely correct. I ran a couple of fingers over her skull between the ears and she gave me a lick. A real old sweetheart, once she knew we were all right.

Mildred came out. I'd a feeling I'd heard another voice in the house, but came to the conclusion that it was the radio. Anyway, it was none of my business if she was entertaining a boyfriend. Handing Nosey the half-dollar, she said: 'Here, and it's more than the stuff's worth: we've got a couple of hundred stacked up there.'

'Ta, all the same,' said Nosey.

'Haven't Ah seen you before?' she said.

'Once seen never forgotten,' he told her. 'Be seeing you again.'

'Bring something useful next time, kiddar,' she told him, and worked her way back to the house. Nosey was still stroking the Alsatian. 'Let's get crackin',' I said. But he hung back. And so did Mildred. She stood in the doorway. In a sense she was telling us to go, without talking. The scent she was using was pretty powerful. It was a mixture of new-mown hay and violets; or maybe it was just violets. Didn't hear the door shut until we were halfway up the hill, and I knew without looking that she'd watched us on our way. A silent, suspicious woman.

'Let's sit down,' suggested Nosey. I was willing. It was a good night: red sky over the city, hardly dusk, a gentle sort of time. I lay back with my hands behind my head and counted grains on one seed-head of grass, admiring the way they folded over and fitted into each other.

'Ah've got an idea,' said Nosey.

'Can't do much with a half-dollar this time of the night.'

'Ten Players and a cup of tea at the milk bar,' he said. 'But that's not the idea.'

'Give,' I told him.

'Did you notice her?'

'More or less – what d'ye mean?'

'Nothin' on under that robe thing,' he said.

'What about it?'

'Let's have a look.'

'You're crazy, man. The dog'll eat us alive. Anyway, they give ye gaol for peeping.'

'Dog's okay,' he said. 'Made sure of that. Let's have a look down.'

'Have a look yourself, if you want. Ah've no fancy.'

'Bet she's walkin' about stark naked,' he said. 'Ever seen a naked woman?' He was leaning over me, chewing a piece of grass-stalk. Didn't know what to say. I had, of course, but thought he wouldn't believe me. In the end I just shook my head: 'What about you, Nosey?'

He nodded. I'd an idea he was lying. In those days I used to think I was unique. 'They look all right,' he told me. 'Knock your eyes out. How about it?'

The dog came out wagging her tail and we gave it a pat or two. My heart was thumping like a diesel. I'd have given anything for that Alsatian to mouth, but she lapped it up and licked us back. We approached the house end on. Nosey was leading the way.

The dog followed us wagging her tail like mad for more love.

There was a curtain over the window but we could see through the middle because the two ends hadn't been pulled far enough to overlap. There was an old oil lamp on the table in front of the fireplace, stirring the fire up. She turned, laughing, and I just about jumped out of my skin because she seemed to be laughing at us. I nearly took off at that moment until I realised there was somebody inside the room with her. The bathrobe fell open all the way down. It wasn't the first time, so it's no use saying I never saw anything like it in my life. But it was a different feeling from before. But lying or not, Nosey was right about one thing. It nearly knocked my eyes out. She stood up and slipped a bracelet off and put it on the mantelpiece. She slipped off the bathrobe. It dropped at her feet. She laughed again. Then a man came behind her. He took hold of her. A split second before I saw his face full on it hit me, and I thought how funny it was that they were so close at such a moment. I mean, two brothers. Because the man was Crab Carron.

Maybe you'll think I'm loopy, but this one finished me. Until this happened it was like watching a film: watching somebody you hardly knew. As soon as I saw Crab I felt guilty and it wasn't just because he could tan the hide off me with one hand tied behind his back. I was excited and sick and felt like running the way old George did in the Hill 60 caper, only away. I tugged at Nosey's sleeve and gave him the nod to leave. Believe it or not he shook his head. He was grinning like a monkey. This made me feel worse.

Yet I didn't want to leave without him. In the end she made up our minds for us by coming over to the window. She turned out the lamp. In the instant before it went out I saw all of her, head and shoulders. All curves and roundness, white and pink. It was still there after the light went down; until she drew the curtains. I was so hypnotised that I didn't react until the curtain had moved; looking back from the gate I saw Nosey stroking the hound dog. Maybe by then he was feeling guilty. He didn't kid me up about running away. We snook along in the opposite direction to the one we used in coming, crossed the barrel bridge, and wandered along past Venice Steps, and were passing the Three-Headed Sheep when Nosey spoke his first word.

'Hang on,' he said. 'Ah'll get us a bottle.'

When he came out there was a bulge in his jacket, which was buttoned, and I knew he'd managed to get the bottle over the off-licence with the excuse that his Old Lady had sent him. I was certainly glad of that bottle. We sat on the steps of a pigeon cree overlooking the river, all shadows and sluggish and oily, with the occasional pilot cutter slugging along through it as if it were tar, which it practically is, and took turns at swigging. I was dry and empty and that brown ale helped to fill me up. After a while old Nosey started rubbing his nose and said: 'Fancy our kiddar!'

'Shook me rigid when I saw his face,' I said.

'Keep it dark,' he said, and it was an order.

'Think Ah've no more sense?' I said.

'Just in case.'

'She's a lot older than him,' I said.

'What's the difference? She's got all he wants, or maybe you're blind. Jam lucky, always was, our kiddar.'

'But when they get married it'll be queer, her being older ...'

'Aw, come off it. He'll not marry her – she's only a good thing.'

'What if he has to marry her?'

'Listen, kiddar, you've no idea, no idea at all. He won't have to marry her. She doesn't want to marry him. Love 'em an' leave 'em, that's the trick.'

'Saw him around here once before,' I said.

'No! Did he know you'd seen him?'

'Yeah – came up and nattered with me a bit.'

'Say anything about her?'

'Said something about her bein' his piggy bank. Said if Ah went down some time an' asked for a drink of water Ah'd find out.'

'You mean he's bein' paid,' said Nosey.

'That's what he told me,' I said. 'Sounded crazy, but he said it.'

'Some women are crazy ... for men.'

'You mean – he gets paid for that – what we just saw.'

'Naturally; that's the way these women are.'

'Well, Ah never heard of a thing like that.'

'Told ye he was jam lucky.'

'He can have the jam. Ah wouldn't meddle with that woman for all the rice in China,' I said.

'Wonder how it started,' said Nosey. 'Wonder how you ever come to the point …'

I could have told him but kept my peace.

All the same, I've often had a kind of dream about it; wondering how it started. It would take a character like Crab to start it moving, because he's tough and can take a chance. Maybe he went down with some scrap the way we did, only alone, and she said come in, with a smile. That smile: I can bring it up like a flash. Or maybe he passed her in the street once or twice and maybe it was Saturday afternoon when the pavement is full of old ladies getting the groceries in, and so they ran into each other. Or maybe he was just hanging around the ravine at a loose end one day, a hot day, and asked for a drink of water. That's the way I think it was, because it was what he told me to do. He didn't dig that one out of his imagination. While he was drinking she'd stand in the doorway and give him a queer smile.

And he'd stop drinking and stare back at her, angry, because none of the Carrons like to be smiled at, and say: 'What's the matter with you – share the joke, Missus.'

And she'd say: 'Ah'm a widow. You remind me of my husband that died in a Japanese prison camp. Just about as old as him when he went away – and just as green.'

'Don't kid yourself.' And then he'd hand her the glass and walk away, angry, but tingling with excitement and glad when she shouted: 'Hey, you. Do me a favour.'

'What's that?' he'd say.

'Fix the curtain hanger for me – the runner things are bent.'

With his heart banging he'd say, 'Well, Ah don't know …' and she'd say, 'Oh, it's all right, little boy. Run away. Ah won't hurt you.' So he'd go in and get up on the steps and pull the curtain on in no time, even with his hands fumbling, and then look down to see her looking up with that queer half smile on her face. And realise that it was all an excuse. So he'd come down and maybe the steps would shake a bit and she'd take hold of his hand. A hand is a living thing and a woman's hand has a wonderful life. His hand would move round until it was holding hers. She'd say 'Yes?' with a kind of little gasp, and then try to draw it away but he wouldn't let go and so in the end her hand would be resting on her soft hip. And only then would he let go of her hand. She'd put that hand behind his neck and he'd see the plump, beautiful whiteness of her arm flash by. Eyes closed, head back, and all of her softness now in the arms. Sometimes it would be upstairs, and then she'd fall back upon the bed and hang on in a kiss until there was no breath left. But mainly it was downstairs and they would go up the dark stairs together, her weight heavy upon him, kissing on the way. Until the door closed and she said: 'Hurry.'

This was my imagination, and it wasn't Crab but me.

What wasn't imagination was that always, afterwards, she gave him money. And always afterwards she laughed at him and told him she didn't care who it was, he just happened to be convenient, and it didn't matter a rap to her whether he came back or didn't. But he always came back. The only thing that changed was that he told her he didn't want the money. So she told him to take it or the next time the door would be locked. Then he'd take the money but try to leave it lying around. But he never got away without it; she'd remind him, slip it into his jacket pocket. The money meant a lot to her. I suppose it was telling her, as well as him, that he didn't count.

That's why she stood in the yard and laughed, the day Crab and me lay in the clayhole. But I still don't know how it started. That dream of mine is a lot of hooey. Maybe it's the way it would have started if it had been me and not Crab. I don't think there was any excuse or talking. It just happened and afterwards Crab would have a bit of a swagger about him and she'd give him the money, smiling, and still there'd be nothing said. I can imagine Crab climbing the bank and stopping to look back: and she'd be standing there in the yard, laughing. You've got to understand this to understand the way Crab felt. All the time he was getting deeper and she was free because of the money.

A terrible thing was happening, and I'm not referring to the action he took. It was the thing that happened to him when she gave him the money and the laugh. I'm not denying that it impressed me a lot; there were times when I envied Crab, because all of us get those moments when you concentrate on what you want, get it, then find you want more.

2

Jumping a fortnight brings us to the day I brought my first pay from the site. I'm telling you this just in case I'm giving the impression that me and the Old Lady led a cat-and-dog sort of existence. We didn't. Most times we managed to live our own lives with sometimes something simmering, and sometimes not. On this occasion, though, it was me that was at fault. Through several jobs the Old Lady had insisted on me tipping up the pay-note intact, and dishing out the pocket-money. This I didn't like.

I'm not saying she was mean, in fact she was always good and generous; but pocket-money's a straitjacket, and that's another fact. What's okay for one week may be pin money the next and you're looking around for scrap iron, or playing beggar. Right or wrong my opinion was that paying board and buying my own clothes would be the right system. There was a lot to lose, on the other hand there was a lot to gain. For instance, I was tired of those Saturday afternoon trips downtown to buy shoes, socks, raincoats, and suits that were always a compromise between her choice and mine.

On the question of clothes the Old Lady is the reincarnation of Queen Victoria.

Before leaving school I ran through a T-boy phase. I lost that and went in for the gimmicks – string ties, for instance, or fancy shirts. I could laugh now, but there was one month when I fought a running battle with the Old Lady to get a glittering shirt with a string tie-up and a glass ornament at the neck. Only twenty-nine bob, but she wouldn't give. At one time or another I fell for skintight black jeans, shot-gold jackets, platform shoes, and satin waistcoats. Some I got, some I didn't. It doesn't matter now, but it did then.

Any character should have the right to buy the clothes he fancies. Maybe he'll make some mistakes. Maybe he'll end up a couple of weeks later wishing somebody had put a pistol to his ear and ordered him out of the shop before the deal was concluded. Maybe he'll make the wrong gamble every time, but that's his own funeral. As long as he brings in the roubles it's his right.

This is my principle, but man, I'm not kidding, I still felt funny when I stepped into the privacy of my own bedroom and took out the first pound note, leaving a little less than four quid in the packet, which I hid under my mattress. For one minute I was tempted to return to the status quo. Then I remembered the outfit which Nosey and I had decided the Manor lot would wear. There was also the fact that I wanted some spending money now, not later when the Old Lady came in from her stint. I hopped it.

But I knew it was going to be a clash of wills.

Anyway, I came in that night about ten-forty-five, and feeling a bit sour on account of a wasted night. Me and Nosey and a few more of the characters had gone to the Regent, which is our local fun-emporium, complete with cinema, billiard saloon, and dance-hall. It was too hot for the pictures so we milled around outside and watched the birds arrive, making maybe a comment or two and getting giggles from the birds and black looks from the lads they had in tow. Growing tired of this we wandered up to the saloon where we found a queue at every table. It was murder. No chance of jumping the queue because there is a character there named Sergeant Minto, an ex-Commando, whose bite is worse than his bark. Tell you about Minto some day; he's a very interesting character.

In the end and against my will we drifted into the dance-hall. Now I can do my share when the floor's packed and nobody cares, but I hate standing in corners making light chatter or beating time to the band when there's a light crowd and the birds are one-partner types or cagey about strangers. And this was the case tonight. We were below the band, which was a collection of tired tramps all playing by ear, and we were just spectators. Being early there was only a light crowd and all experts. Fanatic dancers, girls looking cool in off-shoulder dresses and all fixed-up for every dance with lads who gave them a negative stare if you asked for the pleasure. So there we were, chatting and beating time to the band while the fanatic dancers went round like knitting machines, and I'm telling you there's nothing more sad than watching dancers when you're out.

In my opinion there's something wrong with the organisation. I mean this dancing in pairs all the time. It's another form of capitalism. Maybe you'll think I'm crazy, but I believe if they organised so that everybody could join in, a hell of a lot of frustration that ends in the big smash-up would never rise to the surface.

Which it did this night when Kelly and his boys arrived. One minute we were lost souls, the next on edge. It got worse as the night went on. Seeing us standing under the band platform friend Kelly marched his lads to the opposite end of the room. Naturally, we exchanged glances. Also, in between numbers we put on the swagger and set up some leering laughs. These got under the skin, both sides, and after a bit of this a character in our gang named Roly-Poly Willis said: 'How about goin' over an' clockin' them?'

Nosey shook his head: 'We're clearin' out,' he said, and winked. Then he told us how we'd spread ourselves out on the stairs and catch the Kelly lot coming down, split them up – 'And be careful,' he warned us. 'Those Kelly characters carry chains etcetera an' we're light on the stuff.'

Just at this the MC walked up. He's a tall, thin adult with a moustache and a nervous disposition. 'Hope you lads aren't up to any trouble?'

'Not us,' said Nosey. 'But them characters over there have different ideas.'

'Who are they?'

'Quayside gang – Mick Kelly's lot.'

'Well, for God's sake don't start anything,' said the MC. 'We don't want any trouble – last time somebody smashed the centre light with a pop-bottle – that's ten quid – and we never found him.'

'We don't want no trouble,' said Nosey piously. 'In fact, we've decided to leave.'

'That's a good lad,' said the MC.

So we went out in a casual sort of way, throwing good-byes to the band and a kiss to their tame canary. Once through the door we melted.

The idea was that me and Roly-Poly should hide in the Gents and nip out quickly from the rear. Any feeling the urge and walking in where they weren't wanted would get rapped pretty quickly, leaving less for Nosey and the rest to deal with. The general idea was for all but Nosey to melt out of sight at the base of the stairs while he stood smoking and looking generally innocent and incapable. Kelly-bait.

As it was, a couple of these characters walked into the parlour; I distinctly remember a third looking through the door while I was otherwise engaged but he was all for fair fights and left his pals to look after themselves. Which they didn't. I was behind the door and Roly-Poly was concealed in a toilet when they walked in: not wanting to waste any time I tripped the second lad; the first sort of turned and Roly-Poly came rushing out with his head down, twelve stones, and took him in the tummy. Well, that took care of number one. From thereon all he wanted was air and you could hear him taking it in a mile away, I'll bet. But number two was a more serious proposition, mainly because he'd all his wits about him and fell with his hands close to his chest, which saved him a knock from the marble floor, and enabled him to come up quick like a cat, all spits and spats and a chain in his hand. With which he commenced laying about. You'd have laughed yourself silly to see him whizzing this thing and me and Roly-Poly doing a combination ballet-quickstep to avoid a surgical operation.

Didn't draw any blood but went one worse when he laid the chain over Roly-Poly's shoulder, because the latter is inclined to be a bit of a dandy-boy and doesn't like his clothes creased otherwise than normally. Old Roly-Poly reacted without thinking by coming in with his head again, duck and up, you never saw anything so beautiful in your life. The character, held in the middle and half winded, started belting hell out of Roly-Poly's rear. Whereupon I waited until they'd spun a turn then belted him in the kidneys. I took the chains and Roly-Poly gave him a belt in the eye, which we left him holding.

We charged downstairs. There it was scrumping time, with characters belting each other on piecework, some vertical, others horizontal and trying to keep out of the pounding feet. Maybe three stairs up we met a Kelly-character coming up, or maybe he was just an innocent. Because I took him by the tie and asked him where he was going.

'Any of your business?'

Giving Roly-Poly the wink to extend his leg I remarked, 'Yes,' gave him his tie back and over he went. They were pretty thin by now because a couple of characters evaporated on seeing me and pal Roly-Poly. One or two were sitting around with somebody sitting on them. The only one standing was Kelly.

He pulled a knife.

One second it was something black in his hand. The next it was a bright and shining blade and, boy, that was the finish as far as I was concerned. Everything stopped and I mean stopped because, you see, he had it up against Nosey's midriff. So he said: 'Let them lads away or Ah'll cut a slice of bacon and Ah'm not kidding.'

'Knifer, eh?' said Nosey, but he was sweating.

'Shut up!'

Well, they all cleared out. It was a regular retreat. And when they were all out in the street, Kelly just calmly needled a hole in Nosey's shirt then cut up. After which he took a pill. You'll maybe think this is a tall story: six of us held up by one character even if he did have a knife; but that's the way it was. You get yourself mixed up with a knifeman sometime and see how you slow up. Boy, it's slow motion the moment he draws.

They got across the road and on to a trolley. It drew out before we could have got over, but none of us attempted to follow. For my part, I'd had my pig and you can lay 1000 to 1 that all concerned were feeling likewise. In fact, when somebody mentioned the two characters in the Gents, Roly-Poly suggested only once that we should have another conference with them to even up the knife. Nobody reacted and Roly-Poly didn't make a second try.

In any case we had to melt because you can never gamble on the helpful citizen not calling the slops. Also the MC was coming downstairs in a very cagey manner and while he was no problem we didn't feel like holding a conference. We went to the market-place and cleaned ourselves up in the underground Gents. We had a coffee and a natter. By then the knife was wearing off and most of the characters were enjoying the caper retrospectively, blowing it up, chewing over the tastier bits, etc.

But old Nosey sat with his jacket buttoned.

'Maybe some day Ah'll have his chops for chips,' was all he said. That character had more pride for a half-breed than anybody I've ever known. Maybe I'd have pulled him out of it that night but being preoccupied with other things I let it go. I had my second battle of the night coming up.

3

I walked into a regular little scene of domestic bliss. Oh, I don't mean anything fishy. There was no jumping to attention. It was worse. The Old Lady was sat at one side and Harry at the other, the radio playing softly, and you could see that they'd been having the kind of natter that is possible only between very good friends. It caught me on the raw.

'So you're in,' said the Old Lady, switching rapidly from one tone to another. This is a talent I've noticed among the ladies.

'Hello, all,' I said and sat down at my place, which was set.

'His Lordship wants servin'.'

'Aw, Ma, let's have a meal in peace.'

'Look under your plate for your supper.'

'Ah think Ah'll turn in now,' said Harry.

'Stop in and see the entertainment,' said the Old Lady.

'Yes, stay,' I said. 'Join in the fun – when we know what it's all about.' But all the same I knew what it was all about and also what lay under my plate.

'No thanks, Peg,' he said. 'Ah'll keep me nose out.'

'Which you should do sooner or not at all.'

'What d'ye mean by that?' asked the Old Lady.

'Ye know what Ah mean – fine pow-wow the pair of ye were havin' when Ah walked in!'

'That's enough of that!'

'So long as ye don't try to pull the wool over my eyes.'

'If ye knew your mother at all, ye'd know that she has a mind of her own,' said Harry. 'If she tells me what she thinks of you, that's her business.'

'And now Ah'm gonna tell ye to your face,' said the Old Lady.

'And Ah'm off!' said Harry.

'Pity he didn't stay to hear ye sayin' your lines,' I remarked to his back.

'Now will ye shut your trap or ye'll have the teapot over your head again,' said the Old Lady. 'Ye talk about me goin' on – ye don't give anybody a chance to keep their tempers and say a word in calmness.' Which, of course, was perfectly true. What is it that keeps you talking when you know it's no good? Especially to older folk. I've noticed they're slower to react – with words. They've the experience but the kids have the wit. But on you go stirring up the trouble; what you might call operating and deep without an anaesthetic and sooner or later you go too deep and bring a pain to life that demands to inflict pain elsewhere.

'Anyway,' I remarked. 'What's all the bawlin' about – it's a mystery to me, to date.'

'Ah'll give ye credit for more brains than that …'

'Thanks,' I said.

'Ye know what it's about – your pay.'

'What's the matter – can't ye wait?'

'Ah told you that ye'd be on pocket-money … then you deliberately go and break into your packet. What's the idea?'

'Let me ask ye a question: how d'ye know Ah've broken into it?'

'Well, look under your plate.' But I didn't: I wouldn't give her that pleasure. 'Look under your plate!'

'Ah don't need to look under me plate to know ye've been pokin' about in me room and rakin' about my private property.'

'And Ah don't think much about you,' she said. 'When Ah first started work Ah was proud to go home and hand me pay-packet over to your grandma: proud.'

'Times have changed since then …'

'For the worse. Ah'd burn with shame if Ah were you – after the way Ah've toiled and moiled to bring ye up – and on me own – ye turn round and do this.'

'Listen, Ma,' I said, trying to get things on to a reasonable plane. 'Just listen. *Ah'm* goin' out to work, not you. What was good enough for you doesn't hold for me … oh, it's all right, Ah'll pay me way; Ah'll give you board and lodgings. But Ah'll handle me own money. Ah'll buy me own clothes. Ah'm sick and tired of being taken and told what Ah'm to wear.'

'You'll hand your pay over – intact.'

'Ah'll pay you board and lodgings – that way we'll both be independent.'

'So's you can splash your money on your fancy monkey suits and keep up wi' your low friends, that's your idea. Well, Ah'm tellin' ye now: Ah'm not havin' it.'

Brushing the plate aside I took up the pay-packet and extracted three pound notes: 'There you are. There's your money and be content.' I held them out but didn't get any reaction. So I slapped them bang in the middle of the table. 'All right – Ah'll leave it there an' you can pick it up when Ah've gone in your usual manner.'

'Ah'd burn before Ah'd touch it.'

'Pity you aren't so particular about other things.'

We were both on our feet now and ready to cut. 'What d'ye mean by that crack?'

'That fancy man of yours.'

'Why, you little bastard ...' It wasn't the teapot this time, but the breadboard. Well boy, I'm telling you, I didn't stand to attention. She was berserk, running wild, and coming for me. I ducked and came up and because I was frightened slapped her. She stopped dead. Then she turned and walked over to the chair in the corner and sat down.

'Ah'm sorry, Ma,' I said, following her.

She didn't say a word. She could have said, 'You struck me!' but didn't and I'm bound to admit I admire her for that touch. But I reckon I'd really hurt her. That slap had hit her right on the other solar plexus. 'Ah didn't mean it, Ma, it was just that you were comin' for me. But Ah didn't mean to hit you ... like that.' By this time I was kneeling in front of her and she caught hold of my head and drew me to her. I reckon I was bubbling like a bairn.

'Ah'm sorry, Ma. Take the pay, all that's left. Ah shouldn't have done it.' Well, that's what I said, but I'm bound to admit that at the same time I was thinking myself a mug for giving in so easily. And then I was ashamed.

'No, lad,' she said. 'Ah don't want your money. God knows Ah don't want it. Ah just want to put things right between us, and Ah can't, and it gets me mad. Keep the money but be all right with me.'

'Ah will.'

We sat like this a long time. Then she said, 'What have ye got against him?'

'Ah don't know. He's all right … he's all right as a lodger.'

'Ah've been without a man for more than fifteen years,' she said.

'Ah can't help it, Ma. It just gets me on the raw when Ah think of anything happening between the two of you …'

'He wants to marry me … and it gets lonely.'

She must have felt me stiffen there. 'What would ye do if we got married?'

I didn't answer. After a while I got up and washed my face. Then she fried me some tripe in batter and poured a cup of tea. I sat down and I ate. It was nice and comfortable there in the kitchen, just the two of us and the decision in my favour. But I never felt so miserable in my life. As I laid my head on the pillow I thought of all the fights I'd had and I said to myself: Boy, you can't lose all the time, but sometimes winning is worse than losing.

SIX

1

All things considered, site-work wasn't so bad once you got into the routine. Plenty of variety and not so much of the shovelling as I'd expected – that first day's chewing had been due to the breakdown of some equipment. Most times I was second man to somebody or other; maybe down in the cut loosening up with the windy pick or shoring up the sides when we came into loose stuff. I used to like it down there on account of maybe finding something interesting: in fact, in addition to a seam of nice coal which supplied most of us with the odd bag or two until it ran out there were one or two interesting things. We came across an old mill-race which was arched over to take the water underground and old George told me that it must be pretty old because the bricks were handmade and only about two inches thick. Later we cut through the site of the mill.

We were held up a week or two on the foundations of the old mill. Some of those foundation stones were maybe a yard long and foot square and if that wasn't enough those ancient characters had used a cement that had set as hard as the stone – we had to get in a specialist to blow them apart. We found the place where the big paddle wheel had been and here I found a little hoard. We broke through one morning just about ten o'clock and as soon as possible I hurried down and raked about with my hands. There were one or two green old coins with a woman's face which I guessed to be Queen Victoria's but turned out to be

Queen Anne's, and there was a ring. It was covered with a kind of mould and when I rubbed it on my sleeve I got a flash of green. I shoved this stuff in my pocket without saying anything. I didn't know the regulations about treasure trove but I'd a pretty good idea that Sprogget and Uncle George would flash the stuff away so quick you'd be kidding yourself it had never been there.

Anyway, in the end I showed it to old George Flack. He said the coins were copper but the ring reflected the glint in his eye. 'Ah reckon the miller's wife lost this, lad,' he told me. 'There'd be tears that day. Pin to a penny it came in with a Russian boat. You take care of this till you get a young woman, but make sure she's the right one before ye put it on her hand.'

Which I thought was crazy talk. All the same I took it home and never said a word to anybody about it; in fact I shoved it with the coins under a loose floorboard in my bedroom and rainy nights I'd sit and polish the stuff, but mostly the ring. It was a handsome ring and it had been worn a long time – you couldn't read the writing around the edge. But you could certainly admire that little emerald; the way it was cut it winked like the devil.

That's just by the way. I was telling you about my chores. When I wasn't in the cut I'd take over the bulldozer, which is simple enough to operate, and do a bit grading for the character while he eased himself. Or I'd be directing the digger – a cubic yard job – when the bank was a bit too high and there was a bit spreading to do. The operator was a character named Joe Johnson. He'd been a fairground boxer and was maybe a bit punch drunk, and mean. He wouldn't let me handle her at any price, being afraid of losing his job; in fact he didn't even like me to watch. But I picked it up. Then of course there were the odds and ends, tea-making, sweeping out the shed, running messages for Uncle George or Sprogget.

But mostly I partnered old George Flack at the batching machine. We'd a light mechanical shovel to pick up the sand and pebbles and dump it into the batching machine. There we'd get the correct balance of the stuff from an indicator, then let it run through onto a scoop which tipped into a skip on the concrete mixer. Pull a lever and this skip would run on ropes up to the containers. Then you were set for a run.

When the going was heavy it was a three-man job, but mainly we managed it between us; held it easy, which meant we could talk. The trick was to tickle his imagination and get him talking. It was hard going at first. I've seen me go a whole afternoon and fail to stir him into action, which is to say into speech. I think he lived through his memories. Times you'd shout at him and he'd turn slowly with eyes like glass. But after a time I got to know the buttons.

One was riding. I remember finding out how it was through a riding school, trotting by one fine Saturday morning. We knocked off to watch them lollop by on their frisky little nags, young girls with smooth faces and velvet caps, boys with leather leggings and proud, watchful eyes. 'There's class for you,' I said.

'Not class,' he said. 'Except to you. To others they're like lice. And to those above, nonentities: nowts for short. There's no such thing as class. There's only caste. Caste is what you belong to and what the suckers take in – that's you.'

'Everybody knows there's different classes,' I said.

'Everybody knows,' he snorted. 'And that makes it so. But it's just imagination. You and your pals could get together and make a caste and get as much satisfaction as the nobs among yourselves. Know that. Gang of Teddy Boys or whatever they call them now are no different from the nobs that keep themselves – and the cushy jobs – to themselves. All you need is a bit imagination.'

'Listen, George,' I said, 'how did you work this one out?'

'In the trenches Ah reckon. Not in words. Only vague. And know why? There was only life an' death and it clashed the imagination outa ye. Didn't matter a bugger who led ye over No Man's Land so long as he brought ye back. Class didn't work there – or caste. Some of them class officers were hopeless and helpless and we'd pray for them to get a bullet before we got ours. Best men were them that kept alive; class didn't stop a shell or a bullet, so it's all imagination.'

'But everybody believes it,' I said.

'Makes no odds. The quality had to believe it; that's why so many good men went down. To maintain the idea of caste. They still pull the wool over our eyes – otherwise the entire caper would crash. Doesn't make any difference if they pull it over their own. See?'

I didn't understand this and went off at another tack. 'What was that you said the other week – about being dead?'

'Oh, that!'

'Well, come on, tell us, George.'

'It's simple. When they blew up Hill 60, they blew me up. Nothin' worthwhile left. Proof's in the fact that Ah'm here. By every rights Ah should have been a corpse a dozen times. But there was nothing to kill. What's wrong with the name Flack?' he suddenly asked.

'It's a funny name.'

'Funny?'

'Well, outa the ordinary.'

'Whose isn't? Take yours; Arthur Haggerston. Just think about it.' I did. 'There now, is that less funny than Flack?'

'Funnier.'

'That's it. Every name's a laugh, if ye stop to think. They're relics. Don't go with trousers and braces and television sets. So why the hell bother?'

I told him I hadn't the slightest idea.

'That's right, you don't know. But one name's all right an' you laugh at another – like Flack.'

'Ah never laughed, honest, George.'

'No, not you. But others have.'

'Who for instance?'

'Plenty. You know men have changed their names 'cos they couldn't stand the laughing that went on every time their backs was turned?'

'Nobody down our way ever did that.'

'Well, it's happened. In fact a nephew of mine did that. Came back dead. Wife died in the 'flu epidemic. Sister of mine had a promising lad. Ah wasn't on the beer in them days. Saved all me spare cash. When the day came Ah helped her to send him to a university. Well, he went and it was worse than goin' to the war. He came back a few times but it would have been better if he'd stayed away. Ah used to stay out when he was at home – that's how Ah got on to the beer.'

'He must have been a snob.'

'He lost himself, that's the trouble, and blamed it on the name. Reckon some of the smart lads must have given him hell. So one day after he'd left the university he walked in and said he'd given himself another name.'

'And then what?'

'Nothing. We went on living and he went on living and nobody knew the difference, except that we saw less and less of him.'

'What trade did he go in for?'

'Teacher,' said George. 'Still teaching somewhere around the city. Seen him do a mickey across the road many a time. Mind you, he never did that to his mother. But it gave her a smack all the same.'

'But …' I began to query.

'Know what you're goin' to say – if his mother was me sister his name wouldn't be Flack. Well, you're wrong. She was me sister, but his name was Flack … maybe that had something to do with it.'

We looked at each other for a while. 'Okay, let's get this batch off,' he finally said. 'You think it over. The most comic name there is can be a bloody sad name for somebody.'

We did the batch and all the time I was thinking that maybe this had a funnier twist than he'd dreamt of – was Carruthers-Smith the Flack that changed his name? If so I could understand why he ran that day. As soon as we had a minute – 'What did he change his name to, George?'

'You think you know him?'

'Could be.'

'Think Ah'm goin' to tell you that! Ye've got another think comin' ... he's due to that much protection.'

'Wouldn't be a chap called Carruthers-Smith?'

The glass was back in his eyes. 'You can try me till doomsday but Ah'm sayin' neither yes nor no,' he said.

After a while he said, 'What did you say it was?'

'Carruthers-Smith.'

'Well, he was bloody ambitious, but not so bloody ambitious as that,' he remarked. 'Anyway, there's more than one like him around.'

And this was all he would say. There was a time when I'd have enjoyed the thought of going back to the Dump and brushing up against old Carruthers-Smith to whisper: 'Howya, Flack?' Just to see him take a fit or maybe two. And maybe to make sure it was really him. But not now. I've seen enough of dead men of one kind and another and don't want to trouble them. Often wonder what it would feel like to change my name. Say to Tony Curtis. I reckon it would be like a prisoner on parole. It's bad enough running away from anything, let alone your name. Even Flack. Flack's all right. That character had too much imagination. Or too much to put up with.

2

Meanwhile, the gang was getting organised. Full strength was about fifteen but you couldn't always count on a one hundred per cent turn-out and you could bet your bottom dollar that trouble always came when we were fewest. Not that we had much trouble for a start. One way and another both us and the Quaysiders had learned a lot from the encounter in the Regent.

From then on we kept strictly within our private preserves. Around the perimeter wasn't so very safe so you kept to the centre, and there was plenty there to keep you occupied. A bit boozing, limited because of the expense, pictures twice a week, rolling round the milk bar, and the odd meeting every now and again in the old foundry, which in the absence of anything better we turned into HQ. Saturday nights we'd go to some hop or other. It was a pretty routine existence.

We made a pretty dicey showing in our Saturday uniform – twills, platform shoes, wind-cheater and thin red tie. We kept good care of this outfit. This was primarily animal pride but back of it was Nosey. That man was a stinger for discipline! Everything had to be in tip-top condition or else – not that he'd ever speak to me on this subject since I was fairly chuffed with my outfit. And me and Nosey became close and I mean close and parallel, no tops and bottoms, but close. I liked his sense of humour. Knowing what he was in a fight I had to respect his courage. On the other hand he wouldn't move without me. He'd hatch the plots and I'd pick the feathers.

He was good on the spot stuff – remember the way he master-minded the Regent caper off the cuff? – but I was his man for the long-range strategy. Take the HQ. He took a bit convincing but I pulled him round to the vision. There was this old storeroom, which we cleaned out and fixed with a lock. We put in a table, and borrowed a chair for Nosey – the rest of us squatted on orange boxes and liked it. Why, we even had an old winding-up gramo-phone in there and a pile of old records, begged, borrowed and stolen. There was corny stuff: characters playing stuff from twenty or thirty years or more ago which we used for the laughs. There was one called 'Amy, Wonderful Amy' about a woman that flew the Atlantic or some ocean and broke all records. But there were also some of the old Dixieland characters such as for instance Louis Armstrong, Fats Waller, Jelly Roll Morton, the Mills Brothers, and what have you. We went for the good old jazz. We'd sit hugging our knees for as long as you like, with the odd bottle of pop and a good supply of snouts, or even without. Those were cosy nights. Maybe these were the best nights.

Well, it had to come to an end and it did. Not with a crash but a creep. Crept on us like an old cat after sparrows. It would have come anyway. I know that. All I'm saying is that it came to an end before it should. First thing, Nosey got a job at the sardine factory, which, you might say, made no difference excepting he'd money to flash all the time instead of just sometimes. But one thing leads to another.

Nosey went missing one night. We'd fixed to meet in the milk bar but he never turned up. Man, I don't need to tell you I was lonely all that night even when the rest of the mob turned up. Funny how two characters can get tied up. Not even old Dopey telling the tale about his old man eased the loneliness.

'So the boss-man, he called me to his office and said he'd heard I couldn't read, so I told him we got the "Beano", etc. and read it from cover to cover, and he said less of the impudence, that's a picture paper and what on earth will you do when you get your pay-packet? So I told him Ah could figure enough for that and he jumped up and said it was important to read and write. Everybody should … you listening, Arthur?'

So I said I was listening but all the time in fact I was all churned up. I wanted to reach out and pick up Nosey from wherever he was and set him down beside me. Which I couldn't. There's nothing more baffling.

'Then he said he'd get one of the teachers to come along and give me special treatment, see? And Ah gave him a look. "What you're thinking now?" he asked. Which of course I couldn't tell him on account of the fact that he's against fish and chips and doesn't understand it's like a madhouse when you're in the middle of two females peeling potatoes and one mad old man running back and forth while slices of fish or maybe a two stone block of fat and a stink so high you couldn't push through it with a bulldozer …'

'Hey, that's a good 'un, Arthur.'

'That was lush.'

'Well, in the end he came down to see the old man – and gives him the full strength and all the time the old man's puttin' taties through the chip machine and into a big old bath-tin which we use on Fridays for bath-time when the shop is closed.

'In the end – are ye listenin', Arthur? – he says, he says to the old man: "Are you listening?" An' the old man says: "Ah am, Mister." So the boss man says: "An what do you think?" And the old man comes out pat: "Well, there's one thing certain he'll never be a forger."'

Well, you've got to give a character a laugh when he's one of your lot and he's taken a long jump and a lump of trouble to put it over, but it mustn't have been convincing because old Dopey shoved his face close to mine and said – 'Ah, Ah, Ah! so you don't think it's funny?'

So I said not very and he asked why, upon which I told him straight that if old Rattler had a mind to go out of his way to arrange for some martyr to sacrifice his time teaching a character to read and write then he should be welcomed and not ridiculed. And that it was now ancient history, anyway.

'So what's the good?' asked Dopey. 'Ah'm thick an' Ah know it – because nobody, including you, ever missed a chance of tellin' me.'

'What about when your old man dies an' you have to run the business – a fine cut you'll make of it.'

'Listen, Ah'll hire one of them accountants to keep it in line!'

'You'll have to read. He'll look after the figures and nothin 'else.'

'Okay then, Ah'll be married and leave it to the Missus.'

'Listen, Dopey,' I said. 'You're missin' the point. All Ah'm sayin' is that the boss man wanted to do ye a good turn and you gave him a spit in the eye, you and your old man.'

'Listen the teachers' friend!'

'Listen, all you do is give somebody the laugh. First it's old Rattler, now it's me. And for why – because we try to help you out.'

'Know what's the trouble with you?'

'Stuff it!'

'You're worried because Nosey didn't turn up.'

'Pipe down, pipe down,' said Roly-Poly.

'That's right, pin it up,' said several more of our lot. But man his pride was up, mostly because with both him and his old man the jesting was just a cover-up, and I was getting underneath to that tender, aching heart. I've known one or two illiterates. Some were just dim, and some had lazy minds, and others in the Dopey zone wanted an excuse for taking a slide through life, but they all had one thing in common – they didn't like it. Offer to put a wire thing on their heads with some flashing valves and tubes like in the horror pictures, to put the gift there, instant, and they'd all fall on their knees and worship you.

So as I was saying, the consensus of opinion was all against Dopey but he wouldn't back down.

'Ah'll tell you all about the big white chief – he's runnin' after a jane down the quayside – an' you know who she is? – she's Mick Kelly's sister.'

'You tire me,' I told him.

'That's right, break down an' cry – Pretty Boy.'

'Okay,' I said. 'You asked for it. Let's outside and you can say that again.'

'Yes, Ah'll come outside – *and* Ah'll take me jacket off.'

Got outside and old Roly-Poly said: 'It's a fine caper when two of a lot mix it. Why don't ye call it off, Arthur?'

'If he says he's sorry it's okay – Ah'll call it off.'

'Stuff that for a tale,' said Dopey. 'Ah'm not sorry, not now or never.'

'Let's find a quiet spot,' I said. We walked down the main street and hadn't walked more than fifty yards when Nosey came loping across the road.

'Hi, men,' he said, and we all piled up, milling around a bit while he looked us up and down and came to conclusions. I told you he was smart. 'What's the caper?'

'Dopey and Arthur had a row about one thing and another.'
'Such as?'

'Dopey was retailing that old one about old Rattler offering to learn him to read and write, and Arthur pulled him up about it.'

'I knew that one,' said Nosey, 'two centuries ago.'

'There was some words about you an' Mick Kelly's sister,' said Roly-Poly.

'Well, that's my business – or Ah'm dragging a ball an' chain. The fight's off.'

'Just as well for him,' bragged Dopey. 'Ah'd have his guts for garters!'

'You'd be flat on your back where you deserve,' said good old Nosey. 'You're a troublemaker, an' you're out.'

'For Godsakes, out!'

'Out.'

'Ach, he's all right,' I said.

'You're tellin' me. The Manor lot sticks together. Any mixin' is with any other lot.'

'Ah started it,' I told him.

'Makes no difference who asked who out. He's out and that's the finish.'

Leaving Dopey standing we went back to the milk bar. Maybe I'm soft-hearted but I felt sorry for the lad; mostly because I'd seen the look on his face as we cut off. The look told me that even a low IQ can feel forlorn. Because where was there for him to go? The Quaysiders or any other lot wouldn't have him on account of his dimness, etc. and even if they had, geography was a barrier: whoever heard of a character taking a fourpenny trolley to join his lot? Around the Manor area we were the Lot, the only Lot, excepting for a few half-baked kids not past the duck-stones, hopscotch, follow-my-leader stage. So when we turned him out, boy, he was really out. The Garden of Eden had nothing on it.

In the words of the song: baby, it's cold out there.

You squat in front of the telly and get in a row with the old folk because you're on Channel Nine and there's something startling they've got to see – repeat got – on Channel Eight. Or maybe there's some small article to fetch from the shop at the corner, or the yard to swill, or you're asked when did you last see the bath? So you avoid trouble and hoof it out and around the streets and never a friendly face, or you sit in a clayhole and watch the pigeons, nice to notice in passing, but the most melancholy occupation in the world when you're filling in a night. Boy, you're glad even when the village half-wit stops to say hello.

I've known characters in this condition take up with a girl they wouldn't otherwise have touched with a barge-pole. Spend time looking around furniture shops, and the next thing you know they're walking beside a pram.

See me make a case for Dopey? Not that I said any of this to Nosey or any of the others. But when we were gathered gaily round the juke box and getting rapidly broke on milk-shakes, etc., I spotted the character looking through the doorway like a lost dog. I gave Nosey the nudge. He gave a cold look and said: 'Let him freeze.' So everybody sort of ignored Dopey. Well, after maybe twenty minutes of watching the happy family party, the black sheep edged in sidewise fashion and sat down in a booth. Maybe he thought he was the invisible man, but boy, Nosey had him taped and soon as the record was run-down stopped a character from slipping the next disc. In the resulting quiet he said (and without turning): 'Scram.'

'This is a public shop, isn't it?' said Dopey. 'Ah got a right to walk in and sit down quiet and drink a milk-shake same as anybody else.'

'Ah said scram.'

'Okay then, try throwin' me out.'

Old Milky Joe who runs the outfit said: 'Leave the kid alone, Nosey.'

'On account of the fact he's a hooligan and raised trouble Ah gave him the push from the gang,' said Nosey. 'Ah don't want any trouble, but Ah reckon there will be if that dimwit hangs around much longer.'

'He'll stay as long as he likes,' said Milky Joe. 'Around here Ah say who goes.'

'Okay with you, it's okay with me,' said Nosey.

'Listen, Nosey, I said. 'Give him another chance.'

131

'Try him again,' said Roly-Poly.

With practically everybody else chiming in old Nosey had to give somewhere, so after a short trance he said, 'Okay, Ah'll give him another try but he'd better keep his nose clean, that's all.' And in less than no time Dopey was running around and in between characters like a dog out of the dog-house, but not making any wisecracks. And there was nothing more said about Mick Kelly's sister although you can depend upon it that everybody was busy speculating. I mean, it was obvious that the main reason Dopey got the grand slam was for his crack about the bird. Birds are nerve-work and the biggest breakers of gangs, because the lads around here don't recruit them. Saw a picture once about a gang in the US and it looked to me as if the gang was nothing but a mobile giraffe party – one long neck en-route or static. It wouldn't wear here.

So this was serious news for us because Nosey was always an all-or-nothing character, which meant any minute he might give the whole gang the hot potato. The only ray of hope was the fact that she had the wrong religion and was Mick's sister, but on consideration this was even worse. Tragedy is when one of the lot falls for a bird; high tragedy when his neck is broken in the fall. I don't mind admitting my curiosity but I'd have burned before I asked. So I didn't. Anyway, around ten most of the characters began fading until in the end there was only Nosey and me, and Dopey, who had stayed behind to offer up thanks. Man, I thought that boy was going to weep with gratitude.

He shook hands with me, and he shook hands with Nosey and said he'd always be a true pal and we could depend upon him and did we fancy a walk down to his Dad's fish shop for a free packet? Which we didn't. Some other time maybe, we told him, and off he went wagging his tail, the happiest clown in town.

We went along the edge of the old ravine and it was a great night from the weather point of view but melancholy otherwise; we hadn't a word to say to each other. At last Nosey said, 'You in a hurry, Arthur?' and I told him I wasn't worried, so we sat down on the grass. He was chewing grass like old Nettlefold's nag. In the end he said: 'It's funny the way it happened.'

'What happened?'

'Look,' he said, 'there's our kiddar goin' about like a ghost for that Nettlefold jane and me thinking him crazy and all that until last week – last Wednesday it was. You think Ah'm loopy, Arthur?'

'It happens to everybody, they reckon,' I said.

'Well, this girl is on the packing end; y'know, shoving the tins into big cartons and Ah'm picking the cartons up with a forklift – and wham! before you know where you are Ah'm watchin' her. You could pick her up in your hand. She moves like a feather. She's got a quiet voice, and boy, do Ah need somebody with a quiet voice – no offence, Arthur, Ah'm thinkin' of my sisters and my old lady – fishwives!'

'So she's got you nailed?'

'She has and she hasn't. That would be murder, Ah mean being nailed at my age. But what's to stop me havin' the odd night off, eh?'

'If that's okay with her. But you know these birds. They like you around all the time. They don't like competition.'

'Ah reckon maybe a couple of nights a week.'

'What about Mick?'

'Ah can dodge him.'

'He'll not like it – bein' the wrong religion an' all.'

'Ach – it isn't serious. Anyhow, Ah'll keep out of his way.'

'Next thing you know some kind friend whispers in his ear and he's on the war-path.'

'Could be.'

'With a couple of friends he could make mincemeat of you – and that's not countin' the trouble his sister would be in.'

'He wouldn't touch that little kid!'

'He would – an' the rest of her family.'

'Ah'd burn the house down if they did,' he said. 'If they marked her –'

I could see he'd never be moved. 'Well, kiddar, it's your own business. But keep your eyes pinned.'

He sat looking over the ravine and beyond the two bridges where you can just see the roof-tops of the Quayside district; rotten, rambling old houses pitched on the steep hillside; sloppy cobbled streets leading to crumbling steps and crumby staircases. 'What's her name?'

'Teresa,' he said.

'That's a saint's name.'

'Who was she – the saint?'

'Never heard. Somebody holy, y'know, good.'

'Arthur?' I said yes, I was listening. 'You think Ah'm soft?'

You have to be diplomatic. 'All Ah'm sayin' is that this bird must have something to hit *you* so hard.'

'That's what you think?' he asked.

'That's my solid opinion.'

I left him in a dream-daze, still looking in the direction, maybe waiting for her light to come on. The toughest character in town. Whoever runs the world must have a laugh at the timing of things. I'm saying this because it was around this time that Kelly's lot wrecked the HQ, which lay a little bit further up from where we were sitting. Maybe they came out, spotted him, and took the other road. Or maybe they walked down the bottoms and he never spotted them. Which is possible. His eyes were in the wrong direction.

3

Boy, was that a good night. It was warm and still, soft and sentimental. People were sitting in chairs around their front doors, all shapes and sizes of old wives between forty and ninety, telling jokes or having gossip sessions. Men were standing around or sitting with their galluses off their shoulders for ease, smoking quietly and enjoying themselves. Every now and again you'd hear laughter explode among the hum of small talk.

There's a broadish sort of pavement at the corner of our street, facing onto the main road, where there's a seat under a dry old chestnut tree that never has a full quota of leaves. It's a favourite spot for the old wives in summertime, because of the traffic hopping past and also because even when it doesn't happen here you'll still hear about it in less than ten minutes flat. The Old Lady was there with one or two of her neighbours and to be good company I sat down.

Of course I paid in banter. 'Here's young Romeo,' said Mrs Trotter, who is about ninety and has so many grand-children they're eating on the stairs and in the backyard when all the family go to see her on Sundays.

''Lo, son,' said the Old Lady. 'You're late.'

'Been sitting on the bank-top watching the sunset.'

'With a wench, Ah'll bet,' said Mrs Tappit, sounding off in a laugh like an old donkey.

'One thing Ah'll say for him – he never bothers the lasses,' said the Old Lady.

'What the eye doesn't see …'

'Ah thought our Joe was like that,' said Grandma Trotter. 'Always makin' wireless sets. Then one night he came in and said he had to get married. How he'd found time –'

'Trust 'em to find time for that,' said Mrs Tappit.

I'd more sense than say anything. Anyway I knew they'd soon tire of picking the soft out of me. I let it slide while the Old Lady eyed me; but I felt guilty as hell. These old janes are clever. They know so much they make you wonder at times if you've done something and forgotten it.

'There was Jack Smallman,' said Grandma Trotter. 'Came out of gaol. Out the first night he was home and was caught red-handed in the big Coop shoe department – his pals with the van made a getaway. He was outa gaol exactly nineteen or twenty hours an' gets both himself and his Missus into trouble.'

'He got twelve months an' she got nine!' said Mrs Tappit and off they rocked, including the Old Lady.

'Poor bitch!' said Grandma Trotter, nodding away like an old china doll and chewing her bottom teeth.

'We were all runnin' him down and she turned like a tiger – "Well," she says, "well, there's one thing certain, he always kept himself clean an' tidy – in all me married life Ah never saw him without a collar an' tie."'

'An' her with eight – or was it nine bairns?' shouted Grandma Trotter. 'Can ye see him wi' the collar round his bare neck – an' the tie danglin'.'.'

And, boy, they were off again. If you want to find out about life you find that old bench under the tree halfway down City Road. You'll get an eye-opener and all for frees. But you'll have to be invisible. Those old janes have been around too long to let it flow in front of total strangers. Anyway, in the end we left them there. I went off first, walking a bit sharp because no character around these parts likes to be seen out walking with his Old Lady; the Old Lady caught up with me and brushed my arm, and boy it was like an electric shock, believing that she was going to link me – so I veered off and hung back a bit. And old Tappit got in the last drop of poison: 'You keep hold on him, Peg,' she shouted. 'Tall an' handsome – he'll be outa your hands afore ye can draw breath.'

It was just as if she knew what I was thinking. 'He was a soldier on the Ack-Ack battery down on the coast,' she said.

'Remember you telling me a long time ago.'

'He was a nice man. Good talker. A regular soldier and he'd been all over the show – was in Dunkirk. Your Grandad liked him. I was working in a factory then.'

'Yes, Mam,' I said, trying to brush her off.

'Ah know you must often wonder about him. Well, we were married three months and he was transferred. He wrote a time or two. Then there was nothing for a long time – after me money stopped I wrote to the last address and they said he'd been discharged. So that was that. Ah've me pride. Ah wasn't goin' to chase a man around that didn't want me; Ah'd plenty of trouble, your Grandad dying and you … on the way. So Ah never bothered. But it's been a lonely life.'

'Aw, Ma, don't talk about it,' I said, not knowing which way to turn.

'It was what Grandma Trotter said that reminded me – stirred it all up. Ye'll never leave me high an' dry, Arthur, will ye?'

'No fears of me runnin' away.'

'It's a lonely life,' she said. We went into the house.

Harry's room was showing a light round the door. He shouted: 'That you, Peg?'

'Yes, it's me. You all right?'

'Fine. Thought Ah'd have an early night. Goodnight, lass.'

'Goodnight, Harry.' She went upstairs and I remember wondering what was in the wind. Halfway up she turned and said: 'He'd marry me tomorrow, Arthur.' When I didn't answer she went on. I was all churned up. I went into the kitchen and switched on, filled the electric kettle. When she came down my mind was made up.

'Ma, you do what you want.'

'Ah thought ye'd like to see this,' she said, handing me a sheet of paper. It was the marriage lines. God knows what she was thinking I was thinking – maybe that I was illegitimate. Which I hadn't given a second thought. Anyway, I'd have known soon enough if I had been. We'd always been around there, everybody knew us, and in those circumstances there's always a kind friend with a runaway tongue. Returning the lines I said: 'I didn't need to see this, Ma, but thanks all the same … you heard what Ah said?'

'Ah don't know what to do. There'd have to be a divorce – such an upheaval. Dragging the poor man through the court an' all …'

'Ah reckon ye've still got a soft spot for him, Ma.'

'Ah can't remember his face till Ah see yours.'

'Well, Ah'll not take out on ye, never in a month of Sundays. But it's up to you to enjoy life, Ma. He was never any good to you. It makes no difference to me if you give him his marching orders … and hitch up with the Lodger.'

'You mean that? Ah always thought you didn't like Harry.'

'Harry wouldn't run out on ye.'

'No, that he wouldn't. But, you know, Arthur, Ah've always had a hope he'd walk in through that door.'

'Not a chance.'

At the same time I was wishing he'd walk through that door. Just to see his face, so that I could fix a picture like anybody else and keep it all my life. Until that happened I wasn't complete. I wasn't kidding myself that it'd be all lamb and salad if he did walk through that door – chances are I might have given him bel-fagor for what he did to the Old Lady. He might turn out to be just a happy rascal I could like. On the other hand I might hate him on sight. Whatever, I wanted to see his face. There was I thinking this, and there was the Old Lady thinking her thoughts, mainly about the upheaval if she went for a divorce. It was easy to see that she was dead-afraid and it struck me that it had always been this way. That's us lower orders: we'd rather keep the ball and chain than go to law.

Something else I realised as I tossed and turned after going to bed. We'd practically buried him but I was still hoping he'd walk in through that door.

SEVEN

1

Got up the following morning with a mouth like a sewer on account of all the milk-shakes, etc. of the preceding evening plus a small-hours meal of bacon and egg which I prepared after failing to get to sleep. Being tired I got out of the wrong side of the bed and kept on going wrong all day or most of it. Boy, you should have seen me pedalling uphill half-asleep; or propped up against anything available on the site. I was so tired I was cat-napping between each shovelful.

Sprogget knew I wanted to take it easy so for once was on his toes. His main job was signing the lorry timesheets and looking after any other paperwork, but this day he organised himself for the open air. Every time I took a nap he nipped it in the bud. Mainly by shouting from a distance. In the end I shouted back. So he walked over.

'What you say there?'

'You heard me all right.'

'You should sleep at home.'

'If I got my money as easy as you Ah would.'

'Okay then, get the shed cleaned out – it's stinkin' with tea-leaves and crusts.'

'You're the one that never eats a crust.'

'Less of the lip an' get on with the job.'

'What about George here?'

'He'll have to manage. You get crackin' and get back quick if you're so worried.'

Well, I started sweeping out but in less that a minute he'd jumped me again. 'Thought Ah told ye to clean out?'

'You're kiddin'?'

'Ah want the table and all the gear out – Ah want this place piggin' out.'

'Well, you're out, so what?'

'Clear the show,' he shouted. 'Get cracking! Let's have a bit action.'

'Ah'd manage better without a comic MC,' I told him. I hadn't the sense to see that he was needling me.

'You take your orders,' he said. 'If you weren't a half-wit Ah wouldn't have to stand over ye.'

I walked into the shed, picked up a heavy hammer, and threw it out without turning. It landed on his kneecap. The next thing I knew he was yelling blue murder.

When he'd calmed down he walked back a pace or two, on account of me still spring-cleaning, and laid down the law. 'Ah'm sick an' tired of you,' he said. 'Wait till your Uncle George comes – Ah'll tell him a thing or two.'

'Tell him what ye like,' I said. 'Also, tell him to stuff the job.'

I was back on the machine when the Pasha arrived. After a session with Sprogget he gave me a shout: 'Arthur!'

I shouted back: 'What d'ye want?'

'You come when you're shouted for.'

I went over. Sprogget was supporting the doorway and Uncle George was sitting behind the table like the President of the United States when the Blob from Outer Space has just polished off New York and is due to roll over the White House any minute now.

'What's this about setting up your impitence to Mr Sprogget?'

'Tell him to get off my back an' Ah'll forget it.'

'See!' said Sprogget.

'Why can't ye treat the Man-in-Charge with respect?'

'Ah told ye, he won't get off me back.'

'He's got to chase the work on. You're a disappointment to me,

Arthur. Ah put meself out to get you a job an' this is the thanks Ah get – setting your lip up to the Man-in-Charge. If it goes on I'll have to report ye to the Big Boss.'

'Listen, Ah'm doin' me whack, Uncle George.'

'That's not what he says – eh, Sam?'

'He's a born lay-about; wonder he hasn't broken his neck sleepwalkin'.'

'And you're a born liar.'

'Another crack like that and Ah'll clock ye.'

'Now pipe down the pair of you'se,' said Uncle George, and I suddenly discovered why he was foreman, because we did pipe down, both of us, and glad to. 'When Ah'm not here, Sam takes charge. He's my bumper-up and he bumps who he wants to bump. He's been around long enough to know who and when to bump. That's his merit and Ah'm backin' it.'

'If he bumps me when Ah'm in the wrong there'll be no comebacks.'

'Just out of his short pants,' said Sprogget, 'an' he's after the foreman's job.'

'Ah can fill a timesheet in,' I said. 'One way or another.'

'What's that?' said Uncle George.

'I said it – one way or another.'

'Get back to your work. And get stuck in or else you'll be pickin' your cards up.'

So I got and something told me not to say another word, because I'd shot my bolt. Mind you, it was only a shot in the dark. Old George had been telling me about the lorry trick; that's when a firm hires lorries, and the firm's foreman fixes a price with the haulier. Say fifteen bob an hour, which is a bob over the haulier's own price, and the foreman collects. Say a dozen lorries running eight hours daily each, the bobs mount up, and the only problem is a quiet spot for the payoff, of which there are plenty. Old George had described the trick without any reference to our outfit and it had flashed into my mind that one reason why there had to be a bumper-up was that there had to be somebody around to check on the hauliers when Uncle George wasn't around.

As I say, it was just a shot in the dark with the hope that it would hit and help. I might have known better because in the long run it didn't. Primarily because it happened to be true. The moment I mentioned the timesheets my stew was cooking. I'm no mindreader but from the way the conversation cut off I knew those two characters were worried.

Maybe I shouldn't have said it. Anyway, five minutes after I knew it was a mistake. Not only because, being a runner, Sprogget had some pals among the rough boys, but also because it doesn't do to stamp on a hand that's reaching for the ready money. I knew that there wasn't a chance of me blowing the gaff, but they didn't, therefore they couldn't afford to have me round.

Two things told me trouble was brewing.

First thing was that one of the characters on the site had a quiet talk with me, which he'd never done before, and with a snout included to loosen me up. His name was George Stephenson, but if he'd been the original there'd never have been any iron horses. He was generally too tired to talk. Now he was all sympathy: 'Saw you givin' ol' Sam what-for – that character wants clockin'.'

'Have a try, then; Ah'll cheer.'

'He's a bloody snake – what did the gaffer say?'

'Told me Sam was right and Ah was wrong.'

'Listen,' he said. 'Them two can't afford to split. They know too much about each other.'

'Such as?'

'Work it out for yourself,' he winked.

'Listen,' I told him. 'Listen yourself. Ah don't like Sprogget, an' Ah like him even less for ridin' me into a black mark. But you can take it from me that my Uncle George is not the type of character to get mixed up in anything illegal.'

'Who said illegal?' he said, getting the wind up. 'You jump quicker 'n a cat. All Ah'm sayin' is they've given you the dirty end of the stick.'

'Thanks,' I said. 'But don't you come around to me any more

with any kind of insinuation against my Uncle George or else ye'll get clocked.'

'Ah, you got me wrong,' he said. 'That's the kindest, straightest man Ah ever knew. Knows his job and understands his men; if he's got one fault it's Sprogget.'

'You might have something there,' I told him. 'And all that's wrong with Sam is that the left side of his brain doesn't operate ...'

'Ye mean he's a half-wit?'

'That's an overstatement,' I said. 'For the simple reason that he never had a right side to his brain.'

We were both about as subtle as a pair of brewery horses but, if he did his best, I reckon I bettered it. The interesting thing was the psychology of this character. My opinion is that he knew all about the caper and was satisfied with the odd pint as payoff. The pint satisfied him because he was too dim to organise a bigger dividend, but underneath he dimly resented being used. The way he laughed at the ancient brain-crack proved that much. It was a very sincere laugh.

The conversation, duly reported, won me a reprieve, temporary. But only temporary. The proof of this came the following week, when a new lad started. He wasn't really necessary, excepting for the important messages. The ones I couldn't be trusted with.

2

Now I can stand a fight anyday but a row puts my belly in a turmoil. I always read too much into a row, primarily because I rake over it in my mind, brooding over the bitter bits and losing morale wondering if the other character's best cracks aren't maybe true. I think of the next move in the situation and nine times out of ten worry about moves that the other character never even thought of. I'm absent and I'm off my grub because that big weight in my belly kills my appetite. Which is only telling you that I'm not so tough as it would appear.

It was still with me when I called into the Regent, despite a light blue shirt and slim silver tie with red and black slants, both first time worn. Roly-Poly was there propping the entrance up, and said one or two of the set had gone up to the billiards room, but Nosey hadn't arrived. All the same I was glad Roly-Poly was there to greet me since he has the art of cheering me up. However, he was down in the dumps himself: the butcher he was working for had gone out of business, which may strike you as unusual until I tell you he'd been buying his bottles of whisky out of the till and had gone bankrupt only as the result of great effort.

'And God knows where Ah'll get another job,' he told me. 'They're layin' off men at the shipyards. The docks is dead. Boy, Ah tell you they're not even wantin' cabin boys on the ferry-boats.'

'You get yourself a job on the river tunnel.'

'Can't stand the dark.'

'Try the merchant navy?'

'Didn't you hear – they've abolished it.'

'Well, there's always the dole.'

'I didn't get enough stamps.'

'Well, that's organisation,' I said. 'Come on; let's have a walk up and see the Sergeant.'

Which we did. He was tidying up his little shop, from which he dishes out tickets, chalks up times of letting, and sells cigarettes and sweets, and also gabs with the odd character waiting for a table. The Sergeant is a medium-sized character with nothing military about him except a mechanical leg and a talent for talking. At which he is good.

'What's bitin' you two?' he asked.

'Give me ten Players and Ah'll tell ye,' I said. I broke the packet and scotched three.

'Well, what is it?'

'Roly-Poly here lost a job. Now he's dizzy lookin' for another.'

'He doesn't know he's born. When Ah was his age there used to be queues for a grave-digger's job – Ah seen a thousand fight for a job minding a sewage farm. Ah seen a queue twice around the Labour Exchange.'

'Come off it,' we told him.

'You read the history books. Me, Ah was a Grammar School boy so the search was delayed two years. Ask me why my folk were able to afford to keep me and Ah'll tell ye – my old man was an undertaker's assistant.'

'What's that?'

'Chap that runs around comfortin' the bereaved, finding out the size of the insurance policy, measuring up and stretching.'

'Couldn't you get a job with him?'

'Not likely. Many a time Ah had to drop me homework and get out with him on a rush-job, which they all were. Got used to the work, but never to the customers – Ah like to talk to anybody Ah'm treatin'. Funny, in the end Ah became an undertaker's assistant just the same. Joined up as a boy-soldier. Served in India, got shipped to Egypt, instead of home as expected, rested there till the big push, finished up in Italy and boy it was hot and rough and dusty all the way. Saw more dead men in three-four years than my old man saw all his fifty years in the trade.'

'But in the end you got a job?'

'Took me all of twenty years to do it; plus a leg minus.'

'You're tellin' us this is the first job you ever had, apart from soldiering?' asked Roly-Poly.

'That's right. Left school at sixteen and spent six months searchin'. Me last fling was for a position as clerk to the Public Assistance Committee. Had an Uncle on the Council and a reference from Father Kelly. Another Uncle was the Canon but he wouldn't give me a reference for this particular job – said he wouldn't see a nephew of his run into sin. Went for the interview with promises from the majority of the selection committee that the job was mine ...'

'What went wrong?'

'Somebody else had political influence.'

'You must have had some smashing times in the Army,' said Roly-Poly.

'Sometimes it was rough – and sometimes the apples fell. An' you can bet your bottom dollar that old Jack Minto was there every time with his hands ready to catch.'

'Birds …?'

'Couldn't count them, not if Ah started now and went on to me dyin' breath.'

'You went to bed with them all?'

'If there was time.'

'How d'ye do it, Sarj? How d'ye work it?' asked Roly-Poly.

'Aw, ye're too young yet – time enough for ye to find out.'

'Aw, come on and tell us!'

'Well … OK … Well, briefly, it wasn't so hard. Something gets into these foreign girls in wartime, it's a kind of fever …'

'Go on, Sarj.'

'Also and plus, take the Italian wimmin. They needed food. They needed it so bad they made themselves nice. Ah've seen dogfaced types that no girl – Ah mean top-notchers an' not on the game – would look at in Hong Kong, Karachi and Cairo, find themselves in demand in those little towns on the Po. But Rome was best.'

'What was there about Rome, Sarj?'

'Well, it was home from home,' he said dreamily.

'Go on, tell us about her.'

'Her name was Lucia.' The Sergeant described her with his hands and a rippling whistle. 'Skin like ivory and hair as black as sin.'

At which we whistled.

'Ah, now, don't kid yourselves. She was difficult. It was perfect. She had a flat, she cooked for me and chose my wines: she did everything but …'

'But what?' asked Roly-Poly, nearly falling over the counter.

'She had a wall around her as soon as the coffee was drunk … soon as ye touched her she went rigid. Ah'm not kiddin', that girl was a problem and all the more because Ah was crazy-mad about her … Aye, there, Nosey.'

'Ah'll have ten of the tiny ones,' said Nosey.

'Hi there, Nosey. Listen in to this one,' I said.

'How the Sarj conquered Rome,' said Roly-Poly.

'Hear it another time – Ah'm suggestin' a short stroll.'

'Aw, just a minute, Nosey.'

'Pipe down, this is urgent.'

That was the old Nosey. No interest in anything but the real thing. Roly-Poly went to collect the lads at the tables and Nosey shot off, barking: 'Come on, Arthur.'

To prove my independence I hung back: 'How did you manage it, Sarj?'

He winked: 'Some other time. Full details.'

'You managed it?'

He nodded.

'How?'

To which he gave me a wise look and one word: 'Feet.'

3

Nosey was waiting for me at the bottom of the stairs. 'Something on the boil?' I asked.

'Could be.' And that's all he would say. Soon as we were all collected he jerked his head and off we went under sealed orders. Thinking back I admire Nosey for this stroke. Anybody else would have spilled it. But he wanted it to keep until we saw it with our own eyes. You'll know why. All I'm saying is that he'd the makings of a General and would maybe have been one in the old days before IQ.

Kelly's gang had done a good job. Everything was smashed. They'd smashed the gramophone and all the records. They'd torn the boxes apart and axed Nosey's chair to smithereens. They'd knocked the door clear of its hinges and turned the tables into firewood. They'd enjoyed themselves. Nobody could say anything.

'One of Mick's set told his cousin, and his cousin told a friend that works beside me,' said Nosey. 'But that isn't important.

Anybody like to join in a little caper that might pay this one back?'
Nobody moved an amendment.

'Okay, then, let's clean the place up.'

'For why?' asked an impatient character. 'It's all wrapped-up.'

'Because this is our place and we'll keep it clean and put it to rights.'

'So's they can smash it up again?' said Dopey.

'They won't ever come here again: not after we're finished with them.'

'Well let's start finishin',' said Roly-Poly.

'No fears … we'll take them on our time. Pin to a penny they're waitin' for us tonight – well let them wait.'

'We can take them on anytime an' beat them,' said Dopey.

'Maybe. But we're goin' to make sure, that's all. Last time Mick drew a knife, remember? This time we're goin' to have some old iron with us …'

'Ah'm not carryin' a knife,' I told him.

'Nobody is. But what's wrong with a chair leg? Or a bicycle chain? Or anything interesting you happen to think of?'

'That's still rough stuff,' I said.

'So what's this?'

'Ah don't like it.'

'Well, nobody's forcing you. Come or stay away, it's all the same to me.' He was looking at me.

'Okay, Ah'll come.' But if I'd been able to stand on my two legs I'd have backed out. 'What's the plan?'

'Second house at the Albion. The dance is off at the Regent, so they're sure to be there. We'll go in after the show's started. Roly-Poly and me'll go into the back seats, the rest stay in the side passage beside the emergency exits. Left-hand side, an' be ready. Intermission time me and Roly'll take a walk down to the front to get some ice-cream, or that's the way it'll appear. We'll make sure they see us …'

'They'll massacre ye,' said Dopey.

'They'll not have time. Soon as we see them – and they see

us – we'll start movin' fast showing signs of panic – and make for the left.'

'They'll make back as soon as they see us all lined up.'

'They won't, for the simple reason that there'll be nothing to see: we'll knock off the lights beforehand. Roly-Poly an' me'll keep on running up the passage an' they'll be after us hell for leather – then you lot fall in.'

'Aw, it's too complicated,' said Dopey.

'For you maybe, but not to worry – just keep your eyes on Arthur here, he'll keep you right.'

'Arthur's not too keen,' said Dopey.

'Arthur's all right – aren't you, Arthur?'

'Ah'll take anybody in a fair fight,' I said. 'What Ah don't like is the idea of usin' iron – somebody might get killed.'

'Yeller,' said Dopey.

'No, wise,' said Nosey. 'He's got more sense in his little finger than you have in all that solid between your two lugholes … Okay, Arthur, we'll take them with our fists an' let's pray friend Mick comes without his knife.' He gave me a sharp look. 'So ye'll be there, Arthur?'

'Course, Ah'll be there,' I told him.

'Okay, then, that's all settled.'

So we cleared the place up and flung in half a dollar each, all but Roly-Poly, who was exempt on account of job difficulties, and Dopey went off with a shipping order for fish and chips. Meanwhile we lit a big fire in the main building. We had the fish and chips and followed up with shandy-gaffs. We sat around the fire and one thing led to another until we landed ourselves into the usual filthy story contest. But I was out of it. I wasn't looking forward to the battle at the Albion. Somehow I felt that whatever the outcome we were running into bad trouble; win or lose there'd be trouble. All I could see was that knife. There was the business of the Old Lady and Harry, and my lost old man; and the trouble at work – I'd been having dreams in which the weasel-face of Sam kept blowing up six or seven times life-size and bearing me back until I was smothering to death. The greasy fish and chips didn't suit my stomach and I was a bit too rash with the shandy-gaffs. It all blew up on me and I went into a dark corner to be sick. Nosey followed me over.

'You got the wind up, Arthur?' he asked.

I was too weak to down him. All I could do was shake my head.

'If we're gonna be top dogs we gotta be tough,' he said. 'It's the only way.'

'Ah'm not complainin' – as long as it doesn't come to iron.'

'There'll be no iron,' he said. He was quiet for a bit, then said: 'You mixed up with a bird or something, Arthur?'

'What for?'

'The way ye go off in a thought – like beside the fire a minute or two ago.'

'The bird hasn't been born yet,' I said. I thought of Stella, then decided she didn't count. Easy come, easy go, I thought.

'Don't kid yourself – look at the way it was with me …'

'Ah'm steering clear – it's nothing but a book of troubles. There's my Old Lady wantin' to get married again to the Lodger. That's all she can think about, that and where my old man is.' It's no use trying to tell other people your troubles. All he was doing was putting on an act of listening and nodding.

'You meet up with a kid like Teresa and ye'll change your mind,' he said. 'Ah never knew anybody like her.'

'Furthermore,' I continued, 'the cod-boss at the site – chap named Sprogget – has his knife into me. He's on my back so much we're both saddle-sore.'

'Yes, yes,' he said. 'Give him a poke, a swift jab, some day and get a new job. Listen, as Ah was sayin' about Teresa – that kid's a honey-dish … d'ye know, Arthur, she steadies me up?'

'Well she might,' I said. 'But that won't stop big brother, when it comes to the pinch. What about when you want to marry her – what with her religion an' her family ye don't stand a chance.'

'Marry!' he said. 'Ah never thought of that! It's only fun, kiddar.'

'All the fun you're likely to get is a smash-up hiding.'

'Hey, don't get me wrong – Ah wouldn't touch her!'

'Makes no odds. If ever that Mick gets to know ...'

'Not a chance. Listen, Arthur, we got a perfect assignment – there's an old car on the bankside. We sit there. It's a nest.'

'How d'ye pass all the time?'

'Cut me throat if Ah'm lyin'; a lot of talkin' an' a bit of snoggin', nothing more – Ah never knew Ah'd so much talkin' in me; that kid draws me out.'

'That Lodger's always in conference like that with the Old Lady ... what would you do, Nosey?'

'Take a poke at him – throw him outa the house. Hell, what do old folk want with it at their time of life?'

'They've got it worse than you.'

'Your Old Lady's sensible; kick him out an' ye'll see, she'll forget him quick enough.'

'She's gone on him,' I said and didn't bother to tell him that I hadn't the weight to kick the Lodger out anyway even if I'd felt so inclined. To change the subject I asked: 'How's Crab getting on these days?'

'Ah'll tell ye something: he's serious on the hawker's daughter. He's crazy about her – he'd even marry her.'

'Come off it – she's years older than him, maybe ten years.'

'More – just about twice his age.'

'How d'ye get to know all this stuff?'

'Well, we sleep in the same bed. Ah always know when he's been with her but he never said anything much about her till last week. Came in late one night and awoke me. It was hard gettin' off to sleep again because he was tossing and turning. The next thing Ah knew, he was shaking me. Said he had to talk. Did he surprise me! In the beginning he used to joke and jest about the money part of it – money for jam. Now he doesn't want it, but she makes him.'

'Crazy woman!' I said.

'Crazy man, too,' said Nosey. 'Boy, Ah'll tell ye, the sweat was running off his chin-end he was so worked up about that woman.

But she won't have him. So Ah told him he's lucky she didn't take him up. And ye know what he said to me? He told me Ah didn't know what had got hold of him! So Ah told him Ah've got a girl of my own but catch me shootin' my top.'

He was silent a moment. 'You know what he said? He said: "This is no girl."'

'She's screaming murder,' I remarked.

'Maybe she will someday,' said Nosey. We looked at each other and it was like a flash of ice-cold lightning. I think both of us were glad to get back to the fire again.

4

One of old Flack's favourite expressions is that what has to be, has to be. 'The cards are all decked, lad,' he used to tell me. 'It's all mapped. All ye can do is bite your bottom lip an' bear it.'

Maybe this is all hooey. Simply because when it's all over it seems to dovetail is no argument. All the same, this particular time fits like a ball-bearing. You can almost imagine it spinning out like a stereophonic, technicolor feature. If I hadn't gone to the Albion caper I wouldn't have got blood on my sleeve, and if there'd been no blood I wouldn't have been on a string the following day. And a lot hung on that string.

Don't get any dramatic ideas about the blood. It was near at the time, just too near to be comfortable, and the sight of it was sufficient. The blood marked a boundary I couldn't cross. It might have been the end. Instead it meant a new start.

The Old Lady knew there was something in the wind: 'What's put it into your head to wear those jeans?' she said.

'Don't want to wear the others out.'

'Other Saturdays you're dressed to the eyes.'

'We're only goin' to the pictures. Why get dressed up for the dark. It's only logical.'

'Ah'd rather see ye decent.'

'Make your mind up; last time you mentioned the subject ye were all against twills an' fancy shirts.'

'You're goin' boozin' an' beatin' up the streets, that's why ye're puttin' old things on.'

'Let it lie, Ma.'

'Ah'll not let it lie – Ah've a good mind to keep ye in.'

'You – and who else?' This was going a bit too far. She walked out of the room and I didn't have to rack my brains to know what she was up to. 'Aw, listen, Ma, don't get all het up,' I said when she returned. 'Ah've been out on the bike all day and Ah'm tired. Ah just didn't have the list to get changed.'

'Listen, my lad,' she said, 'ye've got a good poker face and Ah don't pretend to read it like a book – ye're too brazen. But Ah knows your tricks. There's a reason for every move ye make.'

'Honest to goodness, Ma, Ah'm just too idle to change.'

'Workin' clothes – ye're up to some mischief with that Nosey Carron and company.'

'Listen, Ma, we're goin' to the pictures and mebbe afterwards we'll fill up with some fish and chips.'

'Is that all?'

I steeled myself to look straight into her eyes. I hated doing it but it was either that or letting the Manor lot down. 'That's all, Ma.'

She sat down in the old rocking chair, playing with the keys in her lap: 'Are ye sure?' I nodded. 'Ah asked ye a question.'

'Ah'm sure – there's nothin' on.'

Without looking at me she threw the keys on to the floor. 'There you are,' she said. 'You're too big to bray the truth out of so there's the keys.'

'Ah'm tellin' ye, Ma …'

'Ah think ye're telling me a lot of lies.' I picked up the keys. I wanted to tell her the full strength but couldn't. I wanted to tell her that my heart wasn't in it but that I had to go. Maybe it sounds a scream but you think again. What's the difference between old Flack under Hill 60 or my old man waiting for a boat on the beaches at Dunkirk and little Arthur turning up for a caper at the Albion? None at all. You go where you're obligated, and maybe I was more obligated than they ever were. I was sticking to my own personal friends.

I had to go. That's where old Flack had the right angle on what has to be must be. When you laugh around with the lads you've got to face up to the odd time or two when you've got to fight around with them. Or stay out in the cold. You pay your turn and that's all there is to it.

5

From the beginning that Saturday morning bore the mark of doom. Trying to operate the batcher and think about the night's caper led me into trouble. I automatically knocked off without reference to the dial and when old Flack said, 'Bit too quick there, Arthur!' turned on him. 'Who's doin' the job – you or me!' I muttered and started transferring to the mixer.

Sprogget was there when the stuff came out and made the most of it. 'Who the hell turfed this out?' he asked, rubbing it between finger and thumb. 'It's not up to spec.'

'It's according to the book,' I snarled.

Sprogget turned to the chap who was driving the dumper: 'Dump the whole lot,' he said. 'It's no bloody good ...' (turning to me) 'like the man that made it.'

Old Flack took over the machine for the next batch. There was hell to pay because the job had to be done, the first match of the season was coming up, and we were back half an hour. It didn't do my liver any good to see Sprogget and Uncle George looking at the discard, the latter glancing in my direction and shaking his head. Neither did it do me any good to realise that nobody had a down on me; it was my own fault; for which maybe a couple of dozen men would have to suffer.

Working like demons the gang finished the job nearly an hour past time and it didn't do their tempers any good to make the match because they'd worked themselves into a lather for a few shillings. The first match of the season is a treat to be savoured with cosy excitement over a casual, easy-going sort of a Saturday morning shift. I'd spoilt their fun. Sprogget made sure they knew it but it didn't need any underscoring – the sky was clouded with black looks. Even poor old Flack had his share.

As we were picking our things up Sprogget walked over. 'You keep the *skilled* end of the job in future, George,' he said. 'Leave the boy in dreamland where he can't do any harm.'

So I was a failure, moved by Sprogget, seconded by my mates, carried unanimously by myself. It was a dull, hot day without a hint of blue in the sky. All afternoon I pedalled, fixed wheel, my head down low over the handlebars. The wind I rode into didn't cool me. I was moving in a big brass oven along a painted road and I was sure that if I nipped behind the factories on the coast road I'd find an empty space, up and down, like the end of the world. I sat on the cliffs and listened to the noise of people on the sands. There were maybe two thousand kids there, all crying, and if I'd stayed a minute longer I'd have been blubbering too. I rode back in twenty-two minutes flat. There were still four hours to go.

'You can have a table to yourself,' said the Sergeant. 'What's happened – the whole town's dead – not a soul in all afternoon.'

'It's too hot to move,' I said.

'Should be some thunder.'

'Anything to cool a man down,' I said. 'How about a bottle of pop, Sarj?'

We each had a bottle of pop, straight from the neck. It was wet but warm, which is to say I might as well have put my money down the nearest drain. 'Ah'm browned-off, Sarj.'

'Never heard that word for years,' he said. 'In my time being browned-off wasn't an event – it was a state of mind.'

'Which is the way it's gettin' with me.'

'Which it shouldn't,' he said. 'Hell, you've a life to live.'

'What's this life everybody talks about?' I asked him. 'What did it get you, Sarj?' And I looked down at the stiff old leg propped up on a stool.

'It could have been worse – it *was* worse for a lot,' he said. 'Some of the lads lay about wounded, shouting for help when we couldn't get out to them. I was lucky – came through clean. Then came the car smash in Rome – awoke without a leg.'

'Ye were on about that the other day – the girl.'

'Ah yes,' he said. 'The girl.'

'You said something about feet.'

'Feet! You'd have laughed yourself silly but there was nothing funny about it at the time, Ah'll tell ye. Nearly drove me crazy.'

'What – a girl?'

'Ye need be shocked. What d'you know about girls, eh? Walk home from a dance wi' a snotty-nosed ignoramus, hold hands, play around at the street-end – be God ye know nowt about the subject.'

'Ah'm sorry, Sarj,' I said. 'Ah'll admit Ah haven't much experience.' There *are* times when I can play it smooth.

'No, ye wouldn't,' he said, laughing.

'What was this about the feet?'

'Ach, ye're too young – Ah shouldn't be tellin' ye.' But all the same he was brooding. 'Ye've got to understand a soldier's mind. Away from home many a bright year, always on the move, never meetin' anything but a paid woman ...'

'Prostitutes?'

'Cheaters. Same as that warm pop – ye might as well pour it down a drain ... an' that's the hell of it. The kind ye want won't play, see? If they did, ye wouldn't want them.'

'Ah see what ye mean,' I said.

'Oh no, ye don't. Two things ye cannot imagine – killer-pain and the want of a woman. Impossible to imagine. Take Lucia – must have spent a million or two lire on that kid an' she never asked for a single thing an' told me it wouldn't do any good. Went to the well and found it dry ... in the end Ah went mooncrazy. Ah'd say: "Take your shoes off, Lucia *mio*." She'd give me such a look an' Ah didn't have words to say much but Ah'd make me eyes pop an' clap me hands when the shoes were off. She had lovely feet. Perfect feet. Ah used to sit an' stroke them, an' she'd stroke me hair. Then one day Ah kissed them – kissed each foot.'

'Then what happened?'

'Why, Ah made love to them two blessed feet until Ah was worn out and she was blazin' mad. Then one day she let loose. She picked up one o' the shoes and belted the hell outa me, shoutin' all the time in her own language ...'

'Sayin' what?'

'A lot of it Ah forget. But the last bit sticks in me mind: "Am I not a woman!" ... and she was!' His eyes were zooming through space: 'That was the night Ah drew water from the well. That was the night that wiped out all the rest.'

'Would ye have married her?'

'If she'd have had me – but the day after was the day Ah was riding in such a golden dream – and a staff car full of top-nobs – that Ah tried to mount a six-wheel lorry. Ah lost me leg and Lucia all in one go. Ah often think about it. Ah say to myself that if it came to a choice between havin' me leg back and havin' Lucia, it would be me leg every time ... then Ah get to thinking Ah might have lost me leg and me life without the joy of Lucia.'

'It's a mess,' I remarked.

'It's all a mess ... but take my tip, when there's water at the well, take a sup – for consolation.' He looked at my face and saw a joke. Anyway, he started to laugh, rocking with it while he gripped my shoulder with one hand. 'Ah'm sorry, sorry,' he spluttered. 'But if ye could only see your face ...'

6

I took a look at it that night. It was in the Gents at the Albion and I was taking advantage of the last few minutes before the second feature ended. Nosey and Roly-Poly had gone into the snogger's row and we'd removed all the bulbs but one. Now I'd nipped back for a wash. The truth was that the pan of my head contained a raw pain, ripe and ready to erupt at any minute. I thought a soak might do it some good. The place smelled of piss and worse and the bowl was full of toilet paper that somebody had been using as streamers. I leaned my head on the pipe and tried to ignore the drawings of bosoms, bottoms and legs. I was practically delirious with pain and fear. I washed my face with a piece of carbolic soap somebody had sliced off with a razor and dried it with my hanky. Then I took a good long look at myself.

I was astonished to find myself looking like a fish, mouth open, ears sticking out like fins, with freckles for scales. All I could do about it was close my mouth. Then I looked like the characters in a film cartoon called the 'Little Ghosts' which I saw when I was a nipper and affected me very deeply. Big round face and big round eyes and no neck because it had sunk away in despair. But even with the scar it was an innocent face. I couldn't call it handsome or appealing – I'd never be mobbed for my autograph – but it was innocent. Anybody could see that I didn't mean any harm. I couldn't see why anybody should have a down on that ghostly innocent face. But the facts contradicted it. Practically everybody mistrusted that face but Nosey and the Manor lot and maybe they had their doubts. Dopey had for sure. The sad little smile I gave myself wasn't enough to counteract the mean eyes and Saxon nose.

I went racing down the corridor before I changed my mind. A character named Rodney Carstairs was on Dopey's shoulders, extracting the last bulb as I arrived. The place was as black as the pit. I put Mousey Hole in charge of a couple of the youngest to watch the emergency exits and spread the rest out on either side of the corridor. My head was thumping like a Congo drum, so much that I was waiting for somebody to ask where the noise was coming from. The only light we had was a glow from around the bend in the corridor, until the house lights came on for the intermission. Then there was a chink from the edge of the lower door, but just a chink. We could hear some crazy kids' voices shouting for ice-cream in the advertising shot.

'They'll be here any minute,' whispered Dopey.

'Shut up!' I said. 'Everybody all set?'

Nosey and Roly-Poly were late in coming. They just got through the doors as the house lights went off again. They were giggling like lunatics as they raced past us. Then the gang came. We closed up behind them. I heard one shout: 'Where's the effing lights?' Then we began to give them bel-fagor. Everybody was punching wild and sounding off, and the place jerked the sound up a dozen notches like a combined amplifier and echo-chamber. When I went in my heart wasn't there. Then I received a glancing blow on the chin from something hard and solid – possibly a knuckle-duster – which increased my initiative. After that I was in all fours.

You didn't know who you were fighting. Somebody would grab your jacket or your shirt or plant his spread hand on your face and you'd swing for his middle as near as you could guess. One of the kids was crying. Nosey shouted, 'Are you there, Arthur?' and I shouted back. Then they broke away and ran back to the bottom emergency door. It opened with a bang that must have lifted the customers inside completely out of their seats. Nosey shouted – 'After them!' We went pelting down the corridor and it occurred to me on the way that this was just a little bit too easy. We pulled up at the door like a herd of cattle on the edge of a precipice, the reason being the weeping lad. He was one of the two I'd stationed at the emergency doors.

He was sitting in a corner with his hands over his face. His hands were all blood. Nosey got down on his knees and asked him what had happened. He wouldn't answer or take his hands away. Roly-Poly went out in the street. 'It's too quiet,' he said. 'Ah don't like the look of it.'

'It was too easy,' said Nosey. 'There was only one or two of them.'

'Kelly wasn't with them,' said Roly-Poly.

'They tipped it and went straight through the door,' I said. 'We only tacked three or maybe four. The rest went straight through the door.'

'This kid's got a broken nose,' said Nosey. 'We'd better get him out … Rod, take him through the pictures.'

'Come along, kid,' said Rod. They went through the swing doors. It was the best they could do. They might be picked up by the staff, but better the staff than Kelly's lot.

'Maybe we'd better go back into the pictures?' suggested Dopey.

'They'll only wait,' said Nosey. 'Might as well get it over with.' He led the way in the street – one of those narrow lanes leading off the main street – drawing a knife as he did so. 'Put that knife away, Nosey,' I said. He gave me a mean look. 'Get wise,' he said. 'We're up against enough iron to build a ship – our only chance is to rush 'em and break-up …'

'Okay,' I said, 'you do what ye like, but this is the finish for me – definitely the finish.'

'A fine time to resign,' he said and made off. Well, he was right. We met plenty of ironmongery. They came out of doorways swinging chains, bottles, chairlegs and meaning business. All we could do was take it and keep accelerating. There was no squaring up. Everybody was in a hurry. The last thing I saw before reaching the street was Kelly making for Nosey; all I could do was make a swerve into him to give Nosey a chance. Which it did. I heard a string of filth and knew that Kelly had been hammered. I didn't stop to verify but went straight over the road. Cars were weaving like mad or slapping brakes. A trolley just about mounted the pavement. Our men were all over the place with Kelly's lot splitting up and yelling like maniacs because we were on the run.

The fine pieces of statuary standing about were citizens. One woman was standing with a pram, her head back and yelling blue murder. Nosey was running beside me and panting thanks: 'Good for you, Arthur boy,' he said but I hadn't wind to answer. I'll always remember weaving around those long back-streets, ready to drop but not daring, always listening for the following footsteps. After maybe ten minutes we lost them off; and if you think ten minutes is reasonable all I can suggest is a real run under the same circumstances.

We holed up in a warehouse yard. We lay there listening to our own breathing. We were like a couple of shunting engines letting off steam. In the end Nosey started giggling. 'Ye should have seen his face,' he told me. 'Never expected to face the point of a knife himself. Went into a panic trying to recover from that push you gave him – and know what he did?'

'I wouldn't care.'

'Aw, come off it, Pretty Boy,' he said.

'It's no use, Nosey,' I said. 'Ye'll not get a rise outa me. Ah'm finished.'

'Ach, ye'll get over it,' he said. 'Lemme tell ye – ye won't believe it – he got hold of my knife he was in such a panic. Ah wouldn't have cut him up anyway but Ah guessed he'd panic … he didn't hold on long.'

'Ye might have killed him.'

'Not a chance … here, take a look.'

He took the thing out of his pocket and while I watched rubbed the blade with his thumb: 'Oh, it's blood right enough,' he said.

'You're crazy, Nosey. Better get that knife cleaned up.'

'You touch it first.'

'Ah don't want to touch it.'

'Just rub your finger along.'

'No thanks – no!' The knife was under my nose and Nosey was laughing at me. I rolled over – we were both lying flat with our heads pillowed on some sacks – but he pounced upon me. He was straddled over me and jumping like a jockey. 'Ah'll sharpen her up!' He was using my shoulder as a strop and I imagined the blood coming away onto my jacket. Until then I'd been frozen stiff, convinced he was out of his head. At the touch of the knife I drew myself up and bucked hard – 'Whoa there!' he laughed, 'Whoa!' All the time he was jumping into the small of my back and holding onto my collar with one hand like a crazy-mad jockey. He was stronger than me but my fear blazed up white hot and bested him. I gave a twist and simultaneously jabbed back with my elbow. That freed me at last.

He was lying on the cobbles with his face twisted and at first I thought he'd fallen on the knife, the way they sometimes do on the pictures. Kneeling down I said: 'You all right, Nosey? You all right?'

'Boy oh boy,' he said at last, struggling with his giggling. 'That ol' knife gave ye the Willies, didn't it?'

For two pins I'd have kicked him insensible. Then I realised that it didn't matter anyway – I wasn't under his thumb. I could go away and leave him.

'Hey, Arthur, where ye're off to?' He was sitting up now. 'Can't ye take a joke? Arthur!' I didn't answer. 'Come back, Arthur, Ah'm sorry!'

When you're as young as me a friendship means a lot. But I didn't answer. I squeezed through the gap in the fence and started running away from his voice.

It wasn't that he'd made a promise to get me out that night and had broken it, as perhaps he had from the moment it was made. It wasn't that I was scared stiff of the knife, whoever used it, Nosey or Kelly. I was running away from him because I'd never known him. The pal was just a dream. He was a stranger. For all the good times he was still a stranger who'd put on the mask named Nosey. And when his mask slipped there was nothing to do but keep on running.

EIGHT

1

What I'm trying to say is that nobody knows anybody. This was the discovery that made me run. I wasn't just running away from Nosey – man, I was running away from everybody I ever thought I knew. At the same time I realised that I was running away from something I recognised in myself – remember the mirror in the Gents at the Albion? Me hellbent and looking at my face, wondering why anybody should dislike and distrust me.

When we were kids we used to play after the pictures. The game was good 'uns and bad 'uns. Nobody wanted to be a bad 'un but to make the game possible somebody had to take a turn. Speaking for myself, I never managed to convince myself that I was a bad 'un. But to be honest it never spoilt the game, and it slowly dawned upon me that it was just as easy for the others to regard me as a bad 'un as it was for me to regard myself as a good 'un. I'd just seen my best pal as a bad 'un, and that's equal to seeing yourself in the role. Sounds crazy, no doubt, but that's what I saw, and that's what made me run.

I'm not giving a running commentary on how far or fast I ran after leaving Nosey that Saturday night. Just imagine I ran wild, thinking while I ran and not taking much notice of the scenery.

In the end I ran round a corner and into a couple of slops.

'S-sorry,' I said, backing a step or two. One of them moved up. 'In a hurry, son?' he asked. I squeaked something about promising to be in by ten o'clock.

'By gum, Ah wish my young 'uns'd run to be in on time,' he said.

The other slop wasn't so dopey: 'Likely running away from a fight or something,' he said.

'Honest, Ah'm not, Sergeant,' I said. 'Ah've been watchin' the telly at me cousins' and time sorta slipped away. Me old man'll stay me, honest he will.'

'Ach, let him be on his way,' said the other, shoving me off with a friendly pat on the shoulder.

Pounding the pavement I heard them shouting like mad to hold up. Why, I don't know. Perhaps that pat on the shoulder left blood on his hand. I don't know. They chased me the full length of that street and I gained maybe ten yards, then took up the next turning, where the streets were end on. I took a chance, missed the openings of two back streets, then took the third. The first yard door was open. I nipped in and closed it gently behind me. It was dark in there. There was nobody at home and the high walls kept the light from the adjoining houses.

I heard the slops pelting along, gave them five minutes grace, and emerged walking – thanks to Nosey I knew how to keep my head and take a chance – back the way I'd run. Believe it or not, the slops were stuck maybe a hundred yards up. All three parties took off again. In the end I was racing down Shalley Street towards the main road and I knew I'd just about had it when simultaneously I saw the bright lights and heard the whistle go. All that saved me was the fact that they had a corner to turn and I found myself outside the Golden Bowl Mission.

I slipped into a sort of varnished hall. There was a staircase leading up into darkness and a glass-topped door leading into the chapel. They were lifting the roof with a hymn about Beulah Land as I eased the door shut. I was breathing too heavily to join in with the congregation. In fact, that's an understatement: I was breaking my heart for wind. I crawled up those stairs and sat and let my lungs go, and all the time that hymn was swelling and rocking the roof, taking the chorus like the US Cavalry coming down the slope, with Amens and Hallelujahs instead of Yankee yells.

Not that I minded. I thought I was safe.

They stopped singing and somebody started to pray. I guessed it was a girl. If it had been an old woman or a man it wouldn't have mattered to me – when I was a kid I used to go to a local Sunday School and I heard plenty of prayers. But this was a girl and she had a voice like a bell.

What I mean is that her voice was coming out true. It was a cornet of a voice, making words instead of notes. She was half-singing too.

Her prayer was for me and it went like a poem:

And Oh Lord Jesus Christ,
Look down from thy Cross.
And Oh Lord God crucified
Look down from the heavens.
Dear Lord look down from thy Throne,
Dear Lord look down from thy Rapture:
Look down upon us with a Blessing.
Bless this congregation:
Bless with thy blessing this wicked world:
Bless with thy blessing the many young souls
That are lost in sin and darkness.
Oh Lord of heaven and earth send down thy Mercy,
Oh Lord of Grace shower it upon the lost and wandering souls,
And Oh Lord Jesus Christ show thy saving Grace again,
And Oh Lord Jesus Christ make thy servant a vessel –
Let thy Love flow through me
That it might win for thee
Someone lost: Amen.

They sang another hymn and a man said a little prayer but all I could hear was the cornet-girl's wonderful voice. Then they started to come out. I sat there shivering – perhaps I'd had too much to take in one night – and missed the chance to brush through them while they were talking. Also, I hadn't seen the girl. In the end maybe about a couple of dozen had drifted away and the girl still hadn't appeared. I decided to scarper out – the door leading into the chapel was open and I could hear somebody talking but I'd have to chance it. I had reached the bottom of the stairs when the old man came out with his arm around the girl's shoulders – 'The best service we've had for a long time, Dorothy,' he was saying. Then he looked up and saw me. I'll say this for him – he didn't hit the ceiling or take a fit.

'Well, hello, Brother,' he said. It was the first time ever anybody had called me 'brother' and I didn't know where to put myself.

'Hello, Mister,' I said.

'This is my Daddy – Pastor Johnson,' said the girl.

'Pleased to meet ye,' I said. At least I knew her name: Dorothy Johnson; but I'd also discovered that it would be a long time and maybe never before I dared to look directly at her. When I try to think about her now I can't visualise what she was wearing – maybe it was a cottony kind of frock with a belt and a bit of green in it. But that doesn't matter, nor does her height or shape or face. Not much, is it? I mean to carry around with you for a lot of years, perhaps even sixty or seventy. Fair hair and grey eyes, no make up, a natural dresser, by which I mean that she hadn't to try to deck herself, not for me anyway. But minus the voice. And minus the faith.

God's honest truth but I'd never bumped into anything like her in all my born days. Or, for that matter, her old man: tall, thin, death's-head face, kind mouth and machine-tool eyes.

'You must never be shy,' said the Pastor. 'Never hide in the dark. Always walk straight in for salvation. No need to look where ye leap when the mercy seat lies at the other side.'

Keeping my eyes down I said: 'Well; thanks.'

'Shut the door, Dorothy,' said the Pastor.

'Perhaps the young man'll have a cup of tea with us.'

'Ah'll have to go, thanks all the same.'

'The kettle'll be on in a minute.'

'Yes, stay for a cup of tea,' said Dorothy, shutting the door.

'Ah'll have to be away home,' I said. 'The Old – me mother – expects me in. It's getting late.'

'Why then you can tell her you've been to chapel – that'll make her sit up, eh?' Well, man, how could I get out of that one? Dorothy switched on the light and ran ahead and the old Pastor pushed me in front of him and in next to no time there's a white cloth spread and my feet are under the table.

That was the plainest room I ever entered and the plainest food I ever ate but what rocked me was that I was sitting there and welcome, trying to hunch my shoulder out of sight and play up to the best old man I ever met. They must have seen the blood on my jacket shoulder but never gave a sign that they knew it was there.

'You work at something or other?' asked the Pastor.

'Ah'm a labourer on a site – big drain goin' through the other side of the city.'

'Ah worked for my living at every job under the sun,' he said. 'Ah was a strong man in my time – mostly constructional jobs until the Lord called me to preach.'

'Daddy built skyscrapers in America,' said Dorothy.

'That would kill me!'

'Well, now, you never think of it,' said the Pastor. 'Ah was young and sure-footed in those days – didn't believe Ah could fall walking about hundreds of feet up there in the sky on a strip of steel with all the earth below you like an anthill. But I had confidence – not in the Lord mind you, but in my own body, never believing Ah'd fall or even slip. In fact, believing that nothing could happen to me. Even when six good men went sliding through the dizzy heights with a cry on their lips you couldn't make out … well, it didn't shake me. Sometimes I think of it and ask the Lord to forgive my pagan stupidity!'

'Well, Ah can climb a tree with the next,' I said, 'but Ah couldn't move that far up.'

'Ye'll be easier saved than me, then,' said the Pastor. 'All erectors – particularly of skyscrapers – are bound in by darkness.

Arrogance! Ye've never known it until ye've met men like we were.'

'How long have you been working?' asked Dorothy.

'Couple of years,' I said. 'But Ah've had a few other jobs.'

'Since you left school?' I nodded. 'Then you must be about the same age as me.' I couldn't believe it – the same age as me, yet she could close her eyes and pray to God – I'd never thought of God, let alone praying to him.

'You're of an age,' said the Pastor. 'You should get to know each other.'

'Well, Ah don't know …'

'Drop in at a service – Sundays, Wednesdays, Bible Class on Thursdays.'

'But Ah'm not your religion.'

'That doesn't matter – just come. Or come Mondays and Tuesdays and play me draughts – can you play draughts? There you are, then – it's time Ah had a partner worth me mettle.'

'He's a demon for draughts,' said Dorothy. 'What religion are you anyway?'

'Never thought of it – used to go to Sunday School an' it bored me stiff.'

'Our religion won't,' said Dorothy.

Somehow I felt a net fastening around me. I stood up – 'Ah hope ye don't mind but Ah should be on me way.'

'Fair enough – don't forget to come one way or another,' said the Pastor. 'See the lad out, Dorothy.'

At the door she said: 'Come to the service tomorrow.'

'Religion bores me stiff – except when you prayed tonight.'

'That was God using me,' she said. 'Has God ever touched you, Arthur?' And she touched my hand.

'Not like that,' I said. 'Not so that I could feel it – Ah can't feel anything – hymns and whatnot make me want to yawn.'

'Come for my sake,' she said. 'Come tomorrow night. Please.'

'They'll think Ah'm crazy.'

'That's what they thought about the Apostles – crazy with new wine. Surely you're not afraid of what others think?'

'Ah'm as tough as the next!'

'But not tough enough to follow your own heart!'

'Now you're tryin' to force me!'

'Persuade – Daddy says never ram religion down people's throats – he says you can't help embarrassing them when you talk real religion and that can't be helped, but you mustn't drive them.'

'You're driving me!'

'Just guiding – that's all.'

But going home I decided it wasn't as simple as that. If it wasn't the hammer it was the push they were giving me, and well I knew it. So mentally I'd stiffened. Whatever they were trying to give me was good, but I just couldn't take it that way. If God or Jesus Christ would touch me inside the way she'd touched me on the hand, well then maybe I'd turn. But even then I'd turn differently. The way I look at religion it's a secret – real religion, I mean. You go around like an ordinary type and keep mum: no hymns, no prayers, no sandwich boards through the streets; like a kind of secret service man. You obey orders but don't make a song and dance about them and if you do anybody any good you keep dark about it, just in case you fall down on the job and the religion takes the blame.

I couldn't tell my Old Lady I'm 'saved'. Never in a month of Sundays could I tell her – I'd blush for shame. She'd have to find out for herself, picking up the clues, so that she could get used to it maybe and then, in the end, be proud to know. But then again she'd never tell me she knew.

If I was really religious she'd want to be religious too, and go about it in the same way until one day I'd notice, the way she'd noticed me. I'm not saying that it should be this way for everybody. All I'm saying is that I know a lot of people that rant on about their religion and it doesn't do any good. Because why? Because they're trying to convince themselves, maybe? Religion is magic and the less you talk about it the more chance there is for it to operate. God wasn't nailed to a cross so that some crazy fool could brag about it.

2

Awoke on Sunday morning with the sun streaming through the window and a light breeze blowing with it bringing the dry smell of the streets, roast beef warming up, the smell of cats, radio sets blasting away – and down below the Old Lady going it strong with her favourite piece of equipment. But I didn't mind. It was Sunday morning, long-lie-in-day, with plenty to dream about. I nipped out of bed and closed door and window, and drew the curtains. Then I curled up on my side.

But I couldn't settle – and don't kid yourself I was thinking about religion. I was doing a deal with myself. It was a pretty dark deal, with the memory of Dorothy moving about behind it. I was going to finish with Stella. I was finished with the Manor lot. From now on I was squaring up to life. I'd be the best man on the site – forget the dirty deals, Uncle George, Sam Sprogget, etc. – I'd master every part of the job and keep my big mouth shut. I'd make their eyes pop with my silent efficiency, modify the equipment in my spare time, be the first man on the job and the last man off until one day I'd pass the shed and accidentally hear Uncle George say to Sprogget: 'Admit it, Sam – you were wrong about the lad – he's got merit, real merit.'

And I'd go to the Gospel Hall and make friends with Pastor Johnson and Dorothy. I'd be friendly and broad-minded but I'd give them to understand that I was taking an independent line – going religion on my own way. I'd take up that offer to play draughts – I could hold the Lodger and he was no mean player. Yes, I'd wipe the board with Pastor Johnson and Dorothy would look over and wink, and I'd concede one or two pieces. I'd be steady.

Also, of course, I'd help the Old Lady out – see a solicitor and arrange a divorce so that she could marry the Lodger. Man, I'd be so good that even the old janes at the corner seat would notice. Man, I tell you I got myself so worked up that I couldn't settle. Once again I nipped out of bed. When I got back in, with the pillow upright, the cigarette was suffering from one big exultant drag and smoke was curling out of the corners of my mouth, out of my nose, and making a pretty effect with the rings and all the sunbeam motes. Also, my slipper balanced upon my knees on account of the fact that the Old Lady has a mortal dread of smoking in bedrooms leaving a cindered body and thus won't allow ash-trays. I squatted there puffing away, and the glow on the end of the fag had nothing on the great big beautiful glow inside.

The vacuum cleaner stopped. I registered the fact and that's all – any normal day I'd have stubbed the fag and waited the fumes away. So of course she marched upstairs and found me at it. She was carrying the local Sunday paper and my jacket. 'Are ye quite comfortable?'

I muttered something about being sorry but it didn't do any good. 'Ah've told ye time and time again about smokin' in bed.' Then of course I had to stub the thing out in the slipper. She lit up. 'Furthermore, there's something in the paper that might interest you.' It was a big front-page item about 'Young Gangs Battle in Cinema' – evidently the young 'un had keeled over in the pictures and they'd had to take him to hospital with a ruptured inside. The manager had got the whole story out of Rod. There were eyewitness accounts of the fight in the street – but stretched out to a night of horror with dozens of delinquent youth battling hand to hand, knives flashing, bicycle chains going, broken bottles gouging. 'You were in that lot, weren't you – Ah knew there was something up when ye went out in your old clothes.' I didn't say anything. I was praying that Rod hadn't split on us – or there'd be callers any minute. I squinted at my watch – eleven. If he'd split they'd have been round before now – or maybe they were keeping me for the last call. 'It's no use sitting there with your mouth shut – there's proof enough here, on this jacket.'

I said: 'Listen, Ma ...' but it was no use. She was off for the four-minute mile.

'An' the next thing we know the slops'll be at the door,' she concluded. 'A fine carry-on for all the neighbours to talk about.'

171

'It's a bit exaggerated,' I said, tapping the paper.

'Not according to the stains on your coat,' she accused. And what could I say? Certainly not that my dear old pal Nosey had wiped his bloody blade upon it – that would certainly put the tin hat on it!

'Well, that's the finish,' she said, with me silently – so far – applauding. 'From now on you'll act your age. Ah'm puttin' you on the leash. Beginning with today – ye're not stirring out of this house without me.'

Now we'd parted company. In the Manor district the conventions are pretty tight. After you've passed twelve or thirteen you don't go for walks with your parents, unless it's to buy clothes, and there are even some puritans who draw the line so close that they take a different bus and meet their particular Old Lady at the shop. You only walk with a woman when you're courting her; after the honeymoon she's on her own while you go out with the married men of your own age. I've seen characters push a pram and it's held against them for life – they never live it down. So you can understand that my blood was up.

'Ah'm not,' I said.

She gave me a look and went to the wardrobe. Out came my three pairs of trousers and one pair of jeans. 'All right, stay in bed,' she said.

'Ye can't keep me shut up in the house!'

'We'll see,' she said, marching out. Leaving me sitting in a regular panshine. Normally I wouldn't have stood for it, but I'd had a knockout, a real knockout, and had decided to turn over a new leaf, and was in no position to put up a fight. All the good in me was shattered – stuck in the Old Lady's bad books without a chance of putting myself in the clear, trousers out of commission, no chance of following up religion and seeing Dorothy. Finally, my guts all stirred up and a mild sweat in operation wondering if the detectives would be calling.

Also, I was out of cigarettes. I smoked the last man in the packet, rooted out a little cache of fag ends and regretted stubbing them so harshly that they drew badly. Never mind, I smoked them off in a row, then sat and thought how nice it would be to have a nice clean twenty until I nearly drove myself mad. In the end I went out onto the landing in my shorts and shouted down. In between hails, it was so quiet I could hear the Old Lady scraping taties. But I got no response. I felt like a spirit that cannot get through at the seance. I went back into the bedroom and mulled over it for a bit. The old story – if I'd had that straight twenty life would be bearable. Not that I wanted to smoke. All I wanted was the thought that they were around. I made a mental memo to do something about the habit and walked downstairs in my ridiculous shorts.

'Ye're not decent,' she said.

'Ah'm not worried about decency,' I said. 'Ah'm out of fags – let's slip out for a minute an' buy a packet.'

'Ye're agreeing to me terms then?'

'Ye'll have me the laughin' stock of the town.'

'Matter-the-less,' she told me. 'Better a laughing stock than a gaolbird. Ah'm at me wit's end about ye. Ah've come to a finish. From now – seein' ye won't do anything about it yourself – Ah'm keeping ye on the right tracks.'

'Incidentally,' she added. 'Ye look a picture – with the little sentry ready to pop out any minute!'

'Any minute now Ah'll be losing me temper,' I told her. 'Ye can't go on like this – treatin' me like a kid. Ah've got me rights ...'

'And by hell, Ah've got rights too,' she said, waving the knife under my nose. 'Ye've ruled this house long enough. Not eighteen yet an' Ah hardly dare open me mouth. Ye've stood between me an' Harry – an' why? Because ye're just a selfish little brat without a bit of consideration for anything or anybody but your own whim. Well, it's finished, caput, done!'

'Ye can do what ye like with ye're fancy man,' I shouted. 'All Ah want is a bloody packet of fags and all Ah get is a mouthful of bloody misery. Who's stopping ye – not me! Go and do what ye like – but get me a packet of fags.'

'Ye're not budgin' outa this house without me today,' she said.

The trousers were lying over a chair, nice and handy in the fashion of all articles when they can raise a riot. 'Put them bloody trousers down.' Taking no notice I stuck the first leg in. 'Ye'll not master me,' she said and landed me one over the lughole. I recovered and hit her back. It's amazing what you can see in a split second. What I saw was Dorothy's face. Just as if she'd witnessed the whole affair. But it wasn't that which made me beg her pardon. It was the thought that everything I'd planned had been lost for a packet of fags.

Well, she was sitting in the chair with a tragic expression and I was stuttering 'Ah'm sorries' and 'Ah didn't mean tos', etc., which didn't seem to be doing any good. In the end she said: 'Ye'd better look around for some lodgings – Ah can't stand any more of this rough-house, or the worry of wonderin' what ye're up to every time you go out.'

'Listen, Ma,' I said, 'ye drive me to it … honest ye do. Ah could have cut me hand off the minute Ah raised it … if ye'd leave me alone and trust me Ah'll mebbe work out me own salvation …'

'Go and work it,' she said, and now she was crying. 'Get away from me, that's all. Ah knows what it is – if Ah'd brought ye up proper ye wouldn't be like this. It's my fault – Ah've been a poor mother.'

'Ye've been trumps,' I told her. I wanted to go on and say that in my book there wasn't a mother in the world to compare with her, that she had guts, and faith, and a capacity for hard work which had made me a good home which I appreciated even if I'd used it as a camping base. But the convention stopped me. That and the thought that she might think I was sucking up to get my own way. Throwing the trousers down I beat a retreat before I joined in the wake myself.

Five minutes later she went out.

Ten minutes later she came upstairs with my trousers, the whole range, and placed them on the bed-end. Together with a twenty packet. Well, I mean, what can you do with a woman like that? 'Ma,' I said, 'where would you like to go for a walk this afternoon?' She stood with her back to me: 'Ah don't know, Ah'm sure – don't bother about me.'

'We could go to the Exhibition Park and listen to the band.'

'Ah do enjoy a good band,' she said in a queer muffled voice, and I knew we were reconciled. Although I say it myself, we're a queer pair.

3

The trip to the park was torture on two counts, one of which you know, the other being that brass bands of any variety leave me cold. They don't give me any nostalgia and that's a fact. When Harry and the Old Lady were kids I reckon brass still had a glitter, since all jazz had to be exported from New Orleans, Kansas City, Chicago, etc., and there were now home-growns like Humphrey and Chris Barber or even local groups – of which we now have seven or eight around. They were split musical minds – taking little sips of trad jazz with gallons of 'The Maid of the Mountains', 'Belle of New York' and what have you. The old brass bands had the advantage of being seen everywhere, processions, funerals, parades and parks, etc., which was quite something in the days before TV. So for the Old Lady there's still some nostalgia. But there's none for me. All mine comes from the first time I squatted on the steps of a cellar at eight or nine years of age listening to the local group give forth in trad fashion with 'Tiger Rag', 'Basin Street' and hundreds of others; and this nostalgia is mixed up with characters letting rip in a cloud of blue smoke and a joyous perspiration.

The cast-iron stand surrounded by clipped privet, the hanging baskets of geraniums, with hundreds of chairborne citizens surrounding chairborne musicians, is my idea of hell. This afternoon they did everything but 'William Tell'. It was a Military Band. There was a cocky little conductor and, boy, were they under his control – one piece of jam and he'd have slain them. But there was no chance of any jam, none at all, and I took a leaf out of Harry's book and gave myself a ration of shut-eye.

Harry came along with us on account of my nobility – when the subject was raised he yawned and said that it sounded like an interesting way of spending the afternoon and he'd have the house all to himself for the snooze he'd share with the Sunday morning noggin and the Yorkshire pudding. Upon which I said: 'Aw, come along and keep us company,' and the Old Lady nearly took a fit.

'Two's company ...' said the Lodger. 'Wouldn't do for me to break the habits of a lifetime.' But I could tell he was interested in the possibilities. 'Come along and hear *Ave Maria* again,' I said. I could see the Old Lady holding her breath. He gave her a look – 'Think Ah should?'

'It'd be a change,' she said.

So he came and I'll be the first to admit that the idea was only fifty-fifty kindness – taking old Harry along took the edge off escorting the Old Lady. It's wonderful what a load off the mind can do for your general expression of nobility. You see, I'd been worrying about young Rod splitting. After making up with the Old Lady that morning I'd taken the papers upstairs and settled down to review what was happening in the crazy world. Which male star regardless of his lines had taken off with what gorgeous hussy and to where. News of youth in various towns, taken with plenty of salt after reading the hotted-up version of my own personal incident. New instalments of peeping-tom episodes, assaults, rapes, and what somebody's Old Man saw when he took a shift off work to accompany a private eye on a midnight tour of his five-by-four garden. Not news. Just the old routine. About twelve this good work was interrupted by a two-fingered whistle, which I ignored, knowing it was Nosey. However, he wouldn't take no for an answer, so in the end I opened the window and leaned out with the paper in one hand to show that I'd been engaged in my studies. And there he was with his face lifted, ready for another go. 'Go home, punk,' I said.

Planting both hands on his chest he asked: 'What, me? Man, Ah've got good news for ye.'

'Had my fill of bad jokes last night,' I said.

'The Old Lady cheesed off and locked you up?'

'She took a fit when she saw where ye'd cleaned your knife.'

'Ach, never mind. It's all blown over. Ah've good news for ye – the Rodboy kept a stitched lip: we're in the clear.'

'Good or bad doesn't make any difference. As from last night Ah resigned.'

'Come off it, marrer. Nobody resigns. Remember?'

'Ah told ye Ah wasn't having anything to do with the knife.'

'Come an' talk it over in the joint this afternoon.'

'No soap – gotta date.'

He whistled, made a come-off sign with his right hand, and walked away. 'Being seein' ye, marrer,' he hailed over his shoulder. And that was the way we left it. However, it was a weight off my mind to know that the two jollyboys with deadpan faces wouldn't be knocking at my door. So I made the best of the concert. I dozed in the finest possible way, which is to skate along the edge of oblivion with the sun coming through the trees and percolating through your eyelashes to light up the dream-scenes in a kind of mellow haze.

Maybe five or six numbers along the programme the Old Lady clutched my knee. 'My God, Arthur – it's him!'

I came out of my trance, took my bearings, and asked who? But I couldn't get any sense out of her. Just at that moment they were slaying some melancholy piece with a lot of umpaws in it. At the far side of the stand a character was playing the solo part on a trombone. He was standing up, otherwise I wouldn't have known. 'What's wrong, Ma?'

She caught hold of my hand and squeezed until it went dead. 'It's him – it's your father!'

'Can't be,' I said.

'Don't ye think Ah know me own man?'

177

'Well, it's been a long time since ye saw him – ye could be mistaken, y'know.'

'If it isn't him, it's his living spit.'

Old Harry leaned over, and no wonder, for the Old Lady was using her voice and all around us people were wondering what it was all about and taking a gander. 'It's that chap playing the trombone,' I said. 'She reckons it's the Old Man ...'

'Your father?'

'That's what she says.'

'Ah'm goin' down to have a look at him,' said the Old Lady.

'Not now – wait until the thing's over,' said Harry.

'Ah've waited long enough,' said the Old Lady. 'On fifteen years.' And before we could stop her she was shoving out to the aisle.

One thing I'll say for the Old Lady. She's got all her buttons on. I'd been dying the death thinking that she'd rage away down the aisle and walk onto the grandstand to have it out there and then. Instead, she turned her back on the stand. I breathed a sigh of relief and locked my neck to forestall turning. Old Harry nudged me and gave me the message through his teeth: 'Trust her: she's wandering around until she can check him where he can't check on her.' A few minutes later I caught a glimpse of her walking round the far side of the stand. I was waiting for the solo to falter and somebody make a flying leap.

She never came back.

'Settle yourself,' said Harry. 'She's staying put to keep her eye on him.'

'There'll be a row.'

'Not on your life, there won't. We'll join her after the concert's over.'

'You'll come with me?'

'If ye want.'

'If Ah want! Ah'd die if ye didn't.'

'Ah'd have been there anyway,' he said.

'Ye'll give him a hidin'?'

'Depends,' he said. I saw what he meant and settled down to a consideration of my own feelings, now in motion again. Now that I'd my wish I'd have given anything for an out. I'll come honest with you, I was afraid of what I'd find. On the facts he wasn't worth finding, not as far as I was concerned, anyway. He'd shaken the dust and lit out. As far as I knew he'd never worried about the Old Lady, let alone me, in fifteen long years. He was about as low as anything ever featured in the Sunday papers. Yet he was half of me and I wanted to know what that half amounted to.

'Don't jump to conclusions,' said Harry.

'How did ye know?'

'It wasn't hard,' he said, patting me on the knee. 'It's in your face, kiddar. Keep calm, and keep your eyes pinned – and don't do or say anything you're likely to regret.'

Whenever there's something unpleasant to do I generally take a running jump at it. Today was no exception. As soon as the conductor had made his bow and the boys were shuffling about and packing their instruments, I was out in the aisle and beating up against the current. Harry pulled at my arm: 'Let's drift around,' he said.

So we drifted round. The Old Lady was standing back of where my sire was standing: dry eyes but with the hanky clutched in her hand at the ready.

'It's him?'

She nodded and her eyes were following him as he shuffled off the platform and down the steps. 'My, but he's aged,' she breathed. I didn't say it but thought any minute now he's going to age a sight more. Harry took hold of her arm and gently suggested it was time to move.

'Let go me arm!'

'Well, sorry,' he said, and stood off a bit.

'Ah'm sorry, Harry. Ah don't think Ah can go through with it.'

'It's up to you,' he said.

'Ah can't stand the carry-on,' she said. 'Can't bear to look him in the face – fancy that, and him in the wrong!'

'Well, you can do what ye like, Ma, but Ah'm having a word with him.'

'Ye'll leave well alone!'

'Ah've got to see him, Ma. Even if it's just once, Ah've got to see him.'

'Have ye no thought for me?'

'He's the lad's father, Peg,' said Harry.

'Go and ask him his name, then. And if he says it isn't his, just leave him be.'

I set off, then had to come back at the trot: 'What's his first name?'

'Why, what else but yours?'

It took a second or two for the penny to drop. I gave myself a shake and made over to the maybe Old Man. I estimated I could give him a couple of stone and two inches or more. His cap was back and I could see his hair was thin. He'd unbuttoned the tight collar of his jacket and was lighting up from another bandsman's match. I tapped him on the shoulder: 'Your name Arthur – Arthur Haggerston?'

'Who're you?'

'Never mind. Is it Arthur Haggerston?'

'And if it was?'

'Ah've got a message for ye.'

'From who?'

'Soon as Ah'm sure it's the right man Ah'll tell ye.' He had a ratty face and I was beginning to dislike it. The other chaps started to give him a leg-pull about blind dates and what was he keeping up his sleeve? He didn't like it.

'Okay, Ah'm Arthur Haggerston – now what is it?'

'Friend wants to see ye, over here,' and I motioned to a clump of trees.

'Don't see anybody Ah know over there.'

'Listen, chum,' I said, 'Ah'm doing you a good turn. If ye don't want to come it's okay with me. Just say and Ah'll scram.'

'Oh, let's go.' We marched off and I heard Harry shouting: 'Hey, Arthur, wait a minute.'

The Old Man looked over his shoulder – 'That chap shoutin' for you?'

'Which chap?'

'Thin dark feller with the woman – over there.'

I gave a look and shook my head. From then on my mind was made up; from the minute he said 'with the woman'. We reached the trees and he looked around and asked: 'Where's this character that wants to see me.'

'Right here,' I said. Out of the corner of my eye I could see the Lodger running hard. I hadn't much time. I drove for his plexus and he gave a grunt but didn't double up so I knew I'd missed. The blow had belted hell out of my fist – it was like thick leather under his tunic – but I had to come in quick and hit the gold. My fist landed on his elbow. 'You crazy?' he shouted. I shook my head. There was nothing I could do for the right until the juice that numbed it was turned off so I aimed my left like a hammer, end-on, for his nose. Then all hell broke loose. I was hammering away with my one good hand and sometimes hitting his face, and maybe I was also crying and shouting. And he was stepping back and letting me come on for a battering. He kept me for a punch bag for a while and then landed me one on the chin-end. I saw it coming and was glad – he'd been hurting me for a long time.

Two stone lighter and two inches less but it wasn't doing me any good. The next thing I knew I was lying on my back looking through a lovely pattern of leaves at the bright blue sky and thinking how nice it was. The Old Man was looking down at me, looking more ratty than ever but puzzled with it. 'What the hell are ye grinning for?' he asked. I thought of a good crack – my mouth slipped, that's all – but was too shook-up to say it. The Old Lady pulled my head up and asked me if I was all right. I heard Harry say: 'Ah've a good mind to lace ye.'

'Hey, listen, this town gotta grudge against me?' asked the Old Man. A lot of characters, including the military, were gathering round. I could see that old Harry was biting off a bit more than he could chew, with all his sailor-man tricks, and not only because the whole military band might join in.

'Leave him alone, Harry,' I said. 'I started it – got what Ah asked for.'

'That's right,' said the Old Man. 'Told me there was somebody wanted to see me over here. Fell for it. Came over. Next thing Ah knew he landed me in the guts ...'

'The plexus,' I corrected.

'And then he lies there grinning like a Cheshire cat,' said the Old Man. 'What's he grinnin' for – what's the big joke – Ah knocked him, didn't Ah?'

'Reckon he was tryin' to find out what ye were worth,' said the Lodger. 'He happens to be your lad – and this is the wife, if ye're interested.'

The Old Man whistled, and looked away. He said, 'How's things, Peg?' then looked away again.

'Fair enough,' said the Old Lady.

'Let's go for a walk, then.' Putting his hands on his knees he looked down at me. 'You all right – Okay, here's a hand.'

We walked away along the winding path, over the putting green, and along by the boating lake. Nobody said anything the full distance excepting the Old Man, and I reckon it was more to himself. 'Ah should have gone sick,' he said. It was like a dream.

We went through the gate on the Moor, stretching like a prairie over to the long line of bent trees that jointed grass to sky. People were dotted about, singles and pairs, and we were the only group. The Old Man was a couple of yards in front. He kept looking around and I wondered why, until suddenly he spun around and said: 'This quiet enough for ye'se?'

'Suits you, it suits us,' said Harry.

The Old Man sighed and started taking his tunic off. I'll tell you my eyes popped. 'Keep it on, Haggerston,' said Harry. 'We didn't bring ye out here for a belting.'

'Then what ...?'

'Just to ask a few questions and get a few things straightened out.'

The Old Man sighed. 'Ah'd rather it was a fight.'

'Peg here wants a divorce, that's all. You any objection?'

'You want a divorce – there's nothing to stop you. Go ahead, get a divorce. Ah'll not put a sprag in it.' Sitting down he picked a straw and started chewing it. 'Never heard Peg say anything yet.'

The Old Lady manipulated herself onto the grass, and I noticed with surprise how good her legs were. So did the others. 'Ah want to get married again,' said the Old Lady.

'This feller?' She nodded. 'Ye'll get a divorce easy. Like going to the pictures. All cut an' dried. Desertion ... and worse.'

'Ye don't mind?' asked the Old Lady.

'Ah'm fixed up. Have been a year or two.'

'Livin' with her?' asked the Old Lady.

'Married quarters,' said the Old Man calmly.

'You married her – why ye *couldn't* ...' said the Old Lady.

'They call it bigamy,' said the Old Man. 'Reckon Ah'll get a year or two for it.'

'What about Her?' asked the Old Lady. 'Ah mean – the shock ...'

'She'll live through it,' said the Old Man. 'She'll freeze up on me for a week or two.' He made a clicking sound with his tongue. 'Yes, she'll freeze up. But she's okay.'

'Any bairns?'

He shook his head. Gave me a sharp, short look: 'Looks as if Ah've shot me bolt ...'

The Old Lady rose: 'Let it lie, then. Ah'd sooner live in tally than get what Ah want be sending a man to gaol.' With a cut. 'However much he deserves it.' She turned to Harry: 'Ah'm sorry, Harry, but Ah couldn't do it.'

'It's up to you, Peg.'

'No, it's not,' said the Old Man. He was plucking grass and piling it up. 'Ah've let this lie long enough. Said to myself coming up, it'll be a good job if Ah bump into her. Settle the lot for good an' all. That's what Ah said to myself. Got nothin' to do with you. You done enough, fetching the lad up all these years. Now it's my turn. Got to get rid of it for me own sake. So ye

can like it or lump it. Ah'll be in the barracks tomorrow, down
south. Ah'll take a trip down to the local station, see the Inspector.
Pal of mine. Get it over an' done with ...'

'Suit yourself,' said the Old lady. 'Ah wish ye luck.'

'Ah know ye do,' said the Old Man. 'Ah left ye high an' dry but
it wasn't because you were mean – you always had a big heart,
Peg.'

'Coming?' said the Old Lady.

'Ah'll follow on,' I said.

'You go with your Ma,' he said.

'Ah'll be expecting ye for your tea if ye don't catch up to us,'
said the Old Lady to me. Then she went off with Harry. The Old
Man watched them until they were about fifty yards away, when
the Old Lady slipped her arm through Harry's. Then he started
plucking the grass again. We sat a long time. In the end he said:
'Ah'm out of grass. Better move on a bit.' We walked on towards
the trees. Before we reached them he'd started to talk. I wouldn't
have listened maybe, but he'd taken a belting as well as me, and
stood up to it. When you have only one afternoon of your whole
life to spend with your Old Man – well, you make the best of it.

NINE

1

The Old Lady came up trumps, which is to say that she didn't ask any questions about what had transpired between me and the Old Man. For which I was more than glad, not having her fly-paper memory or the gift of letting fly with a string of colourful he-saids and she-saids. Also, what had passed between us wasn't the kind of stuff you want to retail. I give her full marks for guessing the latter. So there was little or nothing said while I scoffed my pineapples and cream and bread and butter and knocked back three or four cups of good strong tea. Then I sat dumb and waited. 'Well, what's the programme for tonight?' she asked.

'Got an invite.'

'An invite – where?'

'What's the use? Can't go unless you go.'

'Try me and see.'

'Got an invitation to the Gospel Hall ...'

'Ah don't believe ye. Who from? And when?'

'Last night. Met the Pastor chap an' he asked me along.'

'And ye want to go?'

'Thought about it; but you said Ah wasn't stirrin' without you.'

'Ah wouldn't stop ye from going to chapel – ye should know that.'

So I said if it was okay with her I'd go, but don't kid yourself I got away without the odd question, such as how come I'd met him, what kind of a feller was he, so he'd a daughter, eh; and so on and so forth. In the end she had the main elements of the situation and let me go. 'Say a prayer for me,' said the Lodger. The Old Lady just looked at me and I guessed what was in her mind. In the end I said a prayer, but it amounted only to a couple of words: 'Help Ma.'

Never thought much about religion excepting to wonder how it all started, and that's a quick way to go crazy if you stick to it; but say you decide God started it all and put up a prayer – what do you get? The sound of your own voice. One-way traffic. Station not answering. Don't get me wrong. Sometimes a stray thought crosses my mind about the neat dovetailing that goes on. And sometimes I think I'm like the character that wants to get to New York, US, or Sydney, Australia, with one of those midget crystal sets. Only maybe it's not so easy as building a radio, even from scratch and without the spares.

Maybe it's like tuning in a billion radio stations simultaneously yet being able to understand each individual programme. Imagine me trying that, me that can't comprehend the Old Lady half the time. Or any other human being you happen to pick out at random, speaking the same language and thinking the same thoughts. Which is not surprising, because the random character doesn't even comprehend himself. Most of the time he thinks he does but this doesn't alter the fact that he doesn't.

Boy, it makes me shiver.

Met up with Nosey on the way over and couldn't shake him off. I told him I was going to the Gospel Hall. 'Okay, Ah'll go along with ye.'

'You're goin' the wrong way, Nosey – if you had any sense you'd be makin' tracks to Teresa's church.'

'Don't go anywhere for a reason; just where Ah fancy.'

There was no arguing with him. We went in. There was a bent old character at the door who gave us a handshake and a hymn book. We sat on varnished forms and joined a congregation of exactly twenty-nine, counting me and Nosey. Dorothy was playing an American organ and gave me a smile. Nosey nudged me: 'Nice piece, eh?' He said it out aloud and all in front, constituting the majority, turned around. Most of them smiled and nodded. Of course they were used to jerks like me and Nosey; in fact one or two rebuilt versions were present.

From the word go that service was full speed ahead, nothing like the Sunday School I'd known. The Pastor came in and announced a hymn, reeled off the first verse without looking at the book, and off we shot. That congregation was one machine and I'm not exaggerating when I say that we went for a ride on it; scared all the time because we'd no control and were going somewhere we knew nothing about. No time to sleep; he prayed, read a lesson from the Bible, and the hymns swept around us and the 'Praise God!'s went up like rockets and then the old Pastor preached.

After five minutes of the preaching my tough old pal Nosey whispered: 'Let's get outa this crazy nut-cracking suite – any minute now Ah'll be blowin' me top.'

'It's only a man talkin',' I said. I'll admit I was scared too, but not that much. I'll also admit that seeing Nosey on the oven-shelf gave me a feeling of quiet enjoyment.

'He's got his eye on us,' he said. 'All the time. Every time ye look up. He's makin' a set for us.'

'He's after sinners,' I said. 'How about the knife, now? No use here, eh, Nosey?'

That man had as smooth a voice for talking as his daughter for singing. It was half-singing anyway, coming out mainly on the toffee range. But sometimes he'd drop to a wind-in-the-wires whisper and then let it come forth, resonant.

Descriptive: how Man had lived in Paradise, which was Home, no death, no disease, no hatred, no evil, no sin. Absolutely safe, with a direct connection to God any time of the day. So safe that even the safety we knew in our mother's arms didn't bear comparison; so joyful that the happiest moment of our natural lives was only a shadow of it; so beautiful that ever since man had ached at the memory. Then the Devil had slid into all this and wrecked it. Man was turned out and had to live and sweat and die. He was cut off from God and that was the worst thing of all because it left him lonely. Instead of eternity there was the tread-mill of days. Man travelling across the salt plains of the years where there was no mercy, only Cain killing Abel; no dew of compassion, only shed blood; and the doom of the Flood or the destruction of Sodom and Gomorrah. Again and again God made Himself known to His people; and again and again His people betrayed Him. So God at last came to earth. The Word was made flesh and was crucified for our sins – my sins, your sins.

'Hallelujah.'

'Praise God.'

'That man's got an eye like a big drill,' said Nosey.

Exhortation: Ah, brethren, you'd think this would be the end – Paradise restored. Who can deny the Cross? Who can turn away from that bloodstained brow, those pierced hands and feet, that riven side? Yet millions have, millions have shut their eyes, millions have chosen the Devil. You may ask how can we choose the Devil if we don't believe in him? Because, brothers and sisters, the Devil has performed a marvellous conjuring trick; he has done the vanishing trick. And all the time he's there! But because he appears not to be there people believe that sin is a normal state of affairs without a taint of wickedness. It has nothing to do with God or the Devil, nothing to do with temptation, nothing to do with eternal damnation. It is just a matter of the will and the senses. The will must have scope, the senses must be satis-fied. So the Devil manipulates them by remote control. Brothers and sisters, the Devil is having the time of his life – he's almost without a job! And the young men and women of our time are at his mercy. The joke of it, for he has no mercy. None at all. They run around with their easy morals, their violence, their disregard of God's holy laws. They plunge into the filth and slime. Young people without hope!

My old pal Nosey was sweating on the top line: 'He's got his eye on me an' you all the time ... what's he after?'

188

'Shut up!' But I was in a sweat as well. That man could preach. Don't kid yourself – I wasn't falling for it. I was just embarrassed.

Persuasion: Ah, if only they knew that the only way to get is to give; that the only way to enjoy life is to give it back to God, that only he who hates life shall have it. See through the net of deceit the Devil weaves; see through to the everlasting torment for the senses the Devil has captured, see through it all for your soul's sake. Turn the other way and look at the Crucified, look at the Head crowned for your transgressions, look at the outspread arms and the hands torn by the nails, look at that bleeding side. Look into those wonderful eyes and find the forgiveness you need.

'Ah'm gettin' out of this!'

'Nobody stoppin' ye.'

Invitation: Now let us all bow our heads and close our eyes. Let us all lift our hearts and pray for a decision – let us pray for those who are not in the fold – to throw themselves before the seat of Mercy –

'Are ye comin', Arthur?'

Now let us sing our prayer – softly, softly so that I can speak God's message …

There was a scuffle. When I looked up old Nosey was running for it as hard as his legs would take him.

'Young man, you cannot run away from God. Stay and find peace.'

But he was gone. 'We'll leave him in the hands of God,' said Mr Johnson at the end of the service. He was looking down upon me from a great height; death's head, sunken cheeks and very kind brown eyes. 'I thought for sure there'd be a decision tonight.' I felt like a tailor's dummy. My clothes were hanging down on me like Monday's washing, only it wasn't soap-suds that were drying out but gallons of sweat at a guinea a drop. I was a couple of stone lighter, and I was mad. Why, I couldn't exactly say. It was buzzing in my head and had been ever since old Nosey made a run out.

'But Arthur stayed,' said Dorothy.

'Aye, that he did,' said Mr Johnson. 'Now why, Arthur?'

'You didn't play the game,' I said.

He smiled: 'God sanctifies every instrument.'

'Maybe so. But Ah'd rather sit down quiet and make me mind up. No prayers, hymns or talking. Just a quiet think – then make me own mind up.'

'And sit and think for ever?' said Mr Johnson. 'Never mind, Ah can see ye're a tough nut to crack – better to beat at draughts, eh?'

I'm not kidding. I was amazed at the difference.

Dorothy saw me off again and kept me talking the best part of ten minutes. 'What do you believe in?' she asked. She had eyes like her father; looking at her I had a crazy look into the time when her face would run dry and shrunk and wrinkled like his. But that would never come.

'Give me time,' I said.

'You mean – you're considering about what you've heard tonight?'

'Your father isn't the only one I listen to – Ah'm listenin' all the time.'

'Everybody listens all the time.'

'Listenin's like pickin' flowers.'

'You pick what suits you, you mean?'

'Sometimes, no. Sometimes, you pick up something that slays you. Like your Old – like some of the things he says. About bein' lonely, about everybody bein' lonely, that's the kind of thing I pick up, not because it suits me but because it checks.'

'You're a strange boy,' she said.

'Listen, how old are you?' I asked. 'Maybe a few months older, maybe younger. You got it all on a plate. Well, that's not for me.'

'Well, I thought about it. I thought about it a lot.'

'That's for sure,' I said. 'All Ah'm sayin' is about myself. This listenin' business, for instance. It's like knitting but slower. Take what your father said about the only way to get is to give ...' I told her about old George Flack and his nephew and how before that he was a dead man.

'And that's why you came tonight?' she asked. There was a little laugh in her voice. I felt like grabbing her and saying, 'No, because there was one flower I wanted to pick.'

All I did was to take hold of her hand. She was leaning against the door looking at me with this little smile, daring me on. But all I could do was press her hand and wish I could just lift it against my face so that maybe it would slide around my neck. She was right and I was wrong. She was a century older than me, I couldn't move, and she was laughing. That's what I felt, plus the feeling that she could so easily make a fool of me. In the end I realised I was making a fool of myself. 'Got to go.' Her hand slipped away. The state I was in, it's a wonder I took her hand, thinking she was too religious to touch, let alone to kiss. Maybe if I'd looked I'd have seen that she was disappointed too. Stopped at the first lamp-post on the way and hit it with my fist. Hit it hard, then turned in time to see the door closing.

2

All through the rest of summer and a good way into autumn was just freewheeling, drifting along to the Mission and getting more and more hardened to the preaching but never to Dorothy's voice: it was her voice I first fell for and even now maybe I'm hearing some other girl talking, then, suddenly, she runs into a tone that makes me remember Dorothy's voice: and it pulls me up, rigid. We went walking but always apart excepting for the accidental brush. I was as nervous as a kitten. That girl had patience, but for no return as it proved. What's in it when you can just walk and go to services – no pictures, dances, or fun? But it went on.

Sometimes I wonder what it was all about. I loved this girl. I'd never been shy. But somehow she froze all my initiative – or maybe it was the memory of her voice, that atmosphere of prayers and hymns that put on the brakes. Maybe again, it was because I had a respect for innocence and didn't want to spoil it. And all the time the thought of Stella held me back.

This had been going on all the time. I never told anybody about it. There it was in a strictly private compartment, snug and cosy like a certain kind of dream and always available. When I think of Crab and Mildred I realise how lucky I was to have it that way – to call and be accepted graciously and tenderly and come away free without any demands. Sounds crazy, doesn't it? But it happened, and now that I'm older and wiser I realise that perhaps the real innocence was in Stella. Sometimes things crowded in and I didn't go to see her for days on end; sometimes I'd try to keep away for Dorothy's sake and then in the end I'd go, because she was home, everything about her was home. The door would open and she'd welcome me with the usual glad smile and never mention how it must have been waiting since the last time. I'd sit on the settee in front of the fire and she'd talk on – prattle's the word, I think – about the book she was reading; she was a great reader; breathlessly, gladly and excitedly. Maybe I'd feel guilty about staying away but within a few minutes the guilt would flake off because she made me feel there were no ties, it was enough that I should be there. Man, I'd feel like somebody great, somebody who'd stepped out of an extra chapter of her favourite book as she sat there, laughing and talking, a plump, pretty little woman with very good legs and gentle, happy eyes. More often than not she'd suddenly run out of talk and come over and kiss me. She was a great one for kissing, both hands cupping my face: a kiss on the forehead, a kiss on the cheek, a kiss on each eyelid, all the time coming the long way round to my lips, delaying tactics, you might say, putting it off until I was dying for those soft pretty lips to reach mine and open slightly as a signal for me to pull her down onto my lap. Or perhaps she'd resist the impulse and say: 'I'll cook something for you – what will it be?' And she'd run to the scullery, humming, pulling down one thing and another, and calling out names to me, until, in the end, I'd go through, tiptoe behind her and put both arms around her waist. She'd pretend to be startled. 'Now, what is it you want?' she'd ask with a flushed face, meaning food, and I'd say I'd rather eat her than any meal, any day, any time, and move my hands to her breasts. And her head would move back and I'd see the arch of her neck as I put my face down to kiss her. I used to think it was like Adam and Eve because everything was so easy and simple; and so of course it was, for me. What it was like for her, thinking about the husband roistering round the world as first mate on a merchantman; big, bluff and easy, so easy he never gave a thought or came within an inch of knowing how much of her was going to waste between trips. She never told me. There was a girl at a boarding school. There were pictures of the kid all around the house. She never talked about her husband, excepting once to tell me in a matter-of-fact way who and what he was, but she often talked about the girl, what a good scholar she was, how serious, keen to be a doctor, not in the least like me, she'd laugh.

I used to ring up and sometimes this kid would be home on holiday. 'Who's there?' she'd say, and I'd freeze stiff over the phone because although her voice was very much younger it was very like Dorothy's. 'Who's there?' Thoughts of her mother would flash through my mind; thoughts of her naked and absolutely unashamed with a body as pink and white as her cheeks, and I'd replace the receiver. I'd walk out of the booth feeling like dirt; and full of fear. I never felt guilty about Stella and me, but I felt guilty about being found out, and I used to think of that little girl reading in the newspapers some day about a boy not much older than herself and her mother, a woman nearly twice his age. The thought used to come at odd times and it was like a fist squeezing you.

Yet, at the same time I was jealous of the Old Lady and Harry, so jealous that one night when I heard a scuffling noise from the room downstairs I worked myself into a passion, crept out of bed and downstairs, and flung open the door of his bedroom. Will you believe it, that comedian was standing on his head, up against the wall! I expected the worst and all I found was this character in his pyjamas and in his stockinged feet, bang up against the wall upside down and grinning. He knew what it was all about and no mistake. That grin told everything. Without moving from his position he said: 'Trying to improve the circulation.'

I grinned weakly back and went back to bed like a trampled cockroach. It could have been worse, I realised. I could have kicked myself for not realising it. It stumped me just to find him doing some yogi exercises – what would it have been like to have found him in bed with the Old Lady? Time after that, as before, I'd hear her creeping downstairs and would pull the sheets over my head and try to forget, because there was nothing I could do about it. But I resented it all the same – and on the same caper myself! Worse, in fact.

Perhaps because I wanted to feel self-righteous about the Old Lady, and to put myself on the right footing with Dorothy, I once stayed away from Stella nearly three weeks – usually I'd seen her once a week. I'm not saying it was easy. It was worse than trying to stop smoking. But the more I realised the hold she had on me the more determined I was to stay away. This led to our one and only row. Came home from work one night, had my tea, went upstairs to change and for some reason took a peek outside. I nearly hit the ceiling when I saw her car, just up the street, sitting there like a judgement. Fortunately, the Old Lady wasn't back from her cleaning job. I didn't know how quickly to get downstairs and out along the street. The window was wound down and she was smoking a cigarette woman-fashion with quick little stabs. 'Get in,' she said. Her nose and mouth were pinched around the corners. The car was moving before I was nicely settled.

We went past Shalley Street and something hit me as we reached the bridge. I looked back. It was Nosey, right enough, standing at the corner end with his eyes popping. Believe me, I started thinking up the story I was going to tell him, then it dawned upon me that it was good old Nosey and that the secret was safe enough with him. It's incredible, because what I had on my hands at that particular moment in time was far worse than Nosey knowing all about my most private affair. She drove like a demon through the town, not carelessly, never beating a light, but

194

weaving in and out of traffic like crazy and daring those big yellow Diesels to do their worst. We whipped out into the countryside in less than no time, took a secondary road down to the river, found a bridle and bounced to a standstill.

'Now,' she said, 'give me a cigarette.' It was an order. After we were drawing – 'Understand, Arthur, you're as free as the air. I'll probably be well rid of you. But you'll be man enough to tell me when you want to finish it.'

I looked at my cigarette. 'You won't get inspiration there,' she said sharply, holding herself in. 'After all, you've had three weeks to think up a story – what is it? Have you fallen in love?' She almost choked on the last two words. I nodded. 'Then why didn't you tell me?'

'Hadn't the guts,' I mumbled.

Then she gave it to me. She told me that only a rat would take a woman for granted the way I had, that she'd never tied me and didn't want to tie me, but expected to be treated as a person and not as some kind of slave. She didn't cry at any time, and that made it worse. Then, in the end, she sat with her face drained of all colour.

'It's all true,' I told her. 'There's a girl, and that's the trouble.'

'Then you should have told me,' she said. 'I wouldn't have kept you. It was just cowardice on your part.'

'It wasn't altogether that,' I told her. And suddenly I knew why I hadn't told her – really why. I'm not trying to say that I wasn't a bit of a rat and a coward. I behaved badly. But looking at her I suddenly knew what it was all about; I'd been hanging on to something impossible. I knew it was impossible but at the same time I wanted it to come true.

'Then what – what?' she demanded, urgently.

And it was me that started crying – 'Because Ah don't want ye to go on living alone in that house – Ah don't want to part with ye – Stella, Ah wish to God ye were my age.'

'Oh, my God,' she said and her face crumpled. I drew her to me and comforted her as best as I could and in the only way I

195

knew. In the end we left the car and walked down the river. It was a mellow autumn night and we found an old sand pit. If anybody had walked on top of us they'd have thought we were crazy – we both thought it was the last time. After the hardness and anger she was eager and generous, but it's curious how your thoughts travel. I kept thinking what a pity it was that I'd never again see her, the whole of her, at my ease and in a full light. And afterwards she said: 'If I went back twenty years – well, it wouldn't mean as much as that – it would mean losing a lot. I couldn't give up Polly or the rest of my life. Thank God we're not offered the chance ...' She was silent awhile then said, 'But I'm glad you said it, my darling.'

And I'm glad to say I remembered what it was I'd said. She dropped me off in the town and I caught a trolley home. I remember looking over the edge of the bridge and seeing the gas lamps and the roofs of the few houses far below and thinking there was a lot of sense in this business of marriage. To grow used to a woman, to fall in love with her almost without knowing it, is something deep. And it puts you through a mangle to have to say goodbye and know it's for ever. If I was a little bit relieved I was also grateful and more miserable than I'd ever been before.

3

So it was back to boyhood, or the shadows between boyhood and manhood, deeper shadows than those seen from the bridge. All that winter I was neither here nor there. Sometimes I ran around with the Manor lot, and sometimes with Dorothy and the Pastor. Nosey was going strong with Teresa and either too busy or too preoccupied to hatch up any big wild capers which constitute the life of any lot. The Kelly lot were also out of the running, tied up in a youth club started by their new parish priest, who kept them happy and busy on a programme of discussions, table tennis, gramophone records and Irish dances. Some of them were even buying kilts on the never-never. I somehow couldn't imagine Mick running around in skirts and nobbly knees, but this was the tale.

The Manor lot looked like dying out for want of opposition, leadership and interest, and I can't say that this state of affairs left me miserable. I'd had a bellyful of playing Cowboys and Indians. I was unsettled and in a haze, dreaming of a girl, and wondering how I could find an out from work-misery. Every morning I rolled out of bed with a feeling of being trapped. Day followed day, and every day was too long and the free time between them too short. The site was going ahead and getting more and more like a swamp in the process; I was living in what you might call a misery of rain. We were working a couple of hundred yards from the river and it gave you a pang every time you saw the launches, etc. cutting about and the big mysterious oil tankers gliding along. Maybe they were only running between a refinery down south and our river but every time you saw them you thought of Persia and sunshine. Sometimes, and this was bad, a character doing nothing in particular on the deck would wave and send a pang to your heart.

It's the same the whole world over, they say, and sometimes worse; I wish they'd give everybody a chance to find out for themselves. All they give you is a decko at the TV or pictures. And meantime you're supposed to be making a living on a dead-end site under a pack of phonies like Uncle George and Sam Sprogget, or other characters that think they're doing well for themselves by bearing down on the lambs and shearing the sheep. It makes you sick.

It's all a dirty rotten trap.

Letters were coming and going. The Old Man went on trial for bigamy and achieved a good talking-to from the judge, culminating in a fairly light sentence. The Old Lady and Harry went to see a solicitor and came back with the news that a divorce would go through like greased lightning. So they were busy also. I kept thinking of the Old Man sweating it out behind bars.

It suited my mood. The Old Lady saw him twice, once at the court when she supplied the necessary, and once in gaol when she went along with her successor to say hello, but each time he was as happy as Larry and as chuffed as a butcher sold out on a Saturday night. Said he was catching up on his reading and everybody was very kind. The Old Lady and his second exchanged letters monthly. Don't ask me why.

Everybody was sitting pretty. Harry and the Old Lady, or Nosey, seemed always to be breaking-off on some exciting journey to say hello. It was like smelling Sunday dinner and knowing there's none for you. All my own fault. I could have been in it too, but went on thinking of Dorothy as of some character out of the Bible. Every time I brushed against her I thought of the first time I heard her voice in the Mission and killed any thought of the usual boy-and-girl.

Then came the crack-up.

One night we're sitting in the Regent billiard room when old Nosey came in. One look at his face and I knew something was in the wind. 'Anything wrong?' I asked.

'Not yet.'

Evidently he wasn't in the mood for talking, so nothing more was said. We had a game of snooker. He chain-smoked all the time, tried to use his cue to scissor the table, and ended up the loser by a mile. Snookered, in more senses than one. I bought him a bitter lemon. 'What's biting ye, Nosey?'

'That Mick beat her up. Says he'll beat her up every time she meets me.'

'Surprised ye've got away with it so long.'

'Ah'll murder him!' he said. 'Ah'll cadge our kiddar's gun an' shoot him up.'

'Whose gun?'

'Our kiddar's gun.'

'You don't want to be messin' about with a gun.'

'With or without,' said Nosey, 'Ah'll get him.'

'You forget the gun, Nosey,' I told him. 'And tell your kiddar to get rid of it – guns lead to nothin' but trouble.'

'Aw, cut the cackle,' he said. 'All you have is good advice. You wouldn't help me out in a pinch like a real pal would. None of you would. Too bloody frightened to live – all of ye!'

It's funny how you see a trap and still fall for it.

'You know me better than that,' I said.

'Okay, kiddar,' he said. 'Ah'll keep you to that. If and when Ah give you the word for a showdown with Mick and Co ye'll come. That understood?'

'Ah'll come.'

4

The truth is that I was afraid of that gun as soon as he mentioned it, and I don't mind telling you why. I was never afraid of guns, having, like most of us, been brought up with them, at second-hand. Pirate pistols that never seem to need any priming; six-shooters that appear like magic; little snapping derringers; sleek little automatics and revolvers with or without silencers; tommy guns, Lee Enfields, muskets, automatic rifles. Almost as familiar as knives and forks excepting that you never handle them. The nearest you ever get apart from the pictures is a rifle in a railway carriage or fixed bayonets and holsters in a procession. There was one time I took a closer look. Me and old George Flack were helping the surveyors in the summer, on the old site, when old George picked up a chamois-leather bundle fastened with a shoelace; the better type of shoelace, the kind that cost a shilling a pair. Old George handled it like butter. I fancy he'd already felt the shape of it. I remember how he fumbled unfastening the knot and unfolding the chamois. All the time the surveyor was shouting: 'Hey, where the hell's that marker? What's up with you two?' He couldn't see us because we were among a jungle of sticky bud plants, which grow tall, and in a bit of a dip. It was Army issue with a butt still damp with oil, nice and shiny, and snicking beautifully apart when George broke it. There was one bullet left. 'Let's have a look at it, George!'

He handed it over. Weighed in my hand it was heavier than I'd expected. Then I stuck it in my belt and drew. It's all hokum about these fast draws; the weight pulls your hand down. At a pinch I might have shot off George's big toe. 'How d'ye think it got there?' I asked. 'Reckon a crook or somebody left it?'

'That gun killed three people if Ah'm any judge,' he said slowly. 'Here, give us it back.' I didn't need a second telling.

'Which three?'

''Bout five or six years ago,' said old George. 'Killed a family: wife, kiddie and husband.'

'Why'd he do that – who was he?'

'Crazy young feller wanted the wife to run away with him. She refused. So he went in and shot them: the television was still going when they found them: the bairn was sitting with his thumb in his mouth.'

'And he got away?'

'They chased him so hard he never got a chance to use the last bullet on himself – or maybe he changed his mind.'

'Did they catch him?'

'They caught him and hung him,' said old George. 'But they never found the gun.'

'We'd better hand it over to the slops.'

'More trouble than it's worth,' said old George. He turned and shouted up to the surveyor: 'Will ye hold yer gob!' Then he walked down to the river with the bullet in one hand and the gun in the other. By the time he was back the surveyor had walked down and was raising hell with me. 'You finished playin' ducks and drakes?' he asked old George.

'Ah've finished,' said George. 'Do you always lock the doors when ye're watching television?' Natch, the surveyor, thought he was off his rocker but I can tell you I was receiving at strength ten or whatever is maximum. Looking through a window at a cosy family scene now always reminds me of what a gun can do.

5

Well, I kept my promise to Nosey and attended the battle. It wasn't like any of the others. It wasn't like any fight I'd ever had and it was the beginning of a pile-up that flattened me. That was a long time after the promise. Christmas and New Year had slipped away and I was leading my old double life and waiting for the spring; in fact, Good Friday was coming up, the week it all started. When I say double life I don't mean anything mean. I was definitely finished with Stella, but was still hanging round the Mission and Dorothy two or three times a week and spending evenings in between with the Lot. It wasn't going easily for me, because I was still treating Dorothy like a china doll and worried about her reaction: some nights she'd be all happy laughter and others as cold as an iced cocktail minus the cherry.

But in comparison with Nosey I was having it all sweet and easy. At least I was seeing my girl, and welcomed by all parties. In fact the only drawback was that the Old Lady and the Lodger took it for granted that I was the complete young lover and going steady and it used to burn me up to hear them cracking sly allusions, etc. when I knew my role was no better than a brother's. But poor old Nosey was in purgatory. What with thrashings, pressure and the religious question his Teresa had decided it was no dice and so there he was rubbing shoulders with her in the factory, his hands touching hers as he took a carton from her machine, and to her, or so it seemed, he didn't exist.

Also, he was worried about Crab and in particular about the gun. The gun because it had disappeared and Crab wouldn't say where or why; Crab, because all this payment business was driving him crazy. Nosey was going downhill because of the way Crab talked in his sleep, or boozed, or acted.

'He'll shoot that woman,' he told me. 'Sure as death he'll shoot her.'

'How come when he hasn't a gun, then?' I said.

'He's got it stashed away, ready.'

'More likely sold it to a pal.'

'They've more sense than play around with guns – even empty ones.'

I remembered old George and the murder gun. 'Maybe he got the wind up and slipped it in the river,' I suggested.

'You think Crab's likely to get the wind up ye've got another think comin',' he told me. We dropped the subject for the time being, but it kept cropping up, and when it didn't it was simply because maybe the night before, we'd talked ourselves out on some aspect or other. Like – 'You think maybe it'll do some good if Ah go and talk to that woman?'

'Not a chance.'

'Well, she's a woman.'

'She's all twisted. She's a man-hater. All she wants is to dirt on them.'

'But maybe if Ah went an' told her about the state he's in ...'

'She'd maybe offer *you* the money.'

'You kiddin'?' I just looked at him, and after a while he continued: 'No, Ah reckon ye're right, she'd do it on me, and then Ah'd kill her for sure.'

'You talk about killing easy, Nosey,' I said.

'It's my blood,' he said. 'It's my bringing up. Anybody with pride is prepared to kill.'

'You don't know what killing is.'

'You ever killed anybody?'

'No, Ah never killed anybody, except in me imagination, so Ah know what it's like.'

'Never thought of it,' he said thoughtfully.

'Not even when Mickey boy pulled that knife?'

He thought a minute and shook his head: 'Not even then, but if he'd flackered a minute Ah'd have turned the knife on him for sure.'

'You'd have been sorry for it.'

'How the hell d'you know?'

'Imagination.'

'Ah never had any of this stuff,' he said. 'What's wrong with me? What's in this imagination anyway?'

'Tracking through,' I said. 'Knife, blood, dead man, trial, rope round your neck.'

He nodded slowly but his eyes were puzzled. 'See what you mean,' he said, 'but Ah don't feel it here. Mean to say you feel it happening?'

'To me, or to anybody else!'

'You feel – for somebody else?' I nodded. 'Man, here's somebody doesn't bother his head about stuff like that,' he boasted. 'A man that's somebody does what he has to do, or else he's in trouble.'

'Trouble's the word,' I said. 'The way you and maybe Crab thinks is a single track to trouble.'

'He'd help me to skip out,' he said. 'Or me him.'

What can you do with a character like that? You're right. That's why I should have kept clear of him. But I didn't. When the time came I fell for his idea rock-bottom. I was riding home from work and spotted him at our street corner. It was raining and he was squatting on his hunkers with an old raincoat over his head watching the gutter run. He looked like an old gypsy woman lying down to die, and it wrenched me worse than the other time I met him – when he was waiting for his longest night to pass away and had the idea of stopping time. I pulled the bike into the corner. 'Camping out, kiddar?'

'Didn't want to miss ye – Ah've something in the oven.'

'Come along to our house,' I said.

'No, it's too hot. Even with a wall in between, your Old Lady'd go up in flames.'

'Okay, then, jump on the back an' we'll talk it over where it's dry,' I instructed.

We sat down and lit up in one of those ruinous old houses. You had to smoke to keep the foistiness out of your system. 'Well, boy,' I said.

His face was greasy with rain, his eyes popping: 'She broke

down today, kiddar. Teresa did. Ah was sidin' along as usual when they blew the buzzer, hopin' she'd give me the word – and cook me up if she didn't.'

'You mean it's all on again?'

'No, no, not yet; but could be … she told me to stop givin' her the eye and chasin' along on account of the trouble Ah'd caused and Ah said there was no trouble from my end. Then, boy, she blew up. She said it was all right for me but she'd gone through the mill what with her Old Lady twistin' and the Ould Man and Mick landin' her until she promised to knock it off.'

'So far it's signing the stamp,' I remarked.

'Hold on. Then she said: "You want me, you settle Mick – so far ye've kept well enough out of his way." So Ah said, "That was 'cos he was your brother; you give the word and Ah'll belt him now or any day."'

'So what did she say to that?'

'She said, "Okay, see if ye can bring it off; but that's not all – will ye turn for me?" To her religion. So Ah said that's askin' something, and she said otherwise no dice because she didn't mind going to hell for me but minded about any kids she had. So in the end Ah said Ah'd turn.'

'And ye'll turn for her?'

He gave me a wink, 'We'll see when seeing time comes.'

'You're crazy promising to turn for a girl and get married at your age. She's hooked ye!'

'Well, that's the way it is,' he said. 'You ready to help out?'

'For crying out Jesus Christ, help in what?'

'Ask for help – all ye get is a load of questions.'

'Boy, you're serious. Help for what?'

'Ah'm goin' to strap him tonight. The way Ah see it is this; it's the night for the ceilidh dancing at the church club and he'll be there. Gettin' on for ten-thirty when they break up. They knock around a bit outside; when Mick makes off down the steps to the quayside there's only one with him …'

'And he's mine?'

'You cotton on quick. You look after him, Ah look after Mick. No iron or anything and Ah bet Ah belt hell outa him.'

'An' what good will that do ye?'

'Ah'll get him to negotiate a settlement.'

'Listen, maneater,' I said. 'All you need do is tell him you're willin' to change religions for her an' the next thing you know ye'll be dancin' in the Church Hall and goin' home to put your feet under her table.'

He was shaking his head. 'No, for two reasons. One, he's solid ivory between the ears an' he'll need beatin' down to the right frame of mind. Second, he's got it comin' for liftin' his hand to Teresa and pullin' a knife on me.'

'Ah've got a date tonight anyway.'

'Don't tell me ye can't get away from a prayer meeting by ten. Tell me it's a simple ditch.'

'If ever it comes out, she'll drop me like a hot potato.'

He got up and started stalking out. As I told him, I should have had my brains examined. 'Who's this character, and what's his weight?' I asked. And that was the beginning of my happy Easter holiday.

TEN

So we arranged to meet at a pub called the Barbican about ten o'clock. I had to fight for this: his idea was to meet there before closing time and have some pop, which didn't suit me at all. I knew his temper and wanted a clear head to do what we had to do. Of course, I knew he'd have his pop anyway, and I also knew there was nothing I could do about his temper, but this made me all the more determined to go in cold. Call it self-preservation. That's what it was in the end, anyhow.

It never rains but it pours. I landed at the Golden Bowl Mission feeling clean, fresh and confident, and in a matter of ten minutes had it all knocked out of me. Honest to God, I was never anywhere near their idea of religion. But you can't stop the odd word getting through. I thought a lot of the Pastor. I was guilty about hanging around on account of his daughter and I really liked that old man. He was kind.

He'd gone wandering from our place as a young man and finished up in London without food and had been too proud to beg and in the end had walked off in a trance and landed up in Colney Hatch, the London loony bin. In the grounds, not inside. He'd taken a five-quid passage to Canada and had slaved for a maniac farmer for two or three years; and worked in a West Virginia coalmine where the hand of the Lord had preserved him from the company cops during a strike and stretched out into the mine when it blew up to save him and three more. He'd ended up in a Bronx Mission where the idea came to him to take the trip home and start away for himself preaching the Gospel. He'd lost his wife. His stipend wouldn't have kept a sparrow but he sang like a thrush. He'd been born kind, but he'd stayed kind.

So when he preached about Peter that night it struck home; every time his eyes lit upon me I heard the cock crowing that I was off to beat up an unsuspecting boy; not Mick Kelly, who wouldn't get what he deserved however hard Nosey tried, but the kid walking home with him who had no grudge against me. And I didn't even know his name.

If I'd stayed a minute longer I'd have called the caper off. So about the time Peter was warming his hands at the fire I blew out. I didn't look at anybody or make any sign, just blew, and Dorothy followed me.

'Where d'ye think you're going to, Arthur Haggerston?'

'Ah've got a pal to see.'

'Why couldn't you say before? Everybody's wondering. What will Dad think – a person walking out in the middle of his sermon?'

'Ah'm sorry.'

'Better be sorry before than after,' she said. 'And it's not only the sermon – he was looking forward to a game of draughts with you tonight.'

'Ah'm sorry.'

'Haven't you the gumption to say something else? You haven't even apologised to me.'

I could only look at her.

'You're stupid – stupid,' she said. 'Who is this pal, anyway?'

'One of the lads,' I muttered.

'The ratty looking type you brought along last year?'

'Your Dad wouldn't say a thing like that.'

'Well, somebody's got to tell you something for your own good.'

'He's got an immortal soul – he's a human being.'

'I'm not denying that. But he's blackening it as hard as he can. Anybody can see that. Anybody can see that he'd stick at nothing. He'll get himself into trouble and take you with him.'

Her voice softened. 'Don't go, Arthur. Stay with me. We'll not go back into the meeting – we'll go for a walk. You'd like that better than going with him, won't you?'

'Ah've promised.'

'If I went down on my knees would you stay?' She came close to me, catching hold of my coat lapels and looking at me with her eyes wide open and asking, 'You wouldn't refuse me?'

'Ach, you know Ah'd rather stay with you, Dorothy.'

'Forget about him.'

'Got to keep my promise – Ah'm sorry.'

She laid her head on my chest. The hymn was going next door: 'Guide me, O thou Great Jehovah, Pilgrim through this barren land ...' I kissed her eyes. She said a long 'O' and my lips travelled over her cheek and to her lips.

Now you'll not believe this but it's simple when you think it out. I was the gangster, detective, deputy who has to go out on men's business. That's one way of looking at it. On the other hand I was a Manor character brought up to pay his way, take his turn and stand by a pal. Furthermore, and this is much more important, I was worrying about what would happen to Nosey if I didn't turn up, what he'd say to me, and what would happen to my reputation if it got around. So I just stood her back and walked out. Her eyes were still closed. I didn't even say good-bye. I knew it was all UP with us. If she'd chased, or just shouted, I'd have turned back and missed a lot of misery. But she didn't.

It was eight-thirty and I had about two hours to pass. I went on a big walk to get rid of my big ache. I walked east. It was dark and sharp. At the New Orleans Jazz Club I shunted south to the long ripple of a trumpet that cut me like a knife, but still had enough life left to wish I could play a trumpet and get rid of my misery in making some perfect sounds. Nothing expresses misery so well as a trumpet and anything that expresses misery in that way annihilates it. That's my theory. I walked downhill past a million dim windows and a thousand crouching cats, heard the coal boats screeching for the swing bridge to open, and made for the river. The water was oily. Looking upriver I could see the big bow of the bridge and all the cars rushing across to commit murder. There wasn't one bloody light out of all the thousands to cheer me up. I sat on a capstan and stared at the water. Don't know how long. I counted thirty-eight pieces of driftwood over two-feet long. Gently swaying on the edge of the pack was a spotted dog with his legs out stiff.

Dreamt I'd once been that old spotted dog, when alive. Man, I thought I was going overboard! First I was a kind of little man running around his skull. There was a glow overhead like a fluorescent in a subway and a couple of portholes that turned out to be eyes. I made a turn around this skull-room two or three times. Could hardly breathe for smells so thick you could cut them with a knife: smells I'd never smelled before. Sitting in a corner I decided I was in anyway and would have to get used to it, which I did. After a while I began to enjoy some of the smells and watch out for others. Then I made a jump up to the glow, thinking it would be nice to sit around the fire. But it wasn't a fire. It was sticky and I hung on like a fly while it took me in. I looked through the portholes, or the portholes looked through me, and got an eye-level view of fence foundations, kerbs, grass; and looked down on tarmac flowing in reverse like a conveyor. Working my four legs I could make it start, stop, go slow, faster and faster. My eyes weren't much good but I could certainly smell and the smell was as good as eyesight. I went into wind after chicken smell and made the feathers fly; it was only fun and I stopped as soon as the boots and turn-ups came into view. That's when I learned to wag my tail, and that's when the boot landed.

It was dark inside the water. I couldn't move my legs. The water was inside and out. The smells had gone and the light was going on and off and dimming every second. The mushy stuff around me went dark and set like stone. The last thing I did was to arch the body and stretch the legs. Water was rushing in and air out and there was no radio to call for help. There's no heaven for dogs and it takes a long time to make the sea in a tidal river.

The tide was turning. Glad to be back, I got a bit of fencing out and steered old spotted dog out into the stream: he went away stiffly wagging his tail.

It took a long time for ten-fifteen to come around. After that the works began to shoot as if time, like the living spotted dog, was going on four fast legs. We walked briskly down from the Barbican and planted ourselves in the foundations of an old house, roughly four or five feet above the steps. 'Let's hope they come this way,' said Nosey. His face was yellow and his breath hummed of ale.

'Is it an ambush?'

'Call it a surprise visit,' he said. 'No time for a parley: they'll soon know what we're after.'

'You think you can make him?'

'You look after yourself; Ah've got all my work cut out.'

'What if he pulls that knife?'

'Doesn't go dancing with a knife.'

'Sure you're clean?'

He clicked his tongue. 'Listen, my pal. Trust me. Said there'd be no iron. Want to go over me with a magnet?'

'Ah'll take your word.'

We heard them laughing and talking at the head of the stairs. 'Take a poke round the corner and make sure there's only two of them,' he said. The tall one was Mick and the short one was mine. He was whistling a ceilidh tune and hitching down the steps, swaying at each hitch. He'd the tricky feet of a born boxer, and his whistle was clean, clear and accurate.

'Just two.' Turning round I caught him sliding the thing on. 'You said no iron!'

'Shut your trap.'

'Ah should have had me head –'

'Listen, either shut up or back out.'

I was determined not to let him use any iron. I was also mad because he'd pulled the wool over my eyes. Not caring about Mick and the kid, now nearly on top of us, I went for his hand.

The thing was cold and wouldn't shift: you'd think it was welded to his fingers. 'Let go, you bloody fool,' he hissed, pushing hard against my throat. I brought my elbow back and came down with the edge of the hand – at that moment all I wanted was to break his wrist, hurt him. Instead the iron went flying over the edge. The moment it hit the steps we froze, both of us, and watched it roll and fall. It made a hell of a racket. The whistling had stopped. The kid shouted, 'Who's there?'

Beside me Nosey was shaking. I realised he was giggling.

'Ach, it's just the cats,' said Mick.

'Let them pass,' breathed Nosey. The kid was whistling again, a bit strained and breathless. He knew there was something up. Their shadows drew out and danced; then they were abreast. 'Now,' breathed Nosey and jumped. Something went wrong and I heard him groan; he told me afterwards that his crotch landed right on Mick's elbow. The whistling kid was crouched like a professional, looking after himself and taking no notice of Mick's end. I jumped down and said: 'Scram!' He was as white as the driven snow, easy meat I thought. I pushed him, 'Go on!' He ducked and gave me one right on the breadbasket but not far enough down to put me out, ducking and weaving, flicking me with his left paw.

I could hear Nosey shouting: 'For Gossake, Arthur!' But I was in plenty of trouble myself with that paw whipping me up. He was a good boxer, I'll say that for him, but he was too immersed in his fun. Got on the edge of a step and wham! down he went. I saw he was counting stars and left him to it. Nosey was down on his knees with his hands across his belly and his head drooping like a lily needing water, but it was wind that he needed. My one thought was to stop Mick booting him, at the same time I was wondering if he'd pull the knife the minute I turned. Then I stood on the knuckleduster. I swiped it up and slipped it on, it was made to measure, saw Mick's foot coming out and caught it with my left hand, then straightened up and let him have it. That second when I connected was the best I've ever had and it'll last me for life. It was the neat way I tipped him and connected, the

211

crunch as I landed, the smack like when you hit the ball square with a bat, but better. He went down like a rotten chimney stack, out. Then I felt panic and went as weak as water. He lay like a sack of potatoes and I couldn't turn him. I pulled his hand out and tried to find the pulse. A few steps down the kid was watching me. 'Bloody rotten effers!' he said. 'Ye've killed him.'

'He's all right,' I said, feeling my voice go. 'Come on,' I said to Nosey. 'Let's get outa this quick.'

'Ah know your faces,' said the whistling kid. Nosey pulled himself up, still holding his middle: 'Just you talk!' he said. 'One peep, that's all, an' we'll bash your bloody brains out!'

The kid realised it was two to one, now, and kept his mouth shut. But I knew he'd talk. I was frightened in case Nosey started something else. 'Come on,' I said. Before we'd reached the top of the stairs the whistling kid was running down the stairs hell-for-leather. We did the same, away. Even the main road and plenty of traffic didn't stop us – anyway, any car that hit us would have bounced that night. A couple went into a mad swerve, partly to avoid us but partly also at the sight of Nosey running half-bent, clutching his middle like a dressed-up ape and making faces with pain. We didn't stop until we reached the far side of Venice Steps, where we scrambled through a hole in the fence. He wanted to sit down instantly but I wouldn't let him – I could still hear the whistling kid running down those steps and knew the pack would soon be out. We walked down the edge of the quay and how we didn't fall in is a miracle. I wouldn't allow him to sit down until we'd reached a street of old warehouses that masked us from the roads that ran parallel with either side of the burn.

He just stretched out on the cold stone until the spasms were finished. I watched him coldly. 'There's worse things than knives,' I said.

He rolled over: 'That's why I carried the iron.'

'You said ye wouldn't!'

'Fine pickle you'd have been in otherwise.' He started to giggle again. 'Boy, it's hard to tell who enjoyed that smack most, you or me. Soon as Ah heard Ah looked up and saw your face.'

'He never pulled the knife,' I said, ignoring the crack.

'And that's Laugh Number Two,' he giggled. 'Strike a match, kiddar … these hands are giving me bloody murder.' They were all puffed and turning black and blue. 'Pity he wasn't wearing boots,' said Nosey. 'He'd have broken every bone.'

The flame died out but I'd noticed that he was more interested in my face than his hands – a good general always thinks of his men, and that's a laugh.

'What d'ye mean, Laugh Number Two?'

'That Father made them turn the iron in; bet he'll be wantin' it back now.'

I didn't say a word. I was thinking that this was the way things turned out – if anything went wrong with Mick it would be me for the high jump.

'Come off it,' he said. 'Sittin' there like a stone monument – what's up?'

'Thinkin' what a bastard you are …'

'Because Ah pitched a yarn! Ye should know me by now – Ah knew ye'd turn up trumps in a caper like this. Could have had Mousey or Roly-Poly for the asking, but it was you Ah wanted to make sure his goose was cooked good and proper. Which it is, and thanks to you.'

'Never mind that,' I said. 'You've led me up the garden path good and proper … Teresa never asked you to beat him up, and that's a fact.'

'Another yarn, that's true,' he said. He'd stopped giggling. I knew I'd touched a sore point.

'Okay,' I said. 'Out with it – Ah might do time for this one, so Ah might as well know the full strength.'

He sat a long time. I got up and this time I was really mad, ice-cold, and hearing myself shout. 'Okay,' he said. 'Here it is. I got her wrong, that's what happened. Three months gone now.'

'Why you stupid bastard,' I said. 'Will beating up Mick help her – you can marry her, can't ye?'

'No,' he said.

'What's to stop ye?'

'Them,' he said. 'Expected her old woman to come and see my old woman – usual thing. She didn't. Teresa stopped work. Went down to their house. Bloody Irish pigsty. Said Ah wanted to marry her. Mick and the old man were out – ye know what the old woman said? Said she'd rather see Teresa burn in hell than marry a rat like me – said they'd send her away …'

I couldn't say anything. For anybody to be considered too low to marry a girl they'd got into trouble was something right out of my experience. For the first time that night I began to feel sympathy for him. 'Ye know what she said? She said: "Get outa my house – you stink." Stink!'

'What did ye do?'

'Crawled out, that's what Ah did … Ah wish Ah'd got him with the iron – he wouldn't have breathed again.'

'Ye're well out of it,' I said.

'Ah'll never see her again,' he said. 'Not now, Ah won't.'

I suddenly realised that this was his choice. It was that Spanish pride boiling over. 'Ah wouldn't say that.'

'You watch,' he said. 'You watch! Ah wouldn't marry her now if she went down on her knees.'

There was nothing to say. We sat maybe thirty minutes and at one time during this period I discovered that I was still wearing the iron. I pulled it off. It was sticky. We were sitting in a narrow alley maybe twenty yards back from the burn, but I didn't miss. Hearing the splash Nosey looked up. 'God knows where Ah'll get another,' he said.

'That's your problem, kiddar,' I said.

He laughed. 'Pipe down on the laughs,' I said. 'Mick might be dead, you know.'

'Ye'd need a ten-pound hammer for that!' I turned away. He put his hand on my shoulder. 'Come out of it, kiddar,' he said. 'He'll be swilling hot tea this very minute.' Somehow I believed him. A few minutes later we made our way out of the warehouse territory and over the road into the ravine. There wasn't a soul astir. Nosey started to whistle Colonel Bogey and in spite of myself I hitched into step with him and joined in alto. The cobbles rang out like drums. Over the hump-backed bridge we marched and looked down and saw the moon dead centre over an old bicycle wheel. Up on the hillside we saw the one lighted window of Nettlefold's cottage. 'Wonder if Crab's there tonight?' said Nosey.

'Ah'm not interested.'

'Funny thing,' he remarked, 'the door's open.'

'Maybe they're coolin' off.'

'Ach, no. Old Charlie should be in by now.' He stood biting his fingernails, and I moved on. 'Arthur.' I carried on. 'Arthur – can ye hear that noise?' There was such a note in his voice that I had to stop and listen. There *was* a noise. Nosey came up to me and took hold of my arm: 'Have ye ever heard anything like that?' We stood and listened together.

'Let's go up and see what's happening.'

'Old Charlie's been belting the dog,' I said. 'He's probably crazy-drunk. Best to stay clear.'

'That's no dog.' I knew he was right and wanted to run. I'd never heard a noise like this before.

'Come on, let's get out of it.'

'There's something happening up there,' said Nosey. 'Let's see.' We walked uphill. 'That dog should have been barking her head off by now,' said Nosey.

'She's inside.'

'They never take her inside.'

When the man appeared in the doorway we ducked sharp. Through the fence we could only see his trousers and shoes. The shoes shone in the light from inside, like the stuff on puss-willow; they were those high yellow suede sneakers. Could see him shuffle to look back. He didn't speak. 'Let's get away from this gate!' I whispered. I heard the man turn sharply. 'Who's there?' he said. He wasn't listening or he'd have heard my heart rush up to my gullet like a stone in a geyser. I knew the voice. He came walking over the yard towards the fence. 'Come out of it!' Nosey's hand was squeezing my arm until it seemed no thicker than a pipe stem. 'Oh, God,' said the man. From the note I realised it was he who'd made the noise – crying. He walked back to the door and closed it and while he was doing this we were inching away from the gate. We couldn't see through the fence for piles of scrap, but we heard him walking again, heard the scraping of his feet as he hesitated and turned, heard the door open once more.

That's when we really started crawling.

He wasn't in long and we didn't hear any talking. He walked through the gate without looking anywhere but in front. About twenty yards away from the gate he started running. We watched him pound over the bridge and there a funny thing happened: he pulled up and looked over, into the water. 'Not there, kiddar!' said Nosey under his breath. Whatever it was that Nosey didn't want him to do, he didn't. Then he started running again.

'You saw who it was?' asked Nosey. I nodded. 'Don't ever say anything about what you've seen tonight, Arthur,' he said.

We got up from the ground and walked back to the gate. Now we knew why he'd gone back. The light was out. 'Look!' said Nosey. He didn't need to tell me. The Alsatian bitch was lying on her side, her tongue out and her head at any angle. The chain was lying slack but you could see it had been at full length. You couldn't see the hole in her head for blood.

The house was sitting quiet.

ELEVEN

1

Since then I've heard that it used to be called Maundy Thursday. In the old days the Kings used to come out to the palace gates and wash the feet of the poor and give them alms. They humbled themselves. That's funny.

Maunday Thursday brought me a humbling, which I didn't want and yet for which I'd asked. I was late in getting to bed and a long time in going to sleep, and when calling-up time came I didn't want it. Not that I was wanting hard to sleep. I was lying curled up on my side with my knees pressed against the weight of my belly, knowing it wasn't a bad dream I'd been having but still hoping I'd go off again and awake a second time the right way. I was lying there from the first buzz of the alarum, heard the Old Lady get out of bed and patter downstairs, heard the little movements she made in the kitchen, heard the kettle blowing off: each noise was a little hammer knocking me back into myself. In the end I was wishing I'd die. But I didn't.

'My God, ye took some shifting this morning,' she said. The cold yellow of her eyes was a dead match for the bloody awful plastic hair-curlers she wore, which I always hated from knee-height on.

'You took bloody good care Ah shifted.'

'Oh, go on,' she said. 'Lie on. We can afford it. What counts with you is what happens after work; and that's nobody's business.'

'That's right – my business.'

'When are ye gonna settle? Square yourself up. Act like some-body with a bit sense. Ye've got me worried outa me wits.'

'Every bloody meal in this house is slanging time,' I said.

'And it will be until ye settle,' she rattled. 'Where were ye last night, anyway?'

'Told ye Ah was at the Golden Bowl.'

'With your clothes up to the neck the way they were! Who do you think Ah am – Mary Jane from Strawberry Lane?'

'Ah, Ah, you said it.'

'Go on,' she cried, 'make a mock of me – a mock of your own mother! That's just about your gannin': but if you don't watch out ye'll be in trouble.'

'Okay, then, Ah'll be in trouble,' I said, banging down my knife and fork and leaving the table. 'But there's one bloody certainty – Ah've had plenty of practice in this house, one way and another …'

She was crying when I left the house. Nearly drove me crackers to hear her. There's cruelty for you. When a woman sits in a corner and shrinks up into herself and gives herself up to weeping you can call it a day.

But I had worse things on my mind.

What with the argument and slow pedalling and feverish thinking, I was ten minutes late for work. Sprogget gave me hell. He let out a shout and immediately every manjack, barring old George Flack, started drumming on the nearest piece of metal. I shoved the bike against the shed and waited for the music to die. There was a gun-metal sky and a sort of creeping mist that didn't improve the wreckage of factories, power-stations, and blasted earth. The river flowed like treacle. Sprogget was defi-nitely cast for the part to play against this backcloth.

He circled like a timber wolf. 'Been out on the tiles?' he purred. 'Or maybe ye've sat up all night worrying about your work?'

'If Ah was in your shoes that might make sense,' I said.

'You're headin' for a walk home with your cards in your hands.'

'That would be a bloody relief.'

'For us it would,' he said. 'You go around with a frigging dream in your head an' expect everybody to kow-tow. Well, me lad, you're gonna get a sharp awakening pretty soon. You're gonna come out of that beautiful dream and find that you're nowhere near bein' cock o' the midden yet.'

'Might be a day of reckoning for more than me.'

'If ye're here – but maybe ye'll have been promoted by then,' he said. 'To Borstal, or one of them other high-class colleges ...'

'What d'ye mean – Borstal?'

'Assault an' battery,' he said. 'Tacklin' innercent bits of lads in the dark with knuckle-dusters an' bicycle chains. Real tough gangster stuff that Ol' Joe Kelly was reel pleased about it – was having a noggin with him when they came in an' told him his lad was knocked up – down wi' his glass and up and outs.' He laughed softly. 'Straight up to the slops when he saw the state his lad was in an' afore ye could say Bob's your uncle they were back with a bloody great car and a notebook – into which went *your* name ...'

After a while he said: 'Got nothin' to say for yourself. *That* shut your gob, eh?' he said, staring. 'Suppose the Johnnie Bobbies'll be waitin' for ye tonight when ye go in. Always very polite ... while they're easin' a statement outa ye ... nothin' to worry about.'

I got pitched in. And glad to. A couple of the characters were off on an early holiday so I found myself with old Flack at the bottom of the dig. It had been raining during the night and the pump was half-hearted and not up to the job anyhow. We were scruffing off the two feet of bottom and sides where we'd hit stone, the kind that old George called a hard post. In half an hour our boots were sopping and we were up to the eyes. Those windy picks have a two-way effect in wet weather; they hammer into your hands and give you pins and needles, and they also cough up tiny splinters like coffee grounds into your eyes and nostrils and also between your hand and the handle. It was just dandy, like digging your own grave, with picks and the shovel going like an orchestra in hell. Now and then the pure misery of being there

hit me and I became conscious of that music and then was cata-
pulted back into my thoughts again. I was thinking of slops and
courts and what the Old Lady would say when she heard I was in
it up to the neck; and on top of that a witness in a murder case.

Nosey had said, last thing before we parted, keep your trap
shut, kiddar.

But they'd find out that we knew, for sure. They'd want to
know the far end of everything that had happened and they'd
winkle it out of us – well, maybe not Nosey, but me for sure.
They'd prop me up in a chair with a lamp shining in my face
and ask questions till I'd be glad to give. Then I'd wait in a
room until a voice called my name and I'd walk in and everybody would look at me; the lawmen, the jury, the judge (with
his glasses perched on the end of his nose), Nosey's Old Lady and
Old Man and the rest of the family, and finally Crab himself.

They'd all give me a good, long look. And I'd remember that
first day on the clay banks when Crab and me lay in the sun and
talked about the jam pot.

Then I remembered something else Nosey had said: 'He's
turned eighteen; he shot the gun; they can stretch him for that.'

Most of the morning Sprogget stood with his hands in his
pockets watching us. In the end I couldn't stand him any longer.
I turned off the wind and shouted: 'You wanta get a mechanic
down here and get this pump working 'stead of standing there
like God Almighty.'

'You get used to it – Dartmoor's a dam' sight worse,' he said,
and strolled away.

'Were you in that lot last night?' asked old George. I nodded.
'Daft thing to do,' he said.

'Ah didn't know the other lad was carrying iron,' I said.

'Still a daft thing to do,' he said.

'You mind your own bloody business,' I said.

'Know what it's like to run, now?' he asked, bending down to
turn on the wind. 'Know what that teacher felt like when ye had
him on the run …'

'You turnin' against me now, George?'

He shook his head. 'Ah wish ye were well outa it, lad. Don't like to see anybody take the wrong turnin' … but it's time ye were puttin' your thinkin' cap on. Stop bein' so pig-headed. Think what ye're doin'. Ye've a chance to make something of yourself, like my nephew, but better'n him. Get on intelligent without putting your boot in folks' faces.'

I knew he was a good old sport but I was too full-up to tell him he was right. The way I saw it I was in too deep to get out. The only thing was maybe to scarper before the slops took me in and laid a charge. I could imagine Mousey Hole and Dopey and all the rest hatching up a lifelong nickname, worse than Pretty Boy, say just The Snitch, or The Squealer, or The Crawler.

Once Uncle George came along and stood watching me. He had his hands behind his back and seemed to be weighing me up; I could nearly hear his tongue clicking. When we knocked off at twelve for bait he walked up and said: 'Hear you've got yourself in a bit of a mess?'

All mush inside I managed to mutter: 'That's to be seen.'

'Aye,' he said, 'that's to be seen, me lad.' I was in it up to the neck. 'Fine name you've given the family,' he said.

All I could think of was the injustice of it all. There was him and Sprogget licking the fat off every week at a bob a run, calling at a quiet little pub I won't mention and sitting in a back room until a character sits down beside them, orders a pint, sups off, and when he's gone he's left a nice fat envelope in Uncle George's jacket pocket. And these are the pious bastards that spout social security and all the rest and maybe one or two of there'll be sitting in judgement on me, along with the money-men that have more up their sleeves than Uncle George and Sam ever dreamed of and can afford to sniff at the problem-kids because they never dream of associating their big knock-offs with what goes on in the back streets.

And maybe an ex-bloody brigadier or what have you sitting there too with a regimental tie and a background that started with poison gas and finished up with tactical weapons, which is what they call the nice little A or H bombs.

All sitting there and looking down their noses, which it so happens they've just lifted from the trough, in which their feet and hands have also been.

Not that it does you any good to know all this, whether you pick it up like I did, or know it in your bones, like Nosey and the rest of the lads. I wandered out and sat in the cab of the mechanical shovel to eat slices of compressed sawdust and ham with the goodness mangled out of it, all on my own.

I came to with my mouth open and half a sandwich in my hand, the cause a voice saying: 'What's the strength?' It was Nosey.

'Boy, we're in trouble,' I told him. 'You off work?'

'Catch me being available,' he said. 'I've been lookin' for our kiddar ... he's nowhere around. There'll be no trouble if we keep our mouths shut.'

'Ah'm not talking about *that*. It's the other thing. Mick Kelly's Old Man went to the slops last night ...'

He raised his eyebrows. 'Wish that was all we had to worry about.'

'They'll root it out of us, Nosey.'

'Not if we keep our heads ... until he's had time to clear outa the country.'

'Did it happen – what we thought?'

'Two black cars parked there first thing this morning. Slops crawling all over the place ...'

'You haven't been down!'

'Rest yourself – Ah've more sense than that! Walked over the bridge and cast a glance passing by.'

'What do we do?'

'Lay low, that's all. Keep our traps shut. Go on as if nothing had happened, that's all.'

'It's all right for you,' I said. 'You're used to it!'

'What, murder, treble murder?' he softly said.

'Jesus ... what d'ye mean, treble murder?'

'Man, dog, woman,' he said, so casually he made my stomach roll. 'Came in, paralytic, an' got the full blast.'

'It'll not take them long to find out who ...'

'You're playing chess now, kiddar – Ah twigged that last night. They'll soon enough plump on *him*, but if they take long enough he might dissolve. If they *catch* him ...'

'Well?' I probed.

'If they catch him he'll need all the cards stacked. What we saw might be sufficient to tip the trap. So we keep ours shut. All the time, for ever, understand.' I nodded. 'Can you do that?' he said. 'Have ye enough gumption to play it that way?'

'Ah'll try,' I said, and knew he'd picked up my lack of conviction.

'You'd bloody well better,' he said. 'Failing that, you just might as well take a walk down the river, now. Because – and listen carefully, kiddar – if he swings through you, Ah'll swing for you. That's all.' Without a smile or a nod he took off down the bank, towards the river; at the last ridge, where he knew that a steep plunge of the ground would take him out of eyeshot, he turned. Even at that distance he was all eyes: and they stabbed me. And I knew that, whether I squealed or not, he was my enemy. Our friendship wasn't worth a brass farthing. Me and the world were his enemy, but me in particular because he knew me.

2

I think I'd have done it anyhow, but the pair of them signed and sealed it when knocking-off time came round. Because it was payday and holiday time as well we knocked off about quarter of an hour earlier. I was maybe fifth or sixth in line. As usual Sam was dishing out the packets and Uncle George checking off.

'There's a bit of paper in yours you'd better read,' said Sprogget. I tore the thing open. It took me a while to fish out the paper and because it was cream (but not black-edged) I knew what it was about before I read it. The Boot, Sack, Kick or whatever.

'What for?' I demanded.

'Well, y'see, the job's nearly finished, an' we're cuttin' down,' said Sprogget. The smile was just below, to fool the others.

'Pipe down,' I said. 'Ah'm speaking to my Uncle George – what for?'

'He's told ye,' said Uncle George with a stiff face I could have relaxed a bit for him.

'Who else, then?'

'You're the only one. Ah'm sorry.'

'Ah'll never forget this,' I said. 'Ah should have had me head examined for takin' the job – from you.' I turned round on the others. 'How about the Union – what do Ah get for me two bob a fortnight?' The better ones looked down at their boots; Sam's pals laughed. 'All right,' I continued, 'Ah get the point – Ah'm out, not being one of the forty thieves.'

'Cut that out, boy,' said Uncle George. He wouldn't meet my eye. The man next in line pushed forward and they went on with the paying out. Names called, signatures signed, same old jokes, everything moving but me, the old frozen rock of which nobody took any notice.

When I got out my eyes were too blurred for riding. I started walking the bike uphill. I was dead-beat, dead-scared, touching bottom. Don't know how I wheeled it. All I wanted was somewhere to be myself, and maybe have a good cry.

'Hey, there – Arthur!' It was old George Flack. 'Ah've been shoutin' after ye this last five minutes,' he complained.

I told him I was sorry and went back into my personal shell, snap, like when you poke at a snail. Nobody existed but me and my troubles.

'Ah'm sorry about your notice,' he said. 'But listen, kiddar; don't take it to heart: you're well out.'

'Oh, Ah'll get over it.'

'It never rains but it pours,' he said, shaking his head.

'What d'ye mean?'

'Heard you an' that other lad talkin',' he said. 'Down in the dig. Not all of it, just enough. One thing ye'll have to learn is keep your voice down.'

I stopped dead. 'You know what it's all about, George?'

He nodded. 'Enough to put two an' two together. You're in trouble an' somebody's in worse.'

'Ye won't tell?' He shook his head.

'Honest to God, George, Ah've never been in worse trouble all me life … it was a murder, like the one you told me about when we found the gun.' I went on, words tumbling out red-hot whilst inside I was curled up in cold fear.

'Don't let it get you down, kiddar,' he said. 'You're like me, too much bloody imagination, but ye'll live through it.'

When we reached the main road he shook my hand. 'So long, son. Dinna' do anything desperate. Just live through it, do nothing, let things happen to you, like the pebble on the sea-shore let the waves come and go. It'll come to an end.'

'Thanks, George,' I said, searching for a word to express my gratitude. 'Ah hope we meet again. And thanks – for everything.'

'Think nothing of it,' he said. 'Ah'm on your side.' He was the first one ever to say that to me. Old man turned sixty, me just turned sixteen, but he knew. We had the same disease, I reckon. Trench-fever, shell-shock, confirmed, sleep-walking over something soft that gives and isn't a carpet. Ah, ah, ah! I love that old man.

So I jumped on my bike and took the road east, first south, turning down a crooked cobbled street where half the houses were empty of people and full of filth, until I reached the river again. I stuck my old steed against a wall, jumped a fence, and made my way to the dig almost happy at the thought.

As far as I could make it out my timing was spot on but, remembering my training under Nosey, I double-checked. There was nobody in the shed. The door was open. I nipped in, picked up the stack of lorry checks and chucked them in the fire. That's the mood I was in. I knew the figure was reckoned out well in advance and that the cash was waiting for them in some quiet pub. The checks didn't count, but the cash would be delayed. Somebody on the paying end might get a scare as a result of this. I watched the checks flare up, blacken, crumble and collapse. I wish you could do the same with the twisters. The Pastor would do it with their souls, but I'd settle for their bodies.

I went down to the dig, the clay sucking at my boots, and remembered old George green-as-they-come on his way over Hill 60. Maybe that's what gave me the idea in the first place.

I could hear them talking inside the big pipe, fifty yards from the end, still moving up. I knew they were making up to the junction, to check on some brickwork; that had brought me back. The cleats of their boots echoed like cracked bells. Their voices were low but swelling like the sea. Nipping back to the shed I picked up a couple of shovels – make them both work. I ran all the way back stopping only to switch on the engine, and shoved the shovels gently inside the pipe. As I let go one handle spun round and sang out. Sprogget said: 'What's that? Did ye hear that?'

'Hear what?' said Uncle George.

'Heard something scuffle.'

Something got hold of me. Coming home from the Regent or Albion in the happy times we used to have a laughing go-as-you-please competition. We used to do the 'Happy Jack' laughter you hear on the playground; falsetto crazy women laughter; laughter of mad scientists and things from outer space; assorted chuckles; kiddy laughter, girlish laughter, gossipy-women laughter, deep, deep men's laughter. Try it some time, it's hard work but it's fun and maybe some day it may come in useful. I did a laugh from the haunted house I once heard in an old Abbott and Costello picture. I really let go and kept it going for five minutes. Then I stopped. You couldn't hear a thing but the sound of their breathing as they tried to make up their minds to come or go. I felt like shouting, 'Dig this,' but discarded it as being childish apart from giving the game away.

Then I nipped back to the mechanical shovel – and not per-chance to dream with a sandwich in my hand! She was grunting like a little pig. Warmed up and ready to go. Down went the bucket into the waiting stockpile. Whoa! Slide her, slide her, nicely forward until she's brimming with half a ton of nicely blended graveyard clay and post stone: stiff cream to congeal around your teeth and nuts you'll never crack. Reverse, lift, swing, release. A cascade of the beautiful stuff went pouring over the pipe-end and, without bothering to wait for a target check, I swung the bucket back into action: in five minutes flat I never played a wrong note and cleared eight to ten ton.

Then I knocked off the engine.

They were yelling blue murder inside but I wasn't listening. Jesus, I was too proud of myself. I'd handled that machine better than a professional. I didn't even have to look at the end of the pipe to know it was well and truly blocked. This was me and the machine and that was all I could think about. I went into a beauti-ful golden dream. Arthur Haggerston brings Atomic Submarine successfully below both poles in ten days flat; Arthur Haggerston touches down on Mars, Venus, Jupiter in tremendous treble planet conquest; Haggerston, human computer, surges to stars, etc …

I came out of my trance. God knows how long they'd been doing the trapped miner stunt with the torch, but there it was, knock, knock, who's there? Knock, knock, knock, knock! For Chrissakes get us out of this! Only then did I saunter over. They'd never handled a shovel, the pair of them, in ten or twelve years. Their hands were soft and their guts riddled with brown ale, Scotch ale, bitter and contractors' cheap whisky. My reckoning was: first they'd try to tunnel out and would bury each other in turn. Then after resting from a tug o' war in the dark they'd shift one half inside the pipe until they'd walled themselves in. Then, with the air hot and foul, they'd hit on the correct solution: casting in line to spread the stuff twenty yards or so up the pipe. Dead reckoning in ordinary time? Six hours going it hard. Nightmare time? Six months stretched out into six years in the dour and dripping dark. Unless some wandering child heard their racket and brought help.

Inspiration came. I picked up a spanner and straddled the pipe at the nearest joint. They got the message quickly that their drumming drowned mine, which is saying something, for I only beat three.

Disguising my voice: 'Hello, what's going on in there?'

Uncle George's voice boomed and echoed: 'Some maniac tipped a lorryload of stuff over the pipe-end … we're trapped … can you get help? Get us out, please.'

I liked the 'please'. 'Can't you get out the way you came in?'

For five good minutes there was bedlam with booms tripping over echoes, Uncle George weeping, Sprogget spouting enough filth to overload every sewer in the city.

'Who's that?' yelled Sprogget.

'Police constable,' I said from my belly.

'Get effing moving!'

'No need to get personal,' I said. 'Wait till Ah have a look at this load.' I sat tight and held myself, then tapped on the pipe once more. 'Hope ye've plenty of grub down there,' I said.

This time it wasn't from the belly. Uncle George tipped it and made the mistake of saying my name. I floated away. Passing the shed, I could still hear Sprogget raving. In spite of my load of misery I was laughing and liking it. Some day I'll buy myself one of those machines, plus a stretch of concrete pipe, whatever the cost. Not to use. Just for laughs.

3

'You've got an appetite on ye!' said the Old Lady.

Since I was eating like a condemned man she had every right to comment. I made the two lamb chops stretch out for three helpings of mashed tatie, three of peas, three of cabbage, three cake-tin Yorkshire puddings, and half a gallon of gravy. Plus a medium sized rice pudding with raisins, top of the milk bottle, and half a pound of sugar, topping up with six fig rolls and three cups of tea. Mind you, they were only small cups. Not being able to tell her that I was a man on the run, I only remarked that an appetite like mine and cooking like hers just had to be happy together. She liked that.

'Ah've been thinking,' she said.

'Think quick, please,' I said. 'I've a big date tonight.'

'None of that rough stuff again, Ah hope,' she said.

'No, Ma,' I said. 'Ah'm finished with that.'

'For the sixth or seventh time,' she said, 'Ah'm pleased to hear it. It's time …'

'You were thinking?' I said quickly.

'Oh, nothing, it was just a dream.'

'Come on, Ma, less of the *Woman's Mirror* and more of the give,' I wheedled.

In the end it came out. 'When everything's squared up,' she said. 'When me and Harry can get married – you don't mind us getting married? – we'll have a real holiday, maybe at Scarborough, or Whitby or one of them holiday camps, an' just relax. And maybe you can bring your girlfriend – that Dorothy.'

'Why wait till you get married?' She was really shocked at this one.

'Arthur, Ah don't know where ye get your ideas from! We couldn't go off like that … not without being married.'

'All right,' I said, 'when you and Harry get married we all go off together and have a rare old time. That's a promise.'

She was looking at me with big eyes.

'Now what have Ah said?'

'You said Harry – that's the first time in ages you've called him by his first name.'

'There's many a worse,' I said, and went upstairs and got changed. Downstairs the Old Lady was giving the latest lyric the works. How she picked them up is nobody's business. I changed into my business suit: twills, pullover, cord jerkin, and stuffed a pair of clean underpants and body shirt under the latter. What with loose change and savings I had two pounds eight and fourpence in the bank, plus a bar of nut-milk chocolate two years old stashed away for just such an emergency. I prised up the floorboard and took out a bit of flannel in which I'd wrapped the old ring. I scribbled a note to the Old Lady saying that this would do for a new engagement ring, and that I hoped it would bring better luck than the last. On second thoughts I shoved this one in my pocket and scribbled another one which was restricted to the item about it doing for a new ring and I hoped Harry and her would make a go of it. I added a PS saying I'd write. For a man who habitually used his home as an hotel, I found myself feeling something like heartbroken.

In short, I didn't want to go.

Those who feel like horse-laughing might like to be reminded that the solid soft gold of sentiment lies below hard rock and beer-bearing strata alike. Even cops and judges have it.

I laid the ring on the notepaper and did a mickey as soon as I heard the front doorbell go and the Old Lady march to answer it. I didn't even look to see whether it was Harry or the plain-clothes men. Just hopped it with my heart in my mouth. Pedalled through the dark night under the blazing orange trees with my feet and nothing else going: the rest of me was just a mass of gum shot full of novocaine.

Until I spun away over the big bridge and cast a look down, as had Nosey before me, and saw the yellow glow in the window and the black shark of that cop car lying, patiently waiting.

4

I hadn't a plan in mind and had nowhere to go, but wasn't worry-ing: in fact, I was well below the worrying mark. Some time your feet have got to touch bottom and then you begin to shoot up to surface. This happened to me about two miles out of the city. There's a big hill with an avenue of those orange trees I men-tioned earlier and I remember what a moiling it was going up, thinking it was near-on endless and maybe a bit of hell, with the corpse lights from those bloody fluorescent fruits staining my hands and the tips of my shoes as they came around. At last my feet were pushing against nothing and I realised I'd reached the summit. Funny, that, you don't dream of stopping on the way up but the minute you make it you want to meditate.

Which I did.

The avenue of rotten oranges looped away to the city. They were simple. The other lights were fighting like hell for existence. Street lamps; window lights; pub signs; winking beacons; glass factories like Perspex boxes all lit up for lonely wandering watchmen, roaming like caged hyenas and wondering when and where to kip; advertising neons; car headlamps twisting and turning like indicators of some hellish map; railway signal cabins suspended on invisible stilts and bridge signals over the tracks winking like fruit machines. The sky was shattered with the reflection. It looked as if any minute it was going to blow up. Suddenly I felt so small. There was this great bloody mass of bricks and steel, tarmac and light, all wired up for misery. What was I running away from? From a little bit of misery that was just a drop in the bucket compared with what some of the quarter of a million hidden below the lights had suffered since I first started to climb the hill. I nearly turned back until it occurred to me to think of Mick Kelly, Crab, Nosey and the Old Lady. Too much trouble. Snip go the wirecutters. Nobody would ever have the opportunity to call me squealer, etc., because I wasn't going to be around when squealing time arrived. This was simple. This solved everything. Sacked, wanted by the police on one score they knew and another they didn't, it was better to ride away, the way they all do.

I rode away, pushing the makings back into my breast pocket, aware that even those phoneys on the Westerns settled somebody's hash and cleared the case before riding away.

I rode maybe seven or eight miles due west then grew tired of a road like a ruler and took a by-road winding away downhill. It swooshed like a roller-coaster track and had some sweet bends.

There was nothing to do but navigate and think, so I restricted myself to the former. I went through a metropolis with sixteen houses, and a pub in which three customers went through some yoga exercises to a sleepy piano; skimmed over a narrow bridge and heard fresh water sixteen feet below, beat a crossing gate and broke my heart on the steepest bank north of the Alps. This hill continued for two miles, one and a half of which I walked, and grateful. This time I didn't stop to look back but simply jumped on and took off. By now something was bothering me. I'd never slept away from home before and certainly never under the sky. That's a lie: went to a couple of school camps, but that doesn't count because with thirty or forty more characters around you can always play gin rummy to ease the boredom and homesickness. I thought about a pub and squashed the idea, being convinced my picture was already printed and circulated, so that even village bluebottles ten miles from civilisation would know it by heart. I kept an eye pinned for a barn and that's a laugh: they don't have them anymore.

In the end I decided to ride all night and sleep as soon as the sun was up. But it was tiring. I was making into hilly country and it's sure thing that where there's an up there's a down. And it was bloody lonely.

Ah, but it was bloody lonely out there, riding nowhere and away from home. The moon above was licking along at about sixty miles an hour. Fir trees stood up like iron spikes. It wasn't so bad so long as I had the wind at the back of me, but getting on for ten o'clock it did a complete switch and from then on, boy, it was a battle just to move. A couple of miles farther on I threw in the towel.

This was how it happened: there was a solitary house at the edge of the road, one of those lodges lying through a couple of big pillars with big balls mounted on top, the biggest I'd ever seen. Beyond was a bit of a garden flooded with a light so warm and mellow it made my heart leap. Leaving the bike I crept up the garden path. It was so thick with moss it felt like walking on a carpet with a three-inch pile. All I wanted was that window. It sucked at me like a sugar and soap poultice. I took one or two quick looks, like a scared bird pecking, before I realised there was nothing to worry about. Inside, in front of a television set, were a woman and a girl. They had half an eye for the screen and the rest for wool. You know the caper – one holds the hank, the other winds into a ball. The one holding the hank was a girl with a gamin crop and a nice neck, which is the advantage of those short crops, and if you haven't a nice neck then forget the idea. She was rolling like a sailor to allow the wool to run. The woman with the ball was old, fortyish, with white hair and rosy cheeks. They both had nice smiles; I could hear the even ripple of their talk. It was good, you could almost hold your hands at their warmth rather than the nice glowing fire. I'd have given all my two quid and loose change to have been able to go in there and say, 'How do!' and get a smile from the dark girl with the luscious neck and a good strong cup of tea from the woman. For a moment I thought of knocking at the door and throwing myself on their mercy; poor orphan making it to Penrith and a job with my uncle.

Then something funny happened. The woman took the last of the wool into the ball, threw it in the air with a laugh, and got up and put it on the high mantelpiece. It was a high mantelpiece and she had to stretch to reach it. She was wearing a woollen dress with a leather belt and it stretched right up. She had the most wonderful legs I've ever seen; underneath the skirt I could see her flanks.

I felt so desolate I could have rushed in and embraced her legs, kneeling to do it, I was so certain there was comfort there. I was almost crazy enough to do it. Some types do it, and I can understand what makes them – loneliness and the feeling that a strange woman can offer comfort. So they rush in, and she screams, bites her hand, claws him, and that's the finish.

I didn't know how quickly to get away from that window.

TWELVE

1

Ever tried to kip out on a cold night? Took a trip round the back of the cottage, hoping to find a shed, only to find a tall wall with enough broken glass cemented in to break a brewer's heart.

Pushed on into the interior. Quarter of a mile on explored a thick bunch of fir-trees and was confronted by a regiment of little red eyes. Realised they were pheasants, stretched out and got peppered for my pains – domesticated but not house-trained. Picked up my bike and pushed on.

Passed a big building like something out of 'The Sign of the Cross'; great bare porch, cold flagstones, beautiful stained glass windows and the decaying corpse of an old American organ put out for the vultures to strip. The door was locked. Walked on and met an animal with a long nose, sympathetic eyes and one leg lifted for the word go. Didn't like my smell and off he went, almost airborne.

Pushed on into the interior, passing a big building, minus some of the walls, most of the roof and all of the glass. It was full of bushes growing between stone blocks. Something scuffled and I shot off faster than the animal. The drive gave a last wiggle of its tail, lost its packed earth quality and became a cobbled road splitting off into two which curved apart to meet again in front of a ghost of a house with three rows of windows, fake battlements and a splendid doorway like the opening to a cave, through which

I pushed myself and the bike. There was a room almost as big as the Regent ballroom and a fireplace that could have been double swingdoors until you saw the chimney-flue squinting at the roof a billion miles away.

Piles of rubble, timber, plaster everywhere as I swung round with cycle lamp in my hand. Left turn, the biggest tapeworm on earth had been having fun chewing everything in sight and leaving a trail of nettles. Right turn, passing a dozen or so rooms of varying sizes where the beams hung down with plaster brattice attached like immense kippers picked clean.

At the end of the passage was a room that looked like a kitchen. There was a big cast-iron range and a collapsed sink. Up above my lamp couldn't find any of the fancy plaster border I'd seen in the other rooms – rabbits or maybe hares, oakleaves, ears of corn. I found another doorway. There was no step, just another passage going down, but a passage under cover. It was like a cave. There were little rooms on one side, each lined with stone boxes. There were bits of thick glass scattered around; in one box there was one whole bottle, very heavy and very empty.

Beyond these rooms the passage gave a hiccup, went skidding into a steeper gradient ending in an empty space into which I nearly walked. I don't know what stopped me from going through. It went down like a cliff for maybe fifteen or twenty feet and ended on the edge of a ravine overhung with bushes. Underneath the bushes I could hear something playing a tiny xylophone. I imagined myself lying there day and night, looking up through the branches and listening to the water tinkling: waiting to die of starvation weakness – they say you last longer with water. Round the corner I thought I saw a glow and snapped off the lamp. It was a fire shining through the window of what looked like a kind of basement. Liking the look of that fire I backtracked to the upper regions and walked round. Heard funny noises and some things skittling about. Halfway down I stopped to wonder whose fire it was. I stood maybe a couple of seconds and looked around and up at the scudding clouds tearing the moon to bits. I decided I was more frightened of all this than whatever was down below, and carried on.

Of course, I didn't walk straight in. First I found a window. It actually had glass in it, through which I could see this character sitting nearly on top of a wood fire. He kept stirring it with a stick, and I imagined a trout cooking or at least a kettle on the boil. At the worst, a tin of baked beans. I walked on and made a row and when I walked through the doorway, which had been hanging on one hinge for a couple of centuries, the character was up and in a corner ready to fight. He had a beard that hadn't been trimmed for a couple of months and bloodshot eyes. Also a nose. I'm mentioning the nose because it was a hell of a nose. It had a twist in it and looked bigger than his beard, which was, of course, an optical illusion.

Well, I walked in and tried not to look at his nose, beard or flies. God knows why but on my way in I chirped: 'Okay, *me friend.*' He didn't say anything but, boy, was he humming! He stank like an otter; not the beer smell, more like rotten eggs and cheese that's lain on a burning ash-heap a month or so with a dollop of knacker's yard thrown in. But the place was warm and I looked around for something to sit on. There was an old pail and a deal end. All the time I was warming my hands he was half-turned away from me in his corner. I was dead-scared, but not half so much as I might have been – you see, I'd been half-expecting to find old Crab sitting there, maybe trying to rub the blood off his hands. I was so relieved that even this Nose didn't put me off. Kept rubbing my hands over the fire, giving him the birdish glance in case he gave me the rush, and wondering where the teapot was.

In the end I said: 'Have a snout?'

He just looked at me. I held out the packet. 'Fag?' I asked, just in case he didn't know his English language. 'Fag – snout, y'know.' He came out with a rush and knocked me off the pail and it was only when I looked up and saw that mighty Joe of a nose that I realised there was a bit of misunderstanding. Like most of us, he was sensitive about his flaws. I got up and walked over to him, but boy, I'm not kidding, I was shaking like a leaf. 'Listen,' I said, 'have a fag. That's all Ah said – a fag. That's what the kids call them, now – on account of the fact that they stick out.'

He grunted and took one. I gave him and me a light. He went back into his corner and stood with his back to me, dragging fifty to the dozen. The way he dragged, putting all his shoulders into it, he'd never had a snout for a century. With me it was a cup of tea, so I told him. He went over to a heap of rags in the other corner, and raked about. He brought me an empty blue can with a handle, a screw of paper with tea inside, and a tin of condensed milk. No water, naturally. I'd to go down through the bushes to get that, but I'd have gone over Everest for it. We had our tea passing the can. It was the lushest tea I've ever tasted. I rolled it round my tongue to get the hotness and sweetness and creaminess out of it and never hesitated when he handed it back. In the end he left me with it, about a quarterful, and went out. Thought he was going for a runoff, but he came back with an armful of logs and packed up the fire.

So we laid up for the night, me in my corner and he in his. I remember he was in the corner opposite the door. He didn't lie down, but sat with that old raincoat over his shoulders. He was watching me without seeming to, and I was watching him. Or so I thought. After about half an hour of this he took off the old raincoat and held it out. I said no thanks, not wanting any part of his smell, and he put the thing on again. That was the first time I noticed his eyes: they were bloodshot all right, but fundamentally they were the same as that animal's, the one I met coming in. He was just a big brute beast, absolutely harmless. After a bit he said: 'Trouble?' I nodded. He shook his head. 'Ye canna get away from them,' he said. That was all. I lay and watched him, not frightened but sort of interested. His beard was down on his chest and that long Saxon nose split his face. With his eyes it formed a cross. Once during the night I awoke and he was crying like a baby.

2

The next time it was morning and he'd gone, smell and everything but the makings and the can. That poor wrecked bastard had left me just about all the portable property he had.

I was as hungry as hell and tore into the chocolate as I went for water and waited for it to boil. Then I sat at my ease in the doorway. The sun streaming through the trees at the opposite side, birds were singing, and apart from being stiff and having a red-hot pain in the small of my back I was as happy and relaxed as I've ever been. Uncle George and Sam Sprogget had never existed. This was the life, boy! But at the same time I was pressing the uneasiness underground, wondering what the Old Lady and Harry were thinking, and if Dorothy knew or cared, or if they'd caught Crab, poor old Crab, who was just a poor wrecked bastard the same as that tramp.

In the end this uneasiness became a kind of panic and something had to be done about it, so I went down into the ravine again and washed out the tea can, washed my face, and watched these little spiders buzzing around on a pool, and wished I had a razor as I watched them, because I could feel the whiskers growing on me and the filth with them. Boy, out there you can be wrecked for the want of a razor and a piece of soap. Don't ever forget them. They're more important than food and that's a fact.

The snowdrops poking out of the grass made me feel even filthier. It was the first time I'd ever seen them separately and growing naturally, I was tempted to pick some for myself. I got hold of one. It was as thin as a needle, but soft, and sent cold stinging through my fingers. Suddenly I disliked its little wax face. There was a kid I knocked about with and liked a lot. He fell from the big grandstand at the racetrack, from the top to the bottom of the outside wall onto the tarmac and of course he was killed. They snatched me off the street the day before the funeral and took me into the sitting-room. He was lying in the box all covered up with a frilly thing around his neck. The snowdrop was like his face and his face wasn't the face of any pal.

Well, I strolled back into my bedroom, poked around a bit, tucked the tramp's gear into a corner, then departed. Kept wondering how I'd managed to spend a night in that lot and how all the tramps can face up to it, night after night, nobody to leave in the morning, nobody to come back at night, and realised that this was now my lot. I didn't like the idea, in fact I was so sick I could have thrown up. The sun shining all nice and mellow didn't help one little bit and the fact that my bike was missing was the final shot of misery. Anybody watching me, boy, would have seen the curtain come down. I ran through that Greek temple like a trapped rat, covering the sixty rooms, etc., in ten minutes flat even poking about in bramble bushes, lifting up tiny fragments of plaster and feeling under piles of timber and unhinged doors. Finally I stood like a statue, weeping internally, and when I came to, the first thing I noticed was that comical little lamp I was carrying. I imagined myself walking up-dale down-dale with a cycle lamp in my hand and laughed a hard bitter laugh which I didn't mean and threw it far enough, which means down the long corridor leading to the kitchen.

Fortunately it wasn't damaged so I carried it into the kitchen and found a spot for it in a hole in the wall which had a nice curve. Then I went into a hopeless trance, just standing; Buddha had nothing on me. But I was all activity inside, cursing that self-sacrificing Jesus Christ of a tramp who had left me the makings of a cup of tea in exchange for my two fast wheels. Thinking of his tattered backside on my polished leather saddle and his stinking feet on my bright steel pedals I wished him everything: the coil up and fester; the roll up and rot; the jump up and clag; the good old Beelzebub belt. But it was no good. Only a long time afterwards I thought that perhaps he needed that bike pretty badly, so badly he had to take it and leave me all he had – the tea and the tea-can. That's what I try to believe.

Suddenly the wind meant more than the sunshine, and the thought of going on without the bike cut me even worse than the wind. I couldn't face going on, yet I didn't like the idea of going back and being bang in the middle of it. Then, somehow – and maybe the lingering memory of the two women and the warm fire had something to do with it – the thought of going to Stella's crept into my mind. I thought of that full kitchen and comfortable living-room, the big bed with its cool starched sheets and eiderdown. I also thought of Stella. But the house came first, the house and all that she'd made of it. I couldn't go back. On the other hand, without definitely making up my mind as to where I was going I was definitely moving that way when I started. When I think of all the tricks I played that day I could cry – none of them were necessary. I crept along hedges out of sight of wrecked cottages and empty cow-byres, circled miles out of my way to avoid a farmhouse, and raced across every bridle path. All I could see was my picture in the papers. By a sort of instinct I eventually found a certain river and followed it. I knew it was the right river because I'd once worked with a character who lived near the old wreck of a house in which I'd slept, and during the war when meat was scarce he'd shot a deer and carried it all the way down on his back. Take it from me, he was the nearest thing ever to Superman. I had nothing to carry and still found it tough going. There were more barbed wire fences going down to the water edge than I can remember. It made no difference which way you tackled them, they got you. They were alive and as ravenous as wolves for your private parts. Sometimes there wasn't any shore to walk along, and you had the choice of walking in full view, in open country or a few hundred yards from a road, or wading. I waded.

I've traced it on the map. It doesn't look much. In fact I walked nearly fifteen miles, which is a long way when you're not used to walking, when you're all aches from a night on a stone-flagged floor and when your shoes and socks and the bottom of your trousers are water-logged most of the way. And when you haven't had a square meal all day and you daren't walk on the road, let alone walk into a shop for a half-pound of chocolate.

It was dusk when I reached the Tyne. I sat on the railway embankment and looked over the metals at the grey steel waters in absolute despair. I knew I was a long way from the city and the one thought in my mind was to get there – to reach Stella. There was no mistake about the latter; hunger and fatigue knock all the nonsense out of you. I watched maybe three diesels go rushing by and never saw such a lot of fat contented hogs looking out of the windows. Then a coal train came along. I sat shivering, watching it clank past, and wishing I dare risk jumping on. The signals went against it. It is possible to make a nice warm burrow between the sides of a wagon and washed nuts. I lay there, aching all over but swelling with joy at the thought of riding all the way in. After the worry of finding a jumping-off spot was nothing; anyway, after a time and after your feet have touched bottom you begin to take things as they come.

3

At nine-thirty or so I was on the wrong side of town and making rings around an empty telephone kiosk. I'd already passed three, all occupied, two with people hanging around. Everybody was ringing up his friend that night. The bits of coal in my shoes were giving me hell – chased by a railway slop over a mile of sidings the stuff had spread all over my soles. Not coal, but little rats were chewing my stomach. What frightened me about the telephone kiosk was the light blazing inside; it seemed like walking into a television studio. I darted in and discovered I'd forgotten her number, so I placed the four pennies in a row and scuffled through the book, tearing pages in my haste to be there, and when I arrived the numbers danced. In the end I had to mark her number with a pencil; afraid of losing it, or forgetting it again if I closed the book. Then I put the pennies in. The last penny wouldn't click, three times the machine rejected it. The fourth time I balanced it in the slot and struck it with my fist: this time it clicked. I rang with my heart in my boots.

She gave her name and number, and now my heart was up in my throat.

'Hullo, Stella. This is Arthur … listen, can Ah come and see you, Ah'm in trouble …'

Her voice cut in again with the name and number. I realised I was talking on a dead line because I'd forgotten to punch button A. In a panic I'd struck button B, got the jackpot and lost her voice. I started all over again.

'Oh,' she said, and then with a rush, 'Did you ring up a few minutes ago?'

'Ah got into a panic – pressed button B and got my money back.'

'You gave me a fright – there's nothing more sinister than being rung and then talking into a dead phone, or to somebody who doesn't answer … it always gives me gooseflesh.'

'Ah'm sorry, Stella,' I said, humbly. I asked again, this time conscious she could hear and was relieved to know I'd been ringing. She didn't say anything. 'Ah just want to come round and talk,' I said.

'Polly's at home,' she answered. Now it was my turn to be silent. In the end I said, 'Just for an hour,' and meant it. Anything to get out of the cold for a while and warm my bones, after which I could face anything.

'I don't want to refuse you,' she said. 'I wouldn't turn you away for worlds … d'ye know what day it is?'

I remember looking into the mirror and seeing my face, dusty like a miner's, and searching for the answer while I realised with a shock that there was no problem in taking a bus or trolley – I could pass as a workman coming off night shift. 'Why, it's Friday, Stella,' I said.

'Good Friday.'

'Ach, yes, I'd forgotten – Good Friday.'

'If it had been any day but this … I killed it a long time ago, but it still comes back. You're just a boy, you don't know, no man ever knew what it means to a woman. I don't want all that pain to start all over ...'

'Listen, Stella, Ah'm in trouble. Just let me talk to you.'

'Promise you'll just come and talk,' she said.

'Ah won't touch you.' All the same I knew it didn't mean a thing. Once there she wouldn't be able to keep her hands off me, and if she did, it would only be for a time. I knew how to lead her and was determined it would be more than talking. I was saying to myself that anybody who's slept out all night is due to a welcome and a warm bed with a woman; I was telling myself that six or seven months was too long to go and that tonight was the night. Like the crazy man needing comfort, but I knew where to get it.

'All right, come,' she said. 'How long will you be, Arthur?' In spite of herself her voice shook a little on the question.

'Thirty minutes flat,' I said, and hung up.

I kept my promise. In less than that time I was ringing the door-bell. 'Come in,' she said, then, 'My God, what's been happening?'

'Took a ride on a coal train to reach you,' I said gaily.

'You look like the first time I ever saw you.'

I pushed past her – all I could think of was that bright beautiful fire. 'I should show signs of wear and tear. Slept out all night; had my bike stolen; walked miles; plodged through rivers.' That big beautiful fire! Not being able to sit on it I did the next best thing and shuffled round on the hearth.

'Slept where?' she sharply asked.

'In a ruined old house with the biggest nose in the country.'

'You've run away from home?'

I sat on the hearth with my backside practically rubbing against the grate and pulled off my shoes and socks. Then I changed to a pouffe and warmed my feet through and didn't mind the tide marks left by the river or the black borders of my toenails. She shuffled the settee close to the fire: 'Here, sit down in comfort.' All the problems were forgotten in her attention to my needs: nurses can't help nursing, mothers mothering, or woman giving. 'You're filthy! What made you run away?'

'Trouble.' I told her about the fight and the murder, but not about the episode on the site: I wasn't sure how she'd take that, or what conclusions she'd draw from it.

I was hoping the murder might be a dream.

'It was in the afternoon papers,' she said. 'A terrible thing – the man must be insane. And you with his brother … how awful!'

We talked around it for a time. There'd been nothing in the papers about the fight with Mick, so that was all right; he might be in hospital with concussion, but boy, that's a sight better than death. 'You're too easily led, Arthur,' she said. 'You shouldn't have gone with that boy. The best thing to do is to go to the police and make a clean breast of it.' I knew better to disagree, and nodded. 'You've nothing to be afraid of. You need a bath,' she said. 'I'll run it.'

'Ah need that and a meal – haven't had a proper meal since last night.'

'You poor thing!' she said. 'I'll make you a cup of tea.' She started the bath, rushed through and put the kettle on, was back in a minute with a tray. The kettle had been boiled once before, I knew, but the tea was perfect, just as strong as she knew I liked it, two spoonfuls of sugar and the top of the bottle. I took it off the saucer and held it with both hands, conscious of the warmth and flavour I'd soon be pouring inside me; conscious also of the cleft between her breasts, revealed as she stooped to hand me the cup. Then she was away upstairs again. 'Two warm towels on the rails,' she said. 'Don't splash too much … what will you have for your supper?'

'Bacon and eggs,' I said, laughing. 'That's all Ah prayed for all the way here, and Ah'm not going back on a promise to myself.' I padded to the door like a contented tiger, a devil of a tiger that made a sucker of the elephants, the guns and all the traps and finishes up at day's end with plenty to eat. 'Why did you come here?' she suddenly asked. 'Why didn't you go to that girl?'

Ignoring the reference to Dorothy I said: 'You were the only one I could come to, Stella.'

She smiled and I thought how nice she looked in the plain print frock – nice to a tiger. I smiled back and went upstairs. The big blue bath was full and steaming. Instead of jumping straight in I stripped off to the waist first and washed my head and shoulders: instead of rinsing off I plunged my head right in once or twice. Then I dried off. Now I could really enjoy it.

I slid in and knelt for a while, nose close to the surface so that the fragrant steam gave full value; then lay on my back full stretch; then stood and soaped myself all over. Then, man, I flopped back, right back until the water was lapping my nostrils. I felt as smooth as a statue with strength coiled up in me. With the dirt I'd washed away all the mistakes, all the humiliation of being taken in by Nosey and sold down the river by Uncle George; the shame of running away and swapping my bike for a screw of tea and a piece of tin; the sweat of running away from the world. Or so I thought. I shut out the thought of everything but myself and Stella.

Then I dried myself, pulled on a shirt and trousers and went downstairs. The rashers and eggs were ready for me. I set to. This was the first course. Stella kept me company, drinking a cup of tea, saying very little and never meeting my eyes. Finally, as I was finishing off with a couple of biscuits, she said: 'Frank's been given a shore job – at Liverpool.'

'You'll be moving.'

'It's just as well. I hate this place. I want to get away to something else.'

'Ah've been a burden to you.'

'That's not your fault. I used to think that once we'd finished there'd be no burden, but it doesn't happen that way. It stays with you.'

She got up quickly and went into the kitchen. I followed through. Man, both hot and cold taps were running into the sink and she was crying over it. I touched the back of her neck. 'It's all right, Stella, Ah'm going now, any minute.' You can feel two things at one and the same time. One is a knife being twisted for what you are and what you've done; the other is a determination to get what you want before it's too late. She watched me lacing up my shoes.

'Where will you go?'

'Don't know – home, probably.'

'There isn't a bus.'

'Ah'll walk.'

'You'll think I'm cruel – turning you out on a night like this. But you've got to go back some time or other, haven't you?'

'You've been grand, Stella. This was all I needed.' I stood up. 'Don't come to the door with me – Ah'll let myself out.' I held out my hand.

I held her hand. 'Ah'll never forget you, Stella. You never failed to come up trumps.' Her hand moved in mine like a ball in its socket; to touch and grip was all that was needed. Her eyes closed.

'Kiss me once before you go; then go quickly, before I change my mind.' I drew her to me and kissed her, not hard but gently, and her hand moved to my face and stroked the scar. I kissed her eyes and felt the salt on my lips and tongue. I felt her body shake and took hold of her. With my hands I probed the difference between the stiff material of her dress and the silkiness of the skin that lay below. 'Oh, don't!' she said, and her head fell back. My hands went on exploring, communicating the shape of her body to my imagination, shoulders and narrow back down to the outward curve. 'Good Friday!' was the last thing she said before I started unfastening the buttons for the beginning of love-making as she'd taught it to me. Then I found that so far I'd only been in the infant's school; the tiger had met his match and had to fight to keep up the pace. It was like a thunderstorm. In seconds flat the light was out and she was returning to me, naked as the day, her eyes wide and staring and her face completely without expression. Tiger! I could laugh. She knelt beside me and I looked into those eyes. They weren't the eyes of the Stella I knew. They were the eyes of a strange woman who had lived and suffered through a couple of hundred lives compared to my one and who was now using me for her own ends. I was scared out of my wits. I thought of Mildred. Then somehow, I gave in. If I was the tiger, then now it was my turn to jump through the hoop. This wasn't pleasure but a battle which I had to fight and lose, for her sake. This wasn't a light goodbye but something that would cut us apart for ever. Afterwards I went out like a light.

I went early in the morning. Somehow I felt as if I was leaving school for a second time, but this time I knew that at least I was going out with something I could build upon. I'd touched fire, the biggest fire in the world, and ever afterwards I'd treat it with the respect it deserves.

THIRTEEN

1

I could have caught a workman's bus but preferred to walk all the way home, mainly because I was afraid to arrive. I needn't have worried. Before I'd time to turn the key the door was flung open, and I was welcomed by old Harry, his hair standing up, his pyjama jacket over his trousers and his braces looped. 'Come in, you're as welcome as the flowers in May,' he said. He stood aside for the Old Lady, who came rushing along the passage all laughter and tears and with a slap across the sound-box that sent me weeping with her. 'There,' she said, 'that's for the worry and lost sleep!' But I knew everything was all right, it was what you might call a love-tap.

'When did you last eat?' said Harry. I lied and said a month or so ago, and in a minute I was smelling my second lot of frying bacon since midnight. The Old Lady was reviving her wrist and simultaneously firing questions, and I was trying to keep my wits about me in case I let something fall I'd regret. I told them the necessary stuff about the fight and seeing Crab come out.

'They've got him,' said Harry. 'Picked him up at Waverley Station in Edinburgh yesterday afternoon – wanted for questioning.' Man, I'm ashamed to say I heaved a sigh of relief that I was out of that one. All the way home I'd been travelling with the horrors – away from Stella for good to one hell of a mess; house watched by long low cars with their aerials full out and inside the Old Lady perched on the hardest chair and being questioned by tough and sweating characters about my life and times.

'Poor bastard, that's all tied up,' said Harry.

'Stop blathering and get your jacket off,' said the Old Lady. Then, suspiciously: 'Ye look mighty and clean for a man that's been sleeping rough!'

'Got a wash in the Gents in town,' I lied.

'This looks a nice bit of ham,' said Harry in the nick of time. The Old Lady forgot me and made for the pantry. He winked at me: 'They'll not be wantin' ye, lad. It's all cut and dried.'

'How d'ye know?'

'Got pals in the Force,' he said. 'Still had the gun. Botched the old chap – he'll pull through to tell the tale. But he didn't miss her.'

'Twisted beast,' said the Old Lady.

'You don't know,' said old Harry. I rolled up my shirt sleeves and watched him. He stood there ten feet tall, vertical, the boss with smiling x-ray eyes and a big heart pumping sense into the two of us. 'You don't know enough about it to talk.'

'He shouldn't have done it.'

'He shouldn't, but he was up against something he didn't understand ...'

'You don't believe in hangin'. Hangin's too good for him, and that's the honest truth,' she said.

'All that boy wants is a quick death,' he said.

'How do you know?'

'I know, woman,' he said. That did for her. 'They'll not need you, or the other laddo, his brother. Him they wouldn't use, anyway. So just forget the slops and trials and all that other malarkey.'

Without jesting and joking, I just slumped there. You'll not believe it but in a way I was disappointed; disappointed in a way that was a bit nasty.

'The only mistake you made,' he said, busy turning the bacon, 'was to walk away from the scene. You should have clocked the other one there and then and given the alarm.'

'If that poor old man had died ...' said the Old Lady, and I saw the point.

'You never walk away from death,' said old Harry. 'It's the one thing a man can be excused for wanting to walk away from, but only for *wanting.*'

'And get him outa your system,' said the Old Lady. 'What d'ye want with a character like that?'

'That's my friend,' I said. 'It's all right talking about stayin' with death. What about stayin' with a friend?'

'Lot of bloody sentiment,' said old Harry, taking the sting out of it with a smile. 'It wasn't altogether the old pal business, now was it? That kid's tough and he had you under his thumb.'

'Well, I've got to see him again,' I said.

'Fair enough. But if he acts up, clock him one. And land him one for me. Be loyal to me for a change.'

'He's in trouble,' I said.

'Don't shout,' said old Harry. I told him I wasn't shouting, and he laughed, looked at the Old Lady and laughed again. 'Who the hell do you think you are – thinkin' you can help him? Eh? Think you can save the other from being topped? Think you can stop him feelin' the way he does? Think you can lead him into paths of righteousness, now? Everybody goes to hell their own way and by the time you're privileged to be able to help a lost soul he'll be pushin' up daisies.'

'Okay, so Ah'm no miracle man,' I said. 'But he's still my pal and Ah'm goin' to help him ...'

'Suit yourself,' said Harry. 'You will, if you're anything like your Old Lady. But expect the unexpected. That kid loves nobody, repeat, nobody.'

'And what about Mick Kelly?'

'And what about Mick Kelly? Ask yourself. Use your loaf. He's glad to keep his mouth shut. *And* his old man. A lot of blether. The only way he'll ever visit the slops is with a bracelet round his wrist that isn't made of platinum.'

'Well, you've got everything sewn up,' I said.

'Don't let it bother ye, kiddar,' he said. 'Man is born to trouble as the sparks fly upwards.'

'But it mightn't be so easy next time,' said the Old Lady. 'Let it be a warning ...'

'Ah don't need a warning, Mum,' I said. 'Maybe Ah do know nothing, but Ah know that Ah know nothing, and that's a good start. But Ah'll not guarantee no trouble.'

'What is it now?' stared the Old Lady.

'Leave him be,' said the Lodger, dishing out the breakfast. 'Let your meat stop your mouth.'

'Have you got religion?' she accused.

'He's been out in the wilderness, hasn't he?' stated old Harry. 'Solitude, self-communion, temptation. It's always meant trouble, ever since the dawn.'

'That's right,' I said, 'in every particular.'

'You'll get to know in God's good time,' said the Lodger. 'All Ah've got to say is that he has the one thing to learn – like his mother. When ye've lost something, stand still. Let your body go through the usual motions, especially if there's a knock on the way, but for God's sake stand still and let the rest rush over ye ...' He pointed his fork at the Old Lady. 'She wanted to call the slops but Ah wouldn't have it. Ah laid a bet with her that ye'd be back, sooner or later. And here you are!' Then he started laughing in his tea. 'But if she'd only known what odds were being laid by the old bookie in my brain, she'd have had a fit.'

That was a great breakfast. Afterwards, I went off to bed.

'Where did ye sleep last night?' asked the Old Lady from the bottom of the stairs.

'You'd drop that duster if ye knew,' I told her. 'In a mansion.'

'*That's* what they call a dyke nowadays, is it?' she said. She hesitated. 'And – thanks for the ring.' She held out her hand. It was on the engagement finger.

'That's where it fits best,' I said.

'D'ye know what that fool said? That ye were sure to come back because you'd left the ring. He kept telling me that every time I went off the deep end ... well, Ah'll keep it, on one condition.'

'What's that, Mum?'

'That you'll give it to *your* lass, that Dorothy, when the day comes.'

All you can do is to play up the best you can.

2

Sleeping during the day doesn't do your stomach any good, and mine turned at the sight of the liver and onions old Harry was lashing down. 'No thanks, Mum,' I said. 'Just give me a nice big cup of tea, to give me strength.'

'What for?' asked Harry. 'Not for the Kellys anyway. Went along and saw the old man this afternoon. There's no trouble expected from that quarter – if ever there was, he's changed his mind.'

'Thanks, Harry,' I said, and meant it. 'But it's not that. There's another instalment – Ah'm out of a job.'

'Out of a job?' said the Old Lady. 'Now what have ye been up to there –'

'Nothin' but gettin' in somebody's feet,' I said. And told the full story. When I was finished – 'Our Arthur!' she exclaimed. 'Ye'll be gettin' yourself shot!'

'That's what Ah was thinkin' myself,' I admitted.

'Why, Harry went along in the mornin' – Ah thought they might know something. But they knew nothing. An' your Uncle George never said a word …'

'He looked completely worn out,' said Harry. 'How much muck did ye put in that pipe end?'

'Maybe five or six ton,' I said. I considered. 'Maybe twenty.'

'He looked more like a man that had shifted sixty ton,' considered Harry.

'Hey, my goodness,' said the Old Lady. 'Ye could have killed them. They'll have you in court for sure … it'll be blazoned forth in all the papers …'

'Not a chance,' said Harry. 'They'd never lift their heads again. Even the sewer business'd chuck 'em out after that ... buried alive! Snake's blood, but Ah wish Ah'd been there to see it ... when they finally burrowed their way out ...'

'Each a stone lighter,' said the Old Lady.

'Blebs on their hands and broken backs,' said the Lodger.

'Paid,' I said. It was the best laugh we'd had together since the snails, but this time we were all laughing together. That's what makes a family.

3

And that's how I landed into the sardine factory, thanks to old Harry who sold me to the manager as action-boy, trouble-shooter and super-mechanic, replacing my old pal Nosey – who'd gone without giving notice. Hard to live up to, but better than standing in one spot all day and soaking up the reek of fish-olive-ketchup. Not that it made any difference. Travelling at twice the speed of sound the stuff still caught up with you in the end, and as you oozed out of the doorway oil and ketchup oozed out of you. There's nothing nicer than a nice sardine on buttered toast; plastered on man it's revolting, and I found out why Harry preferred to walk home taking it slowly.

Like the kids in my grandmother's Sunday School prize books I turned over a new leaf. I even tried to read books, real books instead of space fiction or the odd Hank Jansen. But man, I'll be honest, I didn't get very far. I didn't have the grounding. For a time I read with a little dictionary by my side, looking up the odd word and failing to understand the explanation or getting tired of looking up so many. I've seen me look up six words in one solitary sentence and still be baffled. Hell, there was no certainty anywhere, least of all in words. It took a long time for me to catch on.

And this wasn't the only trouble. I'd seen too much and lived too much; experience-indigestion had me by the guts. Never bothered very much with acne outside, I was coming up with bloody great boils inside, swelling like volcanoes and erupting like mad. I was in a swirl, drowning sailor hanging on to a bit of a spar and not even convinced that it was worth hanging on to. The only useful thing that emerged from this period was a bath. We'd always run outside to the netty, wc or whatever you call it and washed in the sink. The weekly bath was in two stages, using a zinc-bath. Remembering the glory of plunging into Stella's bath, I suggested putting one in. The Old Lady and Harry fell in like lightning; we bought a shop-soiled model, a second-hand boiler and a set of pipes and did the job ourselves, from start to finish, shoving the boiler in over one weekend and installing the bath at our ease. Old Harry was a marvel – watching him shamed me. 'One thing at a time,' he'd say whenever I went crazy to push on regardless and trust to luck not to botch the job. He'd a knack for everything and lovely, neat hands. The Old Lady moves in a groove but he seems to take hold of time with the job and twist both to his own ends. Time didn't count with him, he was a real hero, I used to think.

He was like some character in the *Skipper* or *Rover* who goes on for five or ten years without putting on age or anything, but only in his attitude to work. He had an absolute contempt for time, didn't mind growing old but accepted it and hoped for a quick and easy death. Me, I counted and still count every minute. I wear a watch and don't need to, because I can tell you the time without looking. It dribbles away like a slow leak, or a drop from a tap in the middle of the night, and I always know it and it breaks my heart.

In between times I got around. First, by necessity of work, was Mick Kelly. He was as natural and happy with me as the next, and told me why. 'You saved me from a million years in purgatory,' he said. Just like saying: 'You saved me from missing the bus.'

'How's that?'

'Ah'd have killed the bastard.'

'Get away!'

'Certain fact,' he said laconically. 'Ah knew he was out to get me – talked it all round the place – as soon as Ah saw it was him a funny thing happened …' I waited while he screwed up his long, Nanny-goat's face. 'Swapped places with him,' he said. 'Didn't want any trouble, worried about what the Father would say, then something went – an' he was me.' Now it was my turn to screw up my face. 'Honest to God,' he said. 'Ah was in his shoes, Ah wasn't myself, and he was hammering me.'

'That means ye were hammering yourself!'

'Crazy, but that's the way it was,' he said.

'You mean, you swapped places?'

'Kind of, only Ah was still me. See?' I didn't get it. He held his fist up. 'Every time Ah hit him, wherever it was, Ah felt it, on my fist and also on the same spot – but enjoyed it – it was him that was doin' the hammerin' so there was nothing to worry about. That was a crazy thing to happen to a man, and thanks to Our Lady you came along and put me out. The Divil had me and Ah'd have murdered him for sure.'

I looked at him with amazement. Here was a man who'd occupied two bodies simultaneously, and yet went around the same as usual; a man with a miracle in his life who'd go on bossing his set, until one day he'd bounce his old man and clear out and get married. I didn't know why but it seemed like waste.

I never got the chance to talk to Uncle George. I've seen him often enough, sometimes sailing along with Aunt Mary, sometimes alone, always with his nose in the air like a man that's messed his pants. Sometimes his name is mentioned in the papers and the Old Lady says: 'He'll land himself some day.' But he hasn't and he never will. It's useless talking to the Old Lady but if I could I'd tell her that he's in gaol now, sentenced for life, poor bastard. And what's worse, solitary confinement.

But I met up with poor old George Flack. It was a long time after I'd started work in the sardine factory, a long time after the bath was fixed, a long time after the Mildred affair was wound up, a long time after the Saturday afternoon I walked around to where Stella used to live and saw the HOUSE FOR SALE notice. In fact, it was nearly at the end of this particular bit of my life. I'd returned to the book-reading caper. I was reading a poet called Whitman. For once it was coming through – the bit that starts 'Out of the cradle endlessly rocking' and I was sad and melancholy. The interior stuff started up and I couldn't sit, neither could I stand the quiet contentment of the Old Lady and Harry, gazing at each other in the odd off-moments when they thought I wasn't looking. I grudged them everything because I had nothing, but when you're in that state the best thing to do is to get up and go out for a bit of pavement pounding. I walked, man, I walked, and at last found myself up Elswick way where poor old George lives. I came to in one of those long streets running down towards Scotswood Road where the main doors are always open and the stairs uncovered; and where you can see the long slow ripple of the slates where collapse has begun.

I heard the ships hooting and automatically turned to Thames, Humber, Goodwins, Copenhagen, Hamburg, Biscay, New York, New Orleans, The Horn. I was halfway to the river before I realised I'd automatically turned towards the hooters. Thinking of those exotic names and comparing them with what was around me made me sick: cobbles smeared with filth and a sea-fret that in eight or nine miles had picked up more sulphur and fine ash than hell possessed; neglected gardens as hardpacked as asphalt; tumbling walls; unwashed curtains x-rayed by naked bulbs, and unwashed kids darting about like rats in the dark.

Then, listen, I had a thought. Talk about walking along the boundary line of hell – what was I like inside? *There* was a pit to walk around: Arthur's little lot jumping and screaming to be out; the murderer, the sex-maniac, the liar, hypocrite, and smiling coward; the miser with a yen for solid cash and a talent for elbowing the other swine from the trough; or the rubber-faced thief with too much respect for his skin to have a go. There's a patrol for you! See you at the end of the beat and we'll fetch up our vomit together, you at your end of the trough and me at mine.

I came out on the smooth, slick highway to Blaydon Races and found a pub; not because I wanted a drink but because I wanted to get out of my dark. There was a bar a mile long with a dance-hall floor. I walked over to the frog-faced woman at the bar, a dozen pair of eyes machine-gunning my back, and managed to put my voice down in my chest and ask for a Scotch Ale instead of the shandy gaff I'd have preferred. She gave me a hard look but pulled it; the skin was growing around her wedding ring. I took a sip and looked over my shoulder. In the middle table a couple of grandmas who'd never seen their grandbairns were going fifty to the dozen on abortions and disposals and the filthy luck of their missing colleague, the one that the dying girl split on.

A pair of couples were telling each other dirty jokes and rubbing legs under the cast-iron table; a dark Irish girl was lying back with her legs wide open and her mouth wider, singing a ballad; a couple about my own age were mauling each other in the far corner, perhaps thinking their table screened them, or perhaps just pretending for form's sake; a couple of lorry drivers were faking load sheets with the help of a row of pints; and a respectable old working man with a Kaiser William moustache and a stiff collar was glaring at me as if to say, 'For God's sake isn't there plenty of illegitimate drinking going on without you coming in!'

I came back to my drink and gulped without thinking; it went over my chin and there was only one way to look without getting a laugh. That was where old George was sitting, three pint glasses on the counter and one in his fist. He was like the feel of the sheet after a nightmare, or the rising sun after the longest night in your life. I moved over quickly.

'Hi, there, George,' I said.

'You address me proper,' he said.

'It's me, George.'

'An' who the hell are you?' he said, bringing his head round in a half circle and boy, talk about nightmares, he didn't know me.

'Ah'm Arthur Haggerston, that used to work on the site.'

'Passed outa me mind,' he said. 'You bury as many as me an' ye'll know how hard it is to remember ... Sorry, kiddar, had a bereavement. Lost the last livin' blood relative. Ah've seen them all go down, bullets, bayonets, shells, land-mines, drownin', 'flu, pneumonia, galloping consumption, buried under falls, fried in firedamp, but always had one left …'

'Who was that, George?' I asked.

'Carried a coffin on his shoulder for forty years and decided to fill it in the end,' he said. 'Why, if it isn't Arthur, li'l Arthur the undertaker's man.'

'Ah used to be lad on the site,' I said.

'You buried your Uncle George and Slippery Sam,' he said. 'Slippery Sam slipped away from that one. No more load sheets for him where he's gone.'

'Dead?'

'Sanatorium, collapsed lung,' he said.

'Ah'm sorry to hear that,' I said. Something was squeezing my heart.

'You're sorry! Be sorry for me. Ah got his job. Ah'm the bumper-up now.'

'Did that business cause it?'

He shook his head. 'Took them a couple of hours to get out but they kept the appointment and they were so relieved to see the chap that they went into the first pub and knocked the bung outa the barrel … Well, Sam did. Uncle George went home when he saw the ways the wind was blowin'. Poor ol' Sam couldn't get the cold outa his bones … Got mortalious and lay out all night with his nose in the gutter. It was his own fault.'

'Ah started it.'

He shook his head. 'Nothin' to do with you. Don't get big ideas about givin' him the push into the sanatorium. He walked in himself. Nobody needed to give him the push. He'd been after a slow suicide ever since he left his mother's milk.' He tried to put back the empty jar without rising but just couldn't make the counter. I took it and handed him one of the pair of pints on the counter. 'Don't get big ideas,' he said. 'Did Ah tell ye that?' I nodded. 'Course, Ah told ye. Used to think Ah was to blame for Hill 60 – ever told ye that one? Me, the man that made a tunnel or two and set the fuses! Ah was no more responsible than the general in charge … there's a bloody great snake that starts it all. He sits down there (he pointed his thumb to the floor). He opens his mouth and pulls us down. That's all. The Lord put men on earth to sing, but the snake's jealous and draws us down through the soil into his mouth.'

'It is as simple as that, George?'

'That snake gets everybody,' he said. 'There's no arguing against that.' Tipping the glass he killed the better part of the pint in one breath. 'It's all the easier for the snake now that nobody believes in him. He was pullin' you an' all them other kids the day you chased me nevvy down the clay banks. And me poor young nevvy thought he was runnin' away; balls to that, he was bein' pulled down by the snake. Like gravity, see.'

'Carruthers-Smith?'

He nodded. 'That was how the snake first got hold of him makin' him ashamed of his own name. Didn't matter about me. Ye don't pick your relatives. They're foisted on ye and it's up to you whether you drop them or not. From the minute he changed his name, the snake had him. Man that can't face his name can't face kids – man that can't live his name down'll never live anything down. Right? So off he goes like the fox, goes to earth, meets a woman that's the tongue of the snake, and from then on he's finished.'

Once again I saw Carruthers-Smith sheltering in the house at the bottom of the clay-bank: 'The woman that took him in?'

'The woman the snake intended him to meet.'

'So it wasn't us givin' him the treatment …'

'Get that outa ye head. Ye didn't know what ye were doin'. Same as the woman. My nevvy rolled down the hill he'd been climbin' into the snake's mouth. Hard to tell which was the worst; the climb up or the fall down. But she must've liked him. She'd never had a wash for a couple of days when she told me about findin' him with the rope round his neck and she kept askin' why? why? why? Maybe it was because he'd lost the teachin', she said. Maybe it was because he missed his missus and the kids, she guessed. So Ah didn't tell her that this particular mornin' he wakened up and saw her mucky face, the mucky window, the mucky sheets and maybe the black bands under his fingernails … and realised he was in the belly of the snake.' He wagged a finger at me. 'Mind you, ye can live in a posh house, drive a posh car, do a posh woman and sleep under clean sheets and still be in the belly of the snake …'

'Ah suppose ye can,' I said.

'Look at me, look at you, little Arthur,' he said. 'We're there. We don't lift a foot without the snake gives the order. He's the laddo that makes out the load sheets, not me, nor Sam, nor the man wi' the gun. We're just monkeys on a stick.' His fingers worked the invisible toy.

'When Ah was a miner,' he continued, 'Ah often used to think what would it be if one day Ah broke through into a place full of light? Wouldn't it be a wonderful thing? Well, Arthur, me laddo, there's no place full of light, and that's a fact.'

The frog-faced woman came over: 'This chap a pal of yours?' I nodded. 'Sooner ye get him away the better …'

'Ah'll take him home,' I said, and the words were hardly out of my mouth when I heard a splintering sound. Old George was hard up against the bar and the broken jar was an inch from the frogwoman's face. 'You're one of them,' he said in a low voice. 'You're with the snake.'

His wrist was as hard as iron.

'She doesn't know, George,' I said. 'She's not to blame.'

'That's right,' he said, taking his eyes away from her. She took off like a hare. 'Poor little bitch.'

'Let's get out of this,' I said.

'Back to Hill 60,' he said. 'She's ready to blow.'

'They'll need a bit hand,' I urged. A big fellow with a collarless shirt was coming through from the saloon. I felt in my pocket for a half-crown. 'It's all right, Mister,' I said. 'We're goin' now.'

'What about the glass?'

'There's half a dollar.'

'That doesn't take the Missus outa her fit,' he said and ducked under the counter. 'Here's another one, look out!' said old George. The big fellow revealed a naked woman on his bicep as he put his hand up for a chopper. Old George shouldered me out of the way and went in with his head down. The tattooed man collapsed like a rag doll. All the customers, apart from the Irish girl and the old man, who were now together in the spot vacated by the young couple, crowded round. 'Let me get him out,' I pleaded. 'Watch me shift them,' said George pleasantly. He lifted his arm. They scattered.

From the pub to where he lived was maybe a quarter of a mile but it took us a good thirty minutes. After a time it dawned on me that he didn't want to make port. He wanted to dance, swing around lamp-posts, weave, walk the tightrope, sit in a corner and talk. In the end he sobered up. He wouldn't let me come into the house. 'No place for you, li'l Arthur,' he said. 'Leave me be, Ah'll be all right.' He sat on the hard stone steps and looked up into the sky. 'Not a flamin' star,' he said. 'First time Ah've looked for years an' there isn't a peeper in sight.'

'It's the sea-fret,' I said.

'Don't kid yourself,' he said. 'There's hope there, so the bastards put up a smoke-screen, see? Out there there's so much light it would burn the eyes out of their sockets. Harraway home, kiddar, and make something outa yourself.'

'How?'

He looked down and pulled at his old raincoat. 'Ah don't know. There's a million roads if ye forget yourself. Ah'm a self-centred ould man, so Ah know what Ah'm talkin' about.'

'Will ye be all right?'

'Ah'm all right. Be off with ye.'

'So long, then.'

'So long – hey, before ye gan, lad; did Ah tell ye me share of the contractor's money – a clear ten quid last week?'

It was like a body blow. 'Oh yes,' I murmured.

'Oh aye,' he said. 'So whose wake is it? Sam's, the nevvy's, or mine?'

'Better to clear out like me,' I said.

'Listen whose talkin'!' he mocked. 'Can't an old feller feather his nest? It's too late for anything else.'

I wanted to tell him it wasn't too late, but didn't know how, or whether he could anyway. All I could think of was that the whole earth was his if he could enjoy it, not the bit under Hill 60 but the bit above, and the bit above that, with the peepers and all the light beyond. But I wasn't so dumb that I believed he was wanting answers from me.

He was addressing all his questions to himself, like a buried-alive man knocking at the coffin lid knowing that nobody could hear but himself. 'Ah'm sorry, George,' I said. 'Goodnight.'

'God bless,' he answered. It was wrenched out of him. Came like a half-bottle on the head or a knuckle-duster on the ear because behind it was a man without hope, who knew in his bones there was no God to bless but who created Him for my sake.

FOURTEEN

Nobody had cracked down on it, but our world was cracking. The first time I walked into the Regent and asked after Nosey you'd think he'd never existed. Roly-Poly was knocking a pool with a character named Sangster, whose looks I didn't like. Mousey Hole and Dopey were hanging onto bottles of Cola. Both looked dreamy and relaxed. Also slightly bored. I wasn't surprised when Dopey reacted with a woolly look; that was his usual shape. 'Never seen him since their kiddar knocked off little Milly,' he said at last. 'He's retired.' I looked at Mousey and he merely shrugged, Dean Martin fashion, sending up my blood pressure.

'Leaving him alone?' I asked indignantly.

'Ach, you know Nosey,' said Mousey. 'He doesn't want nobody – he's lying low.'

'Maybe he's waiting for a pal to come around.'

'Relax,' said Dopey.

'Hasn't anybody looked him up?'

'You kiddin'?' asked Mousey. 'Their old man snatched an old geezer that called to say a prayer and put his shoulder out! Ask me, Nosey's in the same mood.'

'Who was this old geezer?' I asked, just to confirm a guess.

'Some Pastor bloke,' said Harry Jones.

'They're takin' it badly,' said another type, knocking off a Cola. 'His Old Lady's never been off the booze – sent out for.'

'You were his pal,' said Mousey. 'Pop down and get *your* shoulder put out.'

'Hey, listen, get this, men,' said Dopey. 'Was on the bus last night, messin' about with one bird and another behind. And this bird behind says: "Whoo-oo, I've got my eyes on you!" Quick as lightnin' Ah said, sorta swanky voice, y'know, "Then, kaindly remove them – they're claggy!" Did she dig it! Boy, she went off like a row of crackers. If Ah'd said another word she'd've wet herself.'

'Never mind the bird,' said Sangster, who'd just finished the game. 'What's plans for tonight?'

'There's a good picture at the Pavilion,' said Mousey Hole. *Spawn of the Fifty Foot Woman*. Let's make the five o'clock show then run over to the Majestic for a bit of a whirl.'

'Seen it,' said Dopey. 'Was here last year. Got maggots crawlin' on her, that fifty foot woman.' He turned to me. 'You seen any good pictures lately, Arthur?' I indicated that I hadn't. 'There's a hot Frenchy filum on at one of the Westgate houses. How 'bout that?'

'Fancy the jazz club,' said Dopey. 'Some of those birds there go wild – yep, they even sit on your knee and throw their arms around you when they hear them trumpets go high.'

'Then let's go to the jazz club,' said Sangster.

'An' drink coffee all night?' said Dopey. 'No soap.'

'We can have a pint or two in the pub next door,' said Harry Jones.

'Ach, Ah don't know,' said Dopey. 'We'll meet here at six, maybe, eh?'

'Ask Roly-Poly,' said Sangster. 'Hey, Roly-Poly!'

He came strolling over. 'What might be the happen?' he said, following the rage for mixed-up, crazy language.

'It's unwhere tonight again,' remarked Sangster, who was a Grammar School type.

'It'll sort itself out,' said Roly-Poly. 'Hi, Arthur.'

'Low boy, low,' I answered.

'You worried, kiddar?'

'In a minute Ah'll be browning the other side,' I said.

'Know what you mean,' he answered. 'Napoleon's on Elba, eh?'

'Fancy the jazz club?' asked Harry Jones.

'Fancy a bit private crack with me old pal, here, the Marshall of Dodge City,' said Roly-Poly. We drifted away into a corner. 'He's gone, boy, gone,' he continued, without any preliminary. 'No use lookin' him up – disposition of a tiger. Saw him last Sunday. Chucked his job as from the night of the murder. Says he's goin' to break old Crab out before the trial ...'

'He's crazy.'

'Don't tell me; tell him. He'll end up in the loony bin. Taking it as a personal grudge. Says he'll blow the wall down, if needs be.'

'Ah'm goin' to see him,' I said.

'Like me to come along with you?'

I shook my head. 'Just want to show that we haven't forgotten him.'

'It won't work, brother,' he said. 'All the world's a slop to him, unless they're prepared to take his crazy talk about digging a tunnel to the condemned cell.'

'Ah've got to see him.'

'Take my tip an' stay at home,' said Roly-Poly. 'Otherwise, take a bodyguard.'

But my mind was made up. 'Where will Ah find him?'

'Easy, he's taken over Crab's fruit stall away along beside the Covered Market. Wear gloves, shinguards and a safety helmet.'

If you'll believe what I say, I went in spite of myself. I was afraid in about a dozen directions. I knew the way he worked. That boy was like a jungle tiger; he had to have his will. And he loved his brother. If he'd made up his mind to spring him, then spring him he would and anybody not in favour of springing would be automatically the enemy, along with the slops, judge, jury, etc. But it wasn't only this. Deep down in me and my folk is a horror of murder. It's in our blood. Maybe it isn't of murder, but of the rope. You can't hang thousands and thousands in public without planting something. They were big X shows and the real stuff and they left a memory which is kept alive by what goes on inside the high walls. Looking at old Nosey from a shop doorway opposite was like seeing him for the first time. That enquiring nose with the little twist was no longer comic, part of the makeup that made him a leader, but a sign of the scaffold, and when he turned his head sideways to shout oranges or apples I could see the knot below his ear.

He was part of a Horror that I didn't want to touch yet which, at the same time, drew me to him for all the wrong reasons, not to help but to take. All over town people were talking about Crab and what he'd done and how he'd suffer for it. Most of them liked the thought of that long, last night and the short one-act play that would follow. Nosey and his folk knew this. All this talking and whispering around them spelled enmity; there was only one way to deal with it – to hit back. If the innocent were hurt it didn't matter. All that counted was the insult to their own blood. In a way Crab himself was insignificant before this monstrous thing – the blow to the dignity of the family.

I could see Nosey's eyes darting for the knowing glance, the word whispered behind a hand, the thought that took his tremendous sense of will and belonging so lightly that it could imagine him letting them take *his* brother to the scaffold. I walked over and, dry-mouthed, said: 'How's things, Nosey?'

'Eff off,' he said.

'It's a bit since Ah saw ye – how about a bit talk when ye pack up.'

'Taken you a long time to come round,' he said.

'Didn't know where ye were working. And Ah didn't like to come to the house.'

'Nobody wants ye.'

'Thought maybe Ah could help out somehow.'

For answer he put his head to one side and cried: 'Oranges, beautiful oranges, two bob for ten; apples, apples, one and sixpence a pund. Lovely eaters.' Then, out of the corner of his mouth, 'You're related to the judge? Got a pal on the jury they picked? Won't make any difference. It's all laid down. He killed her with a gun and the ould man saw him.'

'He might get life, you never know,' I said. 'If they can prove he was insane.'

'Ah talked with the man,' he said. 'And as for the loony plea there's no bloody twists in our family.'

'Ach, it's only a formality or whatever they call it.' He turned on me. I'd have run, like hell I would, if I'd had any power in my legs. 'There's no effin' insanity in my family.'

'Okay,' I said at last. 'So there's nothin' to be done. All Ah came for was to show willin' …'

'*Oranges a bob for four, ten for a couple of bob,*' he yelled. 'Show willin',' he hissed. 'If Ah told ye what was in my mind you'd run like a dog wi' a tin on his tail …'

'Ye'll land in gaol as well if ye try any tricks, Nosey.'

'Ah'll spring him,' he said. 'You watch me, kiddar,' he was all smiles and juggler's hands as he selected a pound of eaters for a young woman. There ye are, Missus.' She mumbled something and ran off with the bag. 'Look,' he said. 'Look at her. Her pals told her Crab Carron's brother has a stall up here. Off she gans to brag about it.'

'That's imagination,' I said. 'She'd no more idea …'

He opened his hand. 'Take a look. One and sixpence a pund. So full of it she hadn't time to wait for her change.'

In his hand was a florin.

'Costs sixpence to take a decko at the murderer's kid brother; cheap at the price, eh? Know what she wants? Somebody like me waitin' for her on the Moor some pitch black night. Drag her down and stuff her mouth with grass and tear off every stitch. *Lovely apples, Missus! Beautiful eating apples, one and sixpence a pund. Sweet Gibraltar oranges four for a bob!* Then give her what's good for her and boy, ye'll have to try to make her squeal! Then ye know what? She'll go home and have hysterics and sob away to the slops until they get out the huntin' dogs. *Sweet Gibraltar oranges! Four a shilling! Ten for two bob – melt in yer mouth.* If the dogs run ye down she'll have more of the hysterics as they carry her out of court. But boy, if they never catch ye, she'll remember ye all her life with lovin' affection.'

'How d'ye know? She might be a pretty nice woman for all you know.'

'Don't make me laugh!' he said. 'Our kiddar's got a rope round his neck – know why? Because he wanted to give a woman it for free! But buckshee wasn't good enough for her. So he shot her. He'd every right. That gun was too gentle, that's all. He should'a used a knife ...'

'You go on that way and ye'll finish up in hospital or somethin',' I said. 'Look, Nosey, it's no use taking it this way.'

'God eff me, no,' he said, jovially. 'Here, there's nothin' more doin' today. You got anything on? No? Then give me a hand down with this barrow ...' I'll admit I was too scared to refuse. But at the same time my mind was working; my cunning old mind. Wonder if yours is the same? Never stops in shame, disgust, pity, pain or anguish. Always listening. Always on the alert. Mine had picked up Nosey's secret.

Now I knew why he could buy and sell in a world he hated; lead me by the nose; take over any set, any time, in five seconds flat. He wasn't two ways. Even if his brain was only as big as a pinhead it was bigger than mine because it blazed on one thing all the time – his me, his mine. He didn't think of yesterday, or dream of tomorrow. He was all for now. He blazed for now. Maybe all his ideas were wrong, but they were moving. They weren't half-dead with neglect, smothered in dust, but blazing white hot. If you could do the same with a little bit good! Say you had in your mind – I'm going to help people – and you thought of nothing else, well look out! People would get helped. You wouldn't need money, or an education, or a talent, because all the people needing help would get it, if just from that blaze. But what makes the blaze?

I thought of this all the way down, pushing that load and swinging it for balance and swerving to avoid the traffic – get an idea and make it blaze.

Stashing the barrow away in a dark corner of the market hall he said: 'Would you come in with me?' I didn't answer. 'There's a dozen ways of springin' him, and one that's perfect. It'll take nerve. It's not kid-stuff. It's something that's never been done before – springin' a man that's bound to hang … How 'bout it?'

'What's he say?'

'Crab? Never asked him. But he'll play, he'll jump at the chance.'

'What if he sits tight?'

He grabbed hold of my arm. 'Where'd ye get hold of that shit and nonsense? Doesn't matter what he says now; come the time when he's sittin' waiting, he'll be ready …'

'He'll not cooperate.'

'How did you know that?' he said, thrusting his face close to mine. 'Who passed the word to you? Who's his brother?'

If I'd been cunning I'd have said okay and played around with the idea. It wouldn't have worked. There'd have been nothing lost. Kid-stuff never works, and that was what it was. But I knew he'd land himself in trouble. I knew that I was in danger of saying yes just because he was strong and I was determined to help in the only way I knew – by saying no for the first time in our short and happy life together. I shook my head.

'Ah was only kiddin',' he said, releasing my arm and walking away. That was the saddest moment of my life with him. 'What if he does say he wants to die that way?' he said over his shoulder. 'You're just using it as an excuse. He shouldn't want to die. He did no more than all them chaps that went zum-zum-zum with a gun in the war, or the fellers that dropped the big bomb – only there was more sense in what he did. He knew who he was hitting. But no you're like all the rest; you want him to swing!'

'Honest, Ah don't, Nosey,' I pleaded. 'If it was left to me there'd be no hangin'.'

'A lot of sweet effing talk that means nothin',' he said. And laughed. 'Anyway, it was just a crazy idea. We'd never pull it off, not even with Superman behind us. Just tryin' ye out, that's all,' he muttered. 'Just seein' how much it means. Thought maybe ye'd jump in with both feet an' leave it to me to tell ye there wasn't a chance of pullin' it off – because she's put the sign on him an' all he wants now is to walk up there with his hands tied behind his back.'

At the door he held out his hand. 'No hard feelings, eh?' I was near crying as I mumbled there were no hard feelings and took his hand. 'Now would Ah do a thing like that for you?' he asked nobody in particular. 'Course not. In fact, Ah'd do ye down – and in fact Ah have ...'

He sauntered around with his hands in his pockets, conscious that I was at his mercy, standing like a shot cock, then leaned against the wall. 'Got a snout?' I took one out and threw it to him. 'Ye wouldn't believe it,' he continued, then paused to light up. I was wondering what was coming and he was playing up to me like a comedian. 'Ye wouldn't believe it,' he said at last, 'but that's the hottest bird that ever dragged me into a dark corner.' Shaking his head and looking at me in a queer expectant way – 'Pulled her up one night and told her how sorry Ah was my old man had snecked her old man, on account of the fact that Ah knew her and knew that the Pastor was only tryin' to do his job.' He threw away the cigarette, less than half-smoked. 'Gives me a kick to drop one after a couple of drags ... you listening, Arthur?' I nodded. 'Went for a walk – a long, long walk; talkin' and talkin', boy that bird loves talkin'. Confessed all my sins. We were gettin' along fine. Then she asked what had happened to you – it just slipped out, slipped out.'

'What slipped out?'

'Kind of joke – how you were all right runnin' around with a woman in a flash car – said maybe there was nothing wrong in it, but boy, she went off like a rocket, tears instead of sparks. So Ah comforted her,' he triumphantly concluded. Putting his head to one side he said: 'You with me?' Perhaps he'd expected me to knock him quick, but I'm a slow burner. What was burning me was the discovery that Dorothy was just another kind of bird, different colouring to Stella, Mildred and all the others, but the same species.

And what was burning me in particular was that it had taken Nosey to prove it to me. And oh, man, I was also melancholy at the thought of her voice and everything, and that poor old preaching man; but mostly melancholy at the thought of poor Arthur. So I stood burning. He could have walked out and that would have been the finish. But he wasn't content to leave it at that. He walked over and poked me in the side with one finger. I exploded. I belted him in the guts three times before I started on his face, and I didn't find any difficulty in uppercutting a man bent double. For a few seconds I reached his state of blazing with one single idea; to put him where his brother had put Mildred. Then I got vomit on my hand. I walked out nursing my fist. He was no baby and could clean himself up. At that moment it was the end.

FIFTEEN

1

Every road is a dead-end. Every Saturday night I walk out with five or six crisp pound notes in my pocket and wonder where to go. I have a record player upstairs, but a record player is no company: only a stop-gap. I also have a dinky little VHF radio so that whenever I get sick and tired of the cosy atmosphere downstairs there's a way of retreat. I switch the radio on and am instantly bored stiff; I put on a record and can't sit. I pace like a tiger and wonder where to go. Patronising pal Sangster now runs the gang: Roly-Poly, Dopey and all the rest are just tired cardboard figures who talk but have nothing to say to me. Nosey is a million miles away, blazing with something that doesn't warm me. Stella has left an empty house. I'm finished with Dorothy.

You turn down every possible road even although you know it's a dead-end. Old man Johnson picked me up in Shalley Street one night and took me along home. We'd nothing to say to each other – everything we said was on the surface, and came hard. Now I know that he was taking me along for medicine – for Dorothy. We played draughts while Dorothy read a magazine. Sometimes I caught her looking at me as if I was something poisonous. Yet on the surface she was pleasant enough – looked good enough to eat, too. In the end I said I'd have to go.

'Have another game,' said the Pastor, half-heartedly. I was already on my feet, backing to the door. 'No, Ah've got to go.

Thanks all the same.'

'Come again,' he said. 'You're always welcome, ye know that.' He looked at Dorothy. 'That right, lass?'

'That's right,' she said with a flat little smile.

'Well, goodnight,' I said.

'Dorothy'll see ye to the door, won't ye, Dorothy?' She nodded with an expression that said that this was something she had to do. She walked past me. Old Man Johnson was sitting looking at the board. 'So long, Mister Johnson,' I said.

He knew it was goodbye. 'So long, son.' He knew it was no use adding 'God bless.' Perhaps he was saying it under his breath, like the gambler watching the pennies go up with his last quid, but knowing it was a dead certainty they'd come down wrong. At the bottom of the stairs I held out my hand. 'Well, so long.'

'Not so fast,' she said. 'Where were you all Easter?'

Ping went a little bell. I could hear Stella asking me what day it was and telling me it was Good Friday. 'Run away,' I said.

'How long were you away?'

'Came back on Easter Sunday – was away a couple of nights.'

'Long enough,' she said. I knew what was coming and tried to stop it with silence. Relentless she continued: 'Have you seen Stanley Carron?' I could only stare at her, not realising she was talking about Nosey, until the penny dropped. I nodded. 'Then perhaps he told you already?' She looked at me until my head went down and I mumbled yes, he had. 'Ah don't know what my father'll say when he finds out – Ah don't know which way to turn, Arthur.' I placed my other hand over hers. She wrenched away from me and put both her hands behind her back. 'It's all your fault – treatin' me like a saint or something – then going away from me to that woman. Yes, he told me all about it, just for his own ends. He won't have anything to do with me now. Oh, Ah hate him! He's just a beast, like his brother, just takes what he wants and goes away. And you – you'll not want to see me again?'

'It won't make any difference to me.'

'But it will to him,' she said, giving me a jolt. She began to cry, quietly. 'Now Ah've lost everything – Ah'll never be easy with my father again. Ah'll never be easy in the chapel. Ah'm no better than the rest – the girls that go to pubs and give themselves to anybody that happens along. And what does it mean to him – it's just something he can boast to you about.'

'He thought he was hurtin' me the worst way he could,' I said.

'Oh, Arthur, d'you think so?' she asked, looking up at me with moist eyes. I put my arm around her and she drew close as naturally as could be. 'Ah'm fond of you, too,' she murmured. Her hands crept through my arms and pressed against my shoulders and after this it seemed as though there was nothing to do but kiss her. What wonderful lips a girl can give! They have a life of their own, a softness that draws in the hard narrowness of your own. With your right hand you feel the hollow nape of her neck and the hair reaches down into your fingers and asks them to comb, with your left hand you find the curve that responds and tightens like a bow. And all the time the soft lips move with strawberry sweetness until you want to devour them; but all that remains is to move your lips over the damp, smooth skin towards the eyelashes that flutter like little birds, then return unsatisfied to the lips again.

'Ah,' she said. 'If only you'd kissed me like that before!' And she held me off, smiling. All I wanted was to kiss and kiss again, and take all I could. But there she was, the cause of it all yet quite cool and collected and thinking. All the brakes clamped down.

'Well, it's never too late to mend,' I mumbled. But she wouldn't move. In a split second she'd turned to stone. The tap had been turned off. This was all I could think about. Turned off for me, but not for Nosey. I'm still not sure what was in her mind; whether we'd suddenly remembered that Nosey was the one, and not me; or whether she was just playing me differently, in the way she thought I had to be played, to keep me as a second fiddle. Women are queer.

2

Well, Crab Carron didn't stand a chance and by all accounts he wasn't wanting even one. The funny thing is that he got quite a lot of sympathy, in spite of the family carrying on and clocking quite a number of people and old Carron creating a scene in court. That was when the judge pronounced sentence. Old Carron jumped up and raved on that his son was a good lad, that the woman deserved all she got, and that if Crab swung he'd do for the judge, jury and hangman. There was a picture of him outside the courtroom, shaking his fist, with Nosey beside him, not full face, but looking over his shoulder. I knew that Nosey was reckoning chances, wishing he was twelve feet tall so that he could break the building down and pick up Crab and carry him away under his arm. Or wait until they took him away to the place and ride down with a bunch of gunmen, or blow down the gates and drive a tank right into the courtyard, spitting bullets. Or tunnel into the gaol from a mile away. But you could see from the turn of his shoulder and the way his fist was clenched that there wasn't a hope and he knew it.

All the same I was expecting something. Before, I kept expecting to open a newspaper and read that Carron's brother had laid out some van driver, and then driven the van right into the prison.

Maybe you'll understand why I stayed in That Night. It was on all our minds. We were all waiting for something, although the thing wasn't due until the following morning. The Old Lady was doing her ironing and Harry was tinkering on with a watch. The time signal had just gone nine. I was reading H.G. Wells and grasping one sentence every couple of pages when Harry lifted his head, took the glass from his eye, and said: 'Somebody knocking at the door?'

'It's the wind,' said the Old Lady, but went all the same. She was back at the double: 'It's him,' she said.

Nobody asked who. 'Ask him in,' said Harry.

275

'Ah did an' he won't,' she replied, and I was on my way out. 'Be careful, Arthur,' she warned.

'Leave him be,' said the Lodger, screwing the glass back. 'That was the knock of a chap needin' help ... tell him there's a cup of tea ready, if he wants it.'

'Thanks, Harry,' I said and went into the dark passage. It was Nosey all right, leaning against the jamb and stroking his nose. I couldn't see his face. He was facing away from the nearest street lamp and in the shadows. I put my hand out to the switch. 'Leave it off, kiddo,' he said. 'How's tricks?'

'Fair to middlin',' I said.

'Better'n me. Fancy a walk?'

'The Old Lady says there's a cup of tea ready if you want it.'

'Ah'd rather walk the leather off my shoes,' he said. I pulled on my windcheater and looked in to tell them what I was up to.

'No mischief,' said my mother. I can see her now, looking over with the iron tilted and the look in her eyes.

'He wants to walk,' I said.

'God help him!'

'Got your latchkey?' asked Harry. I nodded. 'Take him ten, twenty miles. Walk yourself to a blister.'

I had a couple of tanners and stopped at the first slot machine to exchange them for chocolate. This was on the coast road. There was a post office down the road. It had a big clock set off from the wall. He was watching this all the time I was getting the chocolate; the second time he jerked I realised it was in time with the click forward of the big hand. We turned in the opposite direction. Although the time of the year was late October, it wasn't cold. We'd had a mellow stretch and summer had died so hard that nobody seemed to have noticed autumn was in. We pounded along pavements towards the coast. Twice he asked me the time and I could have kicked myself for not leaving my watch at home. The third time, I realised he was waiting for every third lamp to ask. I took off the watch and pretended it had stopped. The time was nine-thirty and while we were walking I pretended to wind it, then gave it the two or three twists necessary to over-wind. When I replaced it, the thing was as heavy as lead and I was sweating in case he missed the tick.

'Wish he could have had this walk,' he said. 'Just one last go. He'd have jump – been glad of the chance even although he never walked where there was a bus or a lift.'

'Ah'm sorry, kiddar,' I said.

'Don't let it bother ye,' he replied. 'When ye're up against it there's nothing to do but walk it off … ever seen them lions and tigers pacing it out behind bars? That's the way it is with me. Reckon there's anybody watching us, or him!'

'God's truth, Ah don't know, Nosey.'

He looked up at the sky. 'Them stars are a hell of a long way off,' he said. All so calm that he amazed me. I didn't know then that it's possible to be in a fever and speak slow and solid, as normal. 'How far d'ye reckon it goes before it comes to an end?'

'Nobody knows,' I said.

'Then whoever it is that's lookin' in won't see much more than a couple of dots movin' so slow that ye'd think they were standin' still?'

'If there's nothin' livin' between us and It,' I said,' we might look a lot bigger than dots …'

'And that's an effin' big if,' he said. 'More likely there's nothing at all behind the stars. Somebody wound it up then walked off. Same as the Bloke they've fixed to do the job tomorrow.' He went off the subject. 'Ah'm sorry about what Ah said that night – the night down in the market hall. Wish it wasn't true.'

'Look,' I said. 'Ah'm sorry too. It was all true – all ye told her.'

'Makes no difference,' he said. 'Ah shouldn't have said it.'

The walking wasn't so bad as I'd expected; in fact, at the back of my mind I was enjoying it. We came to the concrete bridge over all the coal lines. He looked up at the sky. 'Ah'm sick of the road,' he said. 'How about strollin' up the tracks?' We went down into the cutting and turned north walking on the sleeper ends, oppo-site sides. 'What about this other bird?' he suddenly asked.

Thinking it would take his mind off the other thing, I told him about Stella. When I was finished he whistled, stroked his nose, and grinned over to me. 'Boy,' he said, 'for a dreamin' man you sure got the trick of falling into the right kind of jam ...' There was a ghost of the old Nosey. It went like a flash. 'Take a tip from me, kiddar,' he said. 'Don't be so free with the dope about yourself.'

'Why, what for?' I asked.

'Come the day when some bright character'll rub your nose in it,' he said. 'Me, or somebody like me. They'll take that true romance of yours and turn it into dog's vomit, sure as life. You're too effin' trusting by a mile.'

We walked on in silence. 'And Ah'm half-dago,' he said. 'But that's something Ah wouldn't touch, not the way Ah'm feelin' now. But ye never know what's goin' to twist a man ...'

We seemed to have walked a long way when we reached the end of the incline, but I knew from the flash of a lighthouse eastwards that we'd covered no more than five or six miles. The line took us through a place that reminded me of Hill 60. It was an old pit-heap and the bulldozers had ploughed into it for red ash until there wasn't a flat surface anywhere. They'd gouged out craters, made trenches, left ridges and stubby peaks, but the thing was still burning. In the dark it was like looking inside a well-trimmed furnace and the wind brought a smell of rotten eggs. There was a little tower, a walled-in pit shaft, at the far end.

'Let's have a sit down,' he said. But instead of sitting down against the side sheltered against the wind he started to walk around it. Then he hefted a brick in his hand. 'Listen,' he said. The brick played knuckle bones against the side of the hole then landed a thousand feet below, maybe, in a crash of big drums that sounded like water below a shell of ice. The noise boomed on a long time. 'That's a long way, man,' he said, then put my heart in my mouth by springing against the side: it looked as if he was after butting the wall down. But he was after one of the stanchions on the parapet. Like a monkey he pulled himself up until finally he was kneeling on the few inches of brick. 'For God's sake, come down,' I urged. I don't suppose he even heard me. He was looking down. '*Nosey!*' I shouted.

Slowly he gripped the stanchion and lowered himself, hanging a second or two while his feet looked for the plinth a few inches above ground level. His face was against the parapet and he was crying wild. Taking hold of him I made him sit down. The barbed wire had ripped his hand and I bandaged it with my hanky. The other hand he kept against his eyes, like a mask, as if trying to stop himself from seeing something.

Sitting against the shaft wall he ate the chocolate. His hand was over the eyes all the time.

'Wonder if he's awake,' he said. Every time he mentioned Crab – and it was never by name – I jumped a mile. Maybe I should have told him to think about something else. You've got to be walking with the brother of a condemned man to understand just how impossible that line is. That was when I stole a look at my watch. 'Ye've smashed it,' he said. I must have looked stupid.

'Why man alive,' he laughed bitterly, 'Ah can play ye at one end and lose ye at the other, even with this on me mind.' I didn't like the remark, and looked away. 'Take no notice,' he said. 'Ah've had time on me mind for a week or two now, and especially since this mornin' … let's walk,' he said. I was as sore as a boil and all the enjoyment in walking I'd felt at the beginning had worn off. I wasn't up to it, and that's a fact. My windcheater was catching under the armpits and rubbing against my neck, there was an ache in my back, and my flat, tender feet were giving me hell, especially whenever I miscalculated a step and slipped off the edge of a sleeper. To add to this I was missing my sleep, there was sand behind my eyeballs, and I was wondering what was in his mind: boy, I'm not kidding, I wouldn't have been surprised if he'd dropped back, then come up on me and landed me one with a spike from one of the neat piles stacked at intervals along the track. 'Clocks,' he picked up about a mile farther on, so suddenly that I wondered what was up or what he was getting at. 'Clocks. Clocks on churches, shops, town halls. Hangin' on watch-chains, and tickin' beside hearts. You canna' get away from them, and say you do then you begin to notice watches. Thin gold straps and tiny faces, pigskin straps and faces so big that ye can see the second hands rippin' around. Some square ones, about the size of the condemned cell with the hands cuttin' round like knives – get outa the way! Never seen so many metal straps in all me life. Stands to reason. Life-cuffs, eh? Could stick them all, but now Ah canna bear to pass a jeweller's shop.'

'Jeweller's shop?' I stupidly echoed.

'Full of clocks and watches, chimers, grandmother, cuckoo clocks. Hands again, all on the move, and the lights flashin' against the glass like smiles – y'know? Times Ah felt like takin' a half-brick …'

'Works both ways,' I said.

'How's that?'

'The only thing ye can hang on to is that time's got to go on, it's bound to pass over, ye'll be out of it. Could be he's feelin' that way.'

'It'll never do what you want,' he said, ignoring my comment. 'Like being in a big river with cliffs a hundred miles high on either side. Sometimes she goes slow, sometimes hard and fast and faster. But there's nothin' ye can do – it takes ye on the way it wants. So ye drink, or dance, or clock a bloke … while you're doin' your bit, it's doing its work an' ye're older by so much. We're bloody well trapped in the effin' works,' he cried. 'What's the use of bein' here if ye can't have ye own way? What's the use of enjoyin' yourself when ye know ye're only a pig with both feet in the trough fattenin' up for the gun?'

We left the railway and made across the fields to the coast. The land was tilted to the east and the trees were bent to the west. The salt fret smarted in my nostrils and the night air stung. I found myself walking with my face turned sideways. Looking at those bending trees, mostly stubby hawthorn, I thought that maybe they had the answer. The wind's there and they have to put up with it. They bend to it and nobody notices that the branches are on the tilt when the blossom comes. Not accepting God's goodness but putting up with his toughness; not only the wickedness of time passing or not passing but all the other shit that flies. Maybe if you do a bit cunning swimming in that monster river and navigate the rapids you can float in the pools and watch the stars go by. I didn't say anything of this to Nosey. It was his night and if blazing up was going to ease him, let him blaze. Anyway, you work these things out for yourself, you ask questions and receive answers ding-dong only when you're ready. Old Nosey wasn't even at the starting post. Whatever he was riding had its tail to the post way round the bend and trying to balance on its hind legs.

'The whole family got an invitation for tomorrow mornin',' he said. I thought instantly of the gaol and could only stare at him in horror. 'Not *there*,' he continued. 'They wouldn't like it. No, old Johnson sent a note round. Said he was opening the Mission at seven-thirty and we were welcome. Welcome!

'A lot of lemonade,' he said. 'One preacher for our lad, another for the family. One to see his neck stretched, another to pacify the bereaved. Slops with their collars turned round! Cunning effers that make ye fold your hands to save using the cuffs. Ah wouldn't give them house room.'

'Old Johnson's a sincere man,' I said. 'He's had it as tough as you.'

'So his effin' nerve broke,' he said.

I'll remember that walk till the day I die. Every time I think of it the soles of my feet tingle. We followed a path that took us in a circle then landed us in a deep lane. The hedges were nine or ten feet above us and we seemed to be heading north so we went over into some more fields and found ourselves in a swampy sort of place where whacking great bull-rushes grew out of stinking mud. We were jumping like madmen from one bit of dry to another and there wasn't much moonlight to help; I could feel the stuff working over my shoetops every time I missed the dry and pulled out. Every now and again we had a glimpse of a lot of lights, Shields and the south bank of the Tyne, all laid out in rows and loops of white, orange and red. Sometimes there was the sound of a tired old cow of a ship coming home late, so loud you expected to fall into the hold any minute. We got ourselves landed in a fox covert, a mile or so of ups and downs thick with hawthorn and brambles, and the whole concern threw itself upon us: I was pulling thorns out of my hands, head and body for days after; the ones in my shoes didn't penetrate but raked my feet. There was a hole in the middle, full of water black as pitch and stinking high as heaven. I didn't like the look of it. 'Bet there's some queer stuff at the bottom of that,' said Nosey. He didn't need to tell me. That was the one place where I was more frightened of something else, don't ask me what it was, more than him. Then we crossed a pasture as flat as a billiard table and hit a dirt road going through some piggeries; you could hear the beasts nosing and grunting. Nosey stopped, picked up a stone, and let blaze. There was a threshing and squealing. 'That stirred them,' he said grinning.

We hit the coast road again at midnight; I remember how quiet it was again, more quiet than up in the fields because of the noise; electric trains and rivet guns going on some rush job in the shipyards; we stood waiting for a lift, and boy, was I pleased when an early fish-lorry pulled up. A couple of minutes before the headlamps came up the clocks started striking midnight; Wallsend first, then one in Newcastle, St Nicholas perhaps, followed by Tynemouth, the two Shields, Jarrow and elsewhere. They came up loud and clear too, a regular orchestra playing the interval. Through it all came a dull regular clang from some shipyard, somebody playing bel-fagor on a plate, but it sounded more like a cracked church bell tolling you know what. I could see Nosey's hands tighten and didn't dare look at his face.

It was a relief to sit on those high, cold fishboxes after this, and relax, with the ice crackling under our feet. We gave the driver a ten packet of fags and landed home, my home, at 12.30 a.m. on the dot; I remember the time because the first thing I did was to carry the clock into the pantry and set it down face downwards to stop it. The Old Lady shouted from the top of the stairs. 'Make yourselves some tea – there's plenty of bacon and eggs.' I looked up and saw her standing like a ghost in a long nightgown, her hair hanging down, hands clasped: 'Are ye all right?'

'Fine, Mum,' I said. 'You go back and get some sleep.'

'Ah canna',' she said. We looked at each other for a second or two, then she sighed and went back to her bed. A minute or two later the old springs sang out that she was tossing and turning. I filled the kettle, filled the area inside the frying pan, and took off my boots. Nosey watched me in silence. 'Ah don't want any grub, mind,' he said.

But he started taking off his boots, hopelessly, like a tired old man who knows he's too sore to sleep. It was then that I wished we'd kept on walking.

3

Every story should have a happy ending, and if you wait long enough it comes; not in a clinch but in a discovery. You go under the bridge any Saturday night in summer and hear the bright new lad testify to the usual true few, including a girl clasping a Bible in her white gloved hands. I went once and heard him. Navy blue suit, spotless white shirt, red tie with diagonal blue stripes, and cleanliness around him like a halo. Boy, standing there I'm always conscious of grubby hands and a face that hasn't known a razor for ten hours. And inner dirtiness. The thing that strikes me first is the hair. The slick oil washed out, it is light and silky; each individual hair flows in the breeze like an anchored feather. I listen hard. He's read the Bible in his hand on piecework and has loyally listened to old Johnson, who stands watching with his mouth open and a joy beyond understanding. It means something to him, but it is gibberish to me and to everybody else that hurries by. He is clean, he is good, he'll help and not hurt, he will be a good husband and father, but boy, I'm sad.

Not time but the book of rules has him now. He thinks he has everything in his hand, and he's just at the starting point. It's simple, but not so simple that you can throw away your pop records one day and start preaching the gospel the next. Listen, I'm not being superior. Maybe I'm being stupid. Maybe some types take a short cut because it's the only way they can go: and it's still good. And maybe others have to take the long road, make a lot of mistakes, hurt themselves and come through in the end to something similar. But they know what it is, and that's what I want.

Before I put the blindfold on, I want to know why. Before I'd give up the whole of the human race for a book of rules, blinkers, a straight and narrow bounded by texts, and a promise of bliss, I'd spit in God's eye; Nosey's version. I'm all right, Jack; do it my way and you'll be all right too. No! The world's too big for the narrow little men who think you just switch from your track to another that they will lay for you, free gratis. You find your own. You walk the way Nosey and me did that night, only you walk alone, and you never give up your soul to God or the Devil for any easy guide, a pair of new shoes, or even one glass of pure, cold spring water. I don't believe God put us under death and time to find salvation through another kind of slavery. Give your souls up, and you're done. You'll end up on Hill 60, dead. Doesn't matter if you're not blown up, you're still dead.

All right, I'm not making myself clear. Skip it. Yesterday was a perfect day and we went down to the coast. Give me sand before gold, sea instead of champagne – what's it like anyway? – and all the common things like air, and wind, and clouds, and people. The Old Lady fell asleep and somehow or other Nosey's name cropped up.

'There's no denying it's a miracle,' said my stepfather. 'Oh, yes, he's a changed lad – but Ah can never settle down in his company. Rags to riches too quick, Ah suppose. Liable to knock anybody off balance but my opinion is that he'll always be the same. So he's got something! Something Ah'd be damn glad to have but never will. It's a gift – no more than a gift – but he seems to think it puts him on a pedestal. Canna' stand him for that. Get me?'

I got him. All I remembered clicked smartly into place. Anything that separates the living from the living or the living from the dead (what happens to the brother whose neck breaks before he's saved?) is not complete. Anything that makes one man feel or seem more superior than another, or makes another man feel or seem more inferior, is worse than the mines under Hill 60, or H-Bombs, or any of the thousand and one other varieties of death. I'm thinking my way aloud. Love one another has lost its meaning now – here's the modern translation: 'Take risks for one another.' That's why I failed Nosey in the first place. The Old Lady and Harry took a risk the night they allowed me to go off with Nosey: which reminds me that taking risks sometimes means keeping quiet, trusting, keeping your nose out of it. The way they acted the night before Crab Carron was hanged.

Something took hold of Nosey that night. He was like a kite in gusty weather: sometimes he held steady against the wind, sometimes he went into crazy dives and loops. He had me guessing all the time. When we returned to the house I thought he was back to normal. I fried bacon and eggs and planted the dish in front of him without bothering to ask after his appetite. Suddenly he said that bar the chocolate he'd had nothing to eat all the day and perhaps he'd better try. Man, that was a crazy meal! We sat there like stokers, feeding our bodies, too tired and scared to enjoy eating but wading into it as if the food might somehow settle the trouble. And for a time it did. We shifted from the table and sat drinking tea – teapot, milk and sugar on the hearth – in front of the fire.

'You know, kiddar,' he said at last. 'It was pretty good of you and your Old Lady to allow me here. Ah couldn't face the old homestead tonight. Had a row before Ah came out because they were bringing a case of beer in. Ah can take a pint with the best, but not ...' His eyes filled and he turned away. After a few seconds he continued. 'A fine old carry-on they'll be having now. There'll be whor Nancy and Jinny and their menfolk; pot-bellied Joe, and squinty Harry with the everlasting bad breath. Five kids on top of that. Nick'll be at home, trust him where there's free booze; the ould man rantin' about slops fryin' in hell and there was never any justice for him, let alone his lads ... the Old Lady gettin' quietly drunk all the time and that effin' old alarm clock knocking off the minutes while Nick turns the house upside down for a bottle opener ... Aye' kiddar, that's what ye've saved me from.'

'Ye're welcome,' I said, feeling my eyelids droop and my head drop. Then he started to talk, mainly just anything that happened to come into his head. If anybody had been watching in they'd have thought us crazy: Nosey talking fifty to the dozen about Carruthers-Smith (I was even too tired to pull him up and tell him that old C. S. was dead and buried in his grave); the pigeon caper; the times we had in the old foundry roasting potatoes among the hot ashes and grilling herring above; the fights we had with Mick Kelly and Co; this girl Teresa; the tales the Sergeant told and were they true; the tricks of selling fresh fruit on the street corner; how their house was once full of two hundred pair of shoes, all left feet, nicked by his old man and some of his pals. Round and round he went, sometimes forcing it, sometimes getting into a true run, sometimes even raising me from the dead, round and round and in the unspoken centre that old scrap-barricaded fortress of Charlie Nettlefold's and the long tawny dog stretched out beside a quiet house. Or so I thought.

I tell you, he went whooping it like a tribe of Red Indians but never let blaze an arrow in that direction. Tired though I was I could sense that much. Talking just to keep me awake, talking to keep me on a towline, talking to keep his wits company. How often the string sagged until the words came back like a machine gun and he was in a swing again. Tight and tugging; too tight and she snaps, and back would go my head. Then he'd soothe with some soft words about the first little girl down the clay banks and how her hands went to work to give him the craziest delight of his life; and how the same one grown a bird passing him by with her nose in the air until one night at last he caught her in the back row of the Albion and sent her mad for a change regardless of her careful makeup and delicate lingerie. That's the stuff to give the troops; old Arthur jacks up the ten-ton gates of solid steel they laughingly call eyelids and listens ... Detail, this time: how fast your fingernails grow, how one half of your life is spent in reminding yourself it's time for a haircut and the other half in wondering what's the use of shaving; it's back again tomorrow, a mask of stubbles creeping down the side of your face and around your chin like a forest fire in reverse; of your breath, how hopeless it is to buy toothpaste when the whole big family has a go and finishes it in a day or so that the next time you come along you can see the mark of the brush-end bristles way down the orifice; the hate you feel for a claggy jamjar with a dusty layer of sweetness at the bottom; the sour smell of beer bottles in the early morning and how, if you were a millionaire, you'd have a bathroom at the base of a mountain of fizzy tablets to flush the functions and turn the sunlight into something to enjoy.

'Me and the kiddar always slept together,' he tells me. 'Had each other for hot water bottles. Never minded the early morning stiffness. Laughed about the birds and the rest of the crazy family and what slobs the slops were.'

'Sleeping so close to a brother you get to know him.'

Through my half-open eyes I saw him shake on the edge of the chair and thought I'd gone over the rim. It was like the start of a nightmare when you know everything's okay and you've still got the sense to whisper to a fast-receding self: 'Everything's all right: Steady the Buffs.'

It shook me out of my easy languor, anyhow, enough to lean forward and touch his knee. There was a vibration, the kind a windy drill gives, small and regular. The mortal cold and frostbite of the body and spirit. I knew then that he was afraid of himself. 'What is it, Nosey?'

'Ah wish Ah'd never looked into that pitshaft,' he said, and looked at the bandaged right hand.

'Forget it,' I said, and threw him a lifeline. 'Here, what about that bird? Did ye ever see her again?'

'Saw a man down there,' he muttered. 'Saw a man shoot down that shaft.' He made a sweeping motion with his hand. 'Going round and round; not fast; slow and steady. Going round. Going down and getting smaller and smaller. Spinning like a little stiff doll with his head on one side and his mouth open. Then it all stopped. Flat on his back with his hands crossed.'

'That's a good yarn,' I said, poking the fire. I wanted to touch something and connect to prove that I was here, solid, heart-beating Arthur going on and on as usual. But the short hairs of my neck went up like a brush. 'It's all been too much for you,' I told him. 'Ye're headin' for a nervous breakdown, kiddar.'

He leaned forward with his hands clasped: 'What d'ye reckon it meant – what was it all about?'

'You had the clocks on your mind and mixed them up with Crab,' I said uneasily.

'It wasn't him,' he said flatly. I stared at him. 'It was me! Ah could see me own face as clear as Ah can see yours at this minute. And Ah'll tell ye something – Ah'd gone up that wall with half a mind to chuck myself down! But the minute Ah saw that, Ah was finished. Couldn't move, like a nut in a spanner. The minute Ah put me head down and saw that thing Ah was locked.'

'They reckon ye see things like that when ye have a break-down,' I said.

'It wasn't a dream,' he declared. 'Look, Ah was on top of that pit wall watchin' it spin like a propeller, waitin' for the head to come round to make sure it was me. Something was making me stay where I was but at the same time Ah was down there, in that thing, and something was spinnin' me and pullin' me down at the same time ... what was it, the divil himself, or God?' I shook my head hopelessly.

'It was your mind; ye were sick,' I said. 'Twisting all your worries and showing them in the pit. What ye saw in the pit was a picture of the fact – there's nothing ye can do to stop ...'

'What's goin' to happen?' he finished for me. Then shook his head: 'It was either Almighty God or Ould Nick himself that was pullin' me down there.'

'It was a picture you made yourself,' I argued, but he wouldn't have it. 'He's after me. Just specially for me He's dropping this remote control business the Pastor talked about. He's reaching out for me the same way as he reached out for whor kiddar.'

I'd have given anything to have been able to look at a watch or clock and see for myself just how much more of this I had to put up with. But there wasn't a chance. If I as much as looked over my shoulder he jumped in the chair. This was maybe about three o'clock in the morning. I remember watching him ceaselessly rub the palm of one hand against the knuckles of the other, looking all the time straight down beyond the moving hands and through the carpet at something else. I remember telling myself I couldn't fall asleep. But I did, on an ordinary upright chair with my chest alone as a pillow for my chin. And when I awoke the sunshine was blazing into the room. But Nosey was gone. All I had was a confused memory which might have been just a dream of old Nosey holding my chin up and saying softly, 'Don't worry, kiddar. Sleep it off. Ah'm okay now.'

Halfway to the door I realised I was shoeless. Rushed back and pulled them on without tying the ends and went ass-over-heels a couple of times before I was halfway down the street. Couldn't think of anything but that pit shaft – thought he might be trying the same caper again, possibly from the bridge over the clay banks. The bridge was empty. I ran along one side and came back along the other, looking down occasionally to see if I could spot anything down below. But there was only the usual rubble, scrap and halfscrap. St Nicholas was striking eight.

Back at the other side I cut towards the river, still looking down towards the sulky tributary with its drunken granaries, crumby bonded warehouses, and ancient factories.

A lopped-off chimney stack caught my eye. Something was lying at its foot. I measured the distance from the parapet of the bridge to the grey, bent figure. Could be. Pelted down the clay banks and ran out of control; nearly finished up in the messy waters of the burn. False alarm. Somebody had got rid of a half-size mattress. Wearily ascended.

The street stretched in front of me like a funnel. Halfway down on the right-hand side, was the Golden Bowl. Out of the open door trickled a little knot of people. Some of them carried little bags for their Bibles. Even at that distance they showed their excitement The hanging had hammered home one cog into one kind of system; he was engaged now and clicking merrily, and all the good people were glad. The younger ones came briskly walking up the hill, recreating the experience with excited, unfinished sentences ... They passed by without stopping the talk.

'Did ye see his face ...'

'Ye'd think Mr Johnson knew it was goin' to happen ...'

'That prayer he said over him!'

'Did ye see him cryin'?'

'The poor lad was in an awful state ...'

'Mrs Potter strikin' up "Rock of Ages" ... an inspiration ...'

'Ah tell ye he ran down that aisle as if something ...'

'Convicted of sin. Convicted ...'

That was the last word I heard. It rang in my brain. Crab convicted, Nosey convicted, each brought to Law. One hung, the other nailed. Perhaps it was at this point that I realised Crab had hung and swung and was dead. It seemed impossible. Some things are bad to beat. It was money for jam and in the end the money turned him into a killer. Very practical people. No use praying for the condemned duly executed. Why cry over the gallows when they lead another lad right into God's noose? I thought of that long, low ruined building where the women used to spin the ropes for ships' tackle or men's necks. The rope-walk. There is another rope-walk where men spin in their minds the one hundred per cent ropes for souls.

The old lady had a round rosy face and kind china-blue eyes.

She was my last chance to make sure. 'Did he come to the service, Missus?'

'Aye, hinny, he came and was taken into the arms of the Almighty.'

'Well, that's all right,' I muttered, embarrassed.

'If you're his friend ye can be glad an' happy – it was a wonderful sight.'

'Thanks,' I said. 'Ah just wanted to know ...'

'It'll do him a world of good,' she said. 'If ye could have seen his face! The living Glory was there! lifting himself outa himself. Ye should go down and speak to him,' she gently urged.

'No. Thanks for tellin' me. Ah'll not bother him now.' I looked over my shoulder and saw her standing, the china-blue eyes still searching me and my need as I slunk round the corner and back to the clay banks. Lifted himself outa himself! That was good! I felt a stab of envy.

Okay, so I'll spin my own thread. But there was a moment when I nearly started running after the two people I loved most in the world outside my home. Then I shoved my hands in my pockets and turned about. I'm not kidding, I was lonely and melancholy. I was scared. I'm still lonely, melancholy, scared. Here I am with five crisp pound notes in the wallet tucked inside my nice fifteen-guinea suit. I can feel that wallet rubbing comfortingly against a good shirt. But it ends there: all dressed up and nowhere to go. Any train, bus or boat will take me to the same place – to me, a quivering mass of jelly full of rushing, bewildered, frightened, crazy thoughts – that's for sure. So I stay put. I watch the sardines moving along the little conveyor; a silver stream from the sea bound for the place where they're shuffled tail to head and head to tail and slid into the boxes. There I go. Stiff and straight and swimming in the gravy, but that's no consolation when the lid's clamped down.

Smart boy, pretty boy, home boy, I say to myself: Where are you going? It's no use asking Mum and Harry, living in a cosy world of their own, far from snails and upside-down-men.

Nosey has nothing to offer but diamond-cut-diamond, stacked cards, a coin he always calls. To the Manor lot I'm the crazy one, crazier than Nosey, odd boy out. Stella has gone. Once I rang her up. I'm not kidding. I rang her, knowing all the time she wasn't there, and stood in the kiosk with the sweat running down my face. Nobody answered. Brother, sometimes I feel that if some character walked up to me and gave me the nod I'd follow on. And never mind the suitcase with the spare shirt and socks.